D0090582

YOU'RE INVITED

ALSO BY AMANDA JAYATISSA

My Sweet Girl

AMANDA JAYATISSA

YOU'RE INVITED

BERKLEY
New York

BERKLEY
An imprint of Penguin Random House LLC
penguinrandomhouse.com

Copyright © 2022 by Amanda Jayatissa
Penguin Random House supports copyright. Copyright fuels creativity,
encourages diverse voices, promotes free speech, and creates a vibrant culture.
Thank you for buying an authorized edition of this book and for complying
with copyright laws by not reproducing, scanning, or distributing any part
of it in any form without permission. You are supporting writers
and allowing Penguin Random House to continue to
publish books for every reader.

BERKLEY and the BERKLEY & B colophon are registered
trademarks of Penguin Random House LLC.

Library of Congress Cataloging-in-Publication Data

Names: Jayatissa, Amanda, author.
Title: You're invited / Amanda Jayatissa.
Other titles: You are invited
Description: New York : Berkley, [2022]
Identifiers: LCCN 2021057360 (print) | LCCN 2021057361 (ebook) |
ISBN 9780593335123 (hardcover) | ISBN 9780593335147 (ebook)
Subjects: GSAFD: Mystery fiction. | Suspense fiction.
Classification: LCC PR9440.9.J36 Y68 2022 (print) | LCC PR9440.9.J36
(ebook) | DDC 813/.6—dc23
LC record available at https://lccn.loc.gov/2021057360
LC ebook record available at https://lccn.loc.gov/2021057361

Printed in the United States of America
1 3 5 7 9 10 8 6 4 2

Book design by Katy Riegel

To my mother, Kanisha—who encouraged me to be fearless, adventurous, and fun. Turns out that I'm none of these things, but I am eternally grateful that you were a part of my life, even if it wasn't for as long as we both wanted.

AMAYA

Morning of the Wedding

I WOKE UP with bruised knuckles and blood under my fingernails, more rested than I have been in years. I guess this is who I am now. The kind of person who would finally get a good night's sleep after attacking someone else. The kind of woman who would fly halfway around the world to stop my ex–best friend from marrying my ex-boyfriend. If that's one too many exes for you, well, it certainly is for me. But I'm also the kind of woman who does whatever it takes, so here I am.

Balancing my teacup in one hand, I opened the sliding door that led out onto the small balcony attached to my room at the Mount Lavinia Hotel. It overlooked the expansive private beach, which was deserted.

Of course it was. It was too early in the day for anyone to be out there. Maybe later on, but then again, who knows how things will pan out? The wedding would definitely be canceled now. The guests would all shuffle home, dispirited and upset. Or maybe they wouldn't. Maybe they would just be grateful for the all-expenses-paid weekend, and take advantage of the beautiful beach and open bar. They would definitely mull around, gossiping and curious about what transpired. Aunties would have their own theories, no doubt, and phones will light up with messages about what happened to the unfortunate bride, Kaavindi Fonseka. This is Colombo after all.

It flickered in my stomach then—the first flutter of nervousness. I knew I couldn't keep it away for long. It had been a simple plan, of course. But like all simple plans, it could be quite complicated unless you teased everything out. Laid everything bare. And like all simple plans, it had the potential to go very, very wrong.

I watched the waves swell and bounce and crash and forgive. The fishing boats were already well on their way out to sea, and a few birds circled the ocean in the distance. Keeping my eyes on the horizon, I took a deep breath and counted to five.

Then exhaled.

My hands were steady on my cup of tea, but a fleck of dried blood had made its way onto the clean white ceramic. I'd better take a shower. Today was a big day for me. Perhaps even more so than yesterday. So much depended on what I did next.

I stepped into the bathroom and made the water as hot as it would go. It felt like a betrayal, washing the last bits of yesterday off me. Knowing she was gone, as I watched the water swirl down the drain. But I went through all the motions, still nervous but also feeling, for the first time in a very long time, that I belonged to myself. That things just might be okay. That I was finally vindicated of everything that happened five years ago.

I shampooed my hair, conditioned it, slathered on soap that smelled like jasmine all over my body.

Deep breath in, Amaya. Now count to five. Let it out slowly. Just like Dr. Dunn said.

It was over. After so many years, I could finally let it go.

Steam clouded around me as I dried and then dressed myself. My small overnight bag was already packed, ready for me to make my exit. My passport was at home, with the rest of my luggage. The flight back to LA wasn't until tomorrow morning, but I could last till then.

I checked the time—6:36 a.m. A pattern. A lucky number. Thank goodness. I felt some of the tension leave my shoulders.

I'll wait until 7:00 a.m. to check out. 7:07 a.m., if I could manage it. I couldn't afford to look suspicious. After all, who checks out of a five-star hotel at the crack of dawn unless it's some sort of emergency? I didn't want to draw attention to myself now. I couldn't leave anything up to chance.

I busied myself by giving the room a once-over—making sure I hadn't left my charger plugged in and forgotten, or left anything hanging behind the bathroom door. There was a T-shirt in a plastic shopping bag that I kept near my purse, waiting to be thrown out on the taxi ride home. It was always better to be safe. I sat down, phone in hand, watching the numbers on the clock tick their way toward when I could leave.

The rap on my door came at 6:51 a.m., ricocheting through my quiet room, lodging itself deep in my heart.

Who would knock on my door now?

It didn't make any sense.

I hesitated a moment.

The second rap sounded more urgent.

"Miss Bloom, this is Alistair Ferdinand, the hotel manager. Sorry to disturb you. Could we have a moment, please?"

The manager?

Well, at least it wasn't the police. They'd come later. I hoped to be gone by then.

I took another deep breath and cracked open the door.

"Yes?" I tried to keep the tremble out of my voice. I knew it even before he said anything. I could feel it in my bones—the writhing. The inherent sense that things were about to go very, very wrong.

"Miss Bloom, my apologies for this, but we have to search your room."

"Search my room?"

But he was pushed aside by someone as she barreled her way inside.

"Where is she?" Her voice was shrill.

"Tehani? What are you doing here? What's going on?" My voice was a whimper. An embarrassing contrast against hers.

"Oh fuck off, like you don't know."

"I—I don't understand." I swallowed. This wasn't what was supposed to happen.

"I'm sorry, ma'am." The manager stepped in. "We have been instructed to search all rooms immediately. It appears that one of our guests has gone missing."

"What? Who?" I asked, even though I knew the answer.

"I'm not at liberty to say right now, madam. We just need to check your room."

It felt like all the breath had been knocked out of me. This was really happening.

The manager was accompanied by two security guards. Let them look. She certainly wasn't in here. It took just less than a minute of them going through my room to confirm.

I glanced at the time, just to make sure. 6:53 a.m. Nothing lucky about that. My chest tightened.

"As you can see, I'm alone in here. But please, let me know if I can help." I sounded far away—like my voice was disconnected from the rest of my body.

"You can help by telling us the truth, you bitch." Tehani's voice slapped me back to reality. She was holding up the T-shirt I'd been meaning to throw away—a basic white tee with the words *Pink Sapphires* emblazoned across the chest in sparkly letters.

My heart started pounding.

"This is my sister's. Why do you have it?"

I could barely get my words out.

"Kaavi, she—gave it to me. I'd—you know, I'd spilled something on myself, and she wanted me to have it."

"You're such a liar! I knew it! I told them you'd have something to do with this! Just wait—"

And with that, Tehani stormed out, T-shirt and all.

What the hell had I gotten myself into?

"Thank you, Miss Bloom. We are going to have to ask you to please stay in your room until further notice."

"Stay in my room?" My heart was a wild animal now. Jumping and pounding and trying to escape out of my chest. "But I was going to check out soon."

"I'm sorry, ma'am, but it is imperative that you do so. I'm told that the investigators will be arriving soon to handle this situation."

Oh my goodness, I couldn't believe this was happening.

This was not the plan. This was not the plan at all.

"How do you know she's missing?" I asked. "Maybe she went for a walk? Or, well, have you checked the groom's room?" I made sure to lower my voice for that last bit, so the security guards couldn't hear me.

"Trust me, Miss Bloom. She hasn't gone for a walk. There were—

and I don't mean to alarm you—signs of a struggle in her room. Right now, I'm afraid we have to believe the worst . . ." His voice trailed off and he eyed my hand. I glanced down to see what he was staring at.

I'd washed away the blood, of course, but the bruise on my knuckles was a little harder to get rid of.

"Anyway, thank you for your time. Once again, please stay in your room until you're called for questioning."

"Okay." It was all I could manage.

I could barely breathe.

"And Miss Bloom—?" The manager hesitated near my door.

"Yes?"

"We have security stationed on every corridor. So please do be kind enough to adhere to our safety measures." He kept his eyes firmly on my face until just before he turned around, when I saw him try to sneak another glance at my knuckles. I held my hand behind my back—out of sight. I wasn't an idiot.

They shut the door on their way out, and I went back into the bathroom. There was a gentleman's grooming kit on the sink counter. I took out the razor and pried out one of the thin metal blades from its plastic casing.

Dropping the lid shut on the toilet, I sat down, bringing my right foot up to rest on the porcelain so I could reach. I took another deep breath and plunged the blade into the side of my big toe. It stung and throbbed, and a livid drop of blood swelled and burst onto the tile below. That was better. I couldn't risk any more damage to my hands, after all.

I finally allowed myself to feel angry.

I thought I was being so clever—coming here, destroying things, trying to stop this wedding from happening. It was all my fault. I've been too smug. As smug as a cat who's about to get the cream. But I'm no cat. I've been so wrong. I've been the mouse this whole time. I should have known.

I went out to the bed and collapsed, phone in hand, watching the numbers. How long did I have to wait?

Many hours, it turned out.

The room service cart visited me twice, and each time I politely thanked the waiter and asked for an update. Both times, I was met with a formal reply that they were still waiting on more information. Both times I couldn't touch my food that stayed, cooling, and then stinking up my room while I contemplated my next move.

It was 3:28 p.m. when the knock that I had been expecting finally pulled me back to where I was. Still no luck with the numbers. A definite sign.

I took a deep breath. Counted to five. Then I stood up.

"Good afternoon," I said, answering the door.

"Miss Bloom." The manager of the hotel accompanied three security officers. They weren't the police, which made me feel marginally better. I think they were from a private security company, judging from their uniforms. And private security couldn't make any arrests, right?

"You need to come with us, madam. And please alert me to any valuables you might have stored here, as we will be searching your room again. More thoroughly this time, I'm afraid."

"That's fine," I replied quietly. "I don't really have any valuables, but there's about three hundred US dollars in my wallet."

He gave me a curt nod, and the officers escorted me down the corridor. There were security guards swarming everywhere I looked, as well as in-house guards. The security were in beige and brown, sticking out against the old portraits and colonial interior of the hotel, but the in-house guards were decked out in their postcolonial glory—white knee-length shorts, white knee-high socks, and wide-brimmed white safari hats. It was like stepping into a time capsule whenever I saw them.

I was led away to a conference room on the highest floor of the old wing. The wooden staircase echoed as I climbed it slowly, surely, making my way to where my life was undoubtedly about to be torn to shreds.

The room itself was really quite cheerful, with two large windows overlooking the sparkling Indian Ocean and soft pipe music chirping away in the background. It felt like sacrilege. Things shouldn't be this bright and happy. Not now. Not when everything was just about to erupt.

I was left alone. I sat down. I looked at the time—3:33 p.m. Finally. Finally, a good sign. I took another deep breath. Everything was going to be okay.

I'll just tell them the truth. That had to work, right? I'll tell them the truth and then maybe I could make them understand that it's all been a mistake.

The door opened and a woman dressed in a smart white blouse and black trousers entered the room. I couldn't help but wonder what that blouse would look like with a splatter of blood sprayed across it.

"Miss Bloom?" she asked. Her voice was clipped—no-nonsense professionalism, but not exactly cold either. A woman who meant business. Who was she and what was she doing here?

"Yes," I replied, standing up and offering my hand. She gave it two curt shakes.

"I'm Eshanya Padmaraj with Silverhawk Securities. I'm sure you've heard of us. We are a private security company and are investigating the disappearance and possible murder of Kaavindi Fonseka."

Possible murder. The words ricocheted through me, tearing a hole in my chest. I just nodded.

"Her father, Nihal, wanted this matter attended to at once, and with the utmost discretion, as I'm sure you'll understand," she continued.

So Mr. Fonseka didn't call the police, then? That's interesting. I would have thought that with his connections he'd have rung up the inspector general himself. I'm guessing Mrs. Fonseka had something to do with that. They probably wanted everything kept under wraps until they had some answers. Things weren't so bad just yet.

I took a deep breath, but it got caught somewhere in my chest and I started to cough.

"Would you like some water, Miss Bloom?"

"Yes, please," I managed, and used this moment to eye her.

Miss Padmaraj looked to be in about her midforties. She was well-spoken and well-mannered, and she must certainly hold quite a senior position if she was allowed to head an investigation herself. It was practically unheard of for a woman, but I'm glad it wasn't a man. Perhaps she'd be more sympathetic to what I was about to say. Perhaps she'd understand.

"I'll be recording our conversation, and it'll be transcribed for documentation purposes. I hope that's okay," she said, but she wasn't asking for my permission. "The police will take your official statement afterward, if or when they are called in. Our conversation won't be as formal. I'm mostly trying to get a clear understanding of everything that happened leading up to the wedding day in order to assist in the search for Miss Fonseka. Time is quite valuable right now, as you are probably aware."

I took a deep breath and nodded.

"Let's start. Could you state your name and address for the record, please?"

1

AMAYA

Three Months before the Wedding

I WAITED TILL the clock on my oven timer turned 8:08 p.m. to leave. I wasn't superstitious, but it never hurt to wait for a good sign.

I took a deep breath and grabbed my small purse and keys off the counter as I made my way out.

The sleek black limousine was exactly where I knew it would be. Where it always was. A blond whose faded suit flapped around his shoulders was waiting near the rear passenger door. I slowed down, my wrestled confidence fading a little.

"Where's Joe?"

"He's off this week. Family vacation, I think."

This was definitely not a good sign. Damn it.

I took a deep, calming breath like Dr. Dunn said, and tried to center myself.

Was it really so terrible that my usual driver wasn't here today?

No, no it wasn't. I was just reading too much into everything like I always did.

It's not like I would turn around and go back inside because Joe wasn't there. Because there was a slight change to the same routine I'd kept up for months now.

I'd be lying to myself if I said I'd just go home. I was already at the car. I'd never turn back. There's no way I could last another month without, well, whatever this was.

"You ready, ma'am?"

"Y-yes." I hated the way my voice trembled, but if the new driver noticed, he didn't show it.

I climbed into the back seat carefully, making sure I didn't wrinkle my black satin dress. It was slippery on the leather upholstered seats. I balanced stiffly, legs wedged into the synthetic carpet that somehow still had that new car smell, until I buckled my seat belt.

The new driver got in and we pulled out. He turned the air-conditioning up all the way, and I shivered, though of course he didn't notice.

I miss Joe. I know it's silly to miss the limousine driver who picked me up once a month, but it was nice to start off the night with a kind face. And he never adjusted the air-conditioning without asking me. I thought about asking the new driver to turn it down, but I rubbed my arms instead. It felt awkward to ask. I'll tell him if I really start to freeze.

It took about forty minutes to reach the Winchester if LA traffic behaved itself, which it did tonight. Thank goodness.

I stared out the window for a while. The buildings looked like sleek, slippery giants as we cruised by, their windows a million eyes that saw everything. I shuddered, pulling out my phone instead.

I usually don't check my phone when I do this. The whole point is to switch out of my normal life and into, well, into something, or someone, else. But I had seen the time on the little digital clock that glinted at the back of this limousine—8:41 p.m., and it annoyed me a little. This wasn't a good number at all. No patterns. No repeats. No signs from the universe to let me know that things were going my way.

I sighed to myself. Of course all of this was bullshit. Of course this weird obsession I have with the time doesn't mean anything. But I knew that distracting myself was the best option right now.

Opening Instagram and scrolling through was a muscle memory. My fingers had found their way there before my brain even registered what it was doing. And I always ended up on her posts.

Her most recent one was from just a few minutes ago. It was still early morning in Colombo, where she lived. Where I used to call home. The post was of her leaning in close to the camera, her finger held to her perfect, full, pink-painted lips like she was asking me to shush.

Exciting news coming soon! the caption read, and of course the crowd had gone wild.

I scrolled through the *Omg, you have to tell me* and the *Are you pregnant?* comments, but of course she gave nothing away.

Maybe she *was* pregnant? Wouldn't that be something? Maybe she decided to break one of the many unwritten social rules of being a Sri Lankan woman and was going to have a child without being married.

Or maybe her charity, Pink Sapphires, was announcing something big? That seemed more likely. She was always working with underprivileged girls—giving them opportunities they wouldn't have otherwise been able to dream about. Enriching their lives. Being their savior.

I commented from my account ForestFern23—*The suspense is killing me, Kaavi!*

Then I scrolled through her feed, looking for any other signs or hints about what the big news was. But of course there was nothing. Just perfect pictures of her looking perfect, being perfect. Pictures with the girls she helps, pictures from her dad's gem business, which she is geared to take over, pictures brunching and on the beach and living her best Colombo 07 life.

I forced myself to turn my phone off and take a deep breath. I needed to focus on the night ahead of me, not fixate on what Kaavi was up to, a million miles away in my hometown.

I took another deep breath.

And another.

But her post still stayed with me, a pebble in my shoe.

Perfectly lined pink lips. A secret just behind them.

Shhh! Exciting news coming soon.

It was 8:55 p.m. when the limousine pulled up to the front of the hotel—double digits again, thank goodness. See, I had nothing to worry about after all.

I waited for the doorman to open my door before I glided out. A soft breeze fluttered around me and I shivered again. I was still cold from the car ride.

I didn't make eye contact with anyone in the quiet, dimly lit hotel lobby on my way to the front desk, not that anyone would be interested anyway. This was Los Angeles, not Colombo. Anonymity and discretion were part of the lifestyle here, if you wanted it, even though I was nowhere near as rich or famous as those who craved it the most.

"Clara White—I believe you have a key for me?"

I didn't make eye contact with the young woman at the reception either. I could feel her studying my dress, noting that I came directly from the front doors and not the restaurant, that I was clearly being left a key by someone who wasn't walking into this building accompanying me.

I looked at the time on my phone. 9:00 p.m., on the dot. See, there was nothing to worry about. Things would go my way this evening after all.

"You're in room 587," she chirped. I balked at the number. So un-lucky. It made me think of the Instagram post again.

Shhh! Exciting news coming soon.

What in the world was she about to announce?

The receptionist passed over a heavy antique key tag. It was part of the Winchester's charm—the open disdain for the modern. It was what he liked about the place.

Him. That's who I should be focusing on right now. Not her.

The old brass elevator doors swung open, and thankfully, no one got in with me. I checked my makeup in the mirrored wall. My lip-stick had bled out slightly on my lower lip, and I fought the auto-matic response to fix it. He liked me slightly messy. I had never been perfect. That was why he wanted me.

I was early, but that didn't stop me rushing, my black heels click-ing down the hallway, the sound reverberating off the gilded mirrors that lined the walls. I don't know why I even bothered with the spiky stilettos that caused me so much discomfort. They'd be off by the time he got there.

Speaking of which, I checked the time again. I was fifteen min-utes early, as always. I was early for everything. It wasn't something I could help. Give me a deadline or a time to meet someone, and I get this lurch in my stomach. Like the clock ticks with the beat of my heart. Like something would explode if I wasn't on time to stop it.

At least in this case, it was good to be early. I can't even imagine what his reaction would be if I kept him waiting, but I'm always early, and he's always noticed, and he's always been amused.

I let myself into the plush art deco room that looked straight out of an episode of *Mad Men* and adjusted the air-conditioning so it wasn't too cold.

My fingers itched to check my phone one last time, so I quickly turned it on and glanced at her feed, but nothing had changed except about forty more comments begging to know the news.

I had a notification on one of my profiles, KimKx, but it was nothing important. Just a heart from someone random probably looking to get more follows.

I took a deep breath to calm myself and brought my hands up to my neck. It was warm, and my icy hands from the freezing limo ride felt good against my skin. I don't know why her big news made me feel so uneasy.

I checked the clock on the vintage side table. Time for me to put my mind in a box. To let go, finally, after waiting for what felt like an eternity even though it was just a month.

I went to the closet and slipped off my shoes, dress, and matching black lace underwear. I only ever dressed up on the off chance that I would run late anyway. I hung up my dress and left everything else neatly on a shelf. Then I went into the bathroom and washed my hands, making sure I didn't mess up the perfectly rolled hand towels or the little bottles of L'Occitane body lotion on the counter. I opened my purse and gave myself a spritz from the travel-sized perfume I kept with me just for nights like this.

Fixing a loose strand of hair, I finally pulled out the short black leather strap. It was soft, about an inch and a half wide, and felt snug against my skin as I buckled it behind my neck. The D-shaped ring glinted in the dim bathroom light, and I brushed my fingers against it for a moment. I took another deep breath. This. This is why I'm here. The soft leather reminded me. It grounded me.

I went back into the bedroom and moved a coffee table to the side, making space between the wall and the large four-poster bed. I took one last deep breath, let myself unwind, and knelt down facing the wall. Lacing my fingers behind my head, I relaxed further.

Most people don't get it. At least, I guessed that most people wouldn't get it. It's not like I'd ever have the guts to tell anyone, after all. But I know most people don't understand the need to give up control, especially when so much of our lives are spent trying to *be* in control.

But no one really accepts that we aren't in control of anything anyway. At least this way, I can control who I give control over to. It was comforting.

Comforting, and my god it was sexy.

The ache I got, that started at my navel and slithered down between my legs whenever I thought about him.

Him. Alexander. Never Alex, not even as a joke. Alexander, even if I could never be sure that was even his real name. Whose face I have never seen. Who summons me once a month in his limousine to this fancy hotel where one night probably costs two months of my little studio apartment's rent.

Alexander, who has laid down his terms, as I've laid down mine— this is all it will be. Nothing more. Nothing less. Nothing less than the absolute freedom of giving up total control to someone else. For someone like me, who spends every moment of every day obsessing over every detail, who plays back every single conversation in her head, who second-guesses every decision she's ever made, he was a godsend. My only chance to let go. My only chance to just *be*.

At least, that's what I'd thought all this time. Until two months ago, when he asked if I'd like to meet for drinks beforehand.

"In person?" I'd replied stupidly, my fingers grazing the blindfold for a fleeting second, making sure it hadn't budged.

"Yes, my dear. In person."

I'd swallowed. This was not the deal. These were certainly not the terms.

"Can I think about it?" I said finally. I was hoping he'd take the hint, and it felt like he had because he never mentioned it again. Things easily slipped back to where they were before, and I've been grateful.

So when I heard the key in the lock, when his woody, musky cologne filled the room, when I heard him mutter the words "Hello, my pet" before he slipped the satin blindfold over my eyes, I exhaled one last time.

I heard the crack of a whip and my body melted, even though he hadn't touched me yet. And he wouldn't. Not with his hands, anyway. Not for hours, while he teased me and tortured me and made me give every part of myself over to him.

I relaxed. My monsters will be kept at bay.

I could finally be me.

It was hours later, aching, breathless, and more myself than I had felt in weeks, that I finally woke up again. Our night was ending. He was getting ready to leave. I was in bed, blindfold still on, but I could hear him. I listened, trying to guess what he was doing. I could hear a zipper being done, and a clink of something, maybe cuff links. As always, I yearned to sneak a peek at him. To catch a glimpse of this man who changed everything for me. But I kept my blindfold on. Those were the rules. And I always, always played by the rules. He knew that. He knew me.

"Thank you for a lovely evening, my dear. You can remove your blindfold when you hear the door close," he said, his voice dripping over me like a luxurious oil.

"Mm-hmm," I replied, feeling the soft folds of the sheets. The room was mine until tomorrow, where I could have breakfast in bed if I wanted before the limousine would drop me back home. I'd have a bath after he left, I thought, touching the welts that were starting to develop on my butt and thighs. Thank goodness for the fancy lotion in the bathroom. That always helped.

But first I needed to check my phone. The urgency of it slapped me out of my warm daze.

It was like he could feel the shift of energy in the room.

"Clara?" he asked, an edge of hesitation in his voice.

"Yes?" I sat up. He never calls me by my name—fake one included. He certainly never makes small talk afterward. I hoped he wasn't asking about drinks again. I didn't think I had it in me to dodge it a second time.

"Is everything all right?"

"All right?"

"Yes. You, well, seemed a little distracted today."

It was her post. I knew it. Every time I thought I'd pushed it out of my mind, it would sneak back in. A thorn in my side. Impossible to ignore.

I thought I'd done a good job pretending that it hadn't taken over my thoughts. I guess I was wrong. But what could I tell him? *Sorry I wasn't all here. My old best friend, who I haven't spoken to in years, whose social media accounts I stalk relentlessly, just said she had a huge announcement, and I'm filled with so much unexplained dread that I can't relax until I figure out what it is.*

No, I could never tell him that. That, especially that, was certainly not part of our arrangement.

"I have a few things on my mind." I kept my voice light. "You know how it is."

"Did you enjoy our time together tonight?" Always the gentleman.

"You know I did." I kept my voice low. Sexy. I was only ever like

this with him. I cringed when I even I thought about being provoca-
tive otherwise.

"I'll see you in a few weeks, then." I felt him reach over and drop
a kiss on my forehead. It was tender and sudden and not something
he usually does while saying goodbye.

But then he was gone, and I yanked off the blindfold with one
hand while reaching for my phone with the other.

I was just unlocking it when I stopped myself.

Is this really who I was? Five years later and a single Instagram
post about announcing a surprise has me worked up all evening?

I took a deep breath. I checked the time. 12:13 a.m.

Not perfect doubles, but consecutive numbers are good, too, right?
I'm sure it's just something about her charity. I'm sure she's just making a big deal about it for the attention, or the Instagram hearts. I sat
on the edge of the bed and pulled up the app on my phone.

There was a new post.

Kaavi had uploaded two pictures.

The first was a close-up of the most breathtaking diamond and
rose gold ring I had ever seen.

My heart started pounding in my chest.

Breathe, I reminded myself.

The next was a picture of her holding her hand over half her face,
so only a part of her wide smile could be seen. The ring shone out
like a beacon from her finger.

She's getting married.

She's getting married and moving on with her life. Of course she
was. I'm just not a part of it anymore.

It was to be expected, I know. We weren't friends now. We haven't
been in years.

I should be happy for her. She's moved on. My own failure to launch has nothing to do with her, even though it had everything to do with her.

It felt like a wave crashed over me and I drowned, feeling myself getting pulled down to the bottom. But after what felt like far too long, my head broke the surface again. I came out, gasping for air. And I realized that even though we haven't spoken in five years, something didn't quite make sense.

She wasn't dating anyone, was she? At least there was no one serious enough for her to post about on Instagram. And Kaavi posted everything on Instagram, from her breakfast to her workouts to her holidays.

Or maybe she just posted what she wanted others to see. Maybe she was private about some things after all. Or maybe it was an arranged proposal? Her parents would certainly have gotten antsy about her being single for so long. But I just couldn't shake off how odd it felt.

I was still logged in through KimKx, so I left a comment— *Congratulations!*

Then I logged in as IllegallyBlonde99 and left another—*So happy for you xxx*

Then as ForestFern23—*How wonderful <3 Congrats!*

There were more accounts I could have commented from, but I suddenly felt exhausted.

I got off the bed.

Time for that bath.

I made it as lush as I could today. All the soap bubbles and oils and fancy salts. I needed all the pampering I could get. My oldest friend was getting married, and here I was, in a ridiculous old hotel, getting my behind spanked once a month by a man whose face I have never even seen.

I looked through the replies from my various accounts as I waited for the tub to fill. They didn't sound too much like they came from the same person, but I doubt she analyzed all her fan responses anyway.

She'd added another picture to the post, because I didn't notice a third one as I swiped between her face and the ring the first time around. It was a typical couples' selfie. He had his arms wrapped around her while she had her phone pointed at a mirror.

It took a moment for me to recognize who it was. I stopped breathing.

My phone slipped through my fingers and clattered down on the marble countertop.

It couldn't be.

There was no way.

But I'd recognize Spencer anywhere. I'd pick him out in a crowd of a thousand people. I'd find him with my eyes closed. I knew his silhouette, his shadow, I knew every part of him there was to know.

And this was definitely, certainly him.

I picked up my phone and looked at the screen again. I was never wrong. After so many years, there he was. No mistaking that it was him. The floor felt like it was tilting up. Like I couldn't maintain my grip on the slippery tile.

So how was the man who shattered every inch of my soul suddenly wrapped around the best friend I didn't speak to anymore?

I was sitting on the floor of the bathroom. I don't know how I ended up there. It hurt to breathe. I couldn't even move. How could they do this? To me? How could they do this to me?

I tried to take a deep breath and calm down. I needed to center myself. I tried counting to five. It was impossible. It felt like a knife was twisting in my side. Or in my back.

I can't believe this is happening. Kaavi can't marry Spencer.

SPENCER

Interview Transcript: Matthew Spencer (abbrev. MS)

Date: January 25, 2020

Location: The Mount Lavinia Hotel

EP: I hope you don't object to me recording our conversation?

[Pause]

This is Eshanya Padmaraj, carrying out this investigation at the behest of the Fonseka family. Please state your name and address for the record.

MS: My name is Matthew Spencer. I am temporarily residing at the Emperor Residencies, in Colombo 08.

[Pause]

Do you know anything yet? One of the lobby managers mentioned to a guest that this was being treated as a homicide. Is that true? Is Kaavi—is she—have you found anything?

EP: Mr. Spencer, I understand that you're upset, but time is of the essence right now and we need to get to the bottom of things. Could you please outline for us the events leading up to Miss Fonseka's disappearance?

MS: Of course.

[Pause]

Sorry, my apologies. It's just that this is rather difficult for me. I—if something has happened to her—you know I told her to please not be stubborn. To please just room in the new wing of the hotel with the rest of the bridal party. But she insisted she would be fine. The rooms were so much bigger in the old wing, and apparently the lighting was perfect for photos and makeup? I guess that's a thing. Her photos were a really big deal to her—for her social media posts, you see. She's so determined. So independent.

[Pause]

You know, it's what I love most about her. Her fearlessness.

EP: Mr. Spencer, like I said, we need to move through this investigation quickly—

MS: Yes. Yes, of course. Sorry, I—yes. How early would you like me to start?

EP: The days leading up to the wedding will be fine for now. Did you notice anything strange? Anyone unknown hanging around?

MS: Anyone unknown? I don't think so. Not really. Well . . .

[Pause]

I am quite new to this whole, you know, setup. There were tons of relatives and service staff and suppliers coming and going. I suppose, if you're looking at it that way, it could be anyone.

EP: And what about Miss Fonseka? Did she seem upset in any way? Distant, perhaps?

MS: Oh gosh, I don't think so. She was, well, she was preoccupied with the wedding, of course. There was quite a bit of pressure on her, I think. More than there was on me, you know. Being an outsider, it's easier for everyone to forgive any slipups I'd make. But she, well, she was always held to this ridiculously high standard. It almost felt like there was no winning, sometimes. There were a lot of customs and traditions that she, that we both, had to be sensitive to.

EP: Tell me about the day just before she went missing. Did you notice anything strange about her? Did she mention anything out of the ordinary?

MS: What? You mean yesterday? Well, you already know that it was the day of the Poruwa ceremony, of course. We couldn't speak much in the lead-up. She spent the whole morning getting ready, and then there was a photo shoot, and the ceremony itself.

EP: And you didn't speak to each other much during this time?

MS: No, of course we spoke. Just not about anything meaningful, I suppose. Mostly about who we were supposed to greet and what we were supposed to do. We were both so exhausted at the end of it, and of course the full-blown church ceremony and the reception was meant to be, well—

[Pause]

It was meant to be this afternoon. So we had both decided to turn in early and get some rest.

EP: And afterward?

MS: Well, I was hoping to sleep in a little this morning, you know? [Laughs quietly] Figured I'd get some rest before the big day. But then I was woken up by Kaavi's mother. She was upset—asking if Kaavi was in my room. She wasn't, of course. Kaavi would never risk something like that with the hotel being so full of wedding guests.

EP: Mr. Spencer, there were reports of strange sounds coming from Miss Fonseka's room last night. Sounds of a struggle. Would you happen to know anything about this?

MS: Sounds of a struggle? [Pause] No.

EP: And we also have a report from one of our room service wait-ers, who said he saw you go into Miss Fonseka's room last night.

MS: Um, yes. About that—

[Pause]

EP: Mr. Spencer?

MS: Yes. Sorry, sorry. [Sighs] My head's just in such a muddle. Look, I didn't mention it because Kaavi would be really upset if it got out. She's very particular about her reputation, you see, and we aren't technically married yet, and her mother would have had a fit if she knew I was in her room alone last night. Kaavi texted me and asked me to come see her. I thought—well, I thought it might be last-minute nerves or something. But it wasn't. She just wanted—

[Pause]

Well, Kaavi was always quite, um, demonstrative, I guess you could say. We've always been—oh gosh, she would hate me if she found out I said this—quite amorous. And last night, she asked me to come to her room, and, well, I'm sure I don't need to spell it out for you. We just spent some time alone. For the first time in days. It was reassuring. Which is why—

[Pause]

I just know something has happened to her. This isn't just cold feet or something like that.

EP: So last night, you went into her room, and then you left?

MS: Yes.

[Pause]

I don't think I'm missing anything.

EP: Are you sure?

MS: [Pause] Yes—yes, I believe so.

EP: And how did you get that scratch on your face?

MS: [Pause] This?

[Touches face]

Oh, I didn't even realize it was visible. It happened when we were, um, well, you know. Kaavi reached out for me, and her nail— she had these long false nails done for the wedding—caught me on my cheek. I think she was a little upset that it would ruin the wedding photos, but I figured the photographer could photoshop it out or something, you know.

EP: Tell me more about your relationship with Kaavindi Fonseka. I gather it's been quite the whirlwind romance.

MS: I guess you could call it that. Kaavi and I, well, we've known each other for years. We met first when she was in college in San Francisco, and we reconnected again a few years ago.

I—I know that every man probably thinks the woman he's marrying is wonderful, but Kaavi, well, Kaavi is truly spectacular. I admire her so deeply. The work she does through her charity, the way she's seamlessly taking over her father's business, but more than that, the way she carries herself. She's been such a strength to me, through and through. I get asked, sometimes, whether it's too much for me—everything she does. My own friends told me that if I married her, I'd be left holding her purse while she took the spotlight. And they are right. Kaavi's a strong woman. The strongest. And I'm honored that she chose me to be her partner. Maybe some men would feel intimidated by her. But not me. I love her for everything she is. If something has happened to her I—I don't know what I would do.

[Voice breaks]

She's a part of me. She's everything good in my life.

EP: I understand.

[Pause]

I still have a few more questions. Can we continue?

MS: Yes, yes. I'm sorry. Please, go on.

EP: We understand that you had a prior relationship with Miss Fonseka's friend. One Miss Amaya Bloom. Could you tell us a little bit about that?

MS: [Pause]

EP: Mr. Spencer?

MS: Yes, Amaya. We dated for a while when Amaya was in college. It's how I first met Kaavi, actually. But Amaya was quite young back then. So was I, I suppose. It was nothing too serious. Our relationship fizzled out around the time she graduated. We were both taking new directions in life, I guess.

EP: And did she end the relationship, or did you?

MS: It was mutual, at first anyway. I actually thought we ended on good terms. But then I heard that—well, look, this probably isn't fair of me to say. I know how it sounds. I don't want to be the kind of asshole guy saying that my ex-girlfriend is crazy. I hate it when men do that—makes us all look bad, you know. I don't think she's crazy. Not at all. But Amaya was, she is, complicated, I guess.

EP: Complicated in what way?

MS: Um, well, look—I don't want to be harsh here, but, well, to use the word *obsessed* doesn't seem fair, but she certainly had boundary issues. With me, certainly, and from what I saw, with Kaavi. But, well, I assumed they also drifted apart after graduation or something. I wasn't sure of the reasons. I never read too much into it. I hadn't met either of them for years when I reconnected with Kaavi, and I just assumed they'd stopped being friends.

[Pause]

But then, well, Amaya turned up to the wedding. It left everyone feeling quite uncomfortable.

2

AMAYA

Three Months before the Wedding

"What's that you got there?" Jessica asked, eyeing my phone.

We were sitting in the LA sun, sipping mimosas at Bella's Bistro while waiting for our eggs to come. It's a beautiful day, and I shouldn't be on my phone. I shouldn't have come at all. It's been two days since I found out, and to say I'm a blubbering mess is the understatement of the year.

I didn't even stay the night at the hotel. I called for the car and left as soon as I could. I needed to get to my laptop. Combing through Kaavi's social media feeds on my phone wasn't going to cut it.

I spent the rest of the night and most of the next day checking each of her posts for a hint of a relationship with him. For a sign on when they got together. For a crumb of anything at all that didn't leave me feeling like my life was spinning out of control.

I pushed aside the questions that kept buzzing through my head—

Had they always kept in touch?

How long had they been together?

Could they have gotten together when Spencer and I were still dating?

And the worst question of all—

Was there always a spark? A spark of something that I had missed because I worshipped the ground he walked on and she was like family to me?

It was late the next day when I got a few answers, but it wasn't from digging through her older posts. I got notifications on all my accounts that Kaavi had uploaded a video to her YouTube channel.

My fingers trembled as I hit the play button. It had already racked up over a hundred views in the few minutes it was online—127, to be exact. It wasn't going to be good. Even the numbers weren't on my side.

She was sitting in her minimalist, rose gold–accented office.

The future is female, a poster behind her read. Her hair was flawless, as always. I have no idea how she kept it so sleek and neat, but then again, nothing about me has ever been sleek or neat, so it's not like I could relate. And, also as always, she was radiant. She usually included the makeup she wore in her videos with links to buy. I had bought every single product in her ensemble. The scrubs and exfoliators and "natural finish" tinted moisturizers. But never, not once, did my skin manage to look like hers.

She was wearing a dusty-pink silk blouse, which matched the aesthetic of her office. She always matched the aesthetic of her office. Every Instagram post, every YouTube video, every picture on Facebook had some sort of filter on it that made it bright and light, with hints of pink and rose gold, of course. She was nothing like the shy girl I grew up with who mostly wore oversize men's shirts and was obsessed with Bruce Springsteen.

She was smiling and happy and positively glowing as she spoke.

"Hi, everyone! I've been getting bombarded with messages congratulating me on my engagement, and I'm so very thankful."

She pressed her palms together in front of her. Just the right amount of tradition for her Sri Lankan audience, as always.

"But so many of you had questions about Spencer, my fiancé"—she dragged out the word like it was two syllables longer than it was—"that I thought I would make a quick video. First off, many of you have asked if this is an arranged marriage."

She gave a little giggle at this.

"No, my lovelies, this was not arranged by my parents at all. Spencer and I have known each other for a very long time. Years and years, in fact. First as friends, and then I guess we grew into our love for each other."

I knocked over the glass of water that was sitting on the desk next to me. Of course they knew each other for *years and years*. It was normal, wasn't it, for someone to get to know their best friend's boyfriend? The three of us were practically inseparable while we were in college. And they *grew into* their love? What does that even mean? This was a relationship, not a pair of shoes that Sri Lankan parents buy their children—three sizes too big so they would fit them for longer.

I wanted to turn it off. Turn it off and throw my laptop out the window.

"Spencer has been quite the supporter of my charity, and this is what really allowed us to get to know each other and build a relationship based on our shared values."

She interspersed this bit with images of her and Spencer meeting with the girls from Pink Sapphires. There was a picture of him handing over one of those silly oversize checks, and one with both of their arms around three girls. My head felt like it was about to burst.

I remember when I first met Spencer. How he had been so different from the immature, idiotic teenagers I had dated back in Sri Lanka. He used to pick me up from my classes with giant bouquets of roses. He was so proud of me. Wanted to show me off. We didn't have to be quiet or discreet like I had to be at home.

"The big question, of course, was why I had never mentioned

Spence before. And I know, I know, it was all very sneaky of me. I hope none of you will hold it against me, because I really do love sharing my journey with you. It's just that Spence is really quite shy and doesn't like the limelight at all, so he asked me if I could please give him some space and not put too many details up on social media. It was something I struggled with at first, because as you lovelies know, I have no filter."

She gave a hearty laugh, but I continued to feel dizzy. There are many words that I could have used to describe Spencer, but shy was definitely not one of them. Spencer was confident. He always knew what he wanted. Unapologetically so. It was what drew me to him in the first place. Unless he's changed. Of course he must have changed. Five years is a long time, after all. Long enough to forget everything that happened in the past and happily move on with your best friend.

"But now that the cat's out of the bag, I guess I can finally share a little bit about him. Apart from being ridiculously handsome, Spencer is quite the successful entrepreneur. His start-ups in San Francisco have done really well. Well enough that he can finally take some time off to plan the wedding! I don't mean to brag, of course, but I am very, very proud of him.

"What plans for the wedding? Well, here's another bit of exciting news! We've decided to get married in January. Now I know, I know. That's only three months away. But you all know how traditional my parents are, and the astrologer told them that this is the most auspicious day for us."

She gave a little eye roll and a laugh at this. She wanted her audience to know that she thought it was silly too. But not silly enough to hold off on the wedding. Three months. I felt like choking. I couldn't believe this.

"I didn't think that Spence would be all right with all this horoscope business, but funnily enough, he thought it was a great idea. Didn't want to wait at all! So now we are gearing up to drive our wedding planner up the wall."

Spencer, *my* Spencer, who gave me a hard time if I ever referred to myself as a Virgo, was suddenly all right with Sri Lankan horoscope readers? I guess people can change after all. But then I thought about the way my stomach would tighten whenever he came home from work, the way my heart would race when he smiled at me, told me I was beautiful. Could things really change that much? We'd dated all through college. Well, college for me. He'd dropped out in his first year to focus on his start-up. But we did date for four years. Long enough to really know someone. Long enough to discover each other's secrets.

"I have time now for just one more question. AliFlowerx3 asked where we would live after the wedding, and some of you had suggested that I would be moving back to the States with Spence after we got married. It's a nice thought, but it won't be the case. My family's business, which I am actively involved in, as well as my charity, Pink Sapphires, are both run from Sri Lanka, where I intend to stay. Luckily for us, Spence has decided to take a step back from the active role in his most recent start-up for a while, until we get settled as husband and wife, at least. So he'll be moving to Sri Lanka, and we'll be living in my parents' guesthouse until our own house is constructed, just down the road from my family home."

I tried to make myself take a deep breath. It didn't work. A shudder escaped from deep within me.

Of course Kaavi would put her charity first. When she founded Pink Sapphires two years ago, I'd thought it was a typical Colombo 07 vanity project. To my surprise, Kaavi was quite serious about it, and the organization's mission—to provide educational opportunities for girls from low-income households—was gaining quite a reputation.

"That's it, my lovelies. I need to start wedding planning. Oh gosh, it feels so funny to say that. Who would have thought I would be a Mrs. at the very start of the new year! And as always, if you loved hearing about my good news, please don't forget to hit that like button and subscribe to my channel. Love and peace to all of you!"

I just sat there, staring at my laptop screen for so long that YouTube started auto-playing a clip from *Say Yes to the Dress*. I didn't even have the energy to turn it off.

"Amaaaayaaaa?" Jessica dragged my name out. "Hello? Are you even here?" She had a point. I had pretty much forgotten that I was still at brunch. When I wasn't watching the video on my phone, I was replaying it in my head, over and over again.

"Sorry. I've just been a little preoccupied."

I would have given my right arm to have skipped this meetup. I had actually messaged Jessica and canceled, saying I wasn't feeling well, but she didn't buy it—probably because I was always trying to bail on her. She showed up at my door with a bowl of soup, a cup of coffee, and some Tylenol, all of which were discarded on my kitchen counter while she shoved me into the shower and picked out my clothes while I was in there. It was forward and pushy and usually why I liked her. Someone to shake me out of my comfort zone of takeout Chinese food and a movie on my couch on Friday nights, and reading in bed on Saturday mornings. And I usually did have a good time going for brunch, or cocktails, or to some gallery opening that Jessica always seemed to be invited to.

So here I was—forcing myself to sip on overpriced mimosas and nibble on artistically plated avocado and poached eggs when my mind was ten thousand miles away, obsessing over a wedding that should never happen.

It wasn't a terrible morning. I was just having brunch with Jessica,

Deepa, and Imogen, all of whom knew one another from the spin class they took three times a week, though I only knew Jessica since she was a supplier for my store. All three women were upbeat without being too intense, friendly, and always up for a laugh. We'd been doing this lukewarm brunch routine for about a year now. The sun was shining and the breeze was light. I should be having a better time. Not constantly checking my phone to see if Kaavi had uploaded anything new.

Maybe I should just talk about it a little? Maybe I'd feel less terrible if I did? At least, that's what Dr. Dunn said, right?

"That'll be $33.55 each," I heard the lady at the table next to ours tell her friends, and I took that as a sign.

I cleared my throat and looked at Jess hesitantly.

"It's just, well, my ex–best friend is getting married. To my ex-boyfriend."

The outpouring of horror was just as I hoped.

"No fucking way."

"That ho."

"Talk about being a backstabbing bitch."

They were good friends.

"Is that why you haven't gotten off Instagram today?" Imogen asked. This, coming from a woman who was dead set on broadcasting her entire life on social media. None of us were allowed to take a bite of our meals until she had artistically messed up the table and taken pictures of everything. It was annoying, of course, especially when our eggs got cold, but no one ever said anything, so I didn't either. There was a time I used to daydream about her choking on her avocado toast, eyes bulging as she gasped and spluttered for air, just so she would let me eat in peace, but I've gotten used to the constant Instagramming now.

I guess I had nothing to lose by talking about it. Dr. Dunn would probably applaud. *Talking about things is one of the best ways to cleanse your soul.* Maybe he was right.

I took a deep breath.

"You guys know my friend Kaavi. She was my best friend growing up and in college?"

"I think you might have mentioned her, but I can't really remember."

"Anyway, yeah. She's marrying the guy I was dating all through college. She posted about it on Instagram. That's how I found out."

I flushed. It was horrible when everyone's focus was on me like this. I stared at my own drink as they made all the right faces, said all the right things.

"What a fucking bitch!"

"I'd be so pissed if I were you!"

"Show us the post!"

And so I hesitantly passed my phone over, while they continued to be aghast at what Kaavi had done to me.

I took comfort in their disdain. It was good to feel validated. To feel heard, for once. To not feel insignificant.

I even finished my eggs. Drank half my mimosa. My friends were getting rowdier, already on their third round of cocktails.

"And you know what I can't stand? That bitch's hair. I mean, honey, please, blond streaks on South Asian hair don't make you look like Beyoncé. They make you look like a fucking German shepherd." Deepa laughed and Imogen reached across the table and high-fived her.

I laughed along with them. It was the easiest thing to do. I finally had people on my side.

"You know what you should do?" The mimosas were starting to get to Jessica. I knew by the way she dragged her "sh"s. It normally made me wish her butter knife would miss her bread and slash her wrist instead, but it was easy to overlook these annoyances when it felt like your friends were finally on your wavelength.

"You should fly down there. And when the priest does that whole, oh, you know, the whole *speak now or forever hold your peace* bit, you should stand up and tell everyone that backstabbing bitches shouldn't be allowed to get married."

Imogen hooted with laughter.

"No way will Amaya do something so cray. Over my dead body."

I was laughing too. Probably the most I've laughed in a long time. That's why I didn't think when I spoke next.

"No way. More like over *her* dead body. I mean, I could just kill that bitch."

Their laughter wilted away.

Jessica turned her head toward me, a smile still on her lips.

"What was that, babe?"

"Oh my goodness, you guys, I was just kidding. It was a joke." It really was. But my voice came out high-pitched and oddly tinny.

There was a beat. The tiniest of pauses. It felt like an entire year.

"Of course you were kidding!" Jessica forced a little laugh, but her eyes met Deepa's for a fraction too long.

All three women nodded with such vigor that their perfectly curled and styled hair whipped around their faces like snakes. Like they were all modern-day Medusas. I thought about grabbing a fistful of Jessica's hair and slamming her head against the table. Of course, it was just a thought. It went away, like all thoughts did.

I averted my eyes accordingly. It hurt to look at them, with their perfect hair and perfect smiles and perfect lives. Why was I always the one left behind?

"So anyways," Jessica carried on, a big forced smile plastered on her face, "have you seen the new honey supplier? Mark something, I think? I bumped into him the other day when I was making my delivery." Jessica makes chemical-free sea salt blends that sell really well at my little spice boutique in downtown LA.

I shrugged, but Imogen jumped in.

"You know, the tall guy? He had a really great ass."

The conversation moved toward rating various men's behinds, and I tried to shake off the sinking feeling in the pit of my stomach.

Great, now the few friends I have think I'm some sort of troubled freak, and I can't say I blame them.

They were right, of course. I wasn't doing myself any favors by being so obsessive. I have a life, regardless of how paltry it is in comparison to everyone else's. I have a successful small business that I built from the ground up. I have a little apartment that I love. I have friends, or something that resembled friendship, anyway. And I have Alexander. I do. Even if I didn't know a thing about him. Because if Kaavi's announcement proved anything, it was that it didn't matter if you grew up with someone or never saw their face; people still have a way of pulling the rug out from under you.

So when we did our goodbye half hugs and the ladies all took turns squeezing my hand and telling me that I was strong and amazing and that Kaavi and Spencer would probably be divorced before their third wedding anniversary, I held it together. I *am* strong. I *am* amazing. Their wedding didn't matter to me.

All of these were lies, of course, but Jessica gave me a look that said maybe she bought it. Maybe, one day, I would buy it too.

"I wouldn't blame you, you know, if you flew down there," Deepa whispered to me, out of the earshot of the others. "I get it. You want closure. You should go. It'll be good for you."

I managed a laugh that I hoped was flippant. "Thanks, Deeps. I'm fine, though, really. Just caught off guard, that's all."

But it was like a disease. I was sick. Sick of the idea of Kaavi and Spencer.

She's marrying the guy I was dating all through college, I had said to the women at brunch. Just a university sweetheart. It was almost painful how dismissive it was.

Because Spencer, well, he wasn't just some guy. He would never be just some guy. It hurt me, like, actually physically hurt me, to think about the early days of our relationship. The days where he would convince me to play hooky and we would go to the movies and then for ice cream. Juvenile, childish things I'd missed out on growing up. He'd listen to me when I cried. When I told him how much I missed my mom or wanted desperately to hate my dad.

I was exhausted as I dragged myself back to my apartment and collapsed onto the couch. It wasn't just the wedding announcement. I always felt this way after hanging out with the girls. So much of my life is spent on recovery mode.

I was so ridiculous, thinking they would understand. Thinking they would be on my side.

Sure, they were great for a weekly attempt at not being a hermit, but Jessica never really *got* me. She never had the need to. I was sweet, polite, calm Amaya. Amaya who spent her week selling overpriced cinnamon to fancy LA millennials. Who tipped more than anyone should and who was always happy to take a cab home by herself when the friends she came out with disappeared with guys they'd just met.

Jessica would have an aneurysm if she found out that I wear a collar and let a stranger I met on the internet put nipple clamps on me and deny me orgasms until he felt I was adequately whipped.

I sighed.

Five years ago I made a decision to walk away from my old life. That meant Spencer, Kaavi, and everyone in between. It hurt, but I had to do it, for my own sake. It was the first of many decisions where I made myself a priority, and while it broke my heart, it freed me. For the first time, I was truly on my own.

Had I flourished on my own? Perhaps not in every sense of the word. But I sure as hell got by. I had my routine. I had my fun. I had carved out some semblance of what I wanted, and I will keep chipping away at it until I can convince myself that I'm happy.

I pulled out my phone and ordered a large Thai tofu salad for dinner, then turned on Netflix and started searching for a show with some good old-fashioned bloodthirsty serial killers, settling into my favorite pastime.

My phone beeped, and I thought it would be a notification from DoorDash about my salad, but it was an email.

An email from Kaavindi Fonseka.

I sat up straight on my couch. No way she's emailing me. Not now, after five years of not speaking to each other.

My fingers were sweaty, and it took a couple of tries for me to unlock my phone.

Hi Amaya,
How are you? I know this might seem really out of the blue, but I wanted you to hear it from me first. I'm getting married!

A little late there, Kaavi, but of course she wouldn't know how obsessively I stalk her online.

It might come as a bit of a shock to you, after the way we left things, but I'm actually marrying Spencer. I just wanted to be straight up about it and get that out of the way. I know you're probably thinking WTF, and I don't blame you, but I would love it if you could come for the wedding. It would give us a chance to clear things up, once and for all, and to be honest, I've always pictured you at my wedding and I can't imagine going through with it without you by my side. We're keeping it small, no bridesmaids, and my baby sister, Nadia, will be my only flower girl. I don't think you've had a chance to properly meet her, but she's really sweet, and she'll love to see you, I'm sure. My whole family misses you, actually. It would really mean so much, to all of us, if you could come.

    I know it's short notice and you probably have a lot going on, but please think about it?

            Love and bubbles,

            (ha ha, remember when we signed off

            all our notes that way!)

            Kaavi

The remnants of the one mimosa I had this morning rose to my throat. It burned. The distraction was welcome, even if it only took my mind off the email for a moment.

Kaavi invited me. Her whole family did.

Does that mean they've decided to forget about our agreement? The one where I was asked to never contact them ever again?

But there was no way I could go. Forget about our understanding. There was no way I could see Spencer. Not like this. Not with him happily marrying my best friend while I was single, alone, and well on my way to spinsterhood.

But the email kept burning in my mind.

My baby sister, Nadia, will be my only flower girl. I don't think you've had a chance to properly meet her, but she's really sweet, and she'll love to see you.

There was a whole new person that I'd never got to know. There was so much that I'd missed. And not just Kaavi, but all of them. Was it possible for me to ever really move away from the only people who treated me like I was their own? The only make-believe family I had?

My heart felt like it was about to burst. Like I couldn't breathe. I pinched the inner part of my arm, hard, relishing the feeling of my nails digging into my skin.

I took a deep breath and counted to five.

I locked my phone, unlocked it again. Closed the email, opened it again. Read through it many, many times. There was a file attached— an image of a wedding invitation. It was rose gold and delicate and perfect, just like I was sure the wedding would be.

There really was only one person I could speak to, and I was silly not to think about this sooner.

Beth, you there?

She didn't always reply immediately. She worked the night shift at a call center, so she kept an odd schedule. But thankfully, I didn't have to wait too long until my phone buzzed back.

Hi babe, yes, I'm here. You okay?

I breathed out in relief. Where would I even begin?

No

At least I could be honest.

What's going on?

I took a deep breath.

Remember my friend Kaavi? The one . . .

How would I even begin to describe that friendship?

The one I'm not friends with anymore?

**Yeah, the one who made you skip
your reunion.**

Well, it's not like Kaavi *made* me skip anything. I'd checked and double-checked that she wasn't going when I first signed up. I mean, she lived in Sri Lanka. Why would she make it all the way to California just to attend a college reunion? Her name wasn't on the list when I checked two weeks before the date. And so I'd RSVP'd that I was attending. Figured I would fly up to the Bay Area a day earlier. Maybe rent a car and take a drive to Napa. I'd always wanted to go wine tasting there, but it seemed like something you'd want to do with a group of your girlfriends, and I just couldn't imagine spending an entire weekend getting drunk with Jessica, Imogen, and Deepa, I was finally feeling confident enough to book a wine tour for one. I was finally feeling confident.

But then I'd logged on to Facebook and noticed that Kaavi had checked into the first-class lounge at Bandaranaike International

Airport, and was en route to SFO. I guess she'd changed her mind after all.

And so I'd unpacked my bags and ordered my body weight in Chinese food that sat congealing in the takeout boxes because I couldn't bring myself to eat more than a few bites.

Beth knew all about that. It was around the time we met.

> **Yeah. Well, she's getting married. To my ex.**

There was a pause while I watched the dancing dots on my screen that showed me she was typing something.

> **No way.**

That was it? It felt like she was typing a lot more. But, well, I guess I wouldn't really know what to say to someone in my position either.

> **Yeah. I just can't believe it. I never even knew
> they were together. She knew us as a couple as
> well. Hell, the three of us were really close.**

> **I'm so sorry, babe. I can't believe
> she would do that to you.**

See, this is why I was friends with Beth. No calling Kaavi a bitch. No mean comments. Just straight-up empathy.

> **Want to know the worst part?**

> **It gets worse . . . ? Oh no**

Yep. She actually invited me to the wedding.

Wow . . .

Yeah, wow.

I didn't know what else to say. I wanted to tell Beth how this wedding couldn't happen. How I would do anything I could to stop it—even though what I could actually do was pretty darn minimal.

So . . . you gonna go, right?

And here I was, thinking Beth understood me. Sure, I had fantasized a million different ways in which Kaavi and Spencer would call the whole thing off. But to actually go?

Um, no. There's no way I could face them all
after so long.

That bad with the family, huh?

Well, actually, the invitation did come from the
whole family.

That's nice of them, right?

How the hell am I going to face Spencer, that's
my ex btw, after so long? It'll be super awkward.

A part of me did want to see him though. Part curiosity, part . . .

well . . . maybe it was some perverse way for me to convince myself that I was finally over everything that happened. Except I don't know if I'll ever be over it. Over him. And now he's marrying Kaavi? I can't let that happen. I can't believe she would do this.

The dancing dots on my screen were there for a while. But Beth's actual message, when I got it, was short.

> I think you should go.

> What? Why?

> Because, babe, no one needs closure right now more than you do. And the entire family asked you? That sounds to me like they want to make it up to you.

Beth didn't know the real terms of our agreement, of course. But maybe she did have a point. I would love to see them again.

But who was I kidding? I would only get closure from one thing, and if it worked, well, it's not like I'd be any closer to making amends.

> You're right about getting closure . . .

Maybe I could burn Kaavi's wedding dress. Now that might give me some closure. A small, delicious wave shuddered through me.

> Trust me, babe. Holding on to all this negativity isn't going to be good for you. Go. Speak to them.

> **Tell them how you feel. You said**
> **they were like your family once.**
> **You can always be honest with**
> **family.**

Not this kind of family.

But still, I was slowly inching my way over to the edge. Beth was right. It would do me good to see them. To see her. If they all wanted me there, I should go.

Besides, I didn't have the slightest chance of stopping the wedding from all the way over here.

> **Who knows, maybe she'll even**
> **ask you to be a bridesmaid? Lol.**
> **You'll be a vision in pink.**

> **Lol. No way. Besides she's not having**
> **bridesmaids. But her little sister is going**
> **to be a flower girl.**

> **Sounds adorable. Now, will you**
> **woman up and go?**

I took a deep breath. I counted to five. I checked the clock on my TV. The time was 5:05 p.m. Not the best of all the signs, but certainly a very, very good one.

I read Kaavi's email one last time, just to be sure.

Beth was right. I had to go.

This is not jealousy. This is protecting what once was and always will be mine.

3

AMAYA

Five Days before the Wedding

THE HEAT CLAMPED down on my nose and mouth like it was trying to choke me the moment I stepped out of the airport. It takes on a life of its own in Sri Lanka. It's easy to forget when you're looking at the postcards and travel vlogs. How the humidity swirls around you like a fog, making it hard to breathe, coating you in a constant, unyielding film of sweat.

But I can't focus on the heat because I have to spend every ounce of concentration on not getting run over by the stampede of trolley-bearing travelers. Cars honked, porters hollered, tearful families embraced. I took a breath to steady myself, even though it felt like I was inhaling through a wet towel that stank of a boys' locker room.

Urgh, I really shouldn't be like this. I'm not one of those stuck-up Sri Lankans who leave for a few years and come back wrinkling their noses at the heat and the smell and the definite inability to line up patiently for anything. Being Sri Lankan was such a cliché at times—we love our country for the sum of its parts, just not the individual components that make up its whole.

Well, that wasn't going to be me. Steeling myself, I forced another deep breath. I looked around for a clock, or a sign, or, well, anything really.

"*Stoothi*," I called out in thanks to a porter who let me pass by, and instantly regretted how terrible my accent was. I've been gone awhile. I needed to ease myself in. Five years is a long time for anyone. Five whole years. Half a decade. And yet, here I was, ebbing and flowing with the crowd, listening to the louder-than-average voices with their lilting melodies, and it didn't feel like it'd been that long. Like I was just waking up from a nap.

"*Ammi!*" a little girl screamed, darting past me and nearly jumping on the lady pushing a trolley behind me. The mother picked up the child and held her close, tears running down both their cheeks. I forced myself to look away. To give them their moment. I missed my own mother. I missed the life I could have had.

Rolling my trolley farther away to an empty spot on the walkway, I wondered whether I'd be able to spot Mahesh. There was usually a lot of fanfare at the arrivals terminal at Bandaranaike International Airport—families turning up in full vans to greet loved ones returning to Sri Lanka. There were flower garlands for tourists, pushy taxi drivers for those who hadn't booked their transport into Colombo. But apart from just a "see you outside," Mahesh hadn't given me any other instructions.

My flight landed at 4:00 p.m., so I'd messaged him to pick me up at 5:00. If I knew anything about the Sri Lankan airport, it was that things took time. And in any case, *I* didn't want to keep *him* waiting.

I checked my phone and it was only 4:22 p.m., so I guess I had overestimated the time, but at least the number pattern made me feel a whole lot calmer than I had been most of the way here.

I sent a message to Mahesh—

I just got out of the airport. A little earlier than I thought, but please take your time.

A message beeped back a second later—

C u soon, Akki!

I figured I'd send Beth a message as well—

Just landed. Can't believe I'm actually doing this!

She replied right away too. I guess I was in luck today.

You got this, babe!

But what have I got, exactly?

A plan A, plan B, and plan C, all increasingly far-fetched and desperate. I'd spent the last few months thinking and rethinking and drawing up various scenarios. If this were a movie, I'd be sitting at my desk with intricately mapped out blueprints and doing my evil villain laugh, but the reality was actually far from it. A lot of antacids, extra CBD oil in my tea to help me calm down, not that it worked, pacing around my apartment so much that I was sure my downstairs neighbors started to hate me. A few notes scribbled in a little notebook I have. Not too many details, of course, but enough to help me keep track of things.

So maybe I didn't have the best plan. But I did have something better, and that was a purpose. I knew I had to stop this. Any doubts

I had slowly dwindled away over the last three months and were steadily replaced by the true gravity of what I had to do. I couldn't fail. This wedding must not happen.

Kaavi made sure she was keeping all her followers up to date. There had been a flurry of wedding-related posts on her social media. The first was choosing the location—Mount Lavinia Hotel, not as modern as some of the more recently built hotels in Colombo, but *a classic*, she said. *And there's something so romantic about getting married where my parents did.* There had been some pressure, she explained, to just book out an entire island in the Maldives, but they'd eventually decided to stick to good old Colombo so that none of their thousand attendees would be inconvenienced.

The next was picking out the wedding outfits—sari for the traditional Sinhala Poruwa ceremony, followed by a ball gown for the church ceremony the next day, where they would actually be signing the marriage certificate, then a reception dress, and a rose gold going-away outfit *because there was no way I could have a wedding without a rose gold sari.* Of course she would have four outfits. Everything was being done by Andre, one of the most popular local designers, except for her reception dress, for which she flew to Singapore over a weekend to place a rush order on a Hayley Paige. *You know me, my lovelies. I always like to have options for everything except my groom!* Who even wears an outfit that costs thousands of dollars rush ordered as their second option?

Why aren't you signing the marriage certificate on the day of the Poruwa? a follower had asked.

Because, my lovelies, and this is supposed to be a surprise, our guest of honor who will also sign as witness to our wedding—now don't ask me who, okay? Like I said, it's a surprise—he's only available to attend the next day.

Knowing the Fonsekas, it was probably the president himself. Come to think of it, it must be, if they weren't following tradition and signing the documents on the day of the Poruwa. It wasn't entirely uncommon for Colombo's elite to request parliamentarians or movie stars to be witnesses at their weddings. I had been to one many years ago where they had the current president sign right next to the previous president. It really was a who's who of affairs.

There were videos about choosing flower arrangements, entertainment, and even the menu options.

I was just watching an Instagram story that encouraged her followers to vote between two dazzling centerpieces when a white Land Rover pulled up next to me and the passenger side window rolled down.

"Amaya *Akki*," Mahesh called out from behind his mirrored aviator sunglasses. He gestured to his driver, who hopped down and opened the back. I started to carry my luggage over, but it was quickly yanked out of my hands and loaded up for me.

"*Stoothi*," I said, giving the driver a smile, but he didn't make eye contact. Was my accent really *that* bad?

"Get in, *men*, it's fine," Mahesh urged, waving to the back seat, and I abandoned my trolley and climbed in. The driver pushed it away to the collection point, and several cars started honking at us, though both Mahesh and his driver seemed completely unbothered by this.

I twisted around in my seat, trying to make eye contact with the person in the car behind us to wave an apology, but Mahesh gave me a little snort.

"Relax, *men*, really. It's fine."

His driver made his way back to us, so I did relax a little.

"Thanks for coming to get me. Really. I could have just taken a cab."

"Are you mad, *men*? I told you it's fine, no? We're family, after all."

I gave him a small smile. Yes, I suppose we are family, even though we're only related in the way Sri Lankans consider themselves to be connected—our parents were distant relatives. Or rather, his parents were a part of the rare few who didn't stop speaking to my mother even after she eloped with a foreigner.

I welcomed the icy blast of the air conditioner as I settled in, even though Mahesh was so generous with his aftershave that it burned my nostrils a little.

He turned around now and gave me a grin, and the vestiges of the little boy who used to follow me around, hanging on my every word, glimmered up for just a minute. Who would have thought that gawky little kid who blushed every time I asked him how his day was would grow up into, well, I don't think I had ever given any thought to what Mahesh would grow into, but boy, had he grown. Folds of flesh dripped down over the collar of his short-sleeved linen shirt, unbuttoned at the neck to show a thick gold chain. The slicked-back hair on his head was thinning, but the tufts on his arms and chest were abundant. There was really no getting around it—Mahesh had transformed into a Sri Lankan uncle.

But here I was being judgmental again. It didn't matter what he looked like, or what he had become. What mattered was that he was probably the only soul in this entire country that I could ask for a favor.

"So, how are things?" I ventured.

"*Shape, Akki.* You know how it is, no? Same shit, different day. Colombo is Colombo."

That's what I was afraid of.

"And how's work?"

Perfunctory questions, but small talk was good. Small talk distracted me from Colombo being Colombo, and why I was really here.

"Work is okay. Waiting for a tender to go through these days. Might need to call the minister again next week. You know how it is with these bloody buggers, no? Always looking to line their pockets only."

Mahesh had been lining other people's pockets for as long as I could remember. I didn't think he would have any problems with his tender. He barely had any problems with anything. He always seemed to know who to charm, or bribe, or threaten to get what he wanted. Sure, he was good to me. We were family, like he said. But an undercurrent of something I could never quite put my finger on floated just under his mischievous smile. And that is why I knew, even though every fiber of my being screamed against it, that's why I knew he was the only person I could ask for help.

My heart sped up at just the thought of it.

I took a deep breath.

"So, how are things with you?" Luckily, I was saved from having to answer this because he just kept talking. "I was so happy when you called, you know? We hadn't heard from you in so long."

"I kno—" I started, but he cut me off again.

"And your friend Kaavi. I can't believe she's getting married." He turned around again and gave me a smile, though his raised eyebrows implied he wasn't quite pleased about the upcoming nuptials.

"Ye—"

"You know, I used to have a bit of a thing for her, back in the day. Can you even imagine?" He gave a loud guffaw. A few beads of sweat had formed around the loose flesh on his neck despite the frosty air-conditioning.

"She's a real piece of work, ah. Of course she'll go and get herself hitched to a *suddha*." A white man. The generic term for any foreigner. It wasn't used as an insult, but it sure sounded like one coming from him. "Actually, I don't even know why I'm so surprised. Those Fonsekas are so full of shit." Definitely an insult, then.

I kept silent, not that Mahesh noticed.

"Sorry, ah. I know they are your friends. I just think they are hypocrites, *men*, that's all. Actually, maybe that's unfair. They are not all terrible. That second sister, Tehani, no? She's quite sweet, ah. At least she doesn't have a big head like Kaavi does. She can cut loose and have some fun every once in a while."

I've known Tehani for the larger part of my life. I would have never thought to describe her as sweet. The cutting-loose part was a little more on-brand for her. But then, maybe she's different now. A lot could change in five years.

"I met her recently. Kaavi, I mean. At Jona's wedding. I don't know if you know him? His father's a rice importer, so you know, no?" I didn't, but I nodded anyway, keen to hear about Kaavi.

"She gave me some super attitude, *men*. Even I was shocked. And for what, I don't know. She's put on a bit also, you know. Not slim like she used to be. Really losing her looks, but still so stuck-up."

I watched the way his chin quivered as he spoke, and the way the flesh on his arms jiggled as we hit even the slightest bump on the road. Okay, Mahesh, *she's* the one who's "put on a bit."

"And you know the worst? Her bloody fake accent, *men*. It's so put-on. Who does she think she is, anyway?"

Colombo has always been divided into two camps about accents. The first lot hates anyone who speaks with an accent (and refuse to think that the Sri Lankan accent is an accent at all). They see it as an affront to national pride—a placeholder left behind from our "stick it to the colonizer" days. The second group, well, they saw accents as a type of social currency, and they weren't exactly wrong. Speak with a Western accent, real or put-on, and you were bound to get better treatment from a society that, you guessed it, was still entrenched in postcolonial trauma. It has been, and probably will always be, a lose-lose situation.

But then, it isn't the worst thing that Mahesh held a grudge against Kaavi. I was here to wreck her wedding, after all. And I needed all the help I could get.

I took a deep breath and checked the time. 5:05 p.m., thank goodness. Maybe this wouldn't be so bad.

I got my chance when the driver pulled into the parking lot of a building and Mahesh handed him some documents. They conferred in Sinhala, and Mahesh sighed and pulled out two five-thousand-rupee notes from his wallet.

"Thiyaganin ithin. Ahuwoth vitharak, therunada?" Keep this. Only if he asks, you understand?

"Sorry, *Akki*. This will just take a minute, ah," Mahesh explained as the driver went inside the building.

"This is the third time I'm sending these forms to these fellows. Bloody useless buggers. They keep telling me that they've lost them, but I'm no idiot. Not to worry though. Piyadasa knows how to handle them."

I watched Piyadasa, in his short-sleeved, untucked white shirt and black trousers. The standard uniform for bodyguards in Sri Lanka. He was definitely more than Mahesh's driver, but I suppose someone like Mahesh needed more than a driver. It made me feel slightly better about what I had to ask him.

"*Malli*, thank you so much for everything you've done for me. But I need to ask you for something else." My heart was hammering against my chest. I had rehearsed this in my head many, many times, but my voice still came out squeaky and weak.

"What is it, *Akki*? Tell me. Anything that's mine is yours."

I swallowed. I just had to spit it out.

And so I asked him.

He didn't react immediately.

Then he turned around in his seat and slid his sunglasses up onto his forehead so I could see his eyes. He didn't look angry or upset, thank goodness. But he did look amused.

"Is this because of what happened the last time you were here?"

Oh my goodness—did Mahesh know? If he knew, then everyone in Colombo knows for sure. Oh gosh.

I took a deep breath.

"The last time I was here?"

"There was a break-in or something, no? At least, that's what my mother said. About why you went and stayed at the Fonsekas instead of at your place."

"Oh, um, yeah. Something like that."

"You're of course mad, *aney*. You should have at least called me, no? I didn't even know you were here at the time."

"I know." I knew about *those* rumors, of course. I even knew who started them.

I had prepped for this.

"I know there's been a bit of talk about the last time I was here in Colombo. But there's a reason I haven't come back all this time."

He was quiet, for once. I could tell he wanted to know why. Everyone I know back home wants to know why.

"The truth is, the last time I was here—well, I was attacked."

His eyebrows shot up.

"Attacked? By who?"

I instinctively looked at the clock on his dashboard. 5:14 p.m. Oh no. Not now. What if I were to stall for a minute? 5:15 was a pattern. I could work with a pattern.

"*Akki*, who attacked you?"

I took a deep breath and cast my eyes down. Held my breath like Dr. Dunn said. Tried to steady myself. When I looked up again the numbers on the clock had changed, thank goodness.

"*Akki*?"

5:15. Finally.

"Your mother was right. There was a break-in. To my house. I think it was a burglary gone wrong."

"My god, *Akki*. Why didn't you tell me? Did you call the police?"

"Yes, but they, well, they weren't too helpful."

Mahesh clicked his tongue.

"Why didn't you tell me, *aiyyo*? The deputy inspector general is a good friend of mine. I could have made sure they looked into it properly, no?"

"You know, honestly, I was too scared. I just wanted to put it behind me. That's why I stayed at the Fonsekas."

Mahesh frowned. I was being vague, and I hoped he wouldn't question me further. I wasn't sure I could keep this up if he did. I was never a good liar. I was brilliant at avoiding the truth, but straight-up deceitfulness wasn't something I was comfortable with. I guess I had to make my peace with it now though.

"I see. Look, getting something like that here—it's not easy, you know. It's not like in America."

That's what I was afraid of.

"I know it's a tough thing to do. But I figured, if anyone could help me feel safe, it's you."

I was worried he'd see through everything. Especially my hesitant expression and the slight flutter of my eyelashes.

But his chest puffed up a little, and I thought I saw a slight smile play on his lips.

Piyadasa, the more-than-just-a-driver, was making his way back to us, and Mahesh turned around.

"I'll see what I can do," he said, sliding his sunglasses back down.

My heart didn't ease up, but I leaned back in my seat. At least that's plan C taken care of.

TEHANI

Interview Transcript: Tehani Fonseka (abbrev. TF) Part 1 of 3

Date: January 25, 2020

Location: The Mount Lavinia Hotel

EP: Thank you for speaking to us. I understand it must be difficult with your older sister missing.

TF: Why are you interviewing me, anyway? This is ridiculous.
My father hired you to get to the bottom of what happened to
my sister. Not waste our time. You should be demanding the
police arrest Amaya. Or questioning her, at the very least.

EP: And why is that?

TF: Because she did it, after all. I know it was her. I found Kaavi's
top in Amaya's room this morning. All bagged up separately,
like she was trying to get rid of it. It was a Pink Sapphires
T-shirt Kaavi had gotten made just before the wedding. There's
no way Amaya could have it without—well, something bad
happened. I'm sure of it. And that's not all—

[Pause]

EP: Yes?

TF: I saw her outside Kaavi's room last night. We bumped into
each other in the corridor. We, well, we had a few words, and
I think—I know she knocked me out.

EP: She knocked you out? Could you please elaborate further?

TF: I—yes, she attacked me.

[Pause]

EP: You sound hesitant.

TF: Okay, look. I—I had a bit too much to drink last night. My room was in the new wing, which, well, do you know how far the new wing is from the beach? It's kind of ridiculous. And I was wearing this monstrosity of a sari that was so hard to walk in, and these ridiculous heels that kept getting stuck in the sand, and anyway, I was struggling to walk all the way back to my room. I was, you know, feeling dizzy and nauseous, and I think I even hallucinated my mother being pissed at me as I was walking down the corridor. I always hallucinate shit like that when I'm drunk. And Kaavi's room was closer, so I figured I'll just go crash there for the night.

I was just about to knock on the door when Amaya stopped me. Told me not to disturb Kaavi, like, who the fuck was she to tell me what to do? I told her not to be ridiculous, and, well, that— that was the last thing I remember.

[Pause]

Okay, look. I know I sound hysterical and upset right now, but hear me out, okay? It was her who did it—who hurt Kaavi. That's what she does. She's had it out for Spencer and Kaavi since she got here. She—well, she's fucking crazy. Completely nuts. She wanted to break up the wedding.

[Pause]

You know that she and Spencer dated when she was in university, right? No one talks about it. I think even my parents don't know. Kaavi was trying to keep it a secret from everyone because, well, you know her. But it doesn't take a rocket scientist to figure it out. Just someone like me who's known them both and was prepared to do a little digging online, back to their university days. Amaya—she's jealous and still in love with Spencer and wanted to stop the wedding. She even trashed Kaavi's wedding dress. I know she did!

EP: You're claiming that the wedding dress she was supposed to wear today was destroyed by Miss Bloom? Do you have proof?

TF: Obviously, I don't have proof. If I did, then she would be locked up by now, wouldn't she? The original dress that Andre designed was destroyed *mysteriously*. Kaavi had no choice but to wear the Hayley Paige she brought from Singapore to the church, and my mother threw a fit because apparently it's too low-cut to wear before God.

[Pause]

Do you—do you think that was Amaya's way of trying to send Kaavi a message or something?

EP: This is a serious allegation, Miss Fonseka. How are you sure it's Miss Bloom who did it?

TF: I know it's her. I know, trust me. If you did your job, you'd know it too.

EP: I can assure you, Miss Fonseka, that we will be investigating Miss Bloom thoroughly, but first, and most importantly, we are trying to investigate what happened to your sister. That would take precedence over any other accusations, wouldn't you say?

TF: Yes. Okay, look, I'm just—I'm worried, okay? How can I help?

EP: You can start by helping us with this.

[EP holds up phone found in Miss Kaavindi Fonseka's room]

We found this in your sister's room.

TF: You found her phone? Kaavi doesn't even go to the bathroom without it.

EP: Would you happen to know the passcode? We could get a team to come down here and unlock it, but that might take some time, which is of great value right now.

TF: Um, sure, the last time I checked it was—could I try?

[Sound of phone being slid across the table]

TF: [Pause] Here we go. Unlocked. Would you mind if I—

EP: Actually, Miss Fonseka, it would be better if we—

TF: Hang on, oh fuck, there's a video from last night. Here, let me play.

EP: Miss Fonseka, please hand—

[Kaavindi Fonseka's voice fills the room]

If someone is watching this, then chances are that I'm already dead.

I don't even know why I'm recording a video. Call it a force of habit. Maybe later on I'll see it and it'll be hilarious. But tonight, well, [nervous laughter] this isn't the kind of nerves I was expecting the night before my big day.

I'm having my dream wedding. I'm tying the knot at this beautiful hotel where my parents got married. Where I spent so much of my childhood playing down by the beach. I should be out of my mind with joy.

And maybe I'm wrong. Maybe I'm just being paranoid. But I've had this feeling for a while now, that things aren't right.

Maybe it's just—

Hang on.

[Whispering] I hear footsteps.

I think someone's outside my door.

[Knocking]

Oh god.

[Louder] Who, um, who is it?

[Whispering to the camera] They aren't saying who it is.

[Knocking again]

Oh god, here goes.

TF: I guess it's time you start taking my accusations seriously, huh?

4

AMAYA
Five Days before the Wedding

IT'S FUNNY WHAT you call home. Some find it in a place, others in people. You can find it in a smell, in a smile, in a feeling. Home is where the heart is, people say. So where's your home if your heart has been broken into a million pieces, over and over again? Do you have to dig through the rubble to find a sense of belonging, or has the idea of home disappeared, along with everything else?

It took two hours to get into Colombo, so it was dark by the time we pulled into the neighborhood I had grown up in.

Cinnamon Gardens, the upscale part of Colombo 07, was, well, upscale in every sense of the word. I didn't really notice my privilege until I went to the US and was shocked by the size of my dorm room, which was roughly the size of my maid's bathroom. So yes, I had an indulgent life, financially anyway. Growing up in the large house that my father built my mother to echo the sprawling colonial-style home she lost her claim to when she decided to run away and marry him, I had little understanding of the world around me. The poverty that laced the Colombo city limits, just one or two streets over from my home, was like the dregs of a bad dream. I was vaguely aware that it existed, but apart from the usual yearly donations at Christmas, and the various charity clubs we used as an excuse to hang out when we were in school, I'm embarrassed to say that I'd lived in my own little bubble where I was both spoiled and neglected in equal parts.

But Cinnamon Gardens had changed. Just like I had, I suppose. Once a carefully sectioned-out collection of beautiful, large villas that housed Colombo's wealthiest, it seemed that most homes had been converted into foreign embassies and official buildings. I noticed a few restaurants that certainly hadn't been there five years ago either.

"So, looks like apartment life has finally taken over, huh?" I asked Mahesh. He'd spent most of our trip into the city arguing loudly on the phone in Sinhala about a shipment delay and had just hung up.

"You know how it is, no, *Akki*? Suddenly, from nowhere all these buggers decided to build these massive apartments and all our idiots decided it would be the fashionable thing to buy one. Everyone's renting out their houses now and living in these soulless concrete monstrosities. How they can manage in such tiny spaces, I'll never know."

What Mahesh called tiny was probably about four times the size of my apartment in LA. But one thing we Sri Lankans were used to is space, and why wouldn't we be? Up until very recently there was plenty of it to go around—if you're from upper-class Colombo anyway. The less than 1 percent that existed in a world of their own. A world that I was a part of, that I'm still a part of, if I was being honest.

We drove by houses with high white walls guarding their secrets. We liked our walls in Colombo. Yes, they kept the other 99 percent out. But they also hid us away. Kept us safe.

"Who's taking care of your place now?" Mahesh asked.

"Seetha is still here."

"Seetha? *Sha!* Still, ah? I wish our servants were as loyal." I tensed at the word. It was normal to call the household help "servants" in Sri Lanka, and I'd definitely get laughed at if I pointed out the political incorrectness of it to Mahesh, but of course the word choice made me uncomfortable. I get accused of this whenever I visit, though— starting from back when I was in university. Accused of being "woke." Made fun of for applying an American context to words that meant something very different here.

Having someone help in the house was another completely normal part of living in Sri Lanka that never struck me as strange until I left. Men and women from the more rural areas of the country would seek employment as gardeners or housemaids in Colombo, often living with families for years. Upper-class Colombo ladies would love to boast about how well they treated their help and how they considered them to be a part of the family. I mean, they'd never make their actual family only enter the house from the back door and use a separate "servants'" bathroom, but there I was, being *woke* again.

Still, it was true that I've never thought of Seetha as a servant. Housekeeper, perhaps, even though it was still quite a stretch. My father had employed her to run the house and take care of me after my mother died, and she had stayed on, working for those who rented the house while I was away. It was my only condition, actually, when letting the place out. My mother loved this house. It's why I never sold it, even though I could probably make a killing off the land value alone. It was the last true part of her to exist. And Seetha is the only person I could trust not to have it erased.

Not that Seetha and I were close. Not that she ever filled the aching gap left behind when my mother died and my father had decided it was better I remained in Sri Lanka under the eye of a housekeeper than disrupt his new family's life in England.

But there she was, standing on the open veranda that wrapped around my once-home, arms crossed, her *lungi* impeccably pressed, hair pulled back tight in a severe bun as always.

"*Baba*," she greeted me politely when I got down from Mahesh's jeep. I could be a hundred years old and she'd call me *Baba*—the Sinhala word for "baby," which is how the help address the children of the house. I would never be the lady of the house to her.

Her hair was still stark black—she'd been dying it herself for years and would probably slap anyone who suggested she stop, but there were certainly a few extra wrinkles around her eyes, and she seemed frailer than I remembered.

"Hullo, Seetha. *Kohomada?*" How are you? I made to give her an awkward hug, but she pulled back and thumped me on the back instead. She wouldn't risk appearing improper in front of Mahesh. Hugging a "servant" was just not done.

"*Mahansi athi ne?*" You must be tired, she replied, ignoring my question about how she was. Maybe it wasn't Mahesh, then. More likely she still hadn't forgiven me for sending her away the last time I was here. It was only for a few months, and I paid her salary in full the entire time, but she was bitter about it, just the same. I had thought five years would have been enough for her to let it go, but, well, if there's one thing about Sri Lankans, it's that we are certifiable experts at holding a grudge.

"A little bit," I said, switching to English. Seetha spoke it better than most maids. I think it's why my father hired her in the first place because it wasn't like she was warm, or comforting. But she could communicate with him enough to give him weekly (or was it monthly?) updates about me. So he'd feel less guilty about having left my mother when she was sick and dying to restart his life back in England. That he made me stay here afterward, with a housekeeper as my only family.

Piyadasa had carried my bags to the veranda, and I looked over to Mahesh, who was typing something on his phone. He hadn't gotten out, but he rolled his window down.

"You all set?" he asked.

"Yep. All good. Thanks so much, again, really." I suddenly didn't want him to leave. I didn't want to be left alone in this house. Not after so long.

I wish I could have stayed at a hotel, but I knew I'd have to answer enough questions about where I've been the past five years as it is, and didn't want to add to that list. Besides, Seetha would really never have forgiven me then. And a part of me did crave her forgiveness.

"It's fine, *men*, I told you, no? And don't worry. I'll give you a call soon about that thing you asked me." And with a wink, he was gone.

I hoped he'd come through.

Then it was me and Seetha, just like it had always been. Except before, I could escape to Kaavi's if I got too lonely.

"So, you're here for Kaavindi *Baba*'s wedding, no?" she said, picking up my bags as if they were empty and leading me inside.

"Yes, that's right." I don't really know who Seetha spoke to or how word got around, but she had always been up to date with all the Colombo chatter. Then again, everyone except me seemed up to date with the chatter.

Seetha might have been angry with me, but true to her word, she had kept the house exactly as it had been. Just the way my mother left it.

The house itself worked in layers. The outer ring was the veranda, which was dotted with large cane armchairs that were perfect for snoozing or reading. My mother had never really used them, from what I can remember, and neither did I. The next ring was after you step inside the front door—the open corridor that led to our rooms. The walls were covered in my mother's artwork. I'd never let Seetha even think about removing any of it. My mother had been an avid painter, even if her subject matter was gloomy and depressing. Six-by-four-foot canvases of women weeping—heartbroken and alone. Tears streaming down their faces, which were twisted in despair. I asked her once why she painted them, and she must have told me but I can't remember her answer. I was too fixated on the realization that the women all had her eyes.

Then there were the rooms. My mother's on the left and mine on the right. I'm sure Seetha would have cleared out the medical equipment and hospital bed from my mother's when we were renting out the property, but I'd never gone inside to check for myself.

And finally, the last ring. The epicenter around which the house had been built. A spacious open courtyard sat right in the middle of the house, where a large Araliya tree spread its branches. When the flowers bloomed and the smell wafted through the house, it was like my mother hadn't left at all. It was her favorite flower, and my father had it planted just for her. The first tree had died, my mother told me, shortly after they moved in. She said she should have known that they were doomed. But my father had loved her then, and planted another, announcing that it was a good omen when it finally took root. That sometimes, all anything needed was a second chance. Well, he certainly got his.

I don't remember much of him. He'd realized soon after I was born that life in Colombo wasn't really for him. Or maybe it was life with my mother. Or maybe it was me.

But it hadn't taken him too long to set himself back up in England, where he was from. And of course my mother was to blame. She was the one who ran away from home to marry an Englishman against her parents' wishes, after all. She was the one who couldn't keep her man happy. She practically asked for it.

And when she got sick he left for good. He took care of the expenses, and he left her this beautiful, haunted house full of weeping women. All the fight my mother must have once had in her was already spent on leaving her family and living the life of a high-society outcast in Colombo. She was swept away with her cancer on a wave of painkillers much sooner than the doctors expected.

And then there was just me. And Seetha. And this house I never wanted to stay in for a moment longer than necessary but kept coming back to just the same—like I was a ghost cursed to haunt these walls.

The dining room sat at the back of the house. The table was set at my usual seat. Seetha had made *kiribath*—milk rice. It wasn't customary to eat it in the evenings, but we ate it for special occasions. It was supposed to bring us good luck. And I wasn't wasting even an ounce of any luck I could muster.

"*Shaa!*" I made an appreciative noise, to which Seetha gave me a small smile.

"It's good to have you home, *Baba*. Long time, no?"

"Yes, too long."

But it wasn't too long. There wasn't enough time in the world to put between what happened the last time I was here and now.

SEETHA

Interview Transcript: Ranasinghege Kusumalatha Seetha (abbrev. RKS)

Date: January 25, 2020

Location: The Mount Lavinia Hotel

EP: Thank you for joining us today. I was told you are comfortable having this discussion in English, is that true?

RKS: Yes, madam. My English is not perfect, but we can talk. Anything to help. They are saying that Kaavindi Baba—that she is dead. Is that true, madam? No one is telling us anything.

EP: We are investigating the matter, Miss Seetha. The more you can tell us, the better it will be, understand?

RKS: Yes, madam.

EP: Good. Could you please state your name and address for our records?

RKS: Yes, madam. My name is Ranasinghege Kusumalatha Seetha, but you can call me Seetha. Everyone does. My registered address is 281 Vishaka Road, Bandarawela, but I currently reside in Amaya Baba's home in Colombo 07.

EP: That's her home in Cinnamon Gardens, am I correct?

RKS: Yes, madam.

EP: Miss Seetha, what brings you here to the wedding? Were you invited?

RKS: Fonseka Madam asked me to come so I can help, madam. She has known me a long time, and when she asked for my help I was happy to come. I have known Kaavindi Baba since she was a small girl, madam, and I am happy to help with the wedding. The Fonsekas have been good to me. They are very rich, madam, maybe some of the richest people in Sri Lanka, who knows? But they still ask for me. They remember Seetha.

EP: I see. And how about the Blooms? How long have you worked for them?

RKS: I was hired by Amaya Baba's father, Mr. Bloom, madam. It was around the time that Amaya Baba's mother, I called her Loku Madam, got very ill. Before I came to work as a housemaid, I was an English teacher in my village. Sadly, the salary was not enough, madam, only ten thousand rupees, and when my husband's accident left him unable to work as a farmer, I had to leave home to find work in Colombo. Mr. Bloom gave me a very good salary, madam. He sent money every month for expenses as well, and he trusted me to take care of Amaya Baba.

EP: So to answer my question, Miss Seetha, how long?

RKS: Sorry, madam, sorry. I have been with them for about fourteen, fifteen years now.

EP: And were you and Miss Bloom close?

RKS: I looked after her the best I could, madam. It was not always easy. She missed her mother a lot, and was angry with her father for leaving her. But she's a good girl, madam. I can promise you, madam. She's a very good girl.

EP: I'm sure she is, Miss Seetha. Could you tell me a little about what she's like?

RKS: Oh yes. She's a simple, good girl, like I said. I never had problems with her, you know. She never brought boys home. She wore short skirts, sometimes, when she was a teenager, but when I told her that she must not do that, she always listened to me.

She was very sad, of course, after her mother died. But also very quiet. Amaya Baba never shouted or screamed. She didn't even cry at the funeral. Many people came up to me afterward and asked me why. Wasn't she sad? they said. Why is she just standing there, holding Kaavindi Baba's hand and waiting? But I told them all that was the way she was. She might not show her sadness on the outside, but I know she thought her life was finished.

EP: One of my colleagues just brought in an old police entry made about her. Apparently, there was an incident? Shortly after her mother's funeral. Could you tell me a little about that?

RKS: Everyone has forgotten about that, madam. It was old news. Not really important.

EP: But could you fill me in on what happened?

RKS: Amaya Baba was so sad, you know, madam. Her mother had just died, and she had asked her father if she could go to stay with him in England. I think she was only trying to get rid of some of her father's old things in the house. She didn't mean for the fire to catch on like it did.

EP: But it did catch on to a part of the neighbor's wall? And injure her pet, from what the report states.

RKS: Oh no, madam. The old lady who was next door, she's passed on now, madam. I know we mustn't speak ill of the dead, but she really was not a good person, madam. There was only a bit of soot on her wall, and her cat was fine. She said it breathed in the smoke and felt dizzy. How could she know, madam, if her cat was dizzy? Amaya Baba would have never done it on purpose.

EP: And then there was an accident, wasn't there? One of Miss

Bloom's boyfriends who died in a car crash after leaving the residence. This happened when she was older, I suppose?

RKS: Madam, Amaya Baba didn't have boyfriends. That boy was just a friend of hers and of Kaavindi Baba's. It was very sad when the accident happened, madam. Amaya Baba was upset for months.

EP: What about the last time Miss Bloom was in Sri Lanka?

RKS: Yes, madam. Amaya Baba was doing some renovations on the house at that time, madam. Painting the walls and all, you know. She thought it was better that I went home for a while. So I could be more comfortable. She didn't stay at home either. She stayed with the Fonseka family.

EP: And how long did these renovations take?

RKS: I can't remember now, madam. Five years is a long time.

EP: If you had to guess?

RKS: Maybe seven or eight months, maybe. I'm not sure, madam.

EP: Quite a long time for the walls to be painted.

RKS: There were other renovations also, madam. And you know in Sri Lanka, these things take a lot of time. These painters are very lazy men, madam. Very lazy.

EP: And what about this time's visit?

RKS: Yes, madam?

EP: Did Miss Bloom appear normal to you during this visit?

RKS: Yes, madam. She was quiet, as always, and spent most of her time with Kaavindi Baba, of course. Helping her with wedding preparations.

EP: Do you recognize this book, Miss Seetha?

[Shuffling]

RKS: Yes, madam. Amaya Baba was writing in it when she stayed at home during this visit.

EP: This book was found with Miss Bloom's belongings at the hotel. Would you mind turning to page 4? It's marked—

[Turning of pages]

Could you read out what you see?

RKS: Stop wedding no matter what. Plan C. Kill.

[Pause]

This is a mistake, madam. Amaya Baba must have written this as a story, you know? Like the books you read or a film. She is a good girl, madam. She would never hurt anyone.

EP: Were you also invited to the wedding, Miss Seetha?

RKS: No, madam, but like I told you, I went to help.

EP: Who asked you to come?

RKS: I told you, madam, Mrs. Fonseka did. I asked Amaya Baba and she said it was fine. We were not staying at the hotel, of course. We went back in a van with the driver after the party had ended and things were cleared up. And then came back again today morning so we could help with the evening setup for today's function.

EP: Were any other housemaids asked to come help with preparations?

RKS: A few from Mrs. Fonseka's house, madam. But like I said, Mrs. Fonseka trusts me, so I was happy to come.

EP: Miss Seetha, do you recognize this knife?

[Sound of knife clattering on the table]

RKS: Yes, madam. It is from our kitchen at home.

EP: Home, meaning Miss Bloom's residence?

RKS: Well, yes, except Amaya Baba never came to the kitchen, madam.

EP: And you are sure that the knife is yours?

RKS: See this burn mark on the handle, madam? That was when I accidentally left it too close to the fire.

[Pause]

Madam, how did you get this knife?

EP: We found it at the hotel, Miss Seetha. We were hoping you could tell us how it got here.

RKS: I do not know how it got here, madam. But if you are looking for someone who would want to cause harm to the Fonsekas, there is someone I know. She is here in the hotel. She works here now. I saw her yesterday in a cleaner's uniform.

EP: And who is this?

RKS: Her name is Lalitha, madam. She used to work for Mr. and Mrs. Fonseka, but she was sacked a few years ago. She was very upset about it, madam. I heard that she had been cursing the family. She is from the Matara area—I don't know if you know, madam, but they do a lot of hooniyam—you know, witchcraft—in those places. I think she might have put a curse on Kaavindi Baba. That something bad will happen to her. You should speak to her if you can, madam. She is a very vengeful person, and she is very upset that Mrs. Fonseka sacked her.

5

AMAYA

Four Days before the Wedding

IT'S STRANGE HOW your body does things on autopilot, even if your mind has been closed to it for years.

I waited until the clock read 10:10 a.m. to leave the house the next morning, but I was too nervous, too focused on what Kaavi's reaction to seeing me would be, to really think about how I got to the Fonsekas.

I didn't even think about it as I waved down a trishaw and directed him to Kaavi's family home, which is just two streets over from my own. I could have walked, but I hardly ever did. It was too hot, and as I learned the hard way many years ago, no woman, no matter how wealthy, was privileged enough to walk on the streets of Colombo without facing ridiculous amounts of harassment.

I got off one house away from the Fonsekas', just like I used to, because Kaavi's dad would have a fit if he realized that I took a trishaw on my own, and I gave the bell a cursory ring before sliding my hand behind the latch in the gate and pulling it open.

I smiled to myself a little when I passed the large jack tree near the entrance that Kaavi and I used to change our clothes behind when we wanted to wear something her parents or Seetha would disapprove of.

It was only when I was halfway up the drive that I realized I probably should have waited to be let in. I might have done this a million times, but things were very, very different now.

Along with the wedding invitation, Kaavi had also sent along a link to a wedding website with a detailed itinerary for the week leading up to the wedding. I was invited to any and all events I could make it for, my invitation said. Some of it wasn't even parties—there was flower selection, menu taste testing, meeting with the registrar, and the list went on.

But just because she invited me for all the pre-wedding festivities, it didn't mean I could barge in here. I needed to focus now. Not make stupid mistakes and draw more attention to myself than was necessary. Or draw attention to the fact that I'd just broken the terms of a deal I made five years ago.

I was wondering if I should turn around and walk back outside when a harried man in a striped shirt and sarong ran up to me.

"Good morning, madam." He smiled, dabbing his face with a handkerchief and glancing at the gate that I had, still not thinking about it, closed behind me. Poor guy, I hope he won't get into trouble because of this.

"*Bell eka gahuwa. Kamak naa neh?*" I rang the bell. I hope it's okay.

"*Enna, enna,* madam. *Okkolama athule.*" Come in. Come in. Everyone's inside.

Everyone's inside.

Oh no.

I was hoping for a quiet slip-in. Maybe to catch hold of Kaavi privately and say hi. To thank her for inviting me so she won't suspect that I had other motives for being here. The wedding itinerary said she had a sari jacket fitting at 11:00 a.m., and she posted early this morning on her Instagram page that she was looking forward to a morning of relaxing at home. She'd even put up a picture of herself wearing a robe, snuggled up in bed. I had hoped I could slip upstairs unnoticed. Maybe even to say hello to Mr. Fonseka before his wife saw me. I know they had all invited me, but that didn't help my nerves one bit.

I was awkwardly ushered into the spacious downstairs living room. It was decorated with bunches of fresh flowers today, and the large table pushed against the wall was piled with short eats—what we call finger food in Sri Lanka. A professional photographer was snapping pictures of the bite-size delicacies and elaborate table arrangements, while a group of older women in bright floaty blouses and Louis Vuitton handbags were seated primly on the sofas.

"Likes to keep us waiting, no? Trying to make a grand entrance as always," one of them complained, her heavily painted fuchsia lips in an upside-down U. They were wrapped up in one another and didn't pay me any attention, which was a relief.

Good, so that meant Mrs. Fonseka wasn't down yet. Looks like I had crashed one of her charity brunch gatherings. Kaavi wasn't the only woman in the Fonseka family who ran a charity. Fiona Fonseka hosted her fair share of various women's brunches and gala dinners to raise awareness and donations for a number of worthy causes, though I'd often heard Kaavi complain that it was just an excuse for the women to sip on Moët and gossip. Again, I wondered how Kaavi had convinced her mother to invite me to the wedding. She'd never really liked me, I don't think, but the last time I was in this house destroyed any hope I had of being accepted by her. But maybe it hadn't been as bad as I thought at the time, if she'd changed her mind now.

I took a few steps toward the staircase. I could just go up to Kaavi's room. It would be better than hanging around out here with the aunties, who would devour me in minutes.

The large marble staircase was in the middle of the ground floor, flanked by sitting areas on either side. While my single-storied house was breezy and sprawling, made in the older colonial style, the Fonsekas' house was the epitome of ostentatious luxury. Mr. Fonseka oversaw the renovations to his large family home himself, and there was no shortage of marble and the best quality teak wood trimmings, with fittings flown down from Germany and furniture shipped over from Italy. It was always chilly inside, because they always kept the many air conditioners running. I've heard people describe it as a palace, but I suppose those are the same people who didn't know that the Taj Mahal was actually a tomb.

The aunties never gave me a second glance, which surprised me. Usually, the entrance into any home or restaurant or social gathering was accompanied by craning necks and once-over glances where curious observers surmised whether they knew you, whether they knew someone who knew you, and whether you were worth saying hello to. Maybe luck was on my side and their gossip was extra juicy this morning.

I had almost made it to the staircase when Mrs. Fonseka's voice boomed out, echoing over the cold marble.

"What are you doing here?"

I turned around to face her—this shorter, stouter, older version of Kaavi. She was wearing a yellow chiffon blouse that billowed around her, and she carried a small Louis Vuitton clutch, even though she was in her own house.

I steeled myself and turned around. I could feel beads of sweat course their way down the back of my neck.

"Hi, Aunty. How are you?"

She looked like she had seen me smear mud on her pristine white sofas.

"What are you doing here?" she asked again, more quietly.

"I—I'm here for the wedding." I was trembling. "Maybe I should have called first but I got Kaa—"

"You stay away from her, you understand me?" Her voice rose, made louder now that the aunties had stopped talking and were looking over toward us in hushed silence. This must feel like Christmas had come early for them. Enough gossip to fill up their reserves until the next scandal.

"I—I'm sorry. I thought—"

"I don't care what you thought, you hear me? This is the bloody height of madness, I'm telling you. I can't believe—"

"What's all this now?" Kaavi's voice rang out, interrupting her mother's.

Mrs. Fonseka and I both looked up, where Kaavi stood at the top of the staircase in a delicate embroidered pink silk robe. Her hair was pulled away from her face in a messy bun, and her face was bare of makeup. She was breathtaking.

Neither Mrs. Fonseka nor I spoke. Me, because I was so nervous that I thought I would faint, and her, because I think she finally noticed the aunties gaping in our direction. I looked around for a clock, or a calendar, or anything with numbers on it. There was a random ornament on a shelf in the shape of a number eight. The most symmetrical of numbers. A far cry from a sign, but I clung on to the hope of it all the same.

Kaavi floated down the staircase, looking more like she was wearing a ball gown than a housecoat. Her eyes met mine when she was about halfway. She blinked twice, as something passed over her face.

And then she was next to me, smiling and pulling me into a hug.

"You came," she said. She smelled of Chanel No. 5.

"What is this, Kaavi?" her mother asked.

"Relax, will you, *Amma*? Everything is fine. I invited Amaya. I just didn't think she would make it." She let me go and faced her mother.

"No need to be so surprised, *Amma*. I know you're excited to see her too. Gosh, you're such a drama queen." Was it me or did she say this bit a little too loudly?

"You—?" Mrs. Fonseka's lips pressed together so tightly I thought they would disappear into her mouth.

"Yes," Kaavi replied simply, raising her eyebrows and throwing a smile over at Mrs. Fonseka's pack of wolves, who were teetering on the edge of their seats, bloodthirsty to know what was going on.

"Aunty Josephina, Aunty Rajini, hello. Aunty Preeni, my, look at your haircut. I see you'll haven't started your meeting yet. Has my mother kept you'll waiting by being fashionably late again?" She went over to the ladies, who were suddenly trying to look like they couldn't care less about Mrs. Fonseka's outburst, and she pressed each of her cheeks against theirs in turn.

"I hope *Amma* didn't alarm you'll. This is what happens when we work on our invitation lists separately. And if you ask me," she said in a mock whisper, "I think all this wedding stress is getting to her even more than it is to me." She gave a charming little laugh and the aunties laughed along with her. How was she so at ease with them? She was like a magical piece of pink ribbon that wove her way through the fiercest current—floating along, bending and moving with the tide, never appearing to be anything but smooth and elegant and totally in control. I've missed her.

One of them gave me a quizzical look, and Kaavi beckoned me over.

"You must remember my friend Amaya, don't you, Aunty Josephina? We were in school together. And university, too, in the US."

"Ah, yes, yes. Amaya. Sarita's daughter, no? You look just like her. Fairer, of course. Lucky you. I suppose you get that from your father's side."

"Y-yes. Hello, Aunty. How are you?" I had no idea who Aunty Josephina was, and I doubt my mother would have known her, either, but this was Colombo, where in the '80s, a private school–educated Sinhala Buddhist girl didn't run away from home and marry an Englishman against her parents' consent without word getting around.

"Nice to see you, darling. You're looking *well*," one of the other aunties said, clawing for some attention herself. The way she said it made me feel anything but.

"I have to go get ready now. Aunty Preeni, Aunty Rajini, you will excuse me, won't you? I have a jacket fitting with Andre soon."

The aunties oohed and aahed as was befitting the mention of Andre's name.

"I suppose you are here to accompany Kaavi to her fit-on, then?" one of the aunties asked me.

I wasn't sure how I was supposed to respond, and Kaavi had already managed to extract herself as gracefully as possible and was on her way up the stairs.

"Go on. I'm sure you young ones have plenty to catch up on."

Aunty Josephina flapped out her arms and turned her face toward me, inviting me for a Sri Lankan cheek kiss as well, which I awkwardly obliged with all the aunties, since to kiss just one would be terribly insulting to the others.

"We'll see you soon, no doubt," she said. There was a hint of amusement in her voice.

I was just turning around when I heard one of the aunties whisper—

"Is that the girl . . . ?"

"Shh!" She was silenced by Aunty Josephina, who didn't let her smile slip.

I held my breath. I wonder what the gossips were saying about me now? Was it about Spencer? Or about what happened the last time I was here? I had hoped that word wouldn't get out about either. As far as I was aware, only Kaavi knew about me and Spencer back home (who was I going to tell, anyway?), and the Fonsekas would burn their house to the ground before they let out what happened five years ago.

I wonder how it would feel to add just a little bit of poison to their canapés. Not enough to kill them, of course. Just enough to make them ill. For their skin to suddenly glisten and their cheeks to flush and their stomachs to clench before they started to cramp up. For the sudden and explosive vomiting to begin. For them to start gasping for air.

Mrs. Fonseka had remained near the staircase where we left her. She didn't look shocked or angry anymore—her face was instead arranged into a pleasant, dangerous smile.

She reached for my arm as I walked by her, her fingers gripping hard around my flesh at an angle that the aunties couldn't see.

"Kaavi might have invited you, but don't think for a moment that I have forgotten about our agreement," she hissed, the smile never leaving her face.

I nodded, a tight smile on my lips too. Like I could ever forget, even though I wished to every moment of every day.

AUNTY RAJINI

Interview Transcript: Rajini Thambiah (abbrev. RT)

Date: January 25, 2020

Location: The Mount Lavinia Hotel

RT: Can I know what all this commotion is? We've been treated like criminals—locked in our rooms from morning. Brought measly, cold food that we had to eat like beggars. Nihal and Fiona better have a proper explanation for this, I tell you.

[Pause]

Unless—well, we aren't in any danger, are we? Is there some sort of psychopath or murderer running amok at the hotel? Is that why we've been kept locked away?

EP: I understand your frustration, Mrs. Thambiah, but we are dealing with an investigation here. We believe there is no immediate threat at present. Now, if you could please state your name and address for our records, we need to get started right away.

RT: Well, I'll do this for the sake of Fiona. She must be out of her mind with worry, after all. I'm Rajini Thambiah, and I reside at 34 Francis Road, Wellawatte, when I am in Colombo. We usually spend April in Nuwara Eliya, you know, for the season. And we always fly to Australia to spend Christmas with my son's family, even though it's far too hot there at the time.

EP: But you were in Colombo on the morning of the twenty-first of January, for Fiona Fonseka's brunch.

RT: Yes, we were planning this year's dinner-dance. Preeni had this ridiculous idea to make it a costume party, and we were trying to discourage her. The last time we did that, one of the De Livera girls showed up in her underwear claiming it was a costume and our chapter was almost shut down for encouraging lewd behavior after someone took pictures and circulated them among those wretched gossip sites. You know, I think—

EP: So to confirm, you were at Mrs. Fonseka's brunch on the twenty-first?

RT: Yes, my dear, though I can't say I care for your tone.

EP: Was Miss Bloom present on that day?

RT: You mean Amaya Bloom, I suppose? Yes, she had slunk in. I didn't even notice her at first. I thought she might have been a caterer or something. We were late to start as always. Fiona had kept us waiting, again. But then she came down the stairs and saw the Bloom girl and screamed bloody murder. I almost choked on my smoked salmon canapé.

EP: And what was the nature of her screaming?

RT: It almost gave me a heart attack, you know? I couldn't breathe for a minute, at least. I even—

EP: Did Mrs. Fonseka say anything in particular, Mrs. Thambiah?

RT: Well, if you ask me, it seemed like Fiona had no idea the girl was coming. She looked like she had seen a ghost. I don't blame her, you know. There were so many rumors circulating about that girl. She had quite the reputation, you know?

EP: Could you elaborate on that further, please?

RT: My dear, I thought this was an investigation. Not a place for gossip.

[Pause]

But if you must know, there has been quite a bit of talk about the time Amaya stayed at the Fonsekas'. And while Nihal has done well for himself, I can't speak of his loyalty to Fiona. He's been spotted, you know? At one of those parties where the men put their car keys in a bowl. You know what I'm talking about, I hope. But then again, this is Colombo. It's not out of the blue for a man as rich and powerful as Nihal to have, well, extramarital pleasures. Certainly, men with less have had more. And word around town is that Fiona isn't faultless herself. Of course, that was many years ago, and the rumored man, one of Nihal's friends, mind you, suddenly and conveniently dropped dead of a heart attack. Now, I'm not accusing Nihal of anything, of course. I'm just saying that his relationship with the Bloom girl always seemed very improper, since you asked me.

EP: Did Mrs. Fonseka discuss these infidelities with you?

RT: Ha! Like Fiona would ever let anyone see behind her facade. Fat chance of that. As far as she was concerned, she had the perfect family, and she'd kill to keep it that way. She taught her daughters to behave like that as well, though if you ask me, only Kaavindi made an actual effort.

EP: And how would you describe Kaavindi Fonseka's relationship with her mother?

RT: It doesn't take a detective to gather that Kaavindi had been well trained by Fiona, you know. She was always the model of perfection—so pristine was her reputation. And her manners are impeccable. The moment she sees me it's always, *Yes, Aunty Rajini, I love your dress, Aunty Rajini, how is your cold now, Aunty Rajini?*

She was as different from her sister, Tehani, as night and day. Poor Fiona. No matter how much of an effort they made with Tehani—I heard they had even sent her to some sort of finishing school type thing for troubled girls, but still no luck—she's still seen at all the major nightclubs leaving with some chap or the other. But you know, maybe it's all Fiona's fault after all.

The moment Fiona had her little outburst that morning of our brunch, Kaavi was on it like a professional peacekeeper. Smoothed the whole thing over. Couldn't say I blamed her, to be honest. Fiona was putting up quite the show. But who knows? Maybe they had planned the whole thing, and invited the Bloom girl to distract from something else.

EP: Which would be?

RT: Listen, dear. I'm no detective. I know that Nihal Fonseka likes to believe angels themselves delivered his eldest daughter into this world. And Fiona Fonseka likes to pretend that she does everything by her astrologer's book. But answer me this— have you heard of a wedding being rushed along so quickly without there being another, more pressing, matter of urgency? Like, say, an unplanned pregnancy? And if there *were* an unplanned pregnancy, who would do whatever it took to keep the family reputation safe? I don't think you need to be a head of security to figure that out.

6

AMAYA

Four Days before the Wedding

I THOUGHT I'D have a moment with Kaavi when I went upstairs. That we'd be alone, even for a few minutes. I wasn't going to do anything rash just now, of course. That would come later, if things didn't work out the way I hoped. I just wanted to ask about her email. Why she said her whole family wanted me to come when it was obvious Mrs. Fonseka was horrified to find me in her house.

I wish I'd been able to tell Mrs. Fonseka that. That I hadn't just barged in here. That I had been invited. That I thought *she* had invited me. But of course I'd choked. Now all I could do was ask Kaavi what she had been thinking, and hope she'd be able to smooth this over with her mother.

Her bedroom door was open, but I knocked on it before peering inside. I thought it would be a time capsule, like my own room had been, but of course it wasn't. Not for Kaavi.

The boy band posters and colorful collages of our photographs had disappeared. The bright purple accent wall that her mother detested was painted over in a crisp white. Her wooden double bed where we'd had countless sleepovers was replaced with one that had a padded white pin-tucked headboard. There were pink and rose gold accents everywhere, from the metallic pink light switches to the gorgeous lampshades that flanked her king-size bed.

There was a large bouquet of pink roses in a vase on her dressing table. I snuck a peek at the card that dangled off the side.

I can't wait to marry you. —Love, Spencer it read. My stomach did a flip. Being here, in her room, it was all so unreal that a part of me hoped this wedding was make-believe as well. Just a figment of my imagination. Just a bad dream that I would no doubt wake up from very soon.

But Kaavi wasn't in here. I could hear the shower running in the attached bathroom.

"Kaavi?" I called out, tentatively. I've been in her room alone hundreds of times, of course, but that was in another life. We were both different people now. She was a person who would marry my ex-boyfriend, and I was a person who would fly across the world to make sure it didn't happen.

"Hey, sorry, I just hopped in here," she shouted from inside the bathroom. "Would you mind just hanging out for a bit? I'll get killed if I'm late for this fitting, since everything is so last minute and all."

I eyed the large display of roses again.

Sticking my head out of her room, I peered down the corridor. Mr. Fonseka's office was at the very end. I could go and say hello to him. Maybe he knew about my invitation. Maybe it was even him who asked for me to be included. It made sense. He'd always been so kind to me and treated me like I was part of the family, even when Mrs. Fonseka seemed less than pleased.

The aunties' chatter downstairs drifted up, Mrs. Fonseka's voice the loudest and most assertive of them all, and I knew I would be safe for a few minutes at least.

I tiptoed down the hallway. Not a particularly easy feat with the wooden floors.

His door was closed, and I raised my arm up to knock but couldn't bring myself to. I looked around for a sign, but there were no clocks. 10:38 on my own watch. Not great. Kaavi should be done getting ready any moment now. I'd better just head back to her room.

I was about to turn around but the door swung open.

Mr. Fonseka almost slammed into me, but I just managed to jump out of the way.

"Oh goodness, please excuse me," he called out cheerfully, until his entire face changed when he realized who it was he had barreled into.

"Amaya? Is that you?"

"H-hi. Uncle. Sorry, I was—I was just . . ." but the words didn't come.

"Did Fiona see you?"

"Y-yes. Downstairs."

He ran his hand through his hair, which was much grayer than I remembered.

"Ah, I see. So she knows you're here?"

I nodded.

"Come, come. Come inside." He ushered me into his office. Looks like he wasn't expecting me either. Why would Kaavi lie to me?

Unlike Kaavi's room, I hadn't been in Mr. Fonseka's office very often. But I was in here the last time I was at this house—the moment where my life changed. I pressed my thighs together just remembering. I hadn't been prepared for that much pain.

Unlike Kaavi's room, nothing in here had changed. There was a large desk in the center of the room, with a framed sepia-toned portrait of a stern-looking gentleman, Mr. Fonseka's father, hanging behind it. The walls were lined with bookshelves that held more framed photographs of Mr. Fonseka accepting various awards than actual books, and as always, everything felt very dusty.

He didn't sit down. Instead, he turned to face me and spoke in a low voice.

"You know we had an understanding, Amaya. Why are you here?" His hand grazed my upper arm lightly, but he seemed to think better of it and tucked it away into the pocket of his linen trousers.

It wasn't like I could tell him the truth. That I was here to make sure this wedding never happened.

"Kaavi invited me." It was becoming increasingly obvious that Kaavi had pulled one over on all of us. But this was the simplest excuse, even if it did violate the terms of our agreement. It's been five years—would they still hold me to that? "She asked that I come. I didn't want to let her down."

He sighed.

"But still. I would have thought you would've at least—"

He ran his hand through his hair again.

"I—I'm sorry. I should have checked. But I thought she would have cleared it with you before she invited me." At least, that was what I was led to believe. I couldn't imagine why Kaavi would do this. "I—I don't know what—or how much—you've told her."

He looked directly at me then. The same expression he had when I told him about the teacher who made a pass at me in school, or when I asked him what I should study in college. The same face he had five years ago when I promised to stay away from his family. From him. From her. For the rest of my life.

I blinked back tears. I was an idiot for coming. This was too much. I should have stayed away from their home. I should have figured out some other way to stop the wedding. Some other way that didn't involve me dragging myself and Kaavi's entire family through all the tears and pain from five years ago.

But something in his face softened when he saw me cry. He could never stand to see me sad. I guess that's where all his troubles started in the first place.

He started to lift his hand, maybe to touch my arm again, but the door to his study burst open.

"*Thaththi!*" a little girl screamed, launching herself at Mr. Fonseka and wrapping her arms around his knees. A disheveled nanny followed behind.

"Sorry, sir. *Duwagena awa sir ge kata handa ahunama.*" She came running when she heard your voice.

But Mr. Fonseka didn't seem to mind. He picked her up and swung her onto his hip. I was frozen on the spot. He didn't meet my eye.

"*Kohomada mage Nadia patiyata?*" How's my little Nadia doing?

"*Thaththi, ada* beach *ekata yamuda?*" Can we go to the beach today, Dad?

I turned toward the window, to give them some privacy. The moment was too tender for me to lurk around, a voyeur to a life that I could never have. It felt hard to breathe.

"Hmm, we'll see."

"*Thaththa, Amma* wanted me to ask you whether I could take the BMW at four? The Merc has been put for a service, and I don't know if I'll have it back in—oh! You're here." This time it was Tehani who came barging into the study. The Fonseka's middle daughter, who I've never been particularly close to. I don't think she liked me taking up so much of Kaavi's, and her family's, time. I remember once, it was Mr. Fonseka's birthday and they were meant to do a quiet family dinner. An anomaly, and only because Mrs. Fonseka had just finished throwing a huge gala for Fonseka Jewellers winning some award that year, and everyone was exhausted. Mr. Fonseka had flung his arms around the three of us—Kaavi, Tehani, and me—calling us his three girls and saying this was the best birthday ever, but Tehani had been so sulky when she realized I was coming too. She spent the whole evening glaring at me from behind her phone, and I heard her complaining to Mrs. Fonseka in the bathroom, although they both stopped talking the moment I went in.

And it didn't feel like anything had changed. She narrowed her perfectly lined eyes at me and put her hands on her tiny waist. She was wearing a crop top, jeans with rips in them, and more makeup than I typically wore in a year. Only the very rich and the very privileged could get away with an outfit like that in Colombo. But now that I've had some time away from the Fonsekas, I've realized that it must have been hard being Kaavi's younger sister—being compared to someone so perfect all the time. While Tehani had many of the same physical features as Kaavi, like the same wide eyes and the same full lower lip, they weren't arranged the same way, somehow. It was like looking at Kaavi through a misshapen glass. Or maybe it was just Tehani's hardness that always made me feel that way.

"Hi, Tehani."

I was surprised when she gave me a warm smile.

"Amaya, hi. It's been so long." She stuck her cheeks against mine, which felt even more awkward than the aunties downstairs. I could smell cigarettes under her expensive perfume. I've never cared about her smoking, or her drinking, or her experiments with LSD that got her sent to a fancy rehab center in India, but I know for certain that Mr. and Mrs. Fonseka did.

"You must be here for the wedding. Kaavi will be thrilled. And I see you've already met Nadia. Such a cutie, isn't she? Here, let me take her outside. I'm sure you two have a lot of catching up to do," she said, yanking the toddler out of Mr. Fonseka's hands and leaving, nanny in tow. I guess she'd grown up too. She was certainly the only Fonseka who seemed happy to see me, at least.

"I should go also," I said. I couldn't stay in this room a moment longer. "I don't want to keep Kaavi waiting."

I didn't wait to see what he said, in case he insisted I immediately return to LA or something.

Tehani had already disappeared, and I peeked downstairs to see if that was where she went. I couldn't spot her, but Nadia was at the foot of the stairs with her nanny. She peered up at me and gave me a little smile.

I took a quick step back and returned to Kaavi's room. This was too much. This was all too much. I took a deep breath. Tried counting to five. It didn't work.

Why was Kaavi being like this? I should have known better than to just come here. I was such an idiot, thinking they finally wanted to make amends. And now here I was, sneaking around shamefully, like a dog who had been cast out and accidentally wandered back home.

I looked around Kaavi's room. There was a curling iron on her dresser, plugged in, and the indicator light blinking. I picked it up and felt its warmth. This would do for now. I placed my foot on the corner of the dresser and tugged up the cuff on my jeans. Then, holding my breath, I pressed the barrel of the curler onto the inner side of my ankle. It took a second for the pain to register, but when it did, I felt a little more centered. Like I could finally focus.

I'd just put the iron back when the door to Kaavi's bathroom opened. She stepped out, looking like she did in her posts—flawless. She was wearing a silky champagne-colored jumpsuit, and her hair was in soft waves that fell over her shoulders. How did she even get her hair to behave like that in this humidity? I'd have frizz, and pit stains, and smudged mascara before I even left the house.

"Sorry to keep you waiting." She smiled, but she was tapping away at her phone. She still hadn't made eye contact since she first saw me. I guess it was natural for her to be stiff. The last time we met, I'd told her that I hated her and never wanted to see her again. That I wished she were dead.

"So, I was—" But we were interrupted. Again.

This time by Mrs. Fonseka, who burst into the room, slightly red in the face. I don't remember there being this many constant interruptions in the Fonsekas' house.

"Ah, there you are." She was panting slightly.

Kaavi raised her eyebrows. "Where else would we be?"

"I thought . . ." She peered down the corridor but pulled herself together as quickly as she first appeared. "Anyway, Kaavi, you better get going soon. The car is ready. And also, Laura is awake, and she'll be coming with you."

I had no clue who Laura was, but Kaavi frowned.

"Laura? Is that really necessary? She can go some other time, no?"

"No. She'll come with you now. She's already downstairs. Hurry up or you'll be late."

"Everything okay?" Tehani asked. She'd appeared behind her mother, even though I didn't notice her when Mrs. Fonseka barged in.

"Just trying to get Kaavi to hurry up and go for her fitting," Mrs. Fonseka muttered. She didn't give me a second look as she stormed out of the room. Obviously, she didn't leave her meeting and rush upstairs just to tell Kaavi that she was running late. She wanted to check up on me. And judging from this Laura person joining us, it appeared that she didn't want me to be alone with Kaavi either.

"Amaya, have you seen Kaavi's dress yet?" Tehani asked.

"Um, no. Not yet."

Kaavi was busy at her dresser, applying lipstick and spritzing on some perfume.

"Do you want to see it? Kaavs won't mind, will you?"

Kaavi barely glanced in our direction.

"No, no, go on ahead. Just hurry up or *Amma* will be on my case again."

"Come on."

I followed Tehani out of the room. I didn't really want to see the dress, but I supposed it would have been a strange thing to refuse. When I was with Spencer, I used to be one of those girls who would occasionally sneak in a bridal magazine when I bought groceries. No big deal, just a little guilty pleasure for when, someday in the abstract future, I would be a bride too. I'd thought about how I'd love a mermaid or a sheath, never a ball gown, and wondered whether lace would look classic or outdated. But that was me in a different life. I didn't even know that girl anymore.

Tehani didn't lead me far. Just two doors away to one of the many guest rooms that were never used.

Tehani unlocked the door, rolling her eyes a little.

"My mother wants this kept under lock and key, can you believe it? I think she's worried that a maid will wander in here by mistake and ruin it or something."

She moved away, allowing me to step inside first.

I remember there being a bed in here, but that had been moved out, and the rest of the furniture was covered in white sheets—probably because the room remained unused. But a dress form had been set up right in the center, swathed in chiffon and tulle and silk.

I have to admit, I still do enjoy the occasional bit of wedding porn as much as most women my age do. I mean, we've grown up being bombarded by messages about weddings. We've all lived for that final scene in a Disney fairy tale where the princess wears a breathtaking wedding dress. Kaavi and I even used to rate them when we were younger. My favorite was Ariel's, with the enormously poofy sleeves, and Kaavi's was Cinderella's. But the dress in front of me would blow Cinderella's dress out of the water.

"Gorgeous, isn't it? Andre did most of the embroidery by hand and completely by himself. Apparently, he wouldn't even let any of his assistants help him with it. He's such a bloody perfectionist. It's almost a shame that she'll change out of it for the reception, but well, her Hayley dress will arrive soon, and who can say no to a Hayley Paige?"

I eyed the delicate boned bodice that was overlaid with a fabric so soft and sheer that it looked almost like a second skin. Floral appliqués delicately embroidered in silver and gray thread bloomed down the long net sleeves. The bottom layer of the flowy, full skirt was adorned in hand-printed batik florals to match the sleeves. Another slight hint of batik—the traditional Sri Lankan hand-dyeing technique—rippled through the bodice. It was like looking into a mystical pond that glistened and shone and danced with the light. If I put this dress on, I could make no promises that I would ever take it off.

It took some effort on my part to tear my eyes away from it. I turned to say something polite and appreciative to Tehani, but she was keying something into her phone.

"Oh fuck, I have to take this. You know the way back to Kaavi's room, right? I'll see you later." And with that, she stuck her phone up onto her ear and vanished.

I made myself leave. It didn't do me any good to stay here—alone with this dress. I stepped out onto the corridor again as a man made his way toward Mr. Fonseka's office. He turned beet red when he saw me.

"Oh, hello," he said. His voice was soft and had a slight tremble to it. "I'm Chamara. The interior designer. How are you?"

"Hi. I'm Amaya."

He nodded like it made sense and let himself into the office.

Kaavi was still fussing around when I made it back to her room. Her phone rang, but she sighed and silenced it, and started loading up her Louis Vuitton bag. I've never understood upper-class Colombo society and their fascination with Louis Vuitton. It's not even like it was the most expensive brand around, but maybe that was the point. It screamed wealth without having to shell out five times the amount for a Birkin, and god forbid they spend that much on a Chloé or a Mulberry, where the logo wasn't as obvious.

She finally shouldered her bag but hesitated.

"Look, we can talk properly later, and I know that all this must be a bit much for you, but I need a favor."

I just nodded, caught off guard like I always was. I had questions for her. I needed to know why she lied to me about her parents wanting me at the wedding. But of course she wasn't waiting for me to ask.

"No one here knows about you and Spencer, okay? And I'd like to keep it that way. I hope you can respect that."

I was too dumbfounded to say anything, so I nodded again.

"Great. You ready to go?" she asked, but didn't wait for my answer as she left the room and made her way downstairs.

I followed her for the second time today, my head and my heart and my soul feeling like they were about to explode.

LALITHA

Interview Transcript: Lalitha Chamari Withane
   (abbrev. LCW)

Date: January 25, 2020

Location: The Mount Lavinia Hotel

Interview conducted in Sinhala by request of interviewee.
Translated from Sinhala to English.

EP: Thank you for agreeing to speak with me, Miss Lalitha.

LCW: [Laughs] Of course, madam. It's not like I can say no when manager-sir tells me to stop all my morning work and come here.

EP: Yes, I'm really sorry about the interruption. This is very urgent, otherwise we wouldn't have asked for you.

LCW: I understand, madam. When big, prominent families have emergencies, everything needs to be stopped at once. I understand.

EP: Let's start. You are comfortable speaking to me in Sinhala?

LCW: Yes, madam. I speak Sinhala and some Tamil. Not much English.

EP: That is fine. We may have your statement translated to English on request. I hope that's okay.

LCW: Of course, madam. Thank you for asking.

EP: Okay, so would you mind please stating your name and address for the record.

LCW: My name is Lalitha Chamari Withane. Do you want my permanent address or my current one?

EP: Current is fine for now.

LCW: Okay, madam. I currently live at a boardinghouse that many of the other cleaners share. It's not too far from here—16/2A Station Road, Mount Lavinia.

EP: And your current occupation?

LCW: I'm a cleaner, madam, as you can see from my uniform. I work for the Mount Lavinia Hotel.

EP: As in housekeeping?

LCW: No, madam. Not as fancy as that. Just a cleaner. I do the staff bathrooms and make sure the garbage is sorted before the trucks come to pick it up.

EP: And I'm to understand that you worked at the Fonsekas' residence before this, am I correct?

LCW: I knew that's why you wanted me here. They are bad news, that family. I heard there was some problem with them at the hotel. That Kaavindi Baba was hurt?

EP: Could you please answer the question, Miss Lalitha?

LCW: Seetha would have told you the moment she saw me. She's cunning, that one. Never really liked me, though I don't know why. Not to worry, she'll have what's coming to her soon enough. I don't know why you are troubling me, and not her. She was the one who always covered for Amaya Baba. Tried to act like she was so perfect. Did she tell you about that boy who met with the accident?

EP: Miss Lalitha, the question was whether you previously worked at the Fonseka residence.

LCW: Yes, yes, I did work at Mr. and Mrs. Fonseka's. For a long time. I think maybe nine or ten years.

EP: And when did you leave?

LCW: I didn't leave on my own will. I was suddenly asked to go.
That was about five years ago.

EP: And why were you let go?

LCW: You'll have to ask Mrs. Fonseka that. She didn't give me a
reason. Don't worry, I didn't steal or do anything bad. There
were no complaints about my work before.

Can I go now, madam? I'm losing time on my shift and my supervisor will be angry with me if I don't finish all my work for
the day.

EP: I just have a few more questions for you, Miss Lalitha. Your
manager told me you would comply. Would you like me to
speak with him?

LCW: No, no need for that, madam.

[Pause]

What was your question?

EP: So you have no idea why you were let go from the Fonsekas'?

LCW: Like I said, you'll have to ask Mrs. Fonseka.

EP: Are you upset about being let go?

LCW: Upset? Me? You mean upset that I was treated like the trash
after being a loyal maid for ten years? Sure, I was upset. But I'm
also used to it. This wasn't the first Colombo family I worked
for. I knew my place.

I knew that they think they are better than the rest of us, just because they have money. The rules are different for them. Always have been. You know, the salary I get working here as a
cleaner is less than I got when I worked as a maid, but it's okay.
You know why? They still treat me like garbage here, but at
least I know where I stand. I'm never told that I'm part of the
family. I'm never told that they care for me like their own,

only to throw me out on the street later. Things are clearer here. More simple.

EP: Miss Lalitha, would you mind telling me what your shift times were yesterday and this morning?

LCW: I was here from six thirty in the morning to eleven in the night. Same as every day. You can check with my supervisor if you like. He'll confirm it.

EP: I see. Okay, and—

LCW: Madam, sorry for interrupting you, but I know why I am here. And I'm not afraid to answer what you are not asking me. I didn't hurt Kaavindi Baba. I used to call her Loku Baba when I worked at Mr. and Mrs. Fonseka's. I only met her a few times during the last few years because she was away for her studies and only came back home for holidays. I have nothing against her. She's not as innocent as she seems, of course, but I have nothing against her. In fact, I saw more of Amaya Baba during those last few months I was working at the house than I saw of Kaavindi Baba or Tehani Baba.

EP: And would Miss Bloom—Amaya—know why you were dismissed?

LCW: [Smiles] No. I suppose not. Or maybe she does, who knows? She was rather sick, when I was there. And I was concerned, of course. I asked whether she needed to go to a doctor. I even recommended a good Ayurvedic doctor that I knew. Well, I was asked to leave shortly after that.

EP: And you mentioned earlier, about the boy who died in the accident. What do you know about that?

LCW: All I know, madam, is that everything seemed very strange. Amaya Baba was always asking Kaavindi Baba to come to her house in the night after everyone else went to sleep. And

Seetha, well, I don't think she kept as close a watch on Amaya Baba as she was supposed to, so who knows what Amaya Baba got up to? That boy, Gayan Baba, was leaving her house at two in the morning when he met with the accident, you know. And Seetha, well, she said she knew he was there. That the girls and him were just studying. It's all quite odd if you ask me.

Anyway, madam, like I said, you needn't worry about me. Doing something to hurt Kaavindi Baba isn't my way, in any case.

EP: What do you mean it's not your way?

LCW: Madam, if Seetha told you I was here she must have told you, no, about what I can do?

EP: She did mention it.

LCW: Yes, she always had a problem with it. I learned it from my own mother, who learned it from hers, though neither my mother nor I could ever be as strong as my grandmother. I never did anything serious. I would cut limes, to get rid of evil spirits. And I make offerings to the goddess Kaali—she gives justice for women who have been wronged.

But if I really wanted to take revenge on the Fonsekas, which is not what I want—I don't even waste my time thinking about them—I wouldn't attack anyone. I wouldn't have to do any hooniyam, if you can even call it that. I wouldn't have to do anything. I would just wait.

EP: Wait for what?

LCW: You are a Buddhist, madam?

EP: I was raised Catholic, actually.

LCW: But you might already know—there's something called blessings and sins in Buddhism, you are aware aren't you, madam? Well, the Fonsekas have more sins collected than a prison full of crooks and thieves combined. They pretend to be wonderful people, giving to charity and helping others, but the people that they ignore—the servants, the drivers, the gardeners—we see a side to them that the rest of Colombo doesn't see. We see it because they don't care about us. They barely even see us. But we see. And we know all the lies and all the deception.

So if I wanted to watch them fall, if I wanted to see them hurt, then all I have to do is wait. Because no one with that amount of sins gets away from what is coming to them.

7

AMAYA

Four Days before the Wedding

TEN MINUTES WITH Laura, and I could understand why Kaavi didn't want her around. For one, she Never. Stopped. Talking. Not even for a moment. Not even to take a breath, it felt like. How did she not simply run out of oxygen and suffocate?

Laura was, as she wasted no time telling me, the daughter of one of Mr. Fonseka's American friends, and a longtime supporter of their family business. The Fonsekas insisted she stay at their home when they heard Laura had plans to take a gap year and "find herself" in a "third-world country." Her words, not mine.

"You know what's really interesting about Sri Lanka?" she asked, her words buzzing out of her at full speed. "It's that no one ever says please or thank you. Why is that?"

"It's implied in our tone. You see, the formal—" But she didn't wait for my answer. And here I was thinking that interrupting people was a Sri Lankan thing.

"And eating curry for breakfast? That's so . . . strange, isn't it? I mean, I do love a good fish curry, but not first thing in the morning, you know? It just feels so . . . intense."

She went on, and I gave up trying to answer her after a few tries.

Kaavi sat in the passenger seat, not looking up from her phone, which left me little choice but to nod along to what Laura was saying. That she sat up in front with the driver was a testament to how much she clearly didn't like the girl, because proper Colombo 07 ladies never sat in front—they were chauffeur driven unless, of course, they chose to drive themselves.

"So, Ams, how long will you be in Colombo for?" Kaavi asked, when there was finally a lull in the conversation. She didn't turn around when she spoke, but she did call me Ams, like she always did.

"I'll leave a day or two after the wedding." Not that there would be a wedding if I had anything to do about it.

"Ah, I see. So you won't be here for the homecoming, then?"

"I guess—"

"What's a *homecoming*?" Laura interrupted. "Is it, like, a homecoming game? Will there be a formal?"

Kaavi's polite smile was impenetrable, and her phone beeped right on cue.

I didn't think Laura really cared about the answer, but she threw me an impatient look.

"Well? What is it?"

And so I was left to explain to Laura that a homecoming was the party that the groom's family threw for the newly married couple returning after their honeymoon. It was often as grand as the wedding reception itself—a classic way for the families to one-up each other.

I wondered who was throwing Kaavi's homecoming? The last time I checked, Spencer didn't have any family. I suppose the Fonsekas would just hire a wedding planner and throw it themselves.

They were all for keeping up pretenses. Unless Spencer had changed, too, and decided to foot the bill himself. According to Kaavi's social media posts, he was very successful now.

It's not like he was broke, I suppose. He'd just always been happy to let me pay for things when we were together, and it made sense, because I always had a lot more money than he did. My father never spoke to me, sure, but he had set up a trust in my name that was generous enough for me to pay for Spencer's portion of the rent at the apartment Kaavi and I shared before he moved in.

Laura asked me more questions than should be humanly necessary about homecomings, barely listening to my answers before firing off again—

Was there a ceremony? No, the couple and their parents light an oil lamp, that's about it.

What was an oil lamp? I googled an image of a Sri Lankan oil lamp to show her.

Will there be bridesmaids? Nope. She looked disappointed.

So, like, what happens? The typical Sri Lankan festivities—a lot of eating, drinking, and dancing.

Then why does everyone get so dressed up? Good question, Laura. Because Sri Lankans never let the opportunity to wear all their gold jewelry go to waste.

I thought about Kaavi's car getting T-boned by another vehicle. Something big—maybe a speeding lorry. Something that would just ram in on the side Laura was sitting, crushing her to a pulp. Splattering her blood all over the beige leather seats. Spraying bits of shattered bone over the rest of us.

If Kaavi's car hadn't pulled up at the designer's studio when it did, I would have jumped out of it.

The studio itself was more of a house than the artsy creative space

I had envisioned, but the walls were plastered with pictures of women that the designer had no doubt dressed before. We sat awkwardly in the dimly lit waiting area while dozens of brides grinned down at us. The longer I stared at them, the more I started to feel sick.

Being bombarded with questions on the car ride over here left me feeling nauseous and exhausted. Like I just wanted to go back home and take a nap. Or maybe it was the jet lag. Luckily, we didn't have to wait too long.

"Kaavindi daaaarling." The designer swept into the room. He wore a loose shirt with a Nehru collar and a sarong, but not the regular kind—this was one of those expensive handloom sarongs that were dry clean only and far too delicate for everyday wear.

"Andre, this is my friend Amaya," she introduced me, as Andre made loud smacking sounds against her cheeks. "She's down from LA for the wedding."

"Another American girl, huh?" Andre said, smacking his lips near my ears as well. His cheek never really touched mine, though he did grip my hands. His palms were cold and damp.

"And of course, Laura." He reached for her hands, too, while she beamed at him. "My beautiful, beautiful princess. My assistant has your jacket ready. Why don't you head on up? And Kaavi, step right this way. Your friend can come, too, if she likes."

We were ushered into a room stuffed with mannequins and yards of fabric that pooled out onto the floor. This was certainly no *Say Yes to the Dress*, but then, Kaavi had gone shopping for one of her dresses in Singapore, so I guess she had the full experience there.

I was waved off to a chair in a corner, while Kaavi and one of Andre's assistants disappeared behind a large screen.

"What about you, darling? Who's dressing you for the wedding?"

His smile seemed innocent enough, but I knew what was happening here. Luckily for Andre, he had no competition to worry about.

"I'm probably wearing a dress," I explained. A dress that I had packed but hopefully wouldn't need to wear.

"Ah, you young ones. Can get away with anything these days, no? In our days of course you would be disowned if you didn't wear a proper sari like a good Sri Lankan girl." He pressed his palms together in the traditional Sri Lankan greeting pose and guffawed at his own joke.

I gave a little giggle at this, because it was expected of me, and because it helped mask the discomfort of my freshly blooming headache.

"Andre, is this supposed to fit like this?" Kaavi called out from behind the screen.

"Come out, darling. Let us see."

I don't know what it was supposed to fit like, but Andre and I both sucked in our breath (him more dramatically, of course) when Kaavi came out and stood on the little platform in the middle of the room. She had the perfect body for Kandyan sari—similar to the Indian ones you would normally see, but with an extra frill around the waist, and puffed sleeves on the jacket. My angular frame would look ridiculous in one, but Kaavi looked resplendent, like she did in everything, even without the seven necklaces and the headpiece she would wear on the day. I wondered what Spencer would think when he saw her dressed like that—like a perfect little doll. It made my heart hurt.

Andre fussed about her while she pointed out an issue with the neckline. She also said the sleeves were too tight, to which Andre tutted and told her that was normal. Kaavi tried raising her arms to prove her point (they wouldn't go up to even her shoulders), but Andre just swatted them back down. He pinned the jacket tighter near her ribs.

"Hang on, I won't be able to breathe," Kaavi complained. *"Aney,* darling," she called out to the assistant. "Would you mind bringing me my phone? I think I left it back there."

The meek assistant jumped to attention, her cheeks flushed at being acknowledged.

"Now," Andre continued, still brandishing his pins, "you know it's not nice unless just a little bit here jumps out, no?" He pinched the fold of skin, not fat, just skin, that was sticking out between the gap of her jacket and waistband.

"That's okay, Andre. We all know I'm not that nice anyway," she replied, smoothly and with a smile. "And please loosen the arms also. I don't want to feel like a stiff corpse on my big day." When had Kaavi blossomed into so much confidence? I wish I could take control of things like she did.

Andre tutted again but loosened the pins.

"Here, missy, could you please put your phone away for a minute and turn this way?"

Kaavi gave him a tight smile—she really was attached to her phone—and did as she was told. Who was she messaging all the time? Was it Spencer? Or did she have a new best friend to whom she gave a play-by-play? I mean, Beth and I were close, but I didn't message her every moment of every day. I'd let her know I was here in Sri Lanka, of course, and I'd told her how weird it was being back. But I was never glued to my phone the way Kaavi was.

"Okay, now just give me a minute. I actually have some necklaces we just used for a shoot. They won't be the million-rupee ones that your parents will get you, okay, so don't judge. Just so you get the picture, you know." Kaavi giggled, but Andre was probably right about the price.

Andre and his assistant left the room, and it was just the two of us again.

"What do you think?" she asked, finally meeting my eye in the large mirror in front of her.

I know she was the one with the tight jacket, but my breath caught in my throat. I wasn't ready, even after so long, to see this version of Kaavi in real life. The version that didn't need me anymore. The version that didn't depend on me to take care of things and to make things right for her.

But I couldn't focus on all that now. I needed to know why she asked me here.

"You look amazing." I hoped a compliment would soften things.

But compliments mean nothing to someone who had thousands of likes and loves and followers on Instagram. She was used to being told she was amazing. It's old news to her, no doubt.

"I wasn't expecting to see you, you know."

That was fair. I hadn't RSVP'd. I had thought about it, but I couldn't RSVP without replying to her email, and I didn't know what to say. I wasn't even 100 percent sure I would come. That I would have the guts to go through with this.

"I know." I rubbed my temples. I guess now was as good a time to ask her as any.

"Kaavi, why did you say your parents—"

But Andre fluttered back into the room then, and there was more oohing and gasping as they made Kaavi try on various accessories. Laura joined us at some point also, and gladly relieved me of any duty I had to interact with the designer and his team.

And after a whirlwind of pins and lace and draping and air-kisses, we were done. And not a moment too soon because it genuinely did feel like my head would burst.

"Goodbye, my darling. I'll see you on the big day," Andre said with a final smack on her cheek. I briefly wondered how he'd look if he tripped on his pretentious sarong and bashed his head on the corner of the table that held his sewing machine. The way his neck would probably bend at a strange angle. The way his eyes might roll back into his head.

Kaavi and I made our way outside while Laura hung back to settle her bill with Andre's assistant. This was my chance.

"Kaavs, look, I need to talk to you. I need to know—"

"Now's not really a good time, Ams. We can chat later, okay?"

"No, look, I'm sorry. It's just, this is all so much, and this whole idea of you and Spencer and now your parents and—"

"I really can't talk about this now, Amaya."

I knew I was rambling like I always did when I was nervous, but I had to try.

"No, look, I just want to know—"

"Amaya." Her voice was low and fierce, and she kept glancing around to see if we were being overheard. "I know this must be weird for you, and I think it's commendable that you came given that I'm marrying Spencer. But I honestly don't have time for this, okay? I have a wedding to plan and so much craziness to attend to. I'm glad you're here, but please understand that this wedding is definitely happening."

It felt like she had reached out and slapped me. I know we haven't spoken in years, but I was not expecting this—the sharp edge to her voice, the indifference toward me, her oldest friend. It stung far worse than the burn from her curling iron did.

"So, what are you ladies wearing tonight?" Laura's voice rang out, and for the first time, I was relieved to hear it.

"You know my mother, right? I know she said it's supposed to be casual, but please dress up. I just know her friends are going to show up draped in diamonds and designer wear." Kaavi's voice was different now. Smooth and perky, like she sounded in her videos. I guess the steel was just for me.

I knew, from religiously checking the wedding itinerary website, that tonight was a cocktail party at her parents' house to "officially kick off the wedding festivities" and "welcome everyone who had flown down from abroad."

"That's what I was hoping." Laura giggled as she made her way around the other side of the car to get in. I was about to open the door myself when Kaavi stopped me.

"Hey, so I actually have a meeting I need to get to. Take the car and get yourself dropped home, okay? I'll see you tonight."

I should say something. I should try to talk to her again. But I knew it was no use.

"But why don't we just drop you off on the way?" I said instead.

"Oh no, don't worry. You must be exhausted, and this meeting is just around the corner. I've already called an Uber, see?" She waved her phone in front of me.

"But you're just going to Cinnamon Grand. It's only two minutes away."

She paled a little when I said that—I guess she hadn't expected me to actually look at her phone—and glanced around to see if Laura or the driver heard.

"Don't worry, okay? I'll see you tonight. And remember what I said. Dress fancy."

Her Uber pulled up just in time, and she jumped in without a second glance.

That's strange. Why didn't Kaavi want anyone to know she was going to Cinnamon Grand? It was one of Colombo's many five-star hotels, and one that I'm sure she frequented regularly.

I checked my watch—12:15.

What were you trying to hide, Kaavi?

ANDRE

Interview Transcript: Aumunupalage Asoka Dinesh Kumara
   (abbrev. AADK)
Date: January 25, 2020
Location: The Mount Lavinia Hotel

EP: I understand that this must be a difficult time for you, Mr.
   Dinesh Kumara, thank—

AADK: Andre.

EP: Sorry?

AADK: Please call me Andre. Everyone does.

EP: Yes. As I was saying, thank you for agreeing to speak to us. I
   understand that you must be in considerable shock and—

AADK: I am. In considerable shock. But the Fonsekas are like
   family to me, so it doesn't matter if I still feel like fainting. I
   will do whatever it takes.

EP: Yes. Thank you. Could you please state your full name and
   address for the record?

AADK: My name, as you might already know, is Andre.

EP: Your full name, sir, if you don't mind. We have on your National Identity Card, which you handed in to my colleague
   earlier, Mr. Amunupalage Asoka Dinesh Kuma—

AADK: I told you already, darling—must we keep going over
   this? I haven't been called that since I dropped out of school
   many moons ago. Even my late mother, god bless her soul,
   called me Andre. For heaven's sake, I've been traumatized
   enough as it is.

EP: Yes, Mr. . . . Andre. And your address is 26 Church Road, Moratuwa. Am I right?

AADK: That's my registered address, yes. Though I mostly stay at the annex attached to my studio at 187/1A Ward Place, Colombo 07.

EP: Thank you. And you are the Fonseka family's dressmaker, am I right?

AADK: I'm a designer. I've been designing wedding dresses for the cream of Colombo for many years now. If you need a reference, please feel free to call His Excellency, the president. I did his daughter's bridal a few years back, and his nephews' wives—yes, the ministers, their wives came to me for their bridals as well. I am regarded as a close family friend, after all. Anyone could probably tell you. I am certainly not just a dressmaker.

EP: I see. I was told that it was you who first reported the crime. Would you mind going over what happened this morning and how you came to know Miss Fonseka wasn't there?

AADK: Of course. Like I told the security at the time, I arrived alone to the hotel. From the very moment that I knocked on the door, I knew something was very, very wrong. I could just feel it, you know, the energy was off. I knocked multiple times, but there was no answer. This wasn't my first wedding, you know. I've seen many brides have one too many drinks the night before and struggle to wake up in the morning. I've had to drag quite a few of them into the shower myself.

I sweet-talked a housekeeping boy into opening the door for me. I didn't want Mrs. Fonseka to catch her daughter in a hangover—she'd have really blown a gasket. So I got the boy to open the

door, and I stuck my head in. I didn't want to catch her in a com-
promising position, after all. Who knows what these young
women got up to?

The blinds were drawn and the lights were off, so I stuck my arm
in and flipped the switch.

That's when I saw the mess. And the blood. The place was torn
apart. Like there had been some sort of wild animal attack.
Bless that poor girl.

EP: Could you please describe exactly what you saw in the room?

AADK: You've seen it, haven't you? There was definitely some
sort of struggle there. Her makeup pushed off the dresser.
Things on the floor. The mirror broken like someone . . . like
someone smashed something into it. And blood. Like I said.
There was blood everywhere. The window to the balcony was
open, and there were drag marks leading outside.

EP: And what did you do?

AADK: I immediately screamed for the housekeeping boy to call
security, of course. And then I called Fiona, that's the bride's
mother. Sorry, if you could please just give me a moment.

[Pause]

This was all very traumatic, you know. My hands are still shaking, you see?

EP: Yes. And Mrs. Fiona Fonseka also informed me that you had
some information for us? Something that you hadn't yet di-
vulged to her?

AADK: Well, yes. I thought about it long and hard, you know.
Whether I should come forward or not. You know, I prize my
reputation above everything else, and the last thing I need is
my clients worrying about my discretion. I don't just dress

brides, you know. I do saris and jackets for all occasions, and
my clients, well, they've built a certain relationship with me.
You can call me the keeper of Colombo's secrets, if you like.
My god, the things I overhear about cheating husbands and
office affairs and who is sleeping with who. I would be dragged
out of my studio and whipped if everything I knew got out.

[Giggles]

But of course, I always keep my lips sealed. Sealed with a kiss, I
say. It's important that my clients trust me, after all. I don't just
sew sari blouses for women, my dear. I capture her essence in
nine yards of silk, cocooning her, helping her turn into a beautiful butterfly. I can't do that if I don't know her soul. If I don't
know where her heart lies.

Which is why I didn't want to come forward, at first. I don't want
anyone thinking I'm giving away their secrets. But then I said
to myself, "Andre, darling, that poor thing has been attacked
under the most horrific of all circumstances, and you would
never forgive yourself if you didn't do everything in your
power to help."

And so, here I am.

EP: And the information?

AADK: Ah yes, you see, much like anyone of repute, Kaavindi
Fonseka was . . . is my client. Her mother rang me up the very
day after the engagement and insisted I cancel my entire afternoon to meet her. I couldn't believe the timeline when she told
me. I normally had an entire year, maybe a year and a half to
plan a bridal, but she gave me a few weeks.

"My darling," I said, "are you trying to give me a heart attack? I'm
fully booked until next August, at least."

But she just laughed and said I was the only designer her family
would consider, so how could I say no after that? Besides, I
could only imagine the look on that smug Stephan de Krester's
face if he got to dress her instead. I couldn't stand for it.

And so I sourced the most beautiful lace—got it down all the way
from Vietnam, you know. It's handmade. Only the best of the
best for the Fonseka princess. And I came up with a design
that would—

EP: Mr. Kumara, would you mind stating the information you
said you had for us?

AADK: The informa—ah, yes, yes. Of course. And again, please,
call me Andre. The information I wanted to give you is that I
think I know who did it. I know who had it in for Kaavindi
Fonseka.

EP: And who would that be?

AADK: Look, I'm happy to go on record for this because I care
about Kaavindi, you know. They were like family to me, the
Fonsekas.

EP: Sir, who do you believe to have hurt Miss Fonseka?

AADK: Okay, okay. So listen. She brought this friend along with
her, and I knew, from the moment I saw this girl, that something was off. She was jealous of Kaavindi, I could just tell.
Always staring at her, buzzing around her like some sort of
bee, or wasp. I just knew she was trouble. That's why I came
here. To tell you to investigate that girl.

EP: Are you referring to Miss Amaya Bloom?

AADK: Oh, that skittish thing? No, my god, no. That girl looked
like she would faint if she saw her own shadow. No, I mean her
friend Laura. The American. Gave me the worst vibes, that
one. You know what she said to me? She actually told me that

my designs were too colorful. I mean, she's from Houston—what does she know about sari design?

EP: And why is it that you suspect Miss Laura?

AADK: Well, there was an instance where Laura took Kaavi's phone without her permission or knowledge. It was at one of the earlier fittings, when it was just the two of them. Kaavi was quite glued to it, maybe more so than usual that particular day. I thought she looked a little upset. Maybe she was having an argument with Spencer—young couples do tend to bicker, you know, with the stress of the upcoming wedding and all. But when Kaavi went behind the screen to change, Laura swiped Kaavi's phone and clicked on it. I have no idea how she managed to get the passcode. She turned bright red when she noticed that I saw her, and mumbled some excuse about trying to find the driver's number. Unluckily for her, darling, I can smell bullshit from a mile away.

EP: Anything else you noticed about Miss Laura?

AADK: Well, I don't know about you, but she seemed quite obsessed with Kaavi to me. She even asked me if we could do an off-the-shoulder style sari jacket for her. Well, guess who else was getting an off-the-shoulder jacket? That's right, the bride. I couldn't give Laura the same design as the bride, now could I? Mrs. Fonseka would have had my head on a platter. Especially given the rumors about Laura.

EP: And what rumors are these?

AADK: Surely, you must have heard? Now, this isn't the reason why I think she had something to do with it. After all, I'm not one to judge. It's just that, well, like I said, I service the cream of Colombo, and the cream of Colombo loves to talk. But I have it on good authority that Laura wasn't just staying with Kaavi's family—she was, oh, you know, *doing the dirty*, with Mr. Fonseka himself. You've heard the rumors about him, I'm sure. Especially about his youngest daughter, you know, the toddler—Nadia— that he has supposedly adopted out of the goodness of his heart. Like I said before, darling, I can smell bullshit from miles away. It was definitely not out of the goodness of his *heart* that he got some girl pregnant and decided to adopt the child. I'm just surprised that Fiona went along with it. But then, she's known for putting up with his nonsense. Did you hear what he did on his fiftieth birthday? He apparently got down a whole case of Cristal— you know how hard it is to find in Colombo, right? Everyone is always clawing one another for a bottle. Anyway, he filled his entire king-size tub with Cristal and took a bath in it. Just to show he can. I heard from a very reliable friend of the family who has no reason to lie, you know.

But anyway, yes, back to Laura, maybe she was jealous of the attention Mr. Fonseka gave his eldest daughter; after all, we all knew she was the apple of his eye. Or maybe she felt she could never compete with the perfect Kaavindi Fonseka. Either way, that girl is trouble. I know it in my bones.

EP: Anything else you would like to tell us?

AADK: Hmm? No. No. That was it.

EP: Mr. Andre, thank you so much for sharing your suspicions. Would you mind if we asked you a few more questions, now that you are here?

AADK: Of course, darling. I have nothing to hide. I'm an open book.

EP: Mr. Andre, you dressed Miss Fonséka in her traditional Kandyan sari, yes?

AADK: Yes, I did. Ask anyone, they'll tell you—she looked positively divine. Possibly the most beautiful bride I've ever dressed.

EP: And you were also set to dress Miss Fonseka in her going-away sari later on in the day, am I right?

AADK: Yes. Rose gold to match her engagement ring. That girl was mad about the color. I'm devastated that we can't eventually see her in it. What a tragedy.

EP: But you didn't design her wedding dress, am I right? The one for the church ceremony. I am told that she flew out to Singapore to purchase that particular dress.

AADK: No. Actually, I did design her wedding dress. But apparently the original dress I designed, and *hand made*, mind you, was damaged, somehow? The details are still unclear to me, but Kaavindi called me the day before yesterday, quite late in the night, in absolute hysterics, saying that someone had destroyed her dress.

EP: And did she mention who she thought might have done it?

AADK: She did blubber something about the hotel having to take accountability, but to be honest, I was a little too upset to really pay much attention. I asked if I could salvage the dress—if it was a tear or a rip or something I could mend—but she said there was no point.

EP: And were you upset at Miss Fonseka that the dress was destroyed?

AADK: I was upset that the dress was destroyed, of course. I spent hours upon hours doing all the embroidery by hand. I thought I would lose my eyesight at the end of it, that's how intricate the threadwork was. Of course I was absolutely devastated that she wouldn't be wearing it. That she wouldn't even show it to me. But then, she did have a backup dress. A Hayley Paige that she flew down from Singapore. Can you believe that? Hayley Paige being backup to me? Anyway, Fiona was quite upset, but Kaavindi had decided to wear that to the church, apparently.

[Pause]

It was almost a little too convenient, if you ask me. The lowly local designer's dress gets mysteriously ruined, and the high-profile foreign designer's *backup dress* that cost a hideously obscene amount gets moved to the spotlight. Stephan de Krester would have thrown a party when he heard. But then . . . well, I guess there are more important things to focus on now.

EP: So you weren't meant to be dressing her in your own design this morning?

AADK: That's right. Sadly.

EP: Then can I know, Mr. Andre, if you weren't dressing Miss Fonseka in her church dress, why you went to her room this morning?

AADK: What's that supposed to mean?

[Pause]

Kaavi actually messaged me last night and asked me to come in about an hour earlier than planned. Something about wanting to do a livestream of her interviewing me, so I got there even before the makeup artists and hair people.

[Pause]

Look, she might not have been wearing my dress anymore, but I was overseeing her entire wedding aesthetic, you know. Just because she was wearing a fucking Hayley Paige, that didn't mean I washed my hands of her completely. Like I said, Kaavindi was like family to me. I cared about her deeply and only wanted what was best for her.

EP: I see.

[Shuffling of papers]

Mr. Andre, I wanted to thank you for handing your phone over to my colleagues this morning. We have a few bits of information that we would like to verify. Would you mind stating for the record what these are?

[Shuffling of papers]

AADK: They appear to be printouts of text messages, I think.

EP: Yes, they are text messages sent between you and your assistant—a Miss Kumudini. Would you mind reading the highlighted text on page three?

[Shuffling of papers]

AADK: *Can you believe the audacity of that selfish, spoiled bitch?*

[Pause]

EP: Please continue, Mr. Andre.

AADK: Look, you have this wrong.

EP: Let me read out the rest of it for you. *Can you believe the audacity of that selfish, spoiled bitch? All my hard work and she destroys my dress just so she can wear a trashy fucking gown that makes her look like a fucking chandelier? Fuck that rich bitch. I could fucking kill her.*

8

AMAYA

Four Days before the Wedding

I MELTED INTO my room and turned on the air-conditioning as high as it would go. I would start to shiver soon, but I didn't care. My face felt like it was coated in a layer of oil and grime, and my bra cut into my sides, which were starting to itch from the sweat.

I didn't plan on sleeping, even though the dull thud in my head had developed into a full-blown pounding. I paced around the room, anxious, unsettled, trying to confirm my next move. I had been waffling when I got here—I knew that Kaavi shouldn't be marrying Spencer, but I was also giddy with the thought that the Fonsekas might finally want me back in their lives. It was bittersweet. My chance to make amends marred with the knowledge that I had to stop a wedding. But now that I knew I had been tricked—that the Fonsekas never intended on making peace—there was nothing bittersweet anymore. Just plain old run-of-the-mill bitterness.

Kaavi can't marry Spencer. In the past she'd always depended on me to make things right, but everything wasn't about her anymore. It's time for me to launch my first plan.

Seetha knocked on my door and brought a cup of milk tea. I accepted it but left it on my desk. I was too wired for tea.

Seeing Kaavi was . . . interesting, I suppose. Everything that happened left me so broken, so hurt, so painfully raw that when I finally pieced myself together, I thought no one could get through my armor again. But I guess that's the problem with broken armor. There will always be cracks. And Kaavi knew exactly how to leak through mine.

Often, things we were in awe of when we were younger feel oddly unimpressive as adults. I used to think my house was a palace. I used to think my mother was the tallest woman in the world. Food laid out for me was a feast. Things change as you grow. As you understand the world for what it is. That we overcompensate in our memories because we didn't know any better at the time.

That was how I was expecting things to be with Kaavi and the Fonsekas.

I had hoped that it was all in my head. That I'd put them on some sort of pedestal because I'd missed them so much. That I had been looking at my past through glasses that were so rose-tinted that everything was just fluorescent pink at this point. But with Kaavi, it was the opposite. In our time apart, I'd withered away to less, and she'd blossomed to be more. More than I was and more than I ever could be.

I remembered the quiet girl who used to let me copy homework off her. The girl who was always so shy, who'd only show her true self to me. The girl who fell in love as easily as catching a cold, who needed rescuing, for whom I was more than happy to take the fall. But I couldn't protect her anymore. There was someone more important to me now.

And underneath it all, the questions that itched and irritated and stung: Why did she tell me that her parents wanted me here? Was it just a ruse because *she* wanted me here? And if so, why?

I took out my phone and messaged Beth.

**I saw her today. It was rough. I think I'm going to
do it.**

Her reply beeped back a few seconds later.

**I'm so glad you're finally doing
what you have to do.**

Thank goodness for Beth. She's been such a rock to me. Keeping me steady. Keeping me from spiraling out of control. I haven't told her the entire plan, of course. Just the abstract. I couldn't risk losing the one real friend I had, after all.

I sat down on the cool sheets of my bed for a minute, and the next thing I knew, I was drowning in deep, dark dreams that I couldn't wake up from. The sleep of a million demons choking you, pulling you down into the underworld to join them. I'd forgotten how intoxicating jet lag was—how little control you had over your ability to be conscious.

And when I finally woke up, I felt worse than I did before I fell asleep. My throat itched, and my face was puffed up like a cushion. I had broken into a sweat and was now shivering because of it—no wonder, because the air conditioner had finally turned my room into an icebox.

I dragged myself to the shower and tried to put some effort into making myself look respectable. My skin had already started to break out, which was less than excellent. I should have been prepared for the fresh batch of zits that always accompanied my skin acclimatizing to the humidity, but of course I was too preoccupied to concern myself with self-maintenance. I caked on some concealer and tried not to think about how the feeling of sweat trickling down my back never really went away.

I struggled into a black cocktail dress that I knew wouldn't be a hit with the aunties. Not because of its cut, which covered enough of my cleavage, arms, and thighs to be considered demure. It never mattered if it was tight enough that nothing was left to the imagination. Just that you were covered. Sri Lankan rules on dressing conservatively are not renowned for their logic. But it was black, which was considered unlucky at a wedding. Of course this wasn't a wedding per se, and I didn't have a large selection of Colombo 07–appropriate cocktail wear in my regular rotation anyway, so I had to make do. It's not like I had the presence of mind to go shopping at any point.

I did make sure to put on earrings, though, and a thin gold necklace with a tiny diamond pendant. Not wearing earrings or a "gold chain" in Sri Lanka was the equivalent of social suicide, regardless of your socioeconomic standing. Not wearing them meant your family couldn't provide you with the basic necessities of being a woman. If you also wore a gold bangle, even better. I remember Seetha asking me for an advance on her salary once when her niece pawned her gold earrings to pay off her husband's gambling debts.

"She works at a factory, *Baba*. How can she go to work without her earrings? She'll be so embarrassed." Because the shame of your ears being bare was worse than the shame of not being able to make the month's rent.

But still, I did my hair, put on the appropriate amount of makeup, wore my demure-albeit-black cocktail dress, and carried my brandless, too-large-for-a-cocktail-party handbag that held what I needed for tonight.

I took a moment adjusting the minimal jewelry that once belonged to my mother. I used to watch her get ready, when I was younger.

I'd stand near her doorway and be entranced by the way she'd dab on lipstick, the way she'd suck in her cheeks to dust on blush, the way she'd turn her head from side to side after she put on her jewelry.

"It's not too much, is it?" she'd ask me, and I'd always shake my head. It was never too much. Nothing she did was enough, after all, to keep my father by her side.

It's hard to ignore the catching feeling in my chest when I think about her sometimes, and I've been thinking about her nonstop since I got back. I guess that was the curse that came with holding on to this house—if I closed my eyes and allowed myself to float away, it was like she'd never left.

Grieving for your mother shrinks in value as you get older. Everyone acts like it's the end of the world when you lose a parent as a child, and it certainly felt that way to me. But you lose the right to hold on to that grief as the years tick by. As losing a parent is viewed less like a tragedy and more like nature taking its course. Because holding on to stale sadness didn't do anyone any favors. No one seems to understand that real loss never eases; we just become more adept at carrying a weight that settles deeper in our chests, smiling through it, pretending like we are totally fine whenever someone mentions them.

But once again, I had to tuck my mother away into a corner of my mind. I missed her, of course, but I wasn't like her. I believed in fighting for what was mine.

I called a proper taxi to take me to the Fonsekas', because taking a *tuk tuk* alone while dressed like this would be "asking for trouble." It's true I'd been away for a while, but I hadn't forgotten the rules.

The itinerary on the website said that this was a simple gathering at home. Of course, I knew the Fonsekas weren't capable of throwing something basic, but walking back into their home for the second time today, I wasn't prepared for this—

The front lawn was enveloped in a large marquee that was not there when I left this morning. Every bush and tree was bedazzled in fairy lights. A stage with a band was set up at one end of the marquee, with a small bar at the other end. A large number of round tables with elegant crisp white tablecloths took up the space that was not designated for the dance floor, while taller cocktail tables dotted the garden outside the tent. All the tables held towering vases of pink flowers, and the heady scent made me feel a little dizzy. A separate, smaller marquee off to the side contained a decadent buffet, where I could see an impressive mix of Sri Lankan and Western food being served. There was a photo booth with props off to the other side, and a separate gin and tonic bar for handcrafted cocktails.

Mrs. Fonseka was a planner. Not officially, of course. A woman of her disposition from her generation would never seek employment of any sort. And so instead she planned parties, and galas, and charity events. She planned school fairs, and concerts, and her daughters' lives. She'd even taken a shot at planning things out for me. And while her parties were known to be the best in Colombo, she'd definitely upped her game tonight in honor of her daughter.

Speaking of Mrs. Fonseka, she was marching around barking orders at various waitstaff, who looked petrified every time she went near them. Even though her peacock-blue evening dress sparkled like a Christmas ornament, her expression was strictly no-nonsense. She wore a necklace adorned with blue sapphires that glistened in the flickering low lights. I wonder what it might be like to pull it tight. Not too tight—just enough to make her face turn blue. Blue to match her ostentatious necklace and her gaudy dress.

Not wanting to draw any attention from her, I tried to back away as discreetly as possible into the main house, where it would be quieter.

Smiling politely at an old couple, I waited for them to pass me by before turning around and almost tripping over someone.

Maybe I was about to apologize, but my voice never found the words.

I knew, of course, from the moment I decided to come here, from the moment that I decided to sabotage this wedding, that I'd have to see him. I'd spent so long dreaming of this moment. What I'd do, what I'd say when I finally came face-to-face with Spencer after all these years. I was crying, the last time he saw me. Sobbing. Broken. I was a shell before. Not even half the woman I am now. I wondered if he had changed too. How different can someone be after five years? *Do* we really change? Does what's deep within us, in that place that makes us innately who we are, shift and move and evolve with time? Or are our lives like the window dressing of department stores—changed and updated with the seasons, leaving what's inside in the same chaotic mess?

"Amaya," he exclaimed, and I practically disintegrated at the way my name sounded coming from his lips. He was carrying a bouquet of lilies, and the smell of it laced with his aftershave made it hard to breathe.

"Um, hi, Spence. How are you?" I tried to go for nonchalant, but my voice came out high and squeaky. I put my hands on my hips to stop them from shaking and took a deep breath. I can't look like a wreck now. He has to see that I'm not a wreck. I am strong. I am confident. I have my own life and my own business and my own brunch friends. I'm fine.

"I didn't know you were going to be here," he said. He was smiling. His voice was warm. My breath was shallow. I was going to throw up.

"Um, Kaavi invited me." I tried to go an octave deeper. My heart was hammering in my chest.

"Oh? That's a pleasant surprise." So Kaavi hadn't told him either.

"I'm glad you're here, though, Ams. Really." He sounded earnest. My knees felt weak. "I hated the way we left things. I was horrible to you, of course. I never even had the chance to apologize. And then you, well, you left. If I'd have known then that I wouldn't see you for, how long's it been now? Four years?"

"Five," I said softly.

He raised an eyebrow at the correction, his smile as boyish as ever. I was definitely going to throw up. I needed to get out of here.

"You always had a better memory than me. Five whole years. If I'd known it'd be this long, well . . ." He smiled again, but wistfully this time.

I didn't say anything. My body was frozen. My mind too. I could barely look him in the eye and so I stared at his chest instead. He'd left an extra button undone just like he always did. A part of me almost reached out to button it, but of course I caught myself in time. I remember how he used to press me into his chest and I used to bury my face in it, wishing I could melt into him. Wishing I could melt away.

"You'll be here for the whole wedding, then?"

I forced myself to swallow. To hold my voice as steady as I could.

"Yep. The whole thing."

"That's great. I guess I'll see you around?"

"Sure. See you around."

I started to turn away, but he suddenly reached for my arm. I practically choked.

"Amaya, I don't know how you remember it, but the last time we were together—it really—well, it really devastated me, you know. That you thought of me that way." His eyes bored into mine. There was a time I used to think I could get drunk on his eyes alone. The skin on my arm broke out in goose bumps.

He was devastated.

I took a deep breath.

Gave him an apologetic smile.

Gently shook my arm free.

"It was a long time ago," I mumbled, turning away.

"I'll see you around."

And then I fled.

Thankfully, there were enough bathrooms at the Fonsekas' that it was easy to find a free one tucked toward the back of the ground floor. I locked myself in, slamming the lid down on the toilet and collapsing onto it.

I held my hands up to my face. My cheeks were boiling but my palms were ice-cold.

What on earth is wrong with me?

Years of dreaming about this moment. Sleepless nights spent imagining what I would say when I finally met him again. Afternoons spent perfecting my speech.

I could picture it now.

My confident hair flip. The way I would be in control, yet aloof. In my element. The way I would smile at him so he would know for sure that I was over him. That I didn't need him in my life. That I was certainly, definitely, 100 percent not broken.

And instead, there I was, shaking and floundering and still the same insipid girl who let her heart get stomped on. Who loved so hard she lost herself.

Why was I like this? Why could I never be the Amaya that existed in my head? The version of myself that never made an entrance when I most needed it, instead of this watery, half-boiled counterpart?

I grunted in frustration and launched myself off the toilet. I yanked out some tissues and blotted my upper lip, my neck, and stuffed more into the armpits of my dress. I couldn't splash water on my face without ruining my makeup, so I washed my hands instead.

I looked around the vanity for a pair of scissors or a razor. I couldn't find any of those, but there was a little dish of safety pins and hair clips. I picked up a safety pin, opening it. This will do just fine.

If I was unsure about my plans to ruin this wedding before, meeting Spencer solidified everything. I thought of his earnest smile. The way his fingers pressed into the soft flesh of my upper arm. I had to go through with it. I didn't have a choice.

I took the pointed end of the pin and stuck it under the nail on my thumb. It was exactly what I needed. I felt some of my anxious energy drain out with the drop of blood that oozed into the sink. I inhaled. I counted to five.

I needed Dr. Dunn. He'd have told me to "just get it done." I'd rolled my eyes at the catchphrase when I first heard it, but he was right. I needed to stop procrastinating. I had to take initiative.

Then I remembered the way Spencer's eyes bored deep into mine, and the way I'd feel when he smiled at me. Like the world was mine to take. The exhilaration I felt from knowing that he loved me. That he had chosen me.

Forget Dr. Dunn. What I really need is Alexander. Or at least, the way I felt after Alexander was done with me.

I thought about messaging him, which was still within our agreement, after all, but I knew what he'd say. He'd order me to take off my panties and keep them in my purse the whole night, and not allow me to touch myself until I got home and begged him for his permission. I couldn't handle that kind of distraction right now.

I took out the A5-sized envelope from my handbag.

This was just plan A. I hoped it would work. That I didn't have to make it all the way to plan C. Because meeting Spencer pushed any doubts I had from my mind. I had to do whatever it took.

I KEPT MY eyes focused ahead of me as I wove my way through the crowd. I didn't want to accidentally look at any numbers and see any unlucky signs. I didn't want anything changing my mind. I knew what I had to do. The party had really gone into full swing by the time I made it out of the bathroom. I considered grabbing a glass of champagne from one of the many waiters that whizzed by, but decided it would be best to keep my wits about me, and grabbed a bite-size seafood quiche instead. I could barely take a nibble from it.

I looked around, trying to find the perfect person to help me. It couldn't be just anybody. It had to be someone close enough to the family to be taken seriously, but who wasn't too loyal to the Fonsekas either.

I spotted Andre, the designer from this afternoon. He was chatting to a young woman next to him. Would he work? I inched my way closer, wondering if there was an opening in their conversation.

"I'm telling you, child, she's the fakest attention-seeker I know, but you didn't hear it from me, okay?"

The woman threw her head back and laughed. "Oh, Andre, you're such a devil, I tell you."

"I'm just honest, darling. Karma is a bitch, but, well, maybe not as big a bitch as I am. She'll have what's coming to her, mark my words." More laughter from them both.

It didn't sound like the kind of conversation I'd want to interrupt. I could always tell when someone was out for blood during a Colombo gossip session. But who could help with my own plans?

Luckily for me, the answer presented itself in the form of one of the heavily coiffed, sprayed, and lacquered aunties from this morning.

"Amaya, no? Hello, darling," she called out from her chair, opening her arms to me.

"Hi, Aunty Josephina, how are you?" I matched her energy as I bent over and gave her an air-kiss.

"This is one of Kaavi's dear friends," she explained to the other aunties at the table. Her display of happiness was definitely more for their benefit than mine. "She's flown down from LA for the wedding," she said in a mock whisper, raising her eyebrows like it was a juicy secret.

"I was in LA last year," said one aunty with an over-elocuted British accent that most of the older generation had perfected, having grown up during the overlap of colonial Ceylon. "Didn't like it at all. Quite the madhouse, I tell you."

I smiled. "It definite—"

"I much prefer London," she continued, not caring about my views on LA at all. "It's a madhouse there, too, but at least I'm used to that particular type of madness." She looked around at the rest of the table, which was their cue to burst into laughter.

"And you know, no matter what, I just can't understand what those Americans are saying half the time. They are butchering the English language, I tell you. Absolutely butchering it." Another round of laughter. Sri Lankan aunties have always been more protective of the queen's English than the queen herself.

The aunties might be vicious, but they are old. I bet they would snap like twigs in my hands if I could just have a try.

"What's funny, darling?" Aunty Josephina asked, leaning close to me. Her breath smelled rotten.

"Sorry, Aunty?"

"You were smiling to yourself, just now. Is it Aunty Cynthia and her dry jokes?" She giggled to herself and I joined her. She had a piece of something orange stuck in her teeth.

"But I must tell you, that Spencer, he's not like the rest of those Americans, you know. He's such a simple fellow." It took me a second, but I remembered that we use *simple* over here to mean *humble*, not *simpleminded*. To be known as simple, or humble, or down-to-earth, was one of our highest compliments. Even in a crowd that would bust out a different Louis Vuitton for every occasion.

"You know, he even calls Fiona and Nihal *Amma* and *Thaththa*. Can you believe it?"

That was directed at the table, which responded with a series of appreciative *oohs* and *aahs*.

"I hear he made a few million dollars from his last business venture. Kaavindi is a lucky girl. Not that she needs the money, of course."

Another round of laughter. The envelope burned in my handbag, but I couldn't do it here. It would be far too obvious.

"So, Amaya, what about you? Do you also have a handsome American boyfriend?" Like Kaavi said, no one seems to have caught wind of Spencer's and my past. It surprised me, come to think about it, because information like that usually spread like wildfire.

"No, Aunty. Still waiting for the right guy." I smiled sadly, as was fitting for an unmarried Sri Lankan woman in her late twenties.

"A pretty girl like you, that's surprising!"

"Don't wait too long, ah. You know there are so many complications after you turn thirty."

"Yes, yes. *My*—Kusuma's daughter got married last year. She was thirty-four or thirty-five, I think. They are still trying to conceive, *aiyyo*. I feel so sorry for the girl. Imagine waiting so long and not being able to have children?"

"That's what happens when the parents don't push, no? Kusuma had this ridiculous hands-off approach. Letting her come and go and get married when she pleased. I told her till my mouth hurt, but see, this is what happens."

They all launched into a tirade against Kusuma and her poor childless daughter while I wondered if I should abandon this table and try somewhere else. It was exhausting enough being around all this gossip as it was. I gave up on my initial reservations and started checking both my phone and my watch, but I kept missing any combinations that would shake away my sense of dread. I should have known this wouldn't work.

I was just about to excuse myself when Aunty Josephina reached for my hand.

"My dear, do you know where the washroom is?"

"It's inside, just to the right of the side door."

I was turning to give her directions when I noticed her necklace—the pendant was two gold bars, one suspended above the other. A horizontal eleven. Finally.

"Shall I show you the way, Aunty?"

She held on to my arm, her clawlike nails digging into my skin, as I guided her out of her seat. Our whole table murmured about what a sweet, polite, well-brought-up young lady I was. I gave them a bashful smile and said it was no trouble at all.

Aunty Josephina and I made it inside the house, and I led the way to the same washroom I had taken refuge in earlier. There was a small end table on the wall opposite the bathroom door, and I stood next to it while I waited for her.

She took her sweet time, and I pinched my inner arms as hard as I could and prepared myself, hoping no one would notice me shaking like a leaf. The air conditioner was turned on inside, and the cool air that was an immediate relief from the balmy outdoors turned cruel and icy very quickly.

Finally, I heard the toilet flush, the sink run, and she emerged.

"Here, Aunty," I said, offering my arm.

She had just wrapped her talons around me again when I bumped my hip on the end table, causing the small knickknacks on it to slip off onto the floor. I jumped back, pulling Aunty Josephina off-kilter and causing her to drop her handbag.

The small Louis Vuitton tote slid onto the ground, right next to the envelope I had left out there.

"Oh no, Aunty, I'm so sorry," I huffed. "Are you okay?"

Aunty Josephina clutched her chest, closed her eyes, and took a few deep breaths.

"It's quite all right, darling. I just had a bit of a fright," she said finally.

"*Aney*, Aunty. I'm so clumsy. I didn't see that table at all. *Haiyyo*, I've knocked everything off as well. Let me get your handbag."

I got onto my knees and started picking up the fallen ornaments. Luckily, nothing had broken.

"Here! You! Is there no one here to help this lady?" Aunty Josephina called out haughtily for the help, making no effort to assist me herself. But we were alone. All the waitstaff were outside where the party was, of course.

I picked up her handbag and passed it up to her. Then I handed her the envelope.

"Is this yours, Aunty?" I asked, my heart feeling like it would explode.

Aunty Josephina took the envelope and eyed it genially. There was a large *Private and Confidential* stamped on the front, with a boldly printed *Dryland and Deck Investigative Services* branded in the corner.

"Maybe it fell off the table instead?" I offered, reaching for the bundle of papers, but she snatched it back out of my reach.

"No, no, darling. It must have fallen from my bag," she said, hastily stuffing it away.

I was afraid she would hear me release the breath I had been holding.

Now, I wait.

HUSNA FALEEL

Interview Transcript: Husna Faleel (abbrev. HF)

Date: January 25, 2020

Location: The Mount Lavinia Hotel

EP: Thank you for coming in, Miss Faleel. My name is Eshanya Padmaraj. Can I offer you a glass of water?

HF: No, thank you, Miss Padmaraj. I'm just quite confused. We've been locked in our hotel rooms from morning. I'm told that the wedding has been canceled, yet we aren't allowed to leave. Someone sent me a text saying Kaavi was murdered. Is this true? I'd really like to know what's going on.

EP: I understand, Miss Faleel, and I thank you for your patience. Unfortunately, yes, it does appear that the wedding has been canceled, and we are concerned for the well-being of the bride. While I do have sympathy for your frustrations, I'm afraid that time is of the essence here, and we are doing our best to gather as much information as possible and investigate what has happened to Miss Fonseka. Your cooperation would be much appreciated, and we were hoping you could answer a few questions about Miss Fonseka and her family.

HF: Y-yes. Of course. Whatever to help. Of course.

EP: Could you please state your name and address for the record?

HF: My name is Husna Faleel and I reside at 678 Ferdinand Place, off Hill Street, Dehiwala.

EP: How do you know Miss Fonseka?

HF: Kaavi and I went to school together.

EP: And you'll remained friends from your school days?

HF: Not exactly. We weren't very close in school. Kaavi was very shy and we were in different circles.

EP: And what circles were those?

HF: Well, I'm not sure if you're aware, but I was head girl and athletics captain, so you could say that I was quite involved in school activities. Kaavi was more studious and quiet. She mostly hung out with her best friend, Amaya.

EP: And you were not close with Miss Bloom either?

HF: No. Not that I had anything against the girl, of course, but she was a bit . . . much. She had this, well, loud personality. Very different family life from mine, too, from what I gathered. She came and went as she pleased. Never had to ask anyone for permission to do anything. It just wasn't, well, proper, you know.

And there was that incident with Mr. Dole, our physics teacher.

EP: Would you care to elaborate on that?

HF: Well, it was a long time ago, you know, and now thinking about it, I don't even know how much of it was real and how much were rumors. But the talk was that Amaya developed a bit of a crush on Mr. Dole. I mean, he was very handsome, and young for a teacher. He was only here to get some teaching experience, I think. He'd just graduated from Imperial College London, so he had this faint British accent. Many of the girls, not me, of course, but many of the girls were quite taken by him.

But Amaya is the only one who, you know, did something about it. She'd hang back after school to ask him questions. She was seen leaving an empty classroom with him a few times. Private tuition, she'd say, but, well, you tell me if it's appropriate for a fifteen-year-old to be left unsupervised with a good-looking twenty-three-year-old physics graduate. There were times she would ask Kaavi to cover for her, I'm sure, because Kaavi was sneaking around after school as well.

But then I think Mr. Dole got transferred or something. He just disappeared. It was quite strange actually, because it was right in the middle of term and we didn't have a replacement for an entire month and our O Levels were just around the corner. As you can imagine, the rumor mill really got going. They said she had something to do with him going missing. They said he couldn't handle her so he ran off back to England. They said, well, they said quite a number of things, but as always, people gossiped for a while and then someone got caught making out behind the canteen and things went back to normal. Well, kind of. Amaya had gained a bit of a reputation, you know, and many of the girls didn't want to be friends with her anymore.

EP: So Miss Fonseka and Miss Amaya only socialized with each other?

HF: Yes, pretty much. Like I said, we all thought Amaya was trouble, but Kaavi continued to be her friend. It's not like we *bullied* her, or were mean to her, or anything like that, you know? We just didn't want our reputations to also be ruined the way hers was.

EP: Were there any other incidents concerning Miss Bloom that you believed to be out of the ordinary?

HF: Actually, yes, now that I think about it. Again, this was a rumor. I didn't believe it, of course, I had so many other things going on, but I'd heard she got caught, um, hooking up with Gayan Peiris. He was older too. His sister was in our grade, and when Amaya went for her birthday party, she ended up meeting Gayan, and, well, you know. So it wasn't just a coincidence with Mr. Dole. I guess you could say that Amaya liked older men.

And then, well, Gayan, sadly, well, I guess there's no easy way to say this. Gayan died in a drunk driving incident about a month later. And well, I don't know how far it's true, but apparently he had been leaving Amaya's house when it happened. You know she lived alone with just a maid, right? Pretty unheard of, even now, but she had all this freedom, so of course she would have boys over. Gayan's sister was, well, she was understandably upset. She accused Amaya of killing him, and they had this, well, like a screaming match, I guess you could call it. But again, of course, this was all hearsay and nothing was ever proven, of course. Gayan's family moved to Canada shortly after. I think they wanted a fresh start.

EP: And what about Miss Fonseka? Did she have a string of older boyfriends too?

HF: Kaavi? Ha ha, no way. She'd have probably fainted if a boy so much as looked her way. No, she was quite mousy. You'd never guess it seeing her now. She's really come into her own since we left school. Many say that Kaavi grew up after she and Amaya stopped being friends. And thank god they stopped being friends, after what Amaya did to her.

EP: And what did she do?

HF: Again, this is only what I've heard, but I have it on good authority that Amaya had an affair with her father. It was right after university when Amaya came to Sri Lanka on her own and stayed at the Fonsekas' for some reason. Well, we all guessed the reason.

I mean, we mustn't blame Amaya completely, you know. It must have been difficult for her, growing up without a father. Maybe that's why she has this, you know, strange perversion toward older men. But anyways, I heard that that's why they stopped being friends.

EP: You seem to have recently reconnected with Miss Fonseka. She'd invited you for quite a number of the wedding events. How did that come about?

HF: Colombo circles are quite small, you know. I bumped into her at Colombo Fashion Week last year. She was being interviewed by *Hi!!* magazine about her dress, and I knew the lady who was running the interview and we all got to talking. Like I said, she's really blossomed into something stunning now that she has stepped out of Amaya's shadow.

EP: And were you surprised to see Miss Bloom at the wedding festivities?

HF: To be honest, she didn't recognize me, and I didn't really recognize her at first either. She used to be so . . . confident, I suppose. Like she had the entire world in the palm of her hand, you know. Like she wasn't afraid to just reach out and take what she wanted. But the girl I saw at Kaavi's party was nervous and shy and looked like she'd rather be anywhere else in the world than there. I actually felt sorry for her, you know. I guess this is what you get when you live your life without caring about the consequences. Sooner or later your bad decisions catch up to you. But whatever she did get up to in university or after or whatever must have really done a number on her, because Amaya Bloom was barely the girl I knew back in school. And considering the damage she had done, maybe that's not even a bad thing.

But something odd did happen, now that I think about it.

EP: Would you care to explain?

HF: Well, it might be nothing, but when Amaya was chatting to the group, Tehani came up to her out of nowhere. I thought it was a little strange because Tehani was, well, I don't know how much you know about her, but she could be quite the, um, attention seeker, I suppose you could say. Especially around men. And one moment she had a group of admirers vying for her attention, and the next she brushed them all off and comes over to where we were and whispers something in Amaya's ear. Amaya took off from the party two minutes later. It all seemed rather suspicious, if you ask me.

9

AMAYA

Four Days before the Wedding

BOMBS IN MOVIES usually had those digital clocks that let you know how much time you've got left in big red numbers. I've heard that weapons experts claim this is ridiculous. Real time bombs don't tell the hero exactly how much longer they had to save the day. If you found a time bomb out in the field, all bets were off. You just had to diffuse it as fast as you could and hope for the best.

Just like I had no clue how long it would take for Aunty Josephina to read the letter.

And there were so many variables. Too many things that could go wrong.

I ticked them off in my head as I tried to relax a little and enjoy the party.

What if she didn't read it? Chances: Nonexistent. There was no way she was going to let a juicy piece of potential gossip go to waste.

What if she didn't believe it? Chances: Slightly higher, but this is the same woman who I overheard telling her friends that she's avoiding oily food tonight because she didn't want to attract evil spirits on her way home, so it does sound like she would believe just about anything.

What if she didn't tell anyone? Chances: Slim to none. Information like this can't be kept to oneself. Aunty Josephina would probably implode. The question is who she would tell, who they would tell in turn, and whether everything would move quickly enough.

Would she take the news directly to Mr. Fonseka? Chances: Middling, but she'd have to explain how she ended up with the envelope in the first place, and if there's one thing I could guess about Aunty Josephina, it was that she'd do just about anything to save face. It's not like she could say that it magically appeared in her handbag or something.

I noticed her peering into her tote a few times through the evening, though she had enough sense not to pull the envelope out at the table.

I looked over at Kaavi, who fluttered around, greeting the guests. I couldn't believe how ridiculous I was earlier today. All I had to do was go up to her and ask—Kaavi, why did you say your parents wanted me here when it's clear they had no idea I was coming? That's all I had to do. But yet—

But yet, here I was, my words catching in my throat whenever I thought about it. Why was that? When did I become so intimidated by her? By all of them?

I started to stand up. Perhaps I could just ask her now.

"Excuse me, ladies and gentlemen," Mr. Fonseka's voice boomed out over the speaker. Everyone automatically turned toward the stage that the band had vacated and where Mr. Fonseka now stood, looking smart in a navy blue formal shirt that clashed ever so slightly with his wife's dress. I sat back down.

"I'm sorry to interrupt your evening. I just thought of saying a

few words before, you know, the party really got going and everyone started seeing two of me up on stage." There was a round of
generous laughter at this. Nihal Fonseka was, after all, nothing if not
charismatic and likable. Everyone wanted to be his friend. It was
what stood out most about him.

"I just wanted to thank you'll for being here today to kick off the
festivities. I know this wedding was a bit of a surprise for everyone,
but you know we Fonsekas love our surprises."

I heard a *hmph* go around my table while some of the aunties ex-
changed knowing looks.

"And what a wonderful surprise this is. You know, most fathers
would have a heart attack at the idea of their daughter suddenly de-
ciding to get married, but not me. I have every confidence in my
Kaavi, who is smart and kind and, of course, beautiful. She has done
us proud in every way, from the way she conducts herself, to the way
she has been an essential part of my business, to the wonderful work
she's doing with her own charity—Pink Sapphires—which, mind
you, she set up completely on her own. And now she's brought
us Matthew, who, much like those of us in my own alma mater,
S. Thomas' College, goes by his last name, which is Spencer." There
was a round of laughter and cheers at this, too, especially from a table of uncles who were already red-faced—his classmates, no doubt.
Mr. Fonseka never made a speech without referencing his college at
least once. Imogen once said that guys who refer to themselves by
their last names are douchebags, and I was inclined to agree with her
at the time.

"Spencer, too, is a self-made man. A very successful one, I might
add, and I appreciate how much time he has put into getting to know
my family. It'll be nice to have another man around. We'll still be
outnumbered, but at least I won't be alone."

Another round of laughter.

"Of course, I'm only joking. Everyone here knows how much I simply adore my three girls."

My heart jumped out of my chest, but it was just for a moment. He meant Nadia now. I wasn't one of his three girls anymore. Of course I wasn't.

"Can you believe this, ah?" one of the aunties leaned in and whispered to Aunty Josephina. "I was so surprised that Nihal agreed to give her in marriage to a *suddha*. But then, I guess he's not one to talk about morals, no?"

Aunty Josephina was about to reply, but she was drowned out by Mr. Fonseka continuing.

"Fiona and I are blessed to have a new son, and my girls are lucky to have an older brother." The seafood quiche I ate earlier started to swirl in my stomach. "I couldn't be happier than I am right now to welcome you into our family. I only wish, Spencer, that your parents were alive and here with us today, to share in our joy. But I know they must be so proud of you and the man you have become.

"This is an amazing year for us. Our Kaavi is getting married, and Fonseka Jewellers is opening its new luxury concept store to be headed by my new son-in-law, who has graciously agreed to take some time off from his well-established businesses to give our new showroom a little boost. Spencer, you and Kaavi together have brought us nothing but joy and luck. I wish you a marriage as long and as successful as mine and Fiona's. Cheers."

"If that's what he wishes her, well, good luck," muttered Aunty Josephina, as the applause that burst from the crowd left me reeling. Looks like Spence was getting everything he ever wanted. My stomach hardened. That's not true. Kaavi couldn't keep him happy for long; there was nothing I was more certain of.

He joined Mr. Fonseka up onstage and shook his hand, and then beckoned for Kaavi to join him as well.

The two of them held hands and beamed and I wanted to close my eyes and die. But still, I couldn't help but stare at him—his perfectly styled hair, his broad shoulders. He had rolled up his shirtsleeves, and the muscles in his forearms were visible even from where I was sitting. It made it difficult for me to breathe.

I looked at Kaavi, all but glowing, and felt the familiar stirrings of resentment.

People talk about romantic breakups like it's the worst thing in the world. And it's true, in a way. When Spencer and I ended, I thought my mangled heart would ooze out all the love I had ever known. That I would never really smile again. And I wasn't wrong.

Movies are made about romantic breakups. Books are written. Songs are sung about how the sun stops shining and nothing has meaning anymore and how much, no matter how hard you try to drive yourself forward, how much it hurts.

But there's another type of breakup. The kind that's not romantic. The kind that happens between friends. There are no movies made about that. Perhaps because the pain is too deep, too profound to even encapsulate.

I couldn't write a love song for my lost friendship with Kaavi. I'd lamented for Spencer, yes. I mean, I still lament sometimes. But I mourned just as much when I lost my best friend. Am I allowed that? It's still the same pain of losing someone you loved with all your heart, isn't it?

But it looked like I was the only one in mourning.

I could try to put it all behind me. Be happy for both of them. But I knew, from the moment I saw Spencer's smile on Kaavi's announcement photo, that I could never let that happen.

But I couldn't dwell on him for much longer because I was accosted by Laura, who squealed like she hadn't just met me for the first time a few hours ago.

"Amaya, oh god, there you are. Come join the girls for a drink!"

All the aunties at the table raised their eyebrows at this. In Colombo, some women drank. Most women didn't. But certainly, no one ever admitted to it so openly. At least in their generation.

"I'm more in the mood for dessert," I dodged, "but I'll come say hi anyway. Aunties, will you'll excuse me?" They gave me appreciative smiles as they side-eyed Laura's deep-cut dress, which looked amazing, by the way, but looking amazing wasn't the first priority for Colombo 07 aunties.

The space directly in front of the bar was, as expected, taken up by a group of young men in varying stages of inebriation. There were a lot of "*Machangs*," "*Ados*," and general swaying going around. I took a deep breath and held it till we walked past them, but none of them paid me any attention. All eyes were on Laura in her low-cut dress, but of course no one dared approach her. This was Colombo society, after all. Not some rave on a beach. No one would dare be rejected in public. Any form of interest was conveyed covertly, either through friends, or relatives, or lusty, meaningful eye contact and sly smiles. Straight out of a Jane Austen novel, but usually with a lot more booze.

Laura led me over to a secluded area behind the bar where a group of girls had gathered. They stood around a small cocktail table, discreetly sipping on their cosmos and Long Island iced teas. A little mountain of—of course—Louis Vuitton clutch bags was nestled on the table between them, and they were all dressed in some variation of colorful, flowy maxi dresses. I couldn't have felt more out of place—a crow in the middle of a flock of exotic flamingos. I immediately wished the floor would open and swallow me up.

"Ladies," Laura boomed, "meet Amaya. One of Kaavi's old friends." It felt strange that I, who had known Kaavi since she wore braces, was being introduced by Laura, who had known her all of five minutes. But still, the group, a mix of Sri Lankans and foreigners, all smiled and said hi.

"Hi, lovely to meet everyone," I said, taking care to make sure my voice didn't squeak. Is there anything more intimidating than a group of immaculately dressed women sipping on cocktails?

"Amaya, this is . . ." and Laura rattled off a list of names there was no chance I could possibly remember, but it was strange that I didn't recognize anyone. There was no one from the fancy international school we went to, nor from college.

"So," one of them asked the moment the introductions were over, "how do you know Kaavi?"

"We went to school together, so I've known her since we were kids," I said, and then taking the opportunity, "And how do you guys know her?"

"The three of us," a redhead in a stunning green dress said, pointing to two other girls in the group, "all interned at J.P. Morgan at the same time."

"And Lakshi and I," said a very tall Sri Lankan girl in sky-high heels, "work on Kaavi's charity with her."

So that explains why they are new. The thought hit home more than I cared to admit. Kaavi had a new life after I left. New friends who thought she was important enough to fly halfway around the world for. She'd moved on.

You've moved on too, the voice in my head spoke up, defensively.

You have new friends too. Who cares if I spend a significant portion of my day watching Kaavi's every move on Instagram, Facebook, and YouTube? I had Jessica, Deepa, and Imogen, didn't I? Although my brunch friends seemed more like a dream from a different life that I had shaken myself awake from. I had no idea what was real and what wasn't anymore. Except for Beth, of course. She was real. My only real friend. I thought about discreetly sending her a text, but one of the women turned toward me.

"So, did you know Kaavi and Spencer were dating?" the girl introduced as Lakshi asked. It looked like they had been talking about it when Laura and I arrived.

"Um, sorry?" I wasn't playing dumb. It just caught me off guard. Great, now these women were going to think I'm some sort of moron.

"I mean, I see Kaavi every day. I'd known she and Spencer were friends, of course. He's helped out so much with the charity, and has flown down here quite a few times this last year. But I never got the sense that he and Kaavi were involved romantically."

"Maybe it's not about the romance," one of the intern friends joked. "I heard they've been hooking up for a while now."

"Kaavi? Hooking up? No way. She's far too prim and proper."

"No? She's so secretive though. No one ever seems to know what's really going on with her."

"She is secretive. I'll give you that. I actually did get the sense she's been hiding something these past few months. So maybe that's it. Maybe she just had Spencer locked up in her bedroom the whole time."

The table erupted into giggles, and I joined in, too, even though I had given up trying to feel good about anything this evening.

"But that proposal, good lord."

"Good lord, indeed."

"Is the video up yet?"

"No, she hasn't posted it. I don't know why; now that was something out of a movie."

"I have it," Lakshi, who worked at Kaavi's charity, said. "Spencer asked me to record Kaavi's speech, though at the time I had no idea what he would do." She smiled, smug that she was a part of the in-group.

"You have the proposal on video?" I asked, before I could help myself.

"Of course."

I took a deep breath.

"Any chance you could send it to me? I would love to see it."

A beat of silence.

"It's just that I lose out on so much living in LA. I hate that I've missed so many important moments in her life," I added.

"Sure." She was almost dismissive. "Just promise me you won't post it anywhere until Kaavi releases it herself or she'll kill me."

"Oh, don't worry," I said, reaching for her phone as she held it out and keying in my details, "I'm barely on social media anyway."

"And . . . sent."

"Check that out," one of the women said, tilting her head toward the bar.

It was Tehani, openly laughing and doing tequila shots with the boys.

Maybe I was staring, because she suddenly looked over at me. Something glinted in her eye, though that might have been the light from the numerous outdoor lanterns. She handed her drink over to one of the men and whispered something into his ear, flirtatiously touching his arm. Then, shooting him a dazzling smile over her shoulder, she made her way to where I was standing.

"Amaya, hi, sorry I didn't see you until now. I'm so glad you came," she said, smacking her lips loudly as her cheeks touched mine. "Have you said hi to *Amma* and *Thaththa* yet? I know they'd love to see you."

Oh goodness, there was no way I could talk to Mr. and Mrs. Fonseka now.

"Y-yes. Yes, I did. Briefly. They were super busy so I didn't want to take up too much of their time."

"Ah, okay. Great. Well"—she gave me a little hug so her lips were close to my ear—"if this lot become too much to handle, you just come find me, okay?"

She sashayed her way back to the waiting group of men. At least one of the Fonsekas wasn't shunning me. But then, it's not like Tehani knew about anything that happened.

"What did she want?" a girl with a headscarf asked, mischievously. I thought she might have looked familiar, but if I was being honest, I couldn't care less about this party anymore. All I wanted to do was get home, change out of this uncomfortable dress, and watch Kaavi's proposal video.

I managed to exchange polite goodbyes, feign terrible jet lag, and was just about out the main gate when I heard a commotion. There was far more security at the event tonight than there had been during the day—no doubt because there was a politician or two attending.

About four of these security guards, dressed identically to Mahesh's driver in white short-sleeved shirts and black slacks, were pushing back a disgruntled bald man with a neatly trimmed mustache.

"*Mey mona pissuwak the mey?*" What madness is this? His voice was raised as he tried to duck around the group of men. *"Mata katha-karanna vitharai oney."* I just want to talk.

Talk to whom?

"Pissuda bahng? Yannawa oy yanna. Thamuseta therenne naddha dang party-*ak kiyala?"* Are you crazy? Get lost. Don't you understand that there's a party going on right now?

And with that, one of the larger men shoved him back, causing him to fall—sprawling on the side of the road.

I wanted to step out. I wanted to help him. But as always, something held me back.

He pulled himself up onto his feet, shaking his head and muttering to himself.

"Kiyanna thamuselage miss-*te mama aava kiyala."* Tell your miss that I came to see her. And with a few choice Sinhala swear words, he turned around and made his way down the lane.

"What was that about?" I finally was able to muster, stepping out from behind the gate.

"Some madman, miss. Nothing to worry about," one of the security men answered.

"Madam, good evening." It was Piyadasa, Mahesh's driver. That was strange. I don't remember seeing Mahesh inside.

"Good evening, Piyadasa. Mahesh sir *athuley de?"* Is Mahesh sir inside? My Sinhala felt alien coming out of my mouth. Like my tongue was not used to forming the sounds.

"Naa, madam. *Thawa mahaththayekta podi baduwak* deliver *kar-ranna awey."* No, madam. I came to deliver a package to someone else. Was it me or did some of the other drivers smirk at this?

"Is your vehicle coming, madam?" one of the English-speaking drivers asked, peering down the street to where the angry man continued to walk.

I had called an Uber and it was just turning in.

"Who did he want to see?" I asked, looking in the same direction.

"No one, miss. He was crazy. Don't worry."

I was about to dig for more details when Aunty Josephina's voice rang out.

"Leaving early, darling?"

"Y-yes, Aunty. Not feeling so great. Must be the jet lag, you know, no?"

"Yes, yes. I'm not feeling so well too. I thought I'd head home early. My driver needs to leave for the night as well. Ah, there he is."

Her chauffeur-driven BMW pulled up right alongside my Uber, and we air-kissed our goodbyes. A vision of her blouse getting caught in the car door, dragging her screaming on the gravelly road, crossed my mind, but I shooed it away.

The man trying to make his way into the party was like the forgotten leftovers of a dream. I had bigger things on my mind. Things like the envelope in Aunty Josephina's handbag.

How much longer did I have to wait?

Ticktock.

LAKSHI

Interview Transcript: Lakshi Malalasekara (abbrev. LM)

Date: January 25, 2020

Location: The Mount Lavinia Hotel

LM: I've heard that Kaavi might be in trouble. Please tell me what I can do to help.

EP: Thank you, Miss Malalasekara. Could you please state your name and address for the record?

LM: My name is Lakshi Malalasekara and I live at 56 Jayanthi Mawatha, Pita Kotte.

EP: And you work at Miss Fonseka's charity organization. Is that correct?

LM: Yes, ma'am. I work as a senior project coordinator at Pink Sapphires. I joined as an intern three years ago, was hired as a permanent employee within three months, and received my latest promotion last May.

EP: How well did you get to know Miss Fonseka in this time?

LM: Kaavi was always a welcoming boss. Even when I was an intern, she spent so much time with me, showing me the ropes and encouraging me to make decisions for myself. She's truly an inspiration. You should see the way she encourages women. I've even seen her advise the girls in the program—coaching them through insecurities, giving them a voice. I always knew I wanted to work in this field—you know, helping others. But Kaavi really gave me a direction. So much of who I am today, I owe to her.

EP: So you would say you were close?

LM: [Short laugh] Well, she was my boss. But we had a good relationship, of course.

EP: Did she confide in you about her own problems?

LM: Well, how many problems could a woman like Kaavi have? She would tell us when she got stressed-out with work, I suppose. It was a struggle sometimes, working with her family. It would be for anyone, though, wouldn't it? She rarely saw eye to eye with her sister, Tehani, but she never spoke badly about her or anything. I mean, Kaavi worked directly under her father. Mr. Fonseka had even handed over a significant part of the business duties to her, so Kaavi was as good as the boss. I don't think Tehani liked that much.

EP: In what way?

LM: Oh, you know, just the usual sister stuff. Kaavi's, well, she's perfect. Must have been hard to come second to that all the time. But it's not like they hated each other or anything. Tehani would come by the Pink Sapphires office sometimes— Kaavi had her set up as an art mentor, to coach the girls interested in graphic design, and then she and Kaavi would chat and joke and all would be normal. Tehani even played a huge part in Spencer's proposal. It's a pretty sweet story, actually—Spencer knew he wanted to propose to Kaavi during the award ceremony. After all, working on the charity is what brought the two of them so close together, and it only seemed right. That's what Kaavi told us all afterward. But of course, he needed to figure out a way to get onstage, right? He couldn't just walk on up there, after all.

So he asked Tehani to help him, and she convinced Kaavi to invite him up onstage to thank him. I was in the office when Tehani asked her. Kaavi thought it was ridiculous at first. "I'll thank him in my speech," she said, "but doesn't it defeat the purpose to invite a man up onstage to accept an award given to a woman?"

I remember thinking that she had a point.

But Tehani convinced her that it would be a nice thing to do, and I guess it worked because, well, you've seen the video, right?

EP: Did you know that Matthew Spencer was going to propose?

LM: Oh no, of course not. He spoke to me before the ceremony and asked me to personally make sure everything was recorded, but I thought that was just for her YouTube channel or footage for the charity, you know. I didn't even imagine he would ask her to marry him.

EP: Did you know that they were a couple?

LM: Well, no one did. And you know what? I can understand. You know how it is in Colombo. We all keep our relationships a secret unless it ends in marriage. I do wish she would have told me though. I could have helped them. I know how difficult it can be to sneak around and keep things from our parents.

EP: Tell us about Matthew Spencer. How well did you know him?

LM: We all just call him Spencer. He's been visiting our office very regularly now, and I'm sure you've heard about how much he has helped the charity. He's very well-connected, you see, and quite rich too. He's very generous, though, and has dedicated so much of his time to helping us. Kaavi was right in saying that Pink Sapphires would never be what it is if it weren't for him.

EP: And what was his role in the charity?

LM: He helped set up the study-abroad program. He and Kaavi apparently had the idea when she met him in the US. She had gone back to California for her university reunion, I think, when they met. Anyway, Spencer would arrange for the girls to be introduced to leaders in various American companies who would then guide them and give them some insight into how the business runs and so on. We are hoping that this will lead to internships, and some companies have even mentioned offering scholarships to participants. As you can see, it's not the typical opportunities that most girls in Sri Lanka would get, especially if their families can't afford to spend on their education. We are so proud to have just sent off our first batch of girls.

EP: Did you notice anything strange about Miss Fonseka in the days leading up to her disappearance?

LM: Well, she did seem a little flustered at times, but that would be normal for someone planning a wedding, especially with a mother like hers.

EP: Could you elaborate further?

LM: I mean, well, not that Mrs. Fonseka is a bad person or anything. She's just, well, she and Kaavi don't often see eye to eye on most things. Kaavi never said anything, obviously, but I could tell from the way she would stiffen up whenever her mother mentioned marriage.

And I don't think she really supported what Kaavi did. Mrs. Fonseka would never admit to it, of course—she'd never go against her husband that way—but I've heard her mutter things under her breath about Kaavi never being able to find a husband with the amount of time she worked. I think the horoscope reader had told her that Kaavi needed to get married by a particular date, or she'd never get married at all.

There was an incident on Kaavi's birthday. Her father asked what her birthday wish was, and Kaavi said it was for the charity to grow so she could help more girls. That's the kind of person Kaavi is—always thinking about others. But Mrs. Fonseka blew a fuse. She's always a bit high-strung, but she was extra upset that day. Maybe because she remembered the horoscope deadline? Who knows? But she exploded in front of everyone that Kaavi needed to "settle down" before she "brought shame on the family." Kaavi and Mr. Fonseka managed to smooth everything over, of course, and no one ever spoke about it again.

She was over the moon when Kaavi got engaged. There are even rumors around the office that this rushed auspicious date was less about the astrologer and more about Mrs. Fonseka worrying whether Kaavi would back out at the last moment.

EP: And would Kaavi back out?

LM: I don't think so. Why would she? Spencer is the perfect guy. But I'll tell you one thing: Mrs. Fonseka would rather commit murder than have Kaavi walk out on this wedding.

[Pause]

Oh gosh, that was a horrible thing to say. I didn't mean it like that, you know. I really do hope Kaavi is okay. Are there any updates yet?

EP: Not yet, Miss Malalasekara. Were there any discrepancies at the charity I should be aware of? Anything noteworthy that took place recently?

LM: Well, nothing significant, although Kaavi did mention that there was some issue with the accounts. This was about two months ago, I think. Anyway, she took it to finance, which doesn't fall under Pink Sapphires, but Fonseka Jewellers as a whole. Those things were totally outside of our purview.

EP: You said that Miss Fonseka was always going out of her way to help girls through the charity. Are there any girls that she helped in an individual capacity? Perhaps those she formed an independent relationship with?

LM: I can't think of anyone specifically, but she was always giving the girls advice, you know? They'd always be scared, at first. Scared to speak up. Scared to talk to men.

You understand that this is a normal thing for most Sri Lankan girls to feel—especially those from lower-income backgrounds. We aren't supposed to even speak to boys, or look them in the eye, or ever talk for ourselves. We are brought up to be subservient. Maybe we could work in a garment factory or something, if we were lucky, but most of us are brought up to be wives and mothers, that is all. And then suddenly this entire new world is open to these girls, so of course they would feel scared.

Kaavi would give them a kind but stern talking-to, you know, to help them understand how important it was for them to learn and become independent. She helped everyone.

EP: Thank you, Miss Malalasekara. And the advice and guidance that Miss Fonseka gave out, did that extend to you too?

LM: Yes. Like I said, she was very generous. My parents never supported me working either. You see, everyone isn't as lucky to have a father like Kaavi. My own wanted me to get married right after my A Levels, but I managed to put it off, telling him that I would do it after I finished my internship. But then I met Kaavi and realized how important it was that I become independent. She advised me a great deal about how to stand up to my parents.

EP: And did you finally get married?

LM: No. I am not on talking terms with my family anymore. I moved out of my house and live in a girls' boarding.

EP: That must be a difficult change for you?

LM: Well, yes. My father was very angry, of course. But Kaavi taught me that my freedom was more important. Even though I'm struggling now to make ends meet—it is quite expensive, you know, paying boarding fees and living on your own—it's still worth it to me.

EP: One of your colleagues mentioned you confided in her that you were rather bitter toward Miss Fonseka after you first left your family. Is there some truth to this?

LM: [Pause] Who told you this? Was it Danushka?

EP: I am not at liberty to say right now, Miss Malalasekara, but would appreciate it if you could answer the question.

LM: Look, I didn't mean it. I was angry at the time, that's all. I truly am grateful for everything that Kaavi has done for me. If it wasn't for her I'd have been forced into some arranged marriage and stuck with babies by now. All I said to Danushka was that it was easier for Kaavi to talk about independence and push me to leave my family because she had such a comfortable life. Anyone can be independent if they have enough money in the bank. If they are from upper-class Colombo with plenty of connections and a foreign university degree. I'm not being bitter, I promise. I just think it's not fair that she's had it so much easier than everyone else.

10

AMAYA

Four Days before the Wedding

I HELD IT together until I got home. The last thing I wanted was to get interrupted while I was watching it.

I made it to my room with only the most cursory of greetings to Seetha, who always insisted on waiting up for me when I went out, cranked the air conditioner on as high as it would go, kicked off my shoes, peeled off my dress, and sat on my bed to watch the video.

It was shot decently—clearly, Kaavi's colleague whose name I'd already forgotten had used a tripod or something, because there was no handheld shake, and it was zoomed in on the podium in the middle of a stage.

A middle-aged woman dressed in a sari with her hair in a schoolteacher bun took up most of the screen.

"It gives me great pleasure to bestow the SheGives-Lanka Woman of the Year award on Kaavindi Fonseka, for the selfless work she has carried out with her charity, Pink Sapphires. Kaavindi is the youngest recipient of this award since it was established in 1956."

The camera panned out to show Kaavi, who didn't look surprised in the least. I knew that most award ceremonies like this notified the winners ahead of time so they could prepare their speeches and invite their families.

"So beautiful," someone off camera said in a stage whisper, wistfulness dripping from their voice. They were immediately shushed, but there was no masking the obvious jealousy.

Kaavi sashayed confidently onto the stage, her salmon pink sari with gold accents shimmering delicately under the stage lights. Her hair was swept into a casual updo that would have taken hours to perfect, her nails matched the nine yards of silk draped around her, and her makeup was tastefully understated. How did she manage to look like a goddess no matter what she did?

"Thank you, everyone. What an absolute honor this award is." Her voice was modulated, deep and low. Not a hint of awkward squeakiness. I could never be in such control.

"From the moment I moved back to Sri Lanka, I knew I had to found Pink Sapphires. Being from a family like mine, where giving back to the community is a part of our DNA, I was lucky to always be supported and encouraged in this endeavor. My life was changed and my eyes were opened because of the education I received, and it saddened me that it was my life of privilege that allowed me to have these wonderful experiences.

"We started off Pink Sapphires in a modest way—providing skills training, English language classes, and career counseling to bright young women who unfortunately did not have the financial means of investing in themselves. This year, however, has been our true breakthrough. In two months, we will be sending a batch of five scholarship recipients for our first-ever study-abroad program in California. We have grown from a tiny operation in my bedroom to coaching and mentoring hundreds of applicants to be independent, self-reliant young women, and I couldn't be more proud."

There was a round of applause, and Kaavi beamed.

"Of course, it wouldn't be fair for me to accept this award without acknowledging the hard work and dedication by key members of my team. First and foremost, my parents, without whose love and support none of this would be possible. *Thaththa*, you had laid all the groundwork for me through hours of hard work and sacrifice, for which I am eternally grateful.

"Next, to Lakshi, Priya, Danushka, and the rest of my team. We joke that we are each other's work wives, and I don't know what I would do without you. Nothing in my life has been more satisfying than empowering a group of strong, dynamic women who teach me something new every day.

"And finally, to the man who helped me take Pink Sapphires to the next level. Who introduced me to partner companies abroad, who went to bat for me when it felt like I was losing, who helped me take my little charity truly global. The study-abroad program was his brainchild, and wouldn't exist today without his support. He has been a friend, confidant, and most importantly, an ally. Ladies and gentlemen, I know this is a Woman of the Year award, but I'd like Matthew Spencer to join me onstage. Pink Sapphires could never have scaled up the way it did without him."

The camera panned out to show Spencer rise slowly to his feet. Slightly red in the face, he made his way over to the stage. Kaavi started applauding and encouraged the audience to clap too. Spencer blushed but smiled at her. She handed the award to him and shook his hand—no hugging a man onstage; that wouldn't be proper.

Her smile faltered a little as Spencer took the microphone off its stand and held it to his mouth. Clearly, he was only supposed to accept the award, not make a speech. This was her moment, after all, not his.

The camera adjusted so that both of them were in the frame.

"Thank you for your kind words, Kaavi. I've always said you were too good, and you've proved, yet again, how selfless you are. It's true that I've supported, and will continue to support, Pink Sapphires. Nothing makes me happier than seeing the smiles on those little girls' faces. But I have something equally as important to ask you today."

I felt the remnants of the cocktail party rise up in my throat.

The audience gasped as Spencer took a step backward, and then got down on one knee.

"Kaavindi Fonseka, you give so much of yourself to others. Will you please make me the happiest man on the planet by allowing me to give myself to you?"

Kaavi was frozen. Her hands went up to her face in shock.

"Kaavi, will you marry me?" he reiterated. As if the ring and him being down on one knee wasn't clear enough.

Kaavi remained stone-still—eyes wide, hands covering most of her face.

Spencer turned toward the audience and flashed them a wide smile.

"Looks like Kaavi is having some trouble making up her mind. How about a little support, ladies and gentlemen?"

The audience erupted into loud cheers and catcalls.

"Marry him!" someone shouted.

"Say yes!" said another.

Finally, Kaavi uncovered her face. Her lips were curled into a smile.

"Yes." She nodded. "Yes, Spencer, I'll marry you."

Spencer stood up and gave Kaavi a delicate hug. Just the right amount of affection for their conservative audience. The camera panned out to show the audience on their feet, cheering and hooting.

I paused the video and zoomed in on Kaavi's face.

I'd known her since she was a child. Since we both thought boys were disgusting and daydreamed of being the next Britney Spears. I know her favorite brand of chocolate, and what movies make her cry. I know she hates hot showers, that she has to sleep with at least three pillows, that she loves the smell of rain but thinks the ocean smells like dead fish. That she pretends to drink coffee because she thinks it makes her look more grown-up.

And I know, as surely as I know myself, that that was not happiness on her face.

REBECCA (RED)

Interview Transcript: Rebecca Davies (abbrev. RD)

Date: January 25, 2020

Location: The Mount Lavinia Hotel

RD: My name is Rebecca Davies, but everyone calls me Red because of, well—

[Points to hair]

EP: And your address, Miss Davies?

RD: I live in Chicago. 344 Maladino Drive.

EP: And your address in Sri Lanka?

RD: I've been staying at the Hilton with the other girls from J.P.
Morgan.

EP: And you are currently working at J.P. Morgan?

RD: I left six months ago to start my own consulting firm.

EP: But it was while working at J.P. Morgan that you met Miss
Fonseka, yes?

RD: Yes. Kaavi and I both joined their internship program in Chicago at the same time. She didn't stay on for longer than the
internship, of course.

EP: Could you tell us a little bit about your relationship with Miss
Fonseka? Were you close?

RD: Well, the internship was pretty stressful, especially for us
new grads, so we blew off a lot of steam. Worked hard. Partied
harder. Kaavi was friendly and fun. She never, like, bared her
soul to me or anything. She seemed sad, at times, especially
after a drink or two in her. I figured she had just had a breakup
or something. But we never spoke about it.

EP: But you did keep in touch?

RD: Yes, in the way most people keep in touch these days. Through Facebook, mostly. I do follow her on Instagram, too, and I've donated to Pink Sapphires over the years.

EP: And she invited you to the wedding?

RD: Yes. Along with the rest of the group who interned at J.P. Morgan. Of course, only a couple of us could make it on such short notice.

EP: And how was Miss Fonseka's demeanor when you arrived?

RD: The same as always, I suppose. Cheerful, though closed off. Of course, she's put her partying days behind her, as most of us have. I do have to say, though, that I was a little surprised about her relationship with her family, especially her mother and sister. The middle one—Tehani, I think, the one who's just a couple of years younger than her. She posts about them a lot online, about how close they are, about how family is everything to her. But the vibes I got from her, from them all, just weren't the same.

EP: So you sensed tension within the family?

RD: Look, this is just my gut. It's not based on anything. We're all guilty of making our lives appear better than they are on social media, right?

[Pause]

Oh, and this might be nothing, but I also thought it was super strange that Tehani kept cozying up to this other girl—Amaya. Once at the cocktail party and then again at the bridal shower they were whispering to each other. It could be nothing. It's probably nothing. But I thought it seemed a little off because of what came next.

EP: You said to the security team that you had overheard a threat being made to Miss Fonseka. Is that what you are referring to?

RD: Yes.

EP: Could you elaborate on this a little further?

RD: Yes, well. I wasn't drinking that day so I remember it quite clearly. I was having, um, some digestion issues. I think the Sri Lankan curries hadn't been agreeing with me too well, and so I spent a fair bit of time in the bathroom. That's when I saw Amaya and Tehani together, actually.

By the time I came out, the girls had moved from the hotel terrace to the beach. I was going to give Kaavi a quick hug and leave. I didn't have it in me to stay, and I wanted to save my energy for the traditional ceremony the next day.

I was on my way down the corridor when I heard shouting. I didn't know who it was at first. Many of the girls had been drinking, and I was feeling too ill to get in the middle of anything, so I hung back and hoped they would leave without noticing me. But it soon became obvious that it was Kaavi and Amaya.

EP: How could you be sure it was them?

RD: Well, they used their names, for one.

EP: And you had interacted with Miss Bloom before?

RD: That's Amaya, right? I was introduced to her, yes. At the Fonseka's cocktail party, though she didn't really leave much of an impression, if I'm being honest. She seemed quite boring. Timid. Even with Tehani when they were whispering. Not at all like the person I heard in the corridor later that evening.

EP: And what did the two women say?

RD: I can't remember all of it—not word for word, anyway. It caught me by surprise and I wasn't even sure I should be listening. But I do remember Amaya saying, very clearly, that she wanted to kill Kaavi.

11

AMAYA

Three Days before the Wedding

I DIDN'T GO over to the Fonsekas the next morning. I spent it pacing around my room, and when that felt too small, I paced around my house. I set a timer on my phone and checked Kaavi's social media accounts every fifteen minutes.

There were reposts from the party last night. Boomerangs of glasses clinking, girls twirling, funny moments on the dance floor. There were pictures of the decor, panning videos of the dinner buffet, many, many shots of Kaavi and Spencer staring adoringly at each other. I didn't even know what I was looking for.

That something had gone wrong.

A sign that my plan had worked.

But of course, Kaavi wouldn't post about something so negative immediately. She would find a way to spin it. To frame her failed engagement in a way that made her look good. Empowering to women, perhaps. Or maybe to set her up as a martyr—that she decided to put her charity before her own happiness.

But there was a new thought nagging at me now. A thought that was fixated on Kaavi's face after Spencer proposed. If she wasn't really excited about marrying him, then why go through with everything? I'd bet her mother was putting a ton of pressure on her to get married, but it wasn't like Kaavi to cave so easily. Or was Spencer just a trophy to her? Someone who was Insta-worthy. Someone who fit her perfect narrative.

I scribbled in my notebook between refreshes and pacing. This plan was definitely not going to work.

Poison? I wrote.

Accidental drowning?

Kidnap until everything blows over?

I crossed that last one out. There could be no loose ends.

Seetha made me a typical Sri Lankan lunch of rice and various separately curried vegetables. She'd fried up some *papadam* just the way I liked when I was a teenager. I could barely touch it.

"Why, *Baba*? Too spicy?" she asked. "I didn't put much chili. I know you don't like too much anymore."

"No, no, Seetha, it's great. Thank you." I made myself take a few more mouthfuls. Seetha eyed me eating with a fork but didn't say anything. Rice and curry is typically eaten with your hand, but I'd lost touch and it was struggle enough to force something down my throat as it was.

"*Baba*, are you okay?" Seetha asked. She'd never really asked me if I was okay before. Seetha cooked for me, and took care of my house, and stayed up for me when I went out. She kept an eye on me when I was a teenager, scaring off boys and hovering around if anyone ever came to see me. But we never really spoke. We had a kind of quiet peace between us, which I had grown accustomed to. Which is why I responded immediately.

"I'm fine, Seetha."

But she came and stood near me. She'd never take a seat at the table with me, even though I had asked her to eat with me many, many times. It didn't matter if she was my guardian and took it upon herself to give me a curfew when I was younger—social hierarchies were social hierarchies.

"*Baba*, I know that you and Kaavindi *Baba* are old friends. But *Baba*, please be careful."

I almost choked on my rice and curry.

"What do you mean?"

"I mean that you are a good girl. You have always been. But Kaavindi *Baba* is not like you."

"Don't be ridiculous, Seetha." Kaavi had hurt me, of course, but what I was about to do to her was far, far worse.

She didn't say anything else. Of course she didn't. It wasn't her place. But I could feel her eyes on me as I twisted and turned and wrung myself out waiting for something.

I distracted myself by staring at the painting that hung closest to me. It was a woman wearing a pale gray dress, tipping her toes into a river. Her arm wrapped around the branch of a willow tree as she peered into the water. My mother took a lot of liberties with her art. Nothing was photographic. The woman's hair flowed long and wild, like it had a life of its own. The tears that trailed down her face glistened brighter than the water in front of her. The leaves from the tree floated like confetti in the breeze. The river churned around her greedily, just a moment away from sucking her in. And the woman herself—well, my mother told me she imagined the woman very brave, fearful of the danger she was about to submerge herself into, but willing to move forward, all the same. She used the tree branch to steady herself, my mother said, so the woman could spring forward. To me, the woman simply looked like she was possessed. Someone who had lost her footing on the shore. Who was plunging her foot into the water not because she was fearless, but because she felt the land had nothing left to give her anymore. Someone who was just a step away from drowning.

Was that the way I felt about my mother? Or was that just how I saw myself?

I reached for my phone. I needed to message Beth. I needed to speak to someone before I completely spiraled away.

I did something last night.

Don't know if it worked.

I waited awhile, refreshing Kaavi's social media feeds, hoping for something. It was the middle of the night in the US. I doubted Beth would even reply.

I was in luck though. My phone dinged back a few minutes later.

What did you do?

I fed some information about Spencer to one of the gossips.

The information was real, by the way. Information he hadn't wanted to share with me either. Information that left him feeling embarrassed and upset and made me wish I had never stumbled upon it to begin with. I don't really know, to this day, whether it was the information or the way he reacted after I told him I knew that made me see him as a completely different person.

> **Oh wow. Have you heard anything yet?**

I sighed.

> **No. Not yet. The waiting is driving me crazy.**

> **It must be! But what else can you do now? It would be nuts to go over there and see for yourself, right?**

Would it be so crazy though? Crazier than spiraling over here?

> **You think I should head over there? See what the damage is?**

> **I guess it's not the worst idea, ya know? Maybe it'll help you get some closure too.**

Beth was right. I couldn't accomplish anything from hiding out at home.

I threw in the towel and made my way to the Fonsekas' at 2:22 p.m. There was still no sign of anything online. For all I knew, Aunty Josephina hadn't even gotten around to doing anything yet. Maybe I had left it too late. Maybe I should have come a month earlier. I thought cutting it close was a good thing—that it wouldn't give them enough time to repair their engagement. If the wedding was called off, there was no way they would make amends to go through all of this a second time. It would be too embarrassing.

There were no events scheduled for today, so I took a box of old photographs from our school days in case I needed an excuse to speak to Kaavi. She'd see through it, I'm sure, but it seemed like the kind of thing an old friend who had no secret agenda might do just before a wedding.

THE HOUSE WAS quiet. Eerily so, especially after the hustle and bustle of last night. The tents were gone, the chairs were folded, large garbage bags sat on the edge of the garden, along with crates of glasses and silverware, probably waiting to be picked up. There was no one at the entrance to stop me from going inside, so I gently pushed open the side door, the one that led to the large pantry where the family would usually eat.

Tehani sat at the table, alone. She had a bowl of cereal in front of her, which she pushed around without actually taking a bite, distracted by something on her phone.

"Um, hi," I said softly. "I don't want to disturb you."

She snapped to attention, alert and straight.

"Amaya," she greeted me. Was it me or did her smile flicker a little?

"Um, I was wondering if Kaavi was around. I wanted to give her—"

"She's upstairs. They all are. Family meeting."

Her voice was dry, and I didn't ask why she wasn't included.

"Let me just text her and let her know you're here."

"Oh no, don't trouble yourself. I really just—"

"Done. See." She waved her phone around, though I couldn't really see anything from so far away.

"She wants you to come up."

"I—I thought you said they were in a meeting?"

"Yeah, well, that's what she says—*Tell Amaya to come join us in the office.*" She half-heartedly waved her phone at me again, but I still couldn't see a thing.

"Um, okay."

I made my way out to the living room and just reached the stairs when a tearstained Laura launched herself at me.

"What's going on?" she asked. She sounded stricken.

"I—I'm not exactly sure."

"Oh god, oh god, oh god."

My chest tightened.

"Hey, relax." It was more for my sake than hers.

"Look—" She peered around and then dragged me into a downstairs guest room. Hers, I assumed from the mess and empty suitcases.

"I can't understand Sinhala, obviously, but did you hear about the huge fight this morning?"

"There was a huge fight?" My pulse quickened as a choking sensation made its way into my throat.

"Yes! Oh god. It's Aunty Fiona—she—she—well, she burst into Uncle Nihal's office. And then she started screaming all this—well, I don't know what it was. But she was so angry, and oh god."

Was it working? Were they calling off the wedding as we spoke?

"And then, well, she ran downstairs, still screaming. And she was screaming at Uncle and Kaavi. I—well—I tried to talk to them, but they just asked me to wait in my room. I think they called Spencer and asked him to come over too. Oh god, I don't even know why they would do that, because he showed about half an hour later, looking super upset. I just—" She wrung her hands. "Oh, I just don't know what to do!"

So Spencer was here, in the house. I instinctively looked down at myself to check what I was wearing. A simple shift dress. Would he like that? But I shook myself alert. This wasn't the time for knee-jerk reactions to my ex-boyfriend. I needed to focus.

"What do you mean? There's really nothing for you to do, is there?" I hoped I didn't sound happy about it.

I never really thought this plan would work. It sounded like some-thing out of a middle-grader's handbook. I think there might have been a *Baby-Sitters Club* book that had a similar plot. It was too sim-ple. If I knew they'd call off the wedding because of this, I wouldn't have lost so much sleep over plan B or plan C.

But Laura covered her face with her hands and started to cry.

"It's my fault, you know. All my fault."

"Um, what?"

"I didn't want to, you know," she sobbed. "All this is because of me."

She was nearly hysterical. How self-centered could she even be?

"What do you mean all because of you?" I asked.

"Because." She had started hiccuping now. "Because—" She threw herself onto her bed, facedown, Disney Princess style, and continued to wail.

But I heard a commotion outside and left the crying Laura in her room. The Fonsekas had all assembled in the pantry—Mr. Fonseka looked grave and defiant, Mrs. Fonseka had pursed up her lips but there was a sense of resignation about her, a pink-faced Kaavi held Spencer's hand as he actively stared down at the floor, and Tehani looked puzzled. There were a few other people in the kitchen too—

Fonseka relatives, no doubt, who were staying at the house for the wedding. Aunty Josephina's absence was notable, of course, but Aunty Rajini from Mrs. Fonseka's brunch sat right in front of the group, her arms crossed and her lips pursed as well. She lived in Sri Lanka, as far as I knew, so she wasn't a houseguest. That's a little strange—why would she be here at this time of the day? Especially since the Fonsekas didn't really seem to be in the mood for visitors.

I stayed at the edge of the room, where I could hardly be seen.

Kaavi noticed me, though she looked away as soon as we made eye contact.

Mr. Fonseka cleared his throat.

"I'm sure everyone is wondering what the commotion was this morning. I'm very sorry for disturbing you'll"—he looked toward the relatives—"especially those of you who have traveled from so far and are certainly jet-lagged.

"I'm sure you'll can understand that these wedding times can be stressful for everyone. But it's even worse when the stress comes from totally avoidable matters. Of course, we are all no strangers to gossip and the damage it can cause. My family, especially my soon-to-be son-in-law, was the victim of such gossip. I just want to take a moment now to make one thing very clear—"

He paused and looked around the room, making sure to look everyone in the eye, even me. This was the Mr. Fonseka I used to know. Who wasn't afraid to face things head-on. Who took charge of situations. Who I used to call uncle, who kept me safe, who felt almost like the father I never had. My heart swelled, looking at him now.

A kettle that had been left on the stove started to whistle. It seemed to jerk him back to what he was saying.

"There's nothing, do you hear? Nothing that could be said about my family, and I very much consider Spencer to be my family, that would make us turn our backs on one another. Nothing.

"Now if we could please go back to celebrating Kaavi and Spencer, and focus on their big day, I would appreciate it very much. Thank you."

And with that dismissal, he stormed out of the room.

Mrs. Fonseka didn't say anything, but the way she kept her eyes trained down made me think she wasn't too happy. I knew what was in the envelope. And I knew Mrs. Fonseka. There was no way she'd be as accepting as her husband. But I also knew the way things worked—when Mr. Fonseka put his foot down, and it was rare that he did, but when he did, there was no changing his mind. I knew that from personal experience.

I tried to slink out of the room without being seen. I had just crept past one of the relatives, I think her name was Aunty Geetha, when I heard her mutter—

"Of course they all stand by anything the other does. Even bastard children."

She was quickly shushed by the younger woman next to her, but when I looked back, Aunty Geetha locked eyes with mine and gave me a little smile.

I felt my face heat up. I thought about grabbing the kettle full of boiling water and throwing it at her. The way she would scream as her face melted away. That would get rid of her snide grin. But I swatted that thought away.

Looks like I haven't been as safe from Colombo gossips as I thought.

TEHANI

Interview Transcript: Tehani Fonseka (abbrev. TF) Part 2 of 3

Date: January 25, 2020

Location: The Mount Lavinia Hotel

EP: Tell us about your relationship with Matthew Spencer.

TF: What do you mean?

EP: Were you close? Did you get along?

TF: We got along well enough, I suppose. About as much as you would expect a sister-in-law and a brother-in-law to do.

EP: Did you get along with him more than you did with your other family members?

TF: Well, it wouldn't take a rocket scientist to figure out that I'm not particularly close with the rest of my family. So yes, I suppose I was closer to him than them. He was certainly kinder to me than the rest, not that I cared.

EP: But you did help him with the proposal.

TF: Yes, so what? Plenty of men ask sisters of the bride to help them with proposals. It's totally normal.

EP: So you were aware of Mr. Spencer's relationship with your sister?

TF: Not at first, no. Of course Kaavi wouldn't have told me herself. She loved lording over me like some pure, virginal princess. I had no idea they were even together until Spencer told me. He'd become, well, I guess you can say he'd become a friend of the family by then. He'd fly down here often to help out with charity stuff. My mother certainly was in love with him. I had to admit, Kaavi did a great job hiding it. But then he proposed and everything came out.

EP: So Mr. Spencer first informed you of his intentions?

TF: Yes, he asked for my help. Wanted Kaavi to call him up on-stage and she needed some convincing. Of course she didn't want to share her spotlight. But Spencer knew her well. He knew she'd love a big show in front of everyone. She always cared so much about what others thought. Besides, it was perfect material for her YouTube channel. Good thing she didn't turn him down, because she'd have died from the embarrassment of it. Come to think about it, she'd more willingly marry a total monster than face any sort of public humiliation.

EP: And was he, Mr. Spencer, was he a total monster?

TF: Ha ha, no way. Not Spence. That was just a figure of speech. Spencer is amazing. I have no clue what he saw in Kaavi—she was always so uptight, even more so around him, but to each their own, I guess. No, Spencer was great. This one time, my father had been on my case about some bullshit, I can't remember what now, probably something to do with spending too much on my credit card, and Spencer totally stood up for me. He didn't say anything directly to my father, of course, but he spoke to me about it afterward, and told me he understood where I was coming from. It's more support than what anyone in my family had ever given me.

EP: So you felt loyal toward Mr. Spencer?

TF: What do you mean by that—loyal?

EP: I mean, did you feel indebted to him? Perhaps like you have to take his side?

TF: [Pause] I don't know if I understand your question.

EP: All right, then. Would you be able to let us know what happened to your sister's wedding dress?

TF: I—what?

EP: Your sister's wedding dress. You mentioned during our first conversation that it had been destroyed.

TF: Yes. But surely you don't believe I could have had anything to do with that?

EP: Would you explain to me exactly how you realized that the dress had been destroyed?

TF: I—okay, look. I'd had a few shots by then, and there was this family friend who I hadn't seen in a while who was texting me, so I was pretty distracted. I didn't even notice until someone screamed that there was something in the bonfire down by the beach. By the time we all rushed over there, well, the dress was totally and completely on fire.

EP: And you have no idea how it got there?

TF: Well, I've told you my suspicions about Amaya. It could easily have been her.

EP: What I find curious, though, Miss Fonseka, is that none of the other attendees at the bachelorette party appear to remember you there.

TF: I—um, what?

EP: Did you leave the party at any time?

TF: I—okay, look, my parents would freak out if they heard about this, all right. That's why I didn't really mention it. I kinda want to keep it on the down low. But I wasn't just texting that family friend I told you about. I was, well, I met him. He'd flown in from the US for the wedding, and, well, he had a room pretty close to the beach in the old wing, and I snuck in

there for a while. I was there when the dress was found in the
fire.

EP: So you were in the old wing at the time?

TF: Yes.

EP: The reason I ask is that your sister's wedding dress was signed
and received outside her room in the old wing, during the
bachelorette party that you did not attend, and the delivery
receipt has your name on it.

TF: Mine? That's impossible.

EP: Why don't you tell us about what happened last night? After
the Poruwa ceremony.

TF: I—what? Look, I've told you guys already. Things were supposed to wind up early after the Poruwa—you know, just
some milk rice and maybe a few cocktails. But of course things
got out of hand. Some of the uncles pestered my dad to open
up the bar and, well, you could probably imagine the rest. I
mean, they had Spence ride in on a fucking elephant. What
were they expecting? A quiet affair?

Kaavi and Spence did the rounds, and then Kaavi decided to turn in
rather early. Much too early for a bride, and my mother was furious. Hell, I was furious. My dad drops all this cash on a wedding
for her, and she doesn't even have the decency to stay? Thankfully, the guests were mostly my father's friends, and they barely
noticed she was gone. I stayed instead, thanking everyone for
coming and playing host. I was exhausted at the end of it.

EP: One of the waiters mentioned a commotion with a wedding
guest?

TF: [Pause] I had forgotten about that! You don't think—oh god,
do you think it was him?

EP: Could you tell us what you remember?

TF: I'm sorry. The cocktails I had made the whole thing a bit hazy. But I remember a man. He was middle-aged, I reckon. He was bald, and had a mustache.

EP: Had you seen him before?

TF: No. I don't think so.

EP: What happened?

TF: He burst into the wedding. I think some of the security guys were trying to stop him, but he was shouting something at Kaavi. Thank goodness it was when the party really got going, so most of the crowd didn't notice him.

EP: Did Kaavi speak to him?

TF: I'm not sure. My mother stepped in, though, and had him dragged away before he disrupted things further. I just re-member him shouting something about Kaavi needing to take responsibility. I remember thinking, at the time anyway, that maybe he was some crazy fan of hers, from the Insta posts and stuff, you know? She's had a couple of stalkers over the years, but, well, that's Colombo, right? But then—oh fuck . . .

EP: Miss Fonseka?

TF: Oh fuck. Okay, I had totally forgotten about this. Fuck. I knew I shouldn't have had so much to drink.

EP: Miss Fonseka, could you please tell us what you saw?

TF: I'm sorry—I—I really was so wasted. I—I didn't see. Not ex-actly. But I think I heard someone shout that he had a gun. I'm not sure. Oh god—I should have said something earlier. But then, well, I was so tired. And so drunk. And I just figured, well, I just figured that the security would take care of him.

EP: Miss Fonseka, I've already spoken to the security team. There was no gun found on the gentleman, so they let him go. But they hadn't recorded any identification. You are sure you aren't aware who he is?

TF: No. I've never seen him before.

EP: Would you mind giving a full visual description to my colleague? We can send a circular around the hotel.

TF: Of course.

12

AMAYA

Three Days before the Wedding

SPENCER AND KAAVI went outside to the garden, where they sat on a bench and talked in low voices. Kaavi looked a little irritated, but Spencer was visibly upset—running his fingers through his hair and gesticulating haphazardly. If it were me, I knew what I'd do to calm him down. I wonder if Kaavi knew it too? The way to let him vent, to get it out of his system. To say the right things, to do the right things, to bring him back to her.

My heart hurt.

I thought about going home but figured I should leave the box with the photographs in Kaavi's room first. It would look strange to leave taking it with me, but more than that, I didn't want them anymore. If any of my plans were successful, I would never speak to Kaavi again, and I didn't need any mementos to remind me of her. She'd been cut out of my life, sure, but there was always that little spark of hope. What I was about to do would extinguish any chance we had of rebuilding our friendship.

When my father left and I asked my mother if she was sad, she smiled through her tears and told me that hope only truly disappeared when someone passed away. That's the only thing that could destroy true love, she said. When two people belong together, someone had to leave this earth for that bond to be broken. And then she died, so I suppose she was right.

I slunk upstairs, unnoticed, and made my way into Kaavi's bedroom. It was immaculately arranged—bed made, clothes put away. The roses from Spencer were missing. Kaavi probably got rid of them the moment they started to wilt. Nothing imperfect to be found here. There was a black-and-white picture of Bruce Springsteen that I hadn't noticed before on her dresser. It made me inexplicably happy to see it. That this little part of her still existed. Kaavi had always been such a fan, even when I'd teased her about being a dork. Those really were the before-times.

"Too mopey," I'd complained about the singer. "Too mopey and too whiny and not a beat you can even click your fingers to."

But she had been obsessed.

"Listen to this," she'd keep saying, trying to convince me.

"I still don't get it," I'd said, after she played me "Cautious Man." The more obscure his music, the better it was for her back then. "Why would anyone get *love* and *fear* tattooed on their hands? That's just weird."

"So that he'd always remember that it was the same thing."

Where was this wise sixteen-year-old now? Was she buried under her sophisticated wardrobe and designer handbags? Did the old Kaavi even exist anymore?

I could still see both of them down in the garden from Kaavi's bedroom window. Kaavi was starting to stand up, but Spencer held on to her arm, bringing her back down to him. I remember that move. His passion, his intensity when he wanted something. My legs felt weak just thinking about it.

I scribbled a note to her—*Kaavi, please call me. We need to talk.* "We need to talk" was probably the understatement of the century. I left the note on her bedside table along with the box. There was another picture here. An eight-by-five photograph in a rose gold frame. It was taken here at the Fonsekas' house. A group shot of the entire family standing in front of the staircase—big smiles on all their faces. It was probably before an event because all the women were in saris and Mr. Fonseka was in a suit and tie. He smiled widely, carrying little Nadia, who wore a puffy dress. His three girls.

I put the photograph down. This was wrong. This was all wrong. I shouldn't be here. I should have never come.

It felt hard to breathe, like my throat was closing in on itself, and the magnitude of what I was doing crashed down on me. My legs felt weak. I looked around the room for a clock or a calendar, and when that failed I looked at my own watch. 3:45 p.m. Consecutive numbers weren't the best sign, but they weren't the worst either. Better than no pattern at all.

I sat down on the side of the bed and held my head in my hands. I should just go back to LA. I'd walked away before; I could do it again.

I kept my eyes closed and tried breathing deeply, just like Dr. Dunn says. One deep inhale. Hold it for five counts. Then exhale thoroughly for five. One deep inhale.

Something grabbed my ankles from under the bed and pulled.

I slid right off and crashed down onto the floor, a scream escaping my chest.

It had come for me.

I kept my eyes closed, bracing myself to finally meet my demons.

After so many years, it had finally caught up to me.

"Please . . ." I pleaded.

Pleaded for what?

But I just heard giggling.

Huh?

I was in a heap on the floor. Prying my eyes open, I looked across to the bottom of the bed.

It was Nadia, curled under the white frame, giggling hysterically.

"What are you doing?" I asked. I still had the wind knocked out of me and hadn't recovered yet.

"I was waiting for Kaavi *Akki*," she gasped, giggling harder. "She loves this prank."

"Oh." I didn't have words. My breath was coming in short gasps now, and I willed myself to calm down.

It was just a prank.

I took a deep breath.

Just a prank.

It was also my first time alone with Nadia.

I used this moment to really take a look at her.

Nadia, who I've never had the chance to get to know.

"Do you need help getting out from under there?" I asked, offering her my hand.

"Okay." Her smile was so pure. Who did it remind me of?

I reached in and she held on to my palms. It was getting hard to breathe again.

"On the count of three, okay?"

She nodded.

"One. Two. Three!" I tugged and she shimmied and somehow landed on top of me, still giggling.

This kid was way too trusting. It hurt my heart.

I heard footsteps rushing toward Kaavi's room.

"What's going on here?!" Mrs. Fonseka yelled. Her face was pale and she clutched onto the door.

"Nadia? Are you okay?"

"Ammi!" The little girl shrieked, running up to Mrs. Fonseka and reaching for her. Mrs. Fonseka picked her up and held her close.

"What are you doing?" she hissed at me.

"I—I'm sorry. I was just leaving—"

"I don't want to hear it, Amaya. You just show up here, unannounced. Creep around this house. Spread vicious rumors about Spencer—don't tell me it wasn't you!"

I had tried to interrupt but she practically hollered over me.

"We had an arrangement, Amaya. My husband may be too soft to enforce it, and my daughter might have been misguided enough to invite you to her wedding, but that still doesn't mean you are welcome here. You were supposed to stay away, so stay away. From me. From my husband. And most importantly"—she held Nadia tightly to her chest—"from our daughters."

"I'm sorry." I was trembling. "I didn't mean to—I didn't know she was—"

"You need to leave. And while I can't uninvite you from the wedding celebrations, please know that you are not welcome in this house."

And with that she left, leaving me a quivering mess on the floor, thinking of all the horrible, painful ways she could die.

I WAS SUCH an idiot. Of course I should have known better. I should have known better than to go snooping around that house. Trying to fill in the gaps of the lives I've missed, the moments I could never be a part of.

I tried taking deep breaths to steady myself. I did everything Dr. Dunn said—I did my counting exercises, I gave myself a little pep talk, I thought about how someone I admired would handle this situation and tried to emulate that in my thoughts. None of it seemed to work. What Mrs. Fonseka said, though it didn't really surprise me, well, it broke my heart.

Luckily, no one else seemed to have witnessed her outburst. I gathered myself off the floor and picked up the box of photos, stuffing it into my bag. I was so silly, bringing them in here. I should have just gotten rid of them. Gotten rid of them like the Fonsekas had gotten rid of me. I made my way out of Kaavi's room. I needed to get home and take a long shower and crawl into bed. Maybe I'd message Beth. I know it's still the middle of the night for her, but maybe she'd be awake if I was lucky enough. I needed to do something to feel better. Maybe I'd message Alexander?

The hallway was still deserted since everyone was downstairs having tea, thank goodness. I had made it about halfway down when I heard whispering and a loud sniffle, like someone was crying. I peered off the staircase banister to see who it was.

If Mrs. Fonseka saw me still around she would probably physically drag me out of this house and I'd never live that down. As a matter of fact, it was best if I wasn't seen at all. Especially not by Spencer.

But it wasn't Mrs. Fonseka under the staircase. It was Laura. She had her phone pressed up against her face tightly, and her eyes darted around like she was hiding away from everyone.

I paused, leaning away from the railing so she couldn't see me if she happened to look up. What had she been trying to tell me earlier? I'd been too distracted wondering if my ridiculous plan had worked to care. She'd thought the fight had been about her. But why?

I snuck another look, and I saw her wipe away tears and mutter angrily to herself.

My pulse quickened.

What are you up to, Laura?

"Yeah, look, can you hear me now? I have to be quiet. The cell reception in my room is absolute bullshit."

Her voice was low, but there was no one around to hear her but me.

"Of course I'm being careful. But you don't know—no. No!"

"You're not even hearing me out."

"Look, it's getting dangerous. You don't understand."

What was Laura on about? Who was she talking to?

I wonder if it had to do with Spencer?

I should have paid her more attention.

I clenched my hands into fists, digging my nails into the flesh of my palms. It didn't hurt nearly enough to center me, but it did allow me to think clearly.

I strained to hear what else she was saying, but I could barely make out anything over the beating of my heart. It sounded like whoever was on the other end was doing most of the talking.

Laura's pause was so long that I wondered whether she hung up and left. I was about to peer over once more when her voice rang out again, loud, clear, and half an octave higher.

"I don't want to do this anymore, you hear me? Kaavi is my friend. I can't do this anymore. Please don't make me." She stifled a sob and hung up. I could hear her footsteps echo back toward her room and the door slam shut.

I struggled to keep my breathing even.

Was someone forcing Laura to do something to Kaavi?

This didn't make sense.

It took every ounce of energy for me to make my way outside. No one paid me any attention, thank goodness, and I just about collapsed into a trishaw and gave the driver my address.

Plan A might have been an absolute failure, but I was sure of one thing—I wasn't the only one with an agenda.

AUNTY JOSEPHINA

Interview Transcript: Josephina De Lannerolle (abbrev. JDL)

Date: January 25, 2020

Location: The Mount Lavinia Hotel

EP: Thank you for your patience, Mrs. De Lannerolle. I don't know how much you've been told about our circumstances today, but it would be of great help if you could—

JDL: Answer a few questions, my dear, yes, I was made aware by a few of the other guests who went through this same process. You are trying to get to the bottom of what happened to Kaavindi, am I right? Well, no surprise there. That girl came and went as she pleased. No regard at all about what inconvenience she would put her family through. This is hardly a surprise for me, I'm afraid. I knew this wedding was doomed from the start.

EP: Before we begin, Mrs. De Lannerolle, would you mind please stating your full name and address for our records.

JDL: My name is Josephina De Lannerolle and I reside at Apartment 3/4, Queen's Court Residencies, Colombo 03.

I have been a close friend of Nihal and Fiona Fonseka for many years now. Fiona's elder sister, she now lives in the UK, and I were classmates at St. Bridget's Convent, so you can say that I've always been a friend of the family. I attended their wedding, I believe that was in '91 or '92. I was personally invited by Fiona's parents. I was to be a bridesmaid, but they had a cousin flying down from London just for the wedding, so it was only right that they offer that position to her.

I have known Kaavindi ever since she was a little girl. Now, I know it's not proper for me to say this, of course, but it must be said—Nihal and Fiona, well, Nihal mostly, spoiled that child rotten. She only had to look at a toy and her father would move mountains to get it for her. I remember how she had said she wanted a pony for her eighth birthday, and Nihal got one down all the way from Nuwara Eliya. When she cried about it leaving back to the hill country to be kept in a stable there, he kept it in their garden for an entire week until he made arrangements with the stables at the Colombo Hilton so they would house the pony and Kaavindi could visit it once a week for riding lessons. She lost interest in ponies, as expected, but Nihal never seemed to mind.

So it's no wonder, really, that when Kaavindi decided she wanted something, Nihal would always support her. He even sent her to America, can you believe it?

"What's wrong with London?" I asked him. After all, both my sons went to university there, and are doing very well now. One is a barrister, you know, and the other works at Christie's. He just bought himself the latest Jaguar. I couldn't be more proud. They wanted to come down for the wedding, but unfortunately, they couldn't make the time. My eldest's wife is insisting they tour Italy over the summer, you see, and he can't stay away from his work for so long. I told him to take no-pay and just come, you know, it's not like he *needs* the money, but he's diligent and loyal to his company, just like I've taught him to be.

So yes, Nihal sent her to university in America, and paid for her apartments and cars and shopping while she traipsed around doing god knows what. You know, I'm not at all surprised that something terrible befell her. Now, you mustn't get me wrong. I don't have anything against the girl, you know. I like her. I have always wished her well. But my daughter-in-law showed me once, on this, er, the YouTube, I think it is called? Yes, the YouTube. She showed me a video of Kaavindi acting, well, I wouldn't say inappropriately, I suppose. Just that I would never allow my own daughter to ever appear that way. I mean, it's just not done, is it? Such a cheap thing for a young woman to do. To act like she was some celebrity or actress, speaking in a false accent, begging others to watch more of her videos. I shudder to even think about it.

Of course, Nihal was proud of his daughter. Encouraged this behavior. You know, I wouldn't be at all surprised if some crazy man saw her on the YouTube and became obsessed with her. I was concerned that at least Fiona didn't put a stop to this shameless behavior, but then I've heard that even though she paints a picture of a perfect mother, the eldest two girls used to call their nanny "Amma" until they were six.

So actually, I don't know what I was thinking when I told Nihal what I found out. I should have known that he would just brush me aside and call it nonsense. He can accuse me of anything he wants; I know that I acted out of the goodness of my heart.

When I found out about Spencer, I could have told anyone, you hear? I could have told my good friends the Hewages. You know they own the competing gem business in Colombo, don't you? And that would have been enough to bring the whole Fonseka family to their knees. They would have never been able to live down the shame.

EP: Did you discuss it with anyone else?

JDL: Not at all, you hear? I'm nothing if not a woman of honor. I did ring up my daughter-in-law to get her advice, of course—she and Kaavindi moved in the same circles, at least back when she lived in Sri Lanka, and I thought she might be able to give me some guidance. She said to me "Amma"—you know, she's so well brought up that she called me "Amma" from the moment my son proposed—"you must speak to Uncle Nihal at once."

So that is what I did. I spoke to Nihal directly. I wasn't quite sure if he even knew about this news. It was entirely possible that he did. I told him I was worried for him.

EP: Could you please describe what it was you found out?

JDL: I didn't take it very seriously at first, of course. But the documents did have an air of authenticity about them, so it struck me as genuine.

The documents were about Spencer's, well, his *background*, I would say. I have promised Nihal I would not speak about it, but since I'm being questioned now, I am not afraid to say.

It provided quite a lot of details about Spencer's parents. He had led us to believe that both his parents had died when he was a child, leaving him an orphan, of course, but with a tidy sum of money. That's how he was able to finance his various start-ups, Fiona had said.

But this report painted a very different picture. His father, it said, was very much alive, and in prison. Can you even believe it? He had played out quite a number of people for a bit of a sum, it seemed. His most recent conviction was five years ago, although he had been in and out of prison since Spencer was a child.

And his mother, this is the bit that broke my heart. His mother was an addict, who, according to the report, hardly cared for

her child. Can you believe that mothers like that even exist?
She, too, appeared to be very much alive, although what kind
of life could she possibly be living? It seems that Spencer left
home when he was sixteen and hasn't seen her since.

Now, I'm not judging Spencer, of course. The poor boy can't be
blamed for the mistakes his parents made. But you never
know, do you? They say the apple doesn't fall far from the tree.
He could be harboring some, you know, something in his
genes that turns him this way. I feel sorry for him, of course I
do. It was never my intention to upset any applecarts.

But if it were me, I would never have allowed my child to marry
someone from a family like that. What if his father got wind
of Nihal's fortune and came after it? What if Spencer turns to
drugs later in life? It's in his blood, you know? It's not my fault.
I just thought Nihal would like to know.

So I rang him up the next morning and told him what I had found
out. I wanted to advise him. To speak some sense into him.

Ha, that's the last time I play Good Samaritan. You know what he
told me? He told me to keep my nose out of their business and
to stop being a gossip.

A gossip. Me? Can you even believe it?

I said to him, I said: "My dear, I'm just looking out for your family
like you should be doing."

And since he seemed so unbothered by the type of person he was
inviting into his family, I thought it my duty to inform Fiona
as well. Because I knew, from the bottom of my heart, that she
would not agree with his decision. All I was doing was looking
out for my friend.

And you know what Fiona did? You won't even believe it. You
know she threatened me? Said I should keep my mouth shut or

I would get what's coming to me. *Hmph.* Like the Fonsekas could even touch me. You know, my second cousin is married to the minister of finance. Fiona has forgotten who I am. You know, I even asked my good friend Rajini to go over there that morning. Asked to keep an eye out, you know, in case Nihal or Fiona start bad-mouthing me. Thank goodness they seemed to have come to their good senses and did nothing of the sort, or I'd see to it that they are taken care of.

EP: Taken care of in what way, Mrs. De Lannerolle?

JDL: Oh. Oh no. I didn't mean like that. If I harbored any ill will toward the Fonsekas, then why would I even have come to the wedding? I wanted them to know that I had nothing to be ashamed of. All I did was be a concerned well-wisher and friend.

But you know, come to think of it, maybe it was someone from Spencer's side who decided to hurt Kaavi? You never know, do you? I thought it would take a few more years for Kaavindi to face the repercussions of her father's negligence, but it looks like I'm wrong, and she's already had to pay the price.

EP: One last thing, Mrs. De Lannerolle. How did you manage to come about this confidential information?

JDL: Oh—I had some documents posted to me anonymously. I don't know what they hoped to achieve by doing so. They probably thought to reach out to me because I was an upstanding citizen in Colombo society.

13

AMAYA

Two Days before the Wedding

THE ONLY SILVER lining is that, with the wedding around the corner, the celebrations had now moved out of the Fonsekas' home and into the Mount Lavinia hotel.

Kaavi's bridal shower was the next day—*Don't worry, ladies, the bridal shower part is for the aunties, but you can be assured the night won't end without some dirty, flirty, after-hours fun,* Kaavi had joked in a recent video. The formal bridal shower will be held over afternoon tea at the hotel terrace, with the after-party to continue down by the beach. *No one over thirty-five allowed* was the informal notice given. I guess that's when the transformation into Colombo 07 aunty began, at least in Kaavi's opinion.

The bridal shower was supposed to start at 4:00 p.m., so of course, when I showed up at 3:55 p.m. I was the only one there. I kept forgetting about island time, and how it was an unspoken rule that everyone would always be half an hour late. It did nothing to help my anxiety.

I wondered whether Spencer had checked into the hotel today or if he was coming with the rest of the group tomorrow? My palms felt clammy at the thought of bumping into him again. It's been so strange seeing him here—out of his element but still so smoothly fitting in. But that was what drew me to Spencer in the first place. His understated confidence, overruling the childish arrogance I had once worn like a security blanket. Peeling off the layers I had built up to guard against feeling vulnerable, until he knew every bit of me, every inch. The way he could make me smile and laugh and tremble and gasp and lose my breath, and finally, the way he made me his entirely.

I had to stop thinking about him. He was the center of my plan, yes, but I couldn't have him distract me from it.

I decided to wander around the hotel instead. I hadn't been here in many years and had forgotten how absolutely beautiful it was. Originally the governor of British Ceylon's house, it was converted to a five-star hotel in 1877. The legend goes that British governor Sir Thomas Maitland fell madly in love with a dancing girl, Lovina, during a welcome party held in his honor when he first arrived to the island. So much was he enraptured that he ordered the construction of a secret tunnel that led from his wine cellar to Lovina's home, so that the lovers could meet in secret. Even though no evidence of this passageway has ever been found, the hotel was a beautifully preserved echo of a time long past.

Someone once told me, at a wedding when I was a child, that I shouldn't wander through the corridors in the old wing alone at night. They said the ghost of a dancing girl could be heard echoing on the hardwood floors. The tap, tap, tap of her steps, accompanied by the tinkling of bells on her anklets.

The driveway to the hotel wrapped around a sparkling fountain that housed the statue of Lady Lavinia, as Lovina came to be called, and the white colonial-style building rose up against the backdrop of the sea. The enormous terrace that held the hotel pool overlooked the ocean, and of course, Kaavi had booked out the whole terrace

and the attached restaurant. The Fonsekas had booked out the whole
hotel, come to think of it, but I thought that was from tomorrow.

Kaavi and I both loved the Mount Lavinia Hotel as children. The
Fonsekas would usually come here on Sundays, first to have lunch at the
exquisite Sunday lunch buffet, followed by us jumping in the pool or
hanging out down by the beach. Mrs. Fonseka would not sway from
under a large beach umbrella, chiding us girls for being out in the sun
and "getting dark," but we would ignore her and run along the private
beach, reveling in how empty it would get the farther we moved away
from the hotel. Tehani would try to follow us sometimes, but Kaavi
would threaten to lock her in one of the changing rooms that dotted the
shore until she left us alone. Mr. Fonseka would play with us sometimes
too. I remember how he helped us dig a huge hole once, and then I
jumped in and they buried me in the sand, leaving just my head out. We
couldn't stop laughing. I wonder if there was a picture of that somewhere?

I had hoped being early meant that I would have a chance to speak
with Kaavi before the festivities began. I wanted only that—one last
chance to speak to her. She had brushed me off before, at Andre's,
but maybe with everything that had come to light about Spencer,
she'd be a little more open.

And today was probably my last shot. Tomorrow was the Poruwa—
the traditional Sinhalese part of the wedding, though they wouldn't
be signing the marriage certificate until the church ceremony, which
would take place the next day, followed by the reception, of course.
I'd heard whispers that the guest of honor that was delaying the signing of the papers was the highly celebrated captain of the Sri Lanka
cricket team. Thank goodness it gave me an extra day to work with,
and that was what is important right now.

I went to the bathroom and locked myself in a stall. The Mount
Lavinia Hotel was old-school, which meant they had actual walls in

between cubicles—no sneaking a peek underneath to check if anyone was inside. Once you were in, you were safe.

I pulled the seat down and took out my phone. I had typed out everything I wanted to tell Kaavi, from what happened between Spencer and me to everything I had regretted since. I should have never just walked away. I know that now. I just wished it would have been easier for me to fix what happened.

I ran through the conversation I hoped to have in my head. Rehearsed the little script I had planned out for myself. My brunch friends laughed at me when I told them that I like to be prepared and know what I'm saying before I have a conversation, especially a difficult one.

"Girl, you for real? You know you can't plan out every single conversation ahead of time, right?" Jessica had said, while the others snickered. There had been construction going on across the street, and I thought of all three women being crushed under a falling steel beam, or tripping into an open manhole, or my favorite, being run over by a backhoe. Their bodies popping open like balloons under the weight of the machinery.

That was the last time I'd mentioned it to them, but it made me feel a million times better to know I was prepared. I hated it when I thought of the perfect thing to say after the moment had passed, and that happened to me all the time. I'd lie awake at night, berating myself, hating that I didn't have the right comeback in hand. I know it's not possible to rehearse every single conversation I have, but there was no harm in being ready. Especially if it was a conversation that was about to change my life. And Kaavi's too.

My hands trembled a little, making it difficult to read what was on my phone. I tore off some toilet paper and stuffed it into my armpits. The dress code on the invitation said Champagne Chic, which I had to google, so here I was wearing the only beige dress I had brought with me—a shorter flared number that fluttered up far too easily with the breeze on the terrace. I should have known better, but it was too late to change now. Hopefully, I could just leave after I spoke to Kaavi and would be spared from having a potential Marilyn Monroe moment.

I took a deep breath and counted to five. It didn't work. I removed my watch, brought my wrist up to my mouth, and bit down on the side, hard. Better. I put my watch back on over the reddening skin and swiped through my notes again. My hand didn't shake as much this time.

I was halfway through when I heard the door to the ladies' room open.

"Listen to me," Kaavi's voice rang through the bathroom, though I couldn't see her and knew for certain that she didn't see me.

"Yes," she paused, while the person on the line said something. "Yes, I know it's upsetting. Like I told you the other day, I'm really sorry, but your demands are just—" Another pause.

"I am very sorry, but this is bordering on harassment now. Listen, I told you, I am willing to—"

"Is that a threat? Because you know my family and I don't take very kindly to—hello? Hello?"

Something slammed down.

"That motherfucker," Kaavi hissed, opening the faucet.

I heard her pottering around the washroom—the sound of her clutch opening, the sound of something dropping on the floor, Kaavi swearing again, until she cleared out a few minutes later.

I sat stock-still the entire time. My heart was beating so hard I was sure she'd hear me. My mind raced over everything I heard.

Who was Kaavi on the phone with?

What had she done to upset them?

Why were they threatening her?

I checked the time—4:44 p.m.

How could this be a good sign?

LAURA

Interview Transcript: Laura Abigail Thompson (abbrev. LAT)
Date: January 25, 2020
Location: The Mount Lavinia Hotel

LAT: So, um, I've been trying to talk to you for a while. I've been telling the security since I heard about what happened. I have, well, I have an idea who could have done it. I thought you should know.

EP: Thank you for coming forward. Would you mind giving me your name and address for the record, before we start?

LAT: So, you want, like, my full name, right?

EP: Yes, please. And your current address too.

LAT: I'm Laura Thompson, um, Laura Abigail Thompson, though I haven't really used my middle name in a long time. I'm staying with my host family, the Fonsekas, at their home. I don't, um, I don't, like, really remember the address. Would you mind if I text it to you later?

EP: Could you confirm that this is the address, please?

[Shuffling papers]

28 Maitland Crescent, Colombo 07.

LAT: Yes, I guess that's right.

EP: Miss Thompson, you had mentioned to the security officers that you had your suspicions about who might have had cause to hurt Miss Fonseka. Would you mind filling us in?

LAT: Sure, of course. Um, okay, well, it's not easy to say this, you know. I mean, the Fonsekas have been awesome. They've really, you know, welcomed me into their home. Especially Mr. Fonseka. He's very kind. And Kaavi, she's just, well, she's so awesome. We've known each other since we were kids, you know. Well, kind of. They'd stay with us when they visited Texas, and I've always been in such awe of her. But, you know, she's a bit older than me, so I guess I've always kind of been the brat that hung around. You know, I think—

EP: Would you mind telling us about your suspicions, Miss Thompson?

LAT: Yes, my suspicions. Of course. Yes. Well, I guess there's no easy way to say this. But I think the middle sister, Tehani—I think she did it.

EP: And what makes you think that?

LAT: Well, she hated Kaavi's guts, for one thing. You know, seeing the two of them together made me thank god that I'm an only child. I've heard of competition between sisters, of course, but those two. I mean, that was some next-level shit.

EP: Could you give us some examples? Did the younger Miss Fonseka say anything?

LAT: Oh, well, she didn't need to. You could see it all over her face. Over all their faces. I've spent, what, five weeks with the family now? The beauty of living with a group of people as busy as the Fonsekas is that they rarely notice you floating around. Always on their phones, always working, always keeping up. With their charities and their events. It makes it easy to pick up on things, you know. I guess Kaavi never paid much attention to Tehani, but Tehani, well, I think she's a lot smarter than the Fonsekas give her credit for. Sure, she likes to drink and party, but I mean, don't we all? [Laughs]

[Pause]

She's been quite upset with the way everyone's been handling things. With the wedding, I mean, and especially the wedding expenses. I saw her the other day, looking over the business's accounts and getting quite upset. "Would you spend close to a million rupees on fucking fireworks?" she asked me.

I mean, I tried to tell her that things were so much cheaper in Sri Lanka anyway, but she seemed quite pissed off and didn't want to hear it.

EP: And you think this rift about finances is cause enough for the younger Miss Fonseka to hurt her sister?

LAT: Look, I don't know. All I'm saying is that I know bitterness when I see it, and Tehani was as bitter as a grapefruit spoiling out in the summer sun. I don't know. Maybe it was hard for her. Kaavi was so perfect, so wonderful, it would have been difficult, I guess, growing up in her shadow. Having everyone fawn over Kaavi when Tehani was pretty much forgotten.

EP: Thank you, Miss Thompson. Can I also ask you a few more questions, now that I have you here?

LAT: Sure thing. If you think it'll help us figure out what happened to Kaavi, I'm an open book. I really hope this is all one big misunderstanding. Like, you know, *The Hangover* or something. That she's just locked up on a roof somewhere or—oh my god, *have* you checked the roof of the hotel?

EP: Thank you for the suggestion. The security are combing every inch of the hotel as we speak.

LAT: Oh, that's great. Tell them not to forget to check the roof, okay?

EP: Yes. Now, if you don't mind, could you please tell me what happened on the morning of the twenty-second?

LAT: Um, the twenty-second?

EP: Yes. There had been a disagreement in the Fonseka household. A few of the guests mentioned that you seemed quite upset.

LAT: Um, well, I—I was upset, of course. I didn't understand what was going on, and Mrs. Fonseka, well, she seemed really angry. And I—um, I thought she was upset with me.

EP: And why would she be upset with you?

LAT: I was, um, I had been, well, I wanted to check my email. And the Wi-Fi downstairs wasn't working for some reason. And so I thought I'd try using Uncle Nihal's computer instead.

[Pause]

Aunty Fiona burst into the room, and she seemed quite irritated that I was there. I—I thought she was angry with me. She was speaking in Sinhala, you see, she often does when she's upset, and so I couldn't understand what was going on. And when they called a meeting and asked me to stay downstairs, I—well, I thought they were talking about sending me back or something.

EP: Quite an overreaction to you checking your email, don't you think?

LAT: Well, like I said, I had no clue what was going on because I couldn't understand what she was saying.

EP: And you were on the phone, afterward. May I ask with who?

LAT: [Pause] I don't know what you mean.

EP: One of the houseguests said she heard you on the phone. Her room was quite close by and she had her door open, she said.

LAT: Was it Aunty what's her name? Aunty Geetha? She's always snooping around.

EP: Do you remember who you called?

LAT: No. No, I don't.

EP: It was only three days ago. Would you mind checking your call history now?

LAT: [Pause] I—I suppose I could.

[Pause]

It was—just my father, see?

EP: Tell us about your father. I'm to understand he does business with the Fonsekas, am I right?

LAT: Yes, they've been friends for many years and he has invested in Fonseka Jewellers as well.

EP: Look, Miss Thompson, time is very valuable right now, and we need to get to the point. Do you know the penalty of impeding an investigation?

LAT: Um, well—

EP: It could easily lead to imprisonment, Miss Thompson. So I want you to be very honest with me, understand?

LAT: I—I don't—

EP: Because I don't think, for a moment, that you'd like to spend time in a Sri Lankan prison.

LAT: [Pause] Look, I didn't want to, okay? It was all my dad's fault. It's him. He made me do it.

EP: Please explain.

LAT: My father thought, and I guess he is right to think, that, well, the Fonsekas are broke. Completely and totally broke. The gem business hasn't been doing well for a while, and now they're opening another store and none of it makes any sense. It's just about keeping up appearances in Colombo. He sent me here to try and gather as much information as I could so he could sue them for falsifying their accounts. They've been dipping into company money for years, and now with the wedding— oh gosh, that was all I was doing. I didn't want to snoop in the first place; you have to believe me. I love Kaavi. I didn't want to backstab her. But Daddy, well, he insisted.

That day Aunty Fiona walked in, I was actually trying to download some of the company accounts, and I thought they'd found me out for sure. That they were going to hand me over to the authorities or something like that. I was scared out of my mind.

But that's all it was. My father suspected that Uncle Nihal wasn't being honest with him. He was upset, yes, but none of us ever had anything against Kaavi. I told you, I adore her.

14

AMAYA

Two Days before the Wedding

I WAS RIDICULOUS for thinking I could get even a second of face time with Kaavi the whole evening. I gave it a few minutes before I made my way to the terrace so that she wouldn't realize I'd been in the bathroom the same time as her, but while I was away the party had burst into full swing. I had been to weddings in the US that were smaller affairs than this bridal shower.

There was plenty of pink champagne, lobster, caviar bites, and white chocolate–covered strawberries topped with gold foil being passed around, while everyone squabbled over who would get to take photos with the bride-to-be.

There was a manicure station, a hand-rolled chocolate truffles station, a tarot card reading station, and a temporary tattoo station, where a frantic-looking young woman was offering a choice between rose gold Team Bride or Bride Squad tattoos.

Women in various shades of ivory and nude and dull gold milled about, looking like they were having the time of their lives. As always, I felt insignificant. A scrap of used tissue just floating around that no one even noticed.

Mrs. Fonseka was front and center of the action, probably demanding more attention than the bride herself. I stayed out of her line of sight but needn't have worried. She had plenty more important things that required her consideration.

"What's this?" She was berating a young waiter who looked like he wanted to shrivel up and die. "Please make sure all the champagne flutes are properly polished. You'd never see this kind of thing at the Hilton, you know."

"Yes, madam. Right away." The poor man scampered off while Mrs. Fonseka turned and had a hearty laugh with the aunty standing next to her, her mood switching in the blink of an eye. I had to hand it to her: she really was the original queen of putting on a show for her fans.

"Shall we take the family pictures, madam, before the sun sets and the lighting gets weak?" a man with three cameras slung around his neck and shoulders asked.

"Now? My goodness, I suppose so. You know, I really hate having my picture taken," she announced to everyone around her before stalking toward the wall of off-white roses that had been set up as a photo backdrop.

"Kaavi, where are you? It's time for family photos, it seems."

Kaavi took much longer to make it to her mother, during which time Mrs. Fonseka posed, hand on hip for a few individual shots of her own.

I was too far away now to hear what the two women discussed, but Kaavi's smile looked strained and Mrs. Fonseka kept a good foot between the two of them, despite the photographer encouraging them to wrap their arms around each other. Two shots in and

Mrs. Fonseka beckoned for Tehani to join them. Nadia had been left at home, and was it just me, or could the tension between the three of them be cut by a knife? I supposed they hadn't really recovered from their "family meeting" yesterday after all.

I spent most of the party tucked away in a corner, watching what was posted on Instagram. The tags were already rolling in when I logged on. I had to hand it to these girls: they had mad editing skills.

I saw a woman whose blouse pinched and rolled over her sides—obviously two sizes too small—post a flawless picture of herself looking like she just stepped off a runway.

There was a group of girls taking the same Boomerang of them clinking their champagne flutes for what felt like the twentieth time. I wonder whether you could break off the base of a champagne flute and use it to stab someone?

There were pictures of the food, pictures of Kaavi, and about a million different selfies.

You are stunning xx, I posted from IllegallyBlonde99.

Girl <3 Your dress!! from KimKx.

Congratulations! You're going to be the most gorgeous bride ever x from LVSpeedy45.

This was ridiculous. I was being ridiculous. I got up, meaning to walk around a little—perhaps seek out some of the women I'd met at the cocktail party, but after a few minutes of aimlessly flailing around, I figured I'd just head back into the bathroom for a minute.

I still had my phone out and pretended to be texting while I walked so I wouldn't have to make eye contact with anyone, so his voice was a hard punch to the stomach when I heard it.

"Hello, stranger."

I dropped my phone.

"Um, hi," I mumbled, carefully bending down to pick it up. "I didn't think you'd be at the bridal shower."

Spencer gave me his million-dollar smile. "You got me." His voice was low. My heart pounded.

"Excuse me?"

"You got me. I was just trying to sneak a peek at what was going on down here. I got bored, sitting alone in my room." His smile shifted lightly, suggesting something, even though I didn't let myself think of what that something could be.

I was acutely aware of the sweat snaking its way down my back. I couldn't be around him. I didn't trust myself to be around him.

There was only a small tremble to my voice when I started to speak. "I was just heading—"

"I've been thinking about you, you know, since we met the other day."

I was going to throw up. Oh god, I hope he wasn't too attached to the shoes he was wearing because they were about to be ruined.

"Y-you were?"

"Yeah. I wanted to tell you that I was right?"

My body felt cold.

"R-right about w-what, exactly?"

"Well." He reached over and leaned his forearm against the wall, blocking my path. He was too close to me. Dangerously close. I looked around but the corridor was deserted.

"The ending of *Game of Thrones*, of course. I told you from the start, didn't I? That she was bound to lose her mind. It's always the one you suspect the least, after all."

I was holding my breath. My chest hurt.

"Oh. Yeah. I guess you were right, then." I couldn't remember the ending of *Game of Thrones*, or even having this conversation with him. Neither did I care.

I eyed his arm in front of me again. He'd been working out since we'd ended things. I felt light-headed.

"Anyway, it was just a funny thing I remembered about us and, well, you know, the way things were." He removed his arm from the wall and took a step closer to me. Close enough that I could smell his aftershave. It wasn't his usual Polo Blue by Ralph Lauren that I used to buy him, but some other alien scent. It threw me more than his closeness. Maybe even more than this whole wedding. How much of him had changed? The question echoed in my mind yet again. How much had stayed the same?

"I'd better let you go, Ams. Don't want to keep you away from your party."

And he turned and left, leaving me there feeling like I had to piece myself back together all over again. No one has ever had this much power over me. No one ever would; I'd make sure of that.

I leaned against the wall—the same wall that Spencer had casually leaned on just moments ago—and tried to steady my breathing.

"You okay?" It was Tehani this time, impeccably balanced on a pair of the highest, pointiest heels I've ever seen. I plastered on something that resembled a smile.

"Yes, of course. Thank you."

"You look like you've just seen someone die or something."

Not someone. Just me. Just me over and over again.

I forced a little laugh, trying to come up with an excuse. I was about to reply when the tall redhead I had seen at the cocktail party raced past both of us.

"Excuse me, ladies," she called, not looking over as she made her way into the bathroom.

"God, what a bitch." Tehani giggled before turning back to me. "You sure you're all right?"

"You know, I think the champagne went straight to my head."

Tehani rolled her eyes. "It's the Moët, I'm telling you. Always gives me a headache too. I told *Amma* not to be ridiculous and to serve the Veuve instead, or at least some Dom, you know? But they wanted to save the cases for the actual wedding." She sighed dramatically.

I just nodded like I knew what she was talking about, the politics of expensive champagne the last thing on my mind.

"Shall I get you some water or something?"

"I'm fine, really."

"Want to head back inside, then? I have a secret stash of Cristal behind the bar. You should stick to that from now on."

We made it back to the crowd and Tehani dissolved into it while I continued to float around looking very much like I didn't belong.

And then, finally, as the orange sunset faded away into an inky purple sky, Kaavi took the microphone and announced that the crowd was making its way down to the beach for the after-party. She bade a pointed good night to her mother—making it clear that the older generation was not welcome anymore—and then half the party took off their heels and traipsed, already unsteady after the many glasses of bubbly, across the hotel to the old wing.

The Mount Lavinia Hotel famously divided itself into two sections, old and new.

The new wing, where we were on the terrace, faced the ocean off a small cliff. The old wing had access to a flat beach, dotted with huts and open marquees, perfect for beachside events.

I joined the girls who were staggering over to the after-party, though I figured this was a lost cause. I'll just pop my head in, so I could feel like I tried, at least, and call an Uber home. Tomorrow was the Poruwa, which was cutting it super close, but maybe I could catch Kaavi in the morning?

I looked at the time and groaned. 6:43 p.m.

One of the beach huts had been turned into an X-rated dance floor, with inflatable penises hanging from the ceiling. There were squeals and giggles, while a young woman in glasses kept circling the group, reminding everyone to please not take any pictures.

Of course she wouldn't want any photographs. Bachelorette party pictures of young women being inappropriate were notorious for going viral in Sri Lanka, with plenty members of the older generations shaking their heads and sighing that this is why the rate of divorce was going up. Kaavi could hardly risk such a scandal. I looked around the beach at the other huts, but they were all empty except for the large bonfire that burned a safe distance away. Just like the terrace, the entire beach had been booked out too.

"Tequila shot to enter, biatch!" a girl I had never seen before screamed at me, waving a tray in my face, looking like she'd helped herself to her fair share of shots already.

I smiled politely.

"Maybe later? I need to eat something first."

"Boo, such a loserrr."

A loser. My chest felt tight. Here I was again, such a loser. I thought about the girl having one too many tequila shots and drunkenly staggering into the ocean. They'd pull her body out tomorrow, gray and bloated. Unrecognizable. She deserved it.

I turned around and left, unsteady in my shoes over the sand. My heels kept sinking in and I should take them off but there was nowhere to sit and I couldn't breathe and everything was starting to feel like it was all too much.

I had just reached the corridor that led back toward the hotel when I crashed straight into Kaavi. She had her phone out, as usual, and her brow was furrowed.

She smiled when she saw it was me though.

"Ams? You okay? You're not leaving, are you?"

I nodded. Here was my chance. Come on, Amaya, get it over with.

"No, don't go. It's not my mother, right? I swear she's been on everyone's case lately. Don't tell me she snuck down here after I specifically told her not to."

"No, no. I'm just tired." Come on, Amaya, don't wuss out now.

There was no point beating around the bush. I should just throw in the towel and admit it to myself. I'm a loser. A big piece of chickenshit. About as much gumption as a tapeworm. I thought of how I acted around Kaavi, around Spencer, around Mrs. Fonseka, never being able to spell out what was I feeling even when it mattered. All the advice from Dr. Dunn and rehearsed speeches faltered when I actually had to confront someone. That's why speaking to Kaavi about all of this was so hard. Spreading a rumor, no matter how true, and hoping it would catch on enough to stop the wedding, was a coward's plan, and I knew it probably wouldn't work, but you can't blame this tapeworm for trying, right?

Plan B was a lot simpler. So simple that it was actually a braver person's plan A. But then, a braver person also wouldn't check the time whenever they did anything in search of a sign, or be borderline obsessed with her ex–best friend's family and the life she could never have. So yes, I'm not brave, but I'm trying. I had to tell Kaavi the truth. That was all. I had to tell her everything, well, most of everything that happened between me and Spencer and hope that she believed me enough to walk away. That would really be the most ideal situation, right?

"It's not even seven o'clock, Ams. Look, I'll make you a deal, okay? What if you—"

"You can't marry him, Kaavi. I was with him for four years, okay? You can't marry him." The words exploded out of me like a handful of mud being slung against a wall.

I expected Kaavi to be upset. To cry, or demand I leave.

But she just gave me a pitiful smile.

"I knew that's why you showed up here. You're still in love with him, aren't you?"

"You don't understand."

"I should have known. Really. Look, you'd cut me out of your life, okay? I've tried so many times to reach out to you. I wanted to talk to you about it, of course I did. But come on, Ams, after everything we've been through together you just decided to stop speaking to me. And why? Because I tried to help you all those years ago?"

"Help me?" My voice trembled. "You ruined my life!"

"What the hell do you even mean? You're losing your mind, you know that? You've completely lost it. I mean, you just show up here, following me around, completely uninvited—"

"I wasn't. You invited me, Kaavi."

"What the hell do you mean? How the hell could I have invited you when we haven't even spoken in five fucking years?"

"You invited me, Kaavi. You said you wanted me to come. You even lied to me about your parents wanting me here."

"You've lost your goddamned mind. Everyone said it, I just didn't believe them."

My vision was getting blurry. I was shaking like a leaf. My breath came in short gasps. Why was she doing this? Why was she lying to me? This is not the way this conversation was supposed to be going at all. I wanted to tell her the truth. I wanted to tell her what happened. I wanted her to be on my side.

"Kaavi!" I grabbed her arm. "You'll listen to me if you know what's good for you."

She yanked her arm away, her eyes wide.

"Are you threatening me, Amaya? I'll listen to you or what, huh? Or what?"

Her eyes were flashing and her face was red and she had me pushed back against the wall. I could feel her breath on my face, hot and angry. I felt like my knees were about to give way.

"Or what, Amaya? You'll kill me like you killed Gayan Peiris? Huh? Is that what you'd do?"

"Yes!" My voice ricocheted off the empty corridor. "I'll fucking kill you before I let you do this. You hear me?"

Kaavi took a step back like I had slapped her.

"Well, there you go."

I couldn't stop shivering. This was wrong. Everything had come out wrong.

"Kaavi, I—"

"No need to explain. I guess I finally know how you feel about me. Look, this wedding is happening, regardless of who wants it to happen or not. But do yourself, and me, a favor, will you? Stay the fuck away from me. Stay the fuck away from my family. And stay the fuck away from my wedding."

And with that, she turned on her heel and stalked down toward the beach.

I tried to steady myself, but I was shaking all over. I leaned against the wall and tried to take a deep breath. It barely worked. I felt my knees give away as I slid down to the floor.

How dare she? How dare she speak to me like that? How dare she say the cruel things she did? She knew how much it would hurt me. All this time I thought, deep down, that she'd still be my friend. That I couldn't speak to her because she was busy. Because she was preoccupied with the wedding. Because I was a coward. Now I knew she just didn't care. She had nothing to say to me. Of course she didn't— what was there to talk about? As far as she was concerned she got her trophy man. Why would she need me?

Why did she even ask me to come here? Was it to rub it in my face that she had the life that I could never have? Why would she do this to me?

I tried another round of deep breathing.

If the ghost of Lady Lavinia was here tonight, I would surely have scared her away. That's how angry I was.

I could hear footsteps echoing down the corridor. Thank goodness for the wooden floors. I didn't want to be found like this—a collapsed, defeated lump, crying to myself in a deserted corner of a five-star hotel.

Standing up, I dug in my purse for a tissue and wiped my face.

I would walk out of here with my head held high.

I wouldn't let Kaavindi Fonseka tear me down a second time.

Pushing my shoulders back, I walked to the lobby where I could sit down for a moment and call myself a taxi. I saw Mahesh's driver hanging around near the front desk. I briefly wondered why he was there, again, when Mahesh was clearly not invited to the bridal shower, but I didn't feel like making small talk. I kept my face turned away from him. That's when I saw the wedding dress. It was still as ethereally beautiful as it had been at the Fonseka house. I couldn't even bear to look at it.

It had been delivered to the lobby where it now hung, ready to be transported to Kaavi's bridal suite, on a luggage trolley. It looked even more beautiful than I remembered—the lights in the lobby bouncing off the delicate silver threadwork, making the dress look like it was plucked straight out of a fairy tale.

Well, this was not about to be a happy ending.

"*Meka* bridal suite *ekata nedha?*" This is to be delivered to the bridal suite, right? I heard the porter ask.

The idea sizzled in my mind, and I knew I had to act quickly before I lost my nerve.

I turned back around and walked toward the old wing, to where I knew Kaavi's room was. There was only one room that the hotel used as the bridal suite, and I doubt it had changed in years. I moved quickly. The porter would have to take the service route, so he would get there after I did.

I hung around outside Kaavi's empty room for just a minute when I saw him, wheeling the trolley down the corridor.

"*Gowuma nedha?*" That's the dress, isn't it?

"*Owu,* miss." Yes, miss.

"*Ah,* bride *balagena hitiye. Dhan nidagannath gihilla. Mata kivva baara ganna kiyala.*" The bride was waiting for this, but now she's gone to sleep. She asked me to take it in.

I prayed the porter wouldn't ask me why the bride was in bed so early, but then, most Sri Lankan brides start getting dressed at 3:00 a.m. the morning of the wedding, so I supposed it wasn't too suspicious.

"*Ha,* miss. *Ehenam puluwanda methana* sign *ekak dhanne?*" All right, miss. Then would you mind signing right here?

I took the receipt and signed Tehani's name on it. The porter handed the dress over to me, and I made like I was fumbling in my handbag for the keys until he rolled away.

Then, bundling the dress under my arm, I made my way down to the beach.

The crowd was in the hut, from where I could hear squealing and screaming and loud music. They all must be drunk out of their minds now. Good. They were having far too much fun to pay any attention to me.

I kicked off my shoes and made my way down the beach to the bonfire.

You're still in love with him, aren't you? Kaavi's voice rang through me, grating, piercing into my skull. I took a few steps forward, my feet sinking into the sand.

I mean, you just show up here, following me around, completely uninvited. I'll show you uninvited, Kaavi. I'll show you how wrong you were about me.

It's just like her to invite me and then change her mind. To trick me into this shameful position. Lording over me, trying to control me like she did with everyone else.

I took a deep breath, just like Dr. Dunn said. But, then, I'd never really followed his advice before. I was finally doing something. I was finally "getting it done."

You'll kill me like you killed Gayan Peiris? Huh? Is that what you'd do?
I mustn't let myself spiral.

But I was already gone. It was like someone else—a ghost, or a demon—had possessed my body. I wasn't thinking. I was just acting. For the first time in years.

I didn't check the time. I didn't want to know if the signs were bad.
I was finally in front of the bonfire.

Are you threatening me, Amaya? I'll show you threatening, Kaavi. I'll give you just a glimpse of what I'm capable of.

Taking a deep breath, I hurled the dress into the flames.

It lay there, for just a second, glistening in the firelight—a witch, refusing to burn at the stake. It was more beautiful than ever. But then the fire caught. It was sudden, almost explosive, like an eruption. The flames shot up, high against the darkening sky, as I stood there, panting.

A squeal came from inside.

"The bonfire! Look!"

It was time for me to go. It was dark on the beach, and security had been dismissed on account of all the women prepared to behave badly, so I had no problems slinking back inside.

But not before I heard the screams.

"What's that on the fire?"

"Oh my god, what is that?"

"What? Is that a dress?"

I didn't wait to hear more. It was time for me to go home.

I pulled out my phone, almost dropping it as I fumbled to type out my message to Mahesh.

Mahesh, what we talked about. I need it.
Tomorrow.

MAHESH

**Interview Transcript: Don Samaratungage Mahesh
Senadheera (abbrev. DSMS)**

Date: January 25, 2020

Location: The Mount Lavinia Hotel

DSMS: What is this now? I was just told to come down here and
help with some questions. I wasn't told anything about a statement being taken, you know. If that is the case, then I need to
call my lawyer. Is the Officer in Charge here? Tell him that
Mahesh Senadheera is here and wants to speak with him.

[Pause]

Are you actually recording all of this? Don't you have to get my
permission to do that first?

EP: Mr. Senadheera, my apologies. This isn't a police investigation just yet. We are trying to gather as much information as
we can first. This isn't an official statement. We just need to
ask you a few questions.

DSMS: Not official, huh? Okay, I suppose let's get this done
quickly. We are wasting time, you know. We need to find out
what happened to the poor girl, and fast. This is such a shame.

EP: Could you please state your full name and address for the
record?

DSMS: My name is Don Samaratungage Mahesh Senadheera. Address is 902 Lake Drive, Rajagiriya.

EP: Could you please tell us a little bit about your relationship to
Kaavindi Fonseka?

DSMS: My relationship to her? Ha, that's a hell of a how do you
do, no?

[Pause]

Well, if you must know, I have no relationship to her. She was
best friends with one of my relatives, so I've always seen her
around. A bit too much of a big head, if you ask me. Thinks
that just because she's pretty she can have anyone and anything she wants. This is after she went to the US, of course.
Before that she was quite a nice girl. We even had a small, you
know, a small flirtation when we were teenagers, you know
how it is, no, ah? Young love. Anyway, she thinks she's too
good for me now, and I think she's too full of herself, so that's
how it is.

EP: You did meet Miss Fonseka recently, though, didn't you?

DSMS: [Pause] I can't really remember.

EP: Let me remind you. It was in July 2019 at one Mr. Jonathan
Subramaniam's wedding.

DSMS: Ah yes, it was Jona's wedding. Yes, I think I remember her
being there.

EP: And do you remember your conversation with her that
evening?

DSMS: My conversation?

[Pause]

Listen, I had a few too many that night. You know how it is at
weddings, no? Open bar and all. I think I might have said
something to her. I can't remember what.

EP: We have several witness accounts of you calling her—

[Shuffling of papers]

An "uptight bitch."

[Pause]

There were also accounts of her telling you, in no uncertain
terms, to stop stalking her and that she would never sleep with
you. Or were you too inebriated to remember that as well?

DSMS: What the bloody hell is this bullshit? If you have something to ask me, then ask me. Yes, I made a pass at Her Royal
Highness Princess Kaavindi Fonseka while I was drunk at a
wedding. She wasn't as innocent as she made it out to be, you
know. She was a huge tease, always flirting with everyone but
then pretending to be so innocent. Figures she'd finally only
give it up to a *suddha*. She was always too posh for us locals.

Did I call her a bitch? Maybe. So what? She is a bitch.

As for the "stalking"? Please. She's just desperate for attention.
Puts on this fake face for her Instagram page. She's the biggest
hypocrite I've ever met. You should see how she speaks when
there are no cameras around.

EP: Did you maintain a friendship with her sister, Tehani Fonseka?

DSMS: Tehani? No, not really. Though she was easily the better of
the two sisters. A lot more relaxed than Kaavi, for sure.

EP: But you met her last night, at the hotel. I didn't realize you were
attending the wedding. Your name wasn't on the guest list.

DSMS: I wasn't here for the wedding. I was meeting my friends
for a drink at the bar. I knew quite a few of the guys who were
going to the wedding and they were getting a drink on the
beach. Asked me to come too—one of the guys flying down
from Aussie couldn't make it, so there was a free room and
everything. I was on my way down to the bar when I found
Tehani. She wasn't in a good way. Probably had one too many
and passed out right there in the corridor. She'd always had
problems with—you know . . .

[Makes motion of drinking from a bottle]

I helped her to her room. Her mother would have had her neck if
   she had found her that way.

EP: Did you know Mr. Matthew Spencer?

DSMS: I met the chap once or twice. Seems okay for a foreigner.

EP: And did you have any business with him?

DSMS: Business with him? No.

EP: The front desk at the hotel said you came to see him last night.

DSMS: Yes.

EP: But you weren't invited to the wedding?

DSMS: No, but like I said, this is Colombo. Everyone is friends
   with everybody.

EP: Would you mind answering why you met with Mr. Spencer
   last night?

DSMS: [Pause]

EP: Mr. Senadheera, would you—

DSMS: Look, the fellow was a little nervous, okay? Who wouldn't
   be nervous, marrying someone as high-strung as Kaavindi
   Fonseka. One of the boys called me. He wanted a little something to help him relax. I thought I'd help the guy out.

EP: I see. And was this your first time supplying him with . . .
   these relaxants? You didn't have your driver make a delivery to
   the Fonseka's cocktail party on the night of the twenty-first?

DSMS: This was my first time providing it to Matthew Spencer, yes.
   Though I doubt this was his first time calling out for some. Now
   if we are to proceed with this line of questioning about where
   I send my driver, I must warn you that I won't answer without
   the presence of my lawyer. I know how you security fellows
   work, ah. One slip of my tongue and I end up in Welikada.

EP: Understood. Then tell me about your relationship to Miss
   Amaya Bloom?

DSMS: Amaya? No. I mean, she's family. Her mother, Sarita, and my mother were second cousins. My mother was the only one who kept in touch with her after she eloped and married Amaya's father—what was his name now? I can't even remember. He wasn't around for too long. Never officially got divorced but supported them financially. He even bought that massive house for them, you know, the one in Cinnamon Gardens? Turns out he had another family in England all along, so maybe they didn't even need to get divorced. I'm not too sure of the logistics anyway; all I know is that Aunty Sarita's family disowned her and we are the only ones who kept in touch. My mother cried for weeks when Aunty Sarita died. So yes, I've always known Amaya, though we barely kept in touch after she moved to the US. It was almost a surprise to me when she emailed and said she was coming—but then, she and Kaavindi were best friends, so I suppose it isn't such a big deal.

EP: Were you aware of the strained relationship between Miss Amaya and Miss Fonseka?

DSMS: I had heard through the grapevine that they had some issues—you know how these buggers in Colombo are, no? Love to talk. But I didn't think too much of it. They're women, after all. No offense. You know how their moods can be. One moment they love each other, the next they want to kill each other, until they love each other again. I figured it was the same thing with Amaya and Kaavindi.

EP: Did Miss Bloom reach out to you when she visited Sri Lanka five years ago?

DSMS: Five years ago? That was, when, 2013? 2014? We weren't really in touch at that time. I didn't even know she was here until much later.

EP: And when she visited this time?

DSMS: She emailed out of the blue to say she was coming for this wedding, and that she would love to meet up. I did what my mother would have wanted me to do and insisted I pick her up from the airport. She's family, after all. We've spoken a few times since then, of course, but she's been quite busy with wedding activities, from what I gather.

EP: And did she make any requests of you at this time?

DSMS: What do you mean by requests, ah? The hotel manager just told me this was a friendly chat. Trust you buggers to make this into a whole scene.

EP: Mr. Senadheera, we found a notebook with Miss Amaya's personal belongings. Would you like to see what she has written?

DSMS: [Pause]

EP: *Plan C. Buy gun. Speak to M. Worst case only. Kill.*

Would you happen to know who M is, Mahesh?

DSMS: No. I have no idea at all, and you'll be in big trouble if you continue haranguing me like this.

[Stands up and moves toward the door]

If you have any further questions, you can contact my lawyer. This is a hell of a fucking how do you do, no? First you bring up some bullshit that happened at a wedding months ago, and now this? You bastards better get your facts straight before you come pestering me again. Do you know who I am? I can create a fair bit of trouble for you lot if you push my buttons, you know?

Piyadasa, *yamu.* Let's go.

15

AMAYA

Day of the Poruwa Ceremony

I WAS SO upset I couldn't sleep. I paced around my room, trying to take deep breaths, but that hardly worked.

Sacrifice is important, Dr. Dunn had said. *Sacrifice is one of the greatest things we could do to show someone that we love them. There is no purer gift.*

I liked to remind myself of this. Of my sacrifice. How I had given up my best friend, how I had given up my only chance of love and family. How I gave up a literal part of myself. And for what? For Kaavi to marry the man who shattered my world? For it to all be in vain?

How was I supposed to calm down? How was I supposed to relax when everything that was important to me was about to be ruined forever.

I couldn't make Kaavi understand.

So I had to do something else.

Seetha knocked on my door.

"*Baba*, shall I bring you a tea?"

"No, thank you, Seetha. Why are you up so late?"

Her eyes took in the mess in my room, my tearstained face and smudged makeup.

"*Baba*, it's morning. Haven't you gone to sleep yet?"

"I'm fine, Seetha. Don't worry."

"*Baba*, the van will be leaving to the hotel soon. Is it still okay for me to go?"

With everything that was going on, I had forgotten that Seetha was going to the wedding. Apparently, Mrs. Fonseka had asked her to help and she couldn't say no. Why would she? She was probably happy to see Kaavi get married, like any normal person would be.

I checked my watch. 7:47 a.m. I guess it wouldn't be a bad thing if she wasn't around. Maybe today will be a better day.

As if on cue, my phone started to ring.

"Mahesh," I said in way of greeting, turning my back on Seetha and hoping she'd take the hint. I heard my door shut softly but still took care to keep my voice down.

"Amaya *Akki*, can I come to your place now?"

Finally.

Plan C wasn't my favorite plan, but deep in my heart of hearts I knew it would come to this. From the moment I saw the post on Instagram I knew—things had to finally come to an end. People didn't just get to do whatever it was they wanted. There were repercussions for their actions. No matter how delayed.

I splashed some water on my face. My mascara had smudged into giant raccoon eyes, and it wouldn't really wash off. My hair was in tangles. I pulled off my dress from last night and put on a T-shirt and jeans, but they were so rumpled from my suitcase that I looked like even more of a disaster. I didn't care. There was only one thing on my mind now.

I thought about how I felt when I threw Kaavi's wedding dress into the fire. How I finally felt powerful, how I finally felt in control after years. I got lucky with the dress. No one saw me and I doubt I'd get caught. What I was going to do next wouldn't be the same. But it was a price I was willing to pay. I knew that from the moment I heard about the wedding. That I had to stop it. Even if it meant being locked up.

Mahesh was red in the face when he arrived and looked like he'd rather be anywhere else.

"Amaya *Akki*, if you're in some sort of trouble, you would tell me, right? I'm family, you know. I could help you."

I nodded again. I had to lie. There was no way he would ever understand.

"Amaya *Akki*, I—I'm really sorry. I couldn't it get for you."

"What?" My voice came out a little louder than I hoped. How could he do this to me?

"I—it's just. We have a family rifle on the estate, but that's only for use against wild animals on the property. It would raise so many questions if it was found in Colombo. And an untraceable gun is just—look, you know, this isn't America, right? The penalty for a gun without a license is prison—look, it's not that I don't have the connections, but if you were caught, well, I couldn't risk that."

"I can't believe this, Mahesh."

"Please just tell me. Tell me what you need this for."

"I told you. I don't feel safe."

"Safe from whom? Tell me."

But I stayed quiet. I couldn't tell him. I couldn't tell anyone.

"Amaya *Akki*, you don't look well."

"Well, that's what feeling unsafe does to you, okay, Mahesh?" I was snapping but I didn't care. What on earth was I supposed to do now?

"What's making you feel unsafe? I can take care of that. Look, I can ask Piyadasa to come and stay here in the nights, if that's what you're worried about. Or we could easily arrange for some security, or—"

"It's not that, Mahesh. Come on."

"Then what, *Akki*? What? Please tell me? Let me help you."

I sighed. He couldn't help me. I was in this alone.

I had done everything I could to prepare for this. I'd gone to the shooting range, back in LA, and practiced once a week since I made the decision to come down here. I knew I had to be ready for when the time came. But now I had to go off script. I needed a different plan.

"Look, if you need anything else, absolutely anything else at all— anytime, anyplace—you call me, and I'll come. No questions asked, okay? I promise. You call me and I'll be there."

"Okay, Mahesh. Sure." What else was I supposed to say?

He left pretty quickly after that. Thank goodness.

But what in the world was I supposed to do now?

I KNOW THAT Kaavi had disinvited me from the wedding, but she couldn't stop me from being a guest at the hotel. It took about forty-five minutes of being on hold, but I managed to change the reservation for my room—I was booked into the new wing, but I wanted a room in the old one, beachside, on the second floor, so I'd at least have a half-decent view of the Poruwa ceremony that would take place at sunset on the shore. She could tell me not to come, but she couldn't tell me not to watch.

I made sure I kept a low profile while I checked into the hotel. The last thing I needed was to bump into Mrs. Fonseka. I didn't know if she had heard about my fight with Kaavi last night, but I wasn't taking any chances. I declined the services of a bellboy and carried my small suitcase into my room.

The first thing I did when I got in was throw open the balcony doors and go outside. I had a splendid bird's-eye view of the Poruwa itself—the stage, which was already set up. Florists swarmed around it, fussing about with handfuls of flowers. If Mahesh had actually come through, I wondered if I could've just taken a shot from my balcony. That would have been so much easier. Wishful thinking, of course. Life was never that simple. You always had to end up getting down and dirty if you wanted something done. I had brought along a knife from my kitchen. It felt almost comical, smuggling it out here. It was no gun, of course, but maybe it'd still do if I had the element of surprise on my side? Who knew. And here I was sounding like a deranged person straight out of a badly written movie. Hell, I *was* a deranged person, and this movie would probably not even get made.

I sat on the bed and pulled out my phone at 10:10 a.m. I pumped a fist into the air. I'd take any consolation I could get. Kaavi would be getting ready by now. She'd probably be ready hours before the ceremony for the usual two-hour photo shoot. She was on the ground floor, maybe even just below me, and the thought made adrenaline flood my veins. Andre was probably fussing about her, telling her how gorgeous she was. Or maybe he quit in anger after the dress was destroyed. Who knew?

Sure enough, I clicked on her profile to see plenty of behind-the-scenes action on Instagram. Kaavi sipping champagne with her girlfriends. Kaavi beaming while getting her hair done. Kaavi smelling the flowers that would go in her hair.

"Change of plans, my lovelies," she said in a short clip. "Looks like I'll be wearing my Hayley Paige to the church ceremony after all." Trust her to put a positive spin on a destroyed wedding dress.

I laid my head on the cool pillow.

Kaavi giggling at something the makeup artist whispered in her ear.

My head felt heavy. I hadn't slept all night. Maybe I could just close my eyes for a few minutes. There was plenty of time until the ceremony. I set an alarm on my phone, just to be sure.

I fell asleep while watching a video of Kaavi waving into the camera, blowing her viewers a kiss.

TEHANI

Interview Transcript: Tehani Fonseka (abbrev. TF) Part 3 of 3

Date: January 25, 2020

Location: The Mount Lavinia Hotel

TF: Well, I really don't see why you need to ask me more questions. I mean, all the proof is there, right? Why don't you call the police and ask them to arrest this wedding crasher, already?

EP: We will be making arrests in due time, Miss Fonseka. Until then, I'd love to clear just a few things up.

TF: [Pause] Okay, fine.

EP: So you explained to us that your family and Miss Bloom were not on speaking terms. To your knowledge, she and your sister were not on speaking terms, am I correct?

TF: Yeah, that's right. Why are we going over all this again? I thought we weren't focusing on Amaya anymore.

EP: Bear with me. There's something I can't seem to wrap my head around. I've been informed by numerous parties that your family had cut ties with Miss Bloom. If that were the case, then who invited her to the wedding?

TF: [Pause] I don't know.

EP: Are you sure about that, Miss Fonseka?

TF: [Pause]

EP: Miss Fonseka, did you invite Miss Bloom to the wedding?

TF: [Pause]

EP: Miss Fonseka?

TF: No. Of course not.

EP: Miss Fonseka, I'd like to remind you that while we are not the police, you can be in serious trouble for lying during these interviews. The statements we take are as good as a sworn affidavit. You could be arrested for hindering this investigation. Now, let me ask you once more—did you invite Miss Bloom to the wedding?

TF: Okay, look. I thought—well—yes. Yes, I did invite her to the wedding, okay? So what if I did? I didn't . . . Okay, look. I never thought, not in a million years, that she was *serious*. That she'd actually want to harm Kaavi. They were best friends, after all.

EP: Let's backtrack a moment. How did you send her the invitation?

TF: She wouldn't have come if she thought the invitation was from me. And my sister always left her laptop lying around. As you are already aware, I pretty much know all her passwords. It wasn't too difficult to send Amaya an invitation from Kaavi's account.

EP: And why, may I ask, were you motivated to do that?

TF: [Pause] [TF dabs a tissue over her eyes]

EP: Miss Fonseka?

TF: Because my family is full of lying hypocrites, that's why. Especially my father and my holier-than-thou sister. They lord over everyone else, pretending to be so perfect, but they are full of so much bullshit they could fertilize all the paddy fields in the country.

You know my dad is broke, right? Or about as close to it as you can get when you have half of Colombo at your beck and call—no offense. Don't worry, I'm sure you and your security company will still get paid.

But he's pretty much run Fonseka Jewellers into the ground. My poor grandad would turn in his grave . . . but here we are—booking out the entire fucking Mount Lavinia Hotel, paying for my sister to fly to Singapore on a whim just to buy a ridiculously overpriced dress that she'll only wear once.

He was supposed to help me out this year, you know. He'd promised that if I got my business plan together, he'd give me the cash I needed to start my own fashion line. I spent so long on it, you know? Took me ages to source the fabric and find all the suppliers and get the branding just right. I'd networked with all the boutiques in Colombo, and they'd all promised to carry my designs and everything. And then, well, he just goes and has a change of mind. Says that this isn't the right environment for a start-up. Actually has the gall to tell me that no one in their right mind would spend thirty-five thousand rupees on a dress. All the while he's happy to pay for a fucking lobster station at Kaavi's wedding *and* decides to spend money he doesn't have on some bullshit new store just so he could make a big deal about getting Spencer to run it.

I knew if Amaya came back that their bullshit and secrets and lies would be exposed. Everyone might look like they have their shit together, but I know my family. There's so much simmering just below the surface, waiting for a match. Amaya was that match. It would only be a matter of time until my mother blew her fuse. And my father would be exposed as the hypocrite that he is.

EP: And what about Kaavi?

TF: Okay, look, I didn't want her to get hurt. Not like this. I just wanted her exposed. She deserved to be exposed. She's such a fucking fraud. Forget the years she spent belittling and outshining me. Lecturing me and pretending she was better than everyone else. Forget all of that. What kind of friend marries her best friend's ex-boyfriend anyway? There was something seriously fucked-up in her head. And still, *and still*, she'd never be anything but my father's little princess while the rest of us are just forgotten.

EP: Sounds like you have a lot of pent-up anger toward your sister.

TF: Well, duh. Of course. But I didn't hurt her, if that's what you're getting at. I hate her, sure. But my parents would probably set up some sort of shrine for her or something, if she died. She'd be a fucking martyr if she was murdered. If I can't compare to her while she's alive, could you imagine what a disappointment I'd be if she was dead?

No, I just thought, well, Amaya being here will stir up some old feelings. I mean, I knew what Amaya was thinking—she wanted closure. She told me so. That was all she wanted.

EP: When did she tell you this?

TF: [Pause]

EP: Miss Fonseka, could you please elaborate on when Miss Amaya told you that she wanted closure?

TF: Okay, look. This is going to sound fucked-up, but you have to know that I didn't mean any harm. I just—damn, I'm just sick of being left in the dark about everything, okay?

EP: I understand. Please go on.

TF: Well, I always thought there was something strange about Amaya. The way she lurked around my family. The way she hung on to every word my father said but gave my mother and me the cold shoulder. Even though my sister and her were inseparable, I knew something wasn't right.

And then there was that summer, five years ago, when she suddenly showed up in Colombo and stayed with my family. I wasn't here at the time. I took a leave of absence from my university and traveled to India. It wasn't a rehabilitation center, as many here like to call it, you know. I just needed time off to reset and find myself. College in New York was harder than I thought it would be, my grades were slipping, and I'd met this guy . . .

Anyways, I couldn't shake the feeling that something . . . happened. Something bad. I'm sure you've heard the rumors by now—about her and my father. The timing of Nadia's adoption always felt off to me. My parents had never discussed having another child before, much less adopting. And then Amaya just, well, disappeared. Okay, look, don't get me wrong. I was happy she was finally out of our lives. But like I said . . .

It started out as just a way to keep tabs on her at first. I used to check her Facebook and Instagram, just to see what she was up to. To be sure she was keeping her distance from my family. She was hardly on social media though. I couldn't really get a sense of her life. Then I noticed she had shared a post from some support group—Dr. Dunn's, I think. He's some famous podcast motivational speaker. I joined the group, just to check it out. Just to see what she was up to. Turned out she was very active on there. I just lurked, at first.

Okay, look, I don't want you to think I'm some sort of creep. You have to understand. Amaya went from practically living at our house, to being closer than I ever was to Kaavi, to being adored by my father, to suddenly vanishing from our lives. I was just curious. About what happened, about Nadia, about whether she ever planned on coming back.

But then Kaavi announced that she was going to the US for her college reunion. And I wanted to know whether Amaya and she were meeting up. I tried asking Kaavi but she was cagey about it—she never really spoke to me about shit anyway. I wanted Amaya to stay away. She never brought anything but bad news, and things had finally settled down. And so I created a profile, under a different name, and I sent her a message.

EP: I see, and when did you first establish contact with Miss Bloom this way?

TF: Probably around [Pause] I think it was around August, the year before last.

EP: So that was about one and a half years ago. And what was the nature of these messages?

TF: Nothing damaging. Nothing wrong. I just befriended her. Of course, I couldn't tell her who I really was, you know. She'd never have spoken to me, not honestly anyway. I just wanted to make sure she was still in LA, not San Francisco, where my sister was going for this bullshit reunion. Kaavi tries to be tough, but I know their friendship broke her heart, even though I never learned what happened. That was probably why she was going to the reunion to begin with—to try and speak to Amaya.

And then, my online friendship with Amaya, well, it just got out of control. She was suddenly messaging me at all hours, confiding in me, trusting me. I thought it would be a good idea to keep the conversation open. Just so I could try to learn more. About what happened.

EP: And all this time she thought you were someone else?

TF: Yes, she still does. She thinks my name is Beth, a call center associate from Milwaukee with a history of drug abuse.

16

AMAYA

Day of the Poruwa Ceremony

I WOKE UP to a text from Beth.

How are you holding up?

I didn't feel like responding. How *was* I holding up? I wasn't holding up at all. I was barely holding on. But I didn't feel like talking to anyone right now, because I couldn't face being honest. Not that I had to face Beth at all. Not that I ever had to truly face Beth, if I didn't want to, even though she was easily my closest friend.

In an age where we buy our groceries online and meet romantic partners online and do our banking online, why are online friendships considered any less valuable than real-life ones? So what if I've never met Beth in person? Why is the physical act of meeting considered such a big deal when you can literally grow up next to someone and not know them at all?

Why is Beth a less valid friend than Kaavi? Is it because we've never met?

Maybe that's something to unpack about me. Maybe if Dr. Dunn was my real-life therapist, and not just a podcast life coach, he'd think it was worth exploring. Why do I feel more comfortable around Beth, whom I have never met, and Alexander, whom I have only met under very specific circumstances, and Dr. Dunn, who honestly feels like he's just talking to me and me alone? Tell me, please, how that's less real than the relationship I had with Spencer, who left me in shambles, or my friendship with Kaavi that hurt beyond words?

The truth is that it's so much easier to develop relationships with people when there are healthy boundaries between us. When there's enough space. It keeps us from giving more of ourselves than we bargained for. It keeps us safe.

THE PORUWA CEREMONY was all about auspicious times, so I'd set my alarm to 3:45 p.m. even though there was no way I could get unlucky about this. I turned the chair on my balcony to face the crowd that had gathered on the beach and got myself a cup of tea. I didn't have to wait long.

Usually, the groom enters first with his family, accompanied by traditional drummers in turbans. Spencer had no family with him in Colombo, so the Fonsekas had him ride in on an elephant instead.

Yes. An actual, honest-to-goodness elephant.

The government had banned this years ago, and animal rights groups would have a field day if they got wind of it, but the one constant in Colombo is that the rules don't apply to you if you're rich and powerful.

The wedding guests cheered and clapped as Spencer was led toward the stage, where he disembarked with some difficulty. It wouldn't have been an easy task in regular clothes, but of course

Spencer was wearing the traditional Kandyan *Nilame* outfit, to match Kaavi's Kandyan *Osariya*. You would normally have to be from Kandy to wear this, but then, it's not like there was anything normal about this wedding. Spencer had gone all out—wearing the awkward crown-shaped hat, the jacket with the unnaturally puffed sleeves, and the sarong that was cinched in a bundle at his waist. He was adorned in the same white and rose gold threadwork and sparkles that mimicked Kaavi's, and he even carried a sword.

The drums started up again, and I could tell that Kaavi was walking in with her parents. In Sri Lankan culture, it's typical for both parents to accompany their child to the Poruwa, and Kaavi was no different. I was glad I'd seen enough of her Instagram to know how she looked, because I didn't have binoculars and the balcony view was not doing me any favors. I longed to see her up close—maybe I still could, later.

I could see Spencer smile as Kaavi was led up to him, and they were asked to climb onto the stage with their right foot first. They greeted each other with their palms held together, and when Kaavi smiled at him, it was like the clouds had parted and the sun shone through. Mr. Fonseka took Kaavi's hand and placed it on top of Spencer's—the symbolic handing over.

The familiar feeling of wanting to throw up took root in my throat, and I had to look away, blinking back tears. I couldn't believe this. I never in a million years imagined that this would happen to me. How could he do this? How could she?

I tried to take a sip of my tea, but it had gone cold. I went inside and dumped it in the sink, my hands trembling so much the cup almost crashed down on the counter.

When I returned, they had finished dropping the seven sheaves of betel leaves onto the Poruwa, and Spencer was standing behind Kaavi, attempting to clasp a necklace on her. Kaavi giggled a little at

Spencer's fumbling, and a few guests clapped, cheering Spencer on. They were shushed quickly—it would have been a bad omen if he didn't succeed. The thought cheered me up a little, but it took him a few tries and he finally got it. The necklace was gold—I could see it glinting even from where I was. Of course rose gold or even white gold wouldn't do. It didn't hold its value like real gold did, and besides, it could be mistaken for copper or silver or some other metal, and that simply wouldn't do in Colombo, regardless of Kaavi's usual aesthetic.

A man I didn't know, I'm guessing an uncle of Kaavi's, climbed onto the Poruwa and started to tie their little fingers together with a gold thread. In Sinhala, the term for marriage is *bandinawa*, which means, literally, "to tie." We well and truly believe in tying the knot, in every sense of the word, even if the knot is more of a noose. The uncle poured blessed water over their fingers and climbed off the stage.

Six girls dressed in white *lama saris*—the traditional Sri Lankan outfit of a white skirt and frilly blouse specifically worn by young girls—came before the Poruwa and started to sing *Jayamangala Gatha*, a Buddhist chant meant to bless the marriage. But it was in vain. I don't care what it took: there wouldn't be any blessings here.

There was more to do. There were coconuts to be smashed and lamps to be lit and parents to be worshipped—but I couldn't take it anymore.

Weddings were supposed to bring joy, but this one brought nothing but misery.

I took one last look at Spencer before I went back inside.

I've always tried my best not to think about her. To let her go. To let her live her life. But I've known, from the moment I heard about this wedding, that it could only be about her.

Nadia, this was all for you. So I could at least try to give you the life you deserve.

FIONA FONSEKA

Interview Transcript: Fiona Fonseka (abbrev. FF)

Date: January 25, 2020

Location: The Mount Lavinia Hotel

EP: Thank you for coming up, Mrs. Fonseka. I understand that this is a difficult time for you. I promise to make this as quick as possible. Could you please state your name and address so we can get started?

FF: As you already know, my name is Fiona Fonseka. I am the mother of Kaavindi Fonseka.

EP: And your address, please?

FF: [Sighs]

[Pause]

EP: Mrs. Fonseka?

FF: Are all these formalities important at a time like this?

EP: I just need it for the record, ma'am. I apologize.

FF: My husband is paying for this entire private investigation, Eshanya, and here I am, being treated like a criminal when there's a killer on the loose.

EP: I can assure you, ma'am, that this is just routine questioning and that we are just trying to get as clear a picture as possible about what happened to your daughter.

FF: [Pause] Fine. My address is 28 Maitland Crescent, Colombo 07. Is that enough?

EP: Perfect. Thank you. Would you mind telling us about the days leading up to the wedding? Did anything appear unusual?

FF: Well, we don't have weddings like this every day, you know. Everything was unusual. I wouldn't have settled for anything less.

EP: Let me phrase it this way—was there anyone unusual you saw who might have posed a threat? Anyone who wasn't supposed to be there?

FF: You already know that there was. Actually, there were two people who had no place being there. Honestly, I don't know why we are wasting so much time when you should be investigating them instead.

EP: Could you name them for the record, please?

FF: Well, the first, I believe, was mentioned by my daughter. Some strange man who showed up at the hotel brandishing a gun. A gun, could you believe it? And yet, here I am, answering questions like some sort of criminal.

EP: The hotel security claimed they did not find a gun.

FF: Well, I saw it with my own two eyes, so I have no idea how incompetent those buffoons are.

EP: We still haven't managed to ID this man. Are you sure you have no leads on who he could be?

FF: Look, it's no small wonder that there are people jealous of my family. It could have been anyone.

EP: And who was the other person?

FF: Excuse me?

EP: The other person you said had no place being at the wedding.

FF: I can't believe you even have to ask.

EP: Mrs. Fonseka, I assure you, we are doing a thorough investigation. I just need you to state for the record—

FF: Amaya Bloom wasn't supposed to be there. Did you catch that for your record?

EP: Why was she not supposed to be there?

FF: Kaavindi claimed to have invited her when she first got here, but I don't buy that for a moment. Kaavindi was like that, you know, always taking on charity cases. But she was not supposed to be there because Amaya had promised not to be there. Not now. Not ever. We made a deal, five years ago, that she was to stay away from my daughter, and my entire family.

EP: Could you please elaborate on this deal a little further?

FF: I suppose I don't have a choice, now do I? Amaya has always been in and out of our house since she was a child. I wasn't very happy with Kaavindi mingling with her, you know, given her family background. But my husband, as always, took pity on the girl and welcomed her into our family against my judgment. Look how that has turned out today, hmm?

Amaya was always getting into trouble. Boys especially. You name it. My husband had to step in when she had an affair with her teacher at school—he tried to keep the details quiet from me. Then there was that business with the boy who crashed his car. But this time, well, this time she went too far. She preyed on my husband's kindness is what it was.

She turned up one day on our doorstep—we didn't even know that she was back in Colombo, for goodness' sake. She was supposed to be with Kaavindi in the States. Kaavi was about to start her internship at J.P. Morgan at the time. Anyway, Amaya gave us some excuse about her getting over a bad relationship or something. I know the kind of girl she was. Probably ran off with some foreign man, just like her mother. At least her mother had the sense to get married first.

But my husband took pity on her, as always, and told her to stay with us.

We told everyone that there was a break-in at her house, and that
she was staying with us because she was scared—we couldn't
have the Colombo gossips digging into these matters, no?
Well, thank goodness we had enough sense to make that excuse, because what happened next was truly the height of
madness.

I still can't believe she tried to hide it. What did she think would
happen? That if she ignored things her problems would just go
away? I realized that she was pregnant first, you know. Vomiting at all ridiculous hours. It was such a task to have the tests
done discreetly, but it confirmed my worst suspicions. And
then we had to go through so much to keep the whole thing
quiet. We even had to sack one of our maids who was trying
to be too familiar and asked too many questions.

I thought that she would choose to have an abortion, like most
girls in her position, but she was too far along by then. It's hard
enough to find a doctor to do the procedure in Colombo, but
none of them would take the risk of losing a patient's life. They
would be taken in by the authorities in no time. We ended up
hiring a midwife and having a home birth, right in my husband's office, if you could believe it. So many rooms in our
house and that's the only one that's soundproof.

And of course my husband insisted. Decided that we would take
in the baby. But I had had enough. Don't get me wrong—I
adore little Nadia. She is sweet and kind and obedient, unlike
either of her two elder sisters and certainly unlike her mother.
But I had enough of Amaya and her conniving ways. The
agreement was that we would take in her daughter and raise
her as our own—despite my initial reservations and despite
what it made us look like in society—but Amaya was to keep

away. She was never to contact us, or Kaavindi, again. She agreed. What other choice did she have but to accept our generosity? She could barely take care of herself, much less a child.

EP: Mrs. Fonseka, this, well, this is quite a delicate question, and I apologize for having to ask it. Were you aware of who Nadia's father was?

FF: *Hmph*—if you're really serious about this investigation, my dear, you should probably have the guts to come out and say what you really mean. You're asking, not delicately at all, I might add, whether the rumors are true. Whether my husband is Nadia's father, am I right?

EP: I apologize, Mrs. Fonseka. We are just trying to establish a motive. A possible cause for—

FF: Well, establish this, my dear. My husband is a typical man. I'm sure he has his indiscretions. But his main fault is being too soft. Listens to his children and tries to be their friend without telling them what to do. Look at where that has led us? Children don't need friends. They have plenty of friends. What they do need is someone to look out for them. To make sure that they don't make decisions they regret. To live a life they would be proud to show to society.

We don't know who Nadia's father is. Neither do we care. It was probably one of the many men she no doubt had affairs with in the US.

17

AMAYA

The Night before the Wedding

WE'VE ALREADY ESTABLISHED that I was a wuss, right? That I was happy to float through life having decisions made for me. To have friends who would decide where I went and what kind of social life I would have, to have a lover who would tell me everything he wanted me to do in bed. I was happy to give up control. I've fought before. And it damn near killed me.

They say that what doesn't kill you only makes you stronger. I say that's a lie. What doesn't kill you can sometimes leave you paralyzed. That's what happened to me.

I wish I had died. It's coming close to six years now, and there are times I feel my mind forgets, but my body does not. And so I look for signs. To tell me that things would be okay.

Because we have so little control over what happens to us anyway, why shouldn't we search for signs? For something to help us along. For something, anything, to help me along.

But here I am, about to do something that is very much in my control. I don't want it to be in my control. I'm scared out of my mind. I can't believe this is what I've turned into. More than five years of happily giving over control and now I'm trying to wrestle it back in the worst way possible.

I pulled out the knife and looked it over. It was sharp. I'd made sure of that.

There was no point overthinking this. I shoved the knife back in my bag and checked the time. 9:58 p.m. I waited till 10:10 p.m. just to be sure. I needed all the luck I could get.

I had to be extra careful to make sure my footsteps didn't echo on the wooden floor. The old wing was usually not very busy. Most guests prefer to book a room in the newer section, with the larger bathrooms and more modern trimmings.

I hesitated at the bottom of the staircase. I knew the direction I was supposed to go. I knew what I had to do.

But still, something held me back.

Of course something held me back. This was ridiculous. I was going to do something ridiculous. I would be caught. Arrested.

There was a flight ticket, printed and stored safely away with my passport back at my house. I just needed to lie low afterward. The sooner I got on that plane back to the US the better.

I turned to my left, took a few steps, and paused. There was one last thing I could do.

Then I turned around and walked all the way down to room 112, where I knew Kaavi was staying. The only one in the entire wedding party in the old wing. She would be alone. I tried to think about that, and not how her room number just missed the mark on being lucky. I hoped it wasn't a sign of things to come.

It felt like I was sleepwalking. Like my body moved on its own, without me controlling it.

I reached up and knocked on her door.

"Just a minute," she called out.

I reached into my bag and felt for my knife. It was still there. Of course it was still there.

I took a deep breath. Held it.

1. 2. 3. 4—

The door swung open.

"Look, now really isn't a good time." She was frowning, still in her sari jacket that she was tugging at.

She started to close the door on me, but I pushed my knee up against it.

"Hey, look—"

But I shoved her and made my way inside, pulling the door shut behind me.

Here it is. My last chance.

18

KAAVI
Three Months before the Wedding

THERE'S THAT HORRIBLE clichéd saying that they use in books and in movies—about your life flashing before your eyes just before you die. Well, clichéd or not, that's pretty much what happened to me onstage, with Spencer down on one knee presenting me with one of the ugliest rings I've seen in my life.

I should have known that today would end up being a fucking dumpster fire. First, my usual hairdresser, the one I booked for all my blowouts because he was the only one who could do my "not try-ing too hard" waves just right, called in to say he was "sick." Oh please, like I didn't follow him on Instagram and know he was out partying the night before at some politician's fiftieth birthday party. Even hungover, he would have been better than his less-than-subpar colleague who did such a piss-poor job that I spent an extra hour get-ting my hair swept into an updo instead.

I'd just made it home and was setting up my ring light to make a quick video about my makeup "look" for the evening when my mother rang my cell phone. Yes, that's right, she called my phone when she was just downstairs. She only did this when we had company and she didn't want to yell in the house like she normally did.

"Kaavindi, hi, you're back from the salon, no?" I knew from her put-on, honey-drenched voice that this wasn't going to be good.

"Aunty Rasika and Uncle Laal have dropped in for tea. Why don't you come down and say hello?" Making the call in front of our visitors ensured I wouldn't refuse. She could have just texted me, of course, which she did right after hanging up to tell me to wear the floral Karen Millen dress I'd had delivered from London last week.

It was a trap, and I knew it even before I went downstairs to be introduced to Aunty Rasika's sister's son, an investment banker from New York named Ashwin, who was down in Sri Lanka for "a holiday." Yeah right, he was on the prowl for a bride if I ever saw it.

Not that there was anything particularly wrong with Ashwin, if you disregarded the fact that he had about as much personality as a soggy piece of *papadam*. He was wealthy, as was evident from the designer clothes he was sweating through, and from a reputable family. His father exported seafood, and his uncle was a minister, I was told, emphatically. But if I wanted boring, wealthy, and well-connected, well, I could have had my pick from the never-ending parade of sons and nephews of my parents' friends that have been buzzing around from the moment I graduated college.

"Kaavindi, you know you can't keep doing this," my mother warned, after I spent a good hour being charmingly polite to Aunty Rasika and Uncle Laal, and appropriately aloof to the nephew, whose name I was already forgetting. They had eventually left, and I had to get ready for my event, even though this visit meant I wouldn't have time to shoot my video now.

"Doing what, *Amma*?" I asked, innocently.

"You know what! Why are you like this, *aney*? You know what your horoscope says! You have to get married before next February or you'll never get married at all! If Saturn enters your house, then everything is finished."

Given half a chance my mother would schedule her bathroom visits according to her astrologer's calendar. The threat of Saturn hovering over my house (whatever the hell that even means) has been her worst nightmare for as long as I could remember, but it had never been a problem for me until now. Besides, I was pissed. Today was supposed to be about me and everything I've accomplished. Not about a fucking marriage proposal.

"Are you serious, *Amma*?" My voice was a hiss, just in case anyone else was around. In a house as large as ours, you never knew who might be listening in. "You know what a big night it is for me and you choose today of all days to bring him here? Have you lost your mind?"

"Don't be ridiculous. Your hair and makeup were already done, so why waste the opportunity? Although I don't know why you decided to put your hair up like that. It ages you. Why didn't you get a blow-dry instead?"

I WAS ALREADY late when we pulled up to the auditorium, so I didn't pay attention to the directions I had been given and made my way backstage instead of to my seat, and had to be ushered to the right place by a young intern who kept telling me that I was an inspiration and wanted to take a million fucking selfies with me. I mean, it's not bad press; I just wasn't in the mood. Besides, I hate it when someone takes a selfie on their phone instead of mine—there was no way I could tweak it to make it look right before it got posted.

Thank god everything seemed to settle down from there. I took my seat and listened to the glowing introduction of me and my charity. It wasn't easy, you know. Setting up a foundation like this was hard work. I had to practically beg my dad for the money and space to get started, and even then he only agreed if Pink Sapphires was a branch of Fonseka Jewellers, and not its own separate entity. I suppose he was right—I mean, it was a huge tax write-off.

Thanks to all my hard work, Pink Sapphires was finally starting to take off. We've been providing so many opportunities for these young women to take control of their lives. It really has been rewarding, seeing it grow from a tiny operation to winning national-level awards in just a little over a year. The SheGives-Lanka Woman of the Year award was such a big deal. Fonseka Jewellers had to buy out so much advertising space from the chair's husband's newspaper just to secure it. It really was such an exhausting negotiation.

Anyway, all this talk about how I'm improving young women's lives was really helping my image. I mean, it was worth the long hours and the small talk for the free press alone. I'd been on five different magazine covers since we launched, and the writers at *Hi!!* followed me around like puppies whenever they saw me at an event. It's really helped my social media platform, too, and the brand endorsements have made a significant contribution to my little piggy bank.

And it's not like I didn't have a love life, though it obviously wasn't to my mother's taste. I was just not looking for anything serious right now. I'd hop on Tinder for a quick fuck whenever I traveled overseas; I mean, I *am* a feminist, after all, and it was usually enough to keep me going. I only had one rule—no one ever in Colombo. No one who even has a friend who's Sri Lankan. All you have to do in this godforsaken town is fart before the entire west coast thinks you have diarrhea. Not a chance I was willing to take.

My reputation was my moneymaker. The golden girl of Cinnamon Gardens. And boy, did I have them wrapped around my little finger. Until, of course, Spencer decided to get down on one knee and complicate things.

19

KAAVI

Three Months before the Wedding

"THANK YOU. YES, Aunty, of course I'll give your niece a call about the flower arrangements. My congratulations to her for starting her own business. Please give my love to uncle also." My jaw ached from the smile I didn't dare let myself drop. It's been an hour since the proposal. Didn't these people have lives to get back to? Why wouldn't they stop congratulating me?

I snuck a glance over to Spencer, who was shaking the hand of an older gentleman, also showering Spencer with his good wishes. Spence hadn't moved from my side since the proposal, but we haven't had a moment alone either.

After what felt like a lifetime, the aunties and the uncles and everyone else shuffled away, and Spencer leaned over.

"I've booked a private dining room at the Hilton for dinner. Shall we?"

I nodded. The sooner we could get away from this circus, the better. And it was a smart move, booking somewhere neutral for us to talk. Because Spencer sure had a lot of explaining to do.

He didn't have a Sri Lankan license, and I rode with my parents on the way here, so we couldn't speak freely on the chauffeured drive over to the Hilton. Thank goodness it was only a few minutes. As soon as we were seated and our glasses were filled with my favorite full-bodied merlot that Spencer had obviously preordered, I fixed him with my iciest glare.

"You cornered me into that, Spence. What the fuck?" He knew I'd never be able to turn down such a public proposal without my reputation taking a serious nosedive. Not when I'd stupidly spent so much of my speech gushing about what a wonderful man he was.

"Okay, I know you must be upset with me, but please hear me out first?"

"Go on, then." The damage was done. The best he could do was make sense of it to me.

He must have spoken for about an hour while my mood went from *okay, I guess that makes sense,* to *what the fuck is wrong with him?* and back again. We'd finished our starters and our mains by the time he paused to take a look at me, and as far as I could make out, his argument was starting to make sense.

It pretty much boiled down to this—I needed to get married. I was in my late twenties, hurtling toward middle age by Sri Lankan standards, with no sign of settling down. Yes, I know that Western media made it seem like we women had a choice. That we didn't need a man to complete ourselves. That we were strong, independent, and could do it all on our own. Those advocates didn't know what it was like over here, where I'm often treated like my dad's secretary by his colleagues, and can't even make a police entry without being asked why I'm unaccompanied. And while being a woman in Sri Lanka sucked for a plethora of reasons, tipping over "marriageable age" with no potential groom in sight was a real disaster. It wasn't just my mother who reminded me every waking moment. There were family friends, aunties, and even professionals at business meetings who brought it up. And it would be all well and good to say *screw it* and stay single, like my more liberal friends have started doing, but their businesses and livelihoods weren't staked on their reputations, after all.

Besides, as Spencer reminded me, it's not that I just *needed* to get married. It made practical business sense *to want* to get married. It would give me stacks of content for my influencer platforms, it would make me some significant bucks in endorsements, and it would give confidence to my old-fashioned charity donors who thought it unseemly that a woman stayed single past the age of twenty-two.

That bit made sense. Yes, it was indeed a good move to get married. But why Spencer? We weren't even dating. Hell, we'd only even gotten back in touch a year ago. I flew to the Bay Area for our college reunion and there he was. I don't think I ever even had a proper conversation with him till then. He'd always just been my best friend's boyfriend. I think even I was a bit surprised at how much he'd grown up. At how much we'd hit it off, now that Amaya wasn't in either of our pictures. He's been a huge supporter of my charity—that part of my speech wasn't bullshit—and we've built what I've come to think of as a relatively honest friendship, but apart from the occasional drunken stumble into bed after too many gin and tonics, I hadn't really thought about him as marriage material. If getting married was such a good idea, I could easily take my pick from the mindless, soulless procession of men who were already at my disposal.

I had to hand it to him, though—unlike anyone else, especially my mother's proposals, Spencer did seem to understand what my biggest fear was. All this time, I didn't hold off on getting married because I hadn't found love. I'm mature enough to know that love plays a very tiny part in building a life together, like my parents have. I didn't want to get married because I didn't want to lose the life I had.

I mean, unmarried-woman problems aside, I'd be an idiot not to appreciate the setup I have going for me. I was my own boss (I mean, I know my father kept up pretenses, but let's face it, I had a free hand to do as I liked with my charity), I could travel, I wasn't burdened with any of the mundane family duties that my married friends had thrust on them.

Spencer presented marriage to me in a way that made sense. It was an agreement. I could keep doing whatever I wanted, with no threat to my lifestyle or career. He wouldn't be possessive and lock me up in an ivory tower like most Sri Lankan men would, he wouldn't make demands of me to have children (we'd have to do that at some point for the sake of appearances, I supposed, but we'll cross that bridge later), he wouldn't need me to do anything except what I wanted to do.

And he would get what he always wanted. A family. More specifically, mine.

I knew he had it rough after his parents died, even though he had been provided for, but he was probably not as smart as I thought if he believed the Fonsekas were as picture-book perfect as we made ourselves out to be. But hey, it was his funeral.

He loved Sri Lanka, he claimed, and that was easy to understand. Sri Lanka was the perfect place to live if you had enough money to spend. A five-star lifestyle for a fraction of the price you would pay in the US. A four-course meal like the one we were having tonight would cost as much as a monthly salary for the average Sri Lankan, but was still less than a round of appetizers at the Hilton in Union Square.

He wanted to set up a base, he said. Lay down roots. Start over.

And what better way to start over than as my husband, in a city where my family was equal to royalty. That was a good deal if I ever heard one. There have been marriages that took place for far less.

We'd just have to keep the pesky little detail that he was Amaya's ex-boyfriend under wraps. She's pretty much vanished from Colombo society, but it still wouldn't be a good look for me at all.

"I'm sorry I caught you off guard; I truly am." His eyes glittered in earnest. "But I know you. If I'd spoken to you about it beforehand, you would have overthought it and come up with a million reasons why you shouldn't go through with it. You'd have thought I was crazy." He was right. I was still not convinced this whole thing wasn't absolutely ridiculous.

"But the most important thing, Kaavs, is that I get you. I know this is right. And I'm willing to spend the rest of my life proving to you that this is the best decision you've made."

I thought about my mother and the countless proposals she will continue to bombard me with in the months to come. I thought about the mileage I would get from marrying a handsome, wealthy American man with his own company in San Francisco. I thought about the opportunity to curate my life into something that would really work for me.

"Okay," I said, finally, after we had finished dessert and had started on our coffee. "Okay, let's give it a shot."

I could always get rid of him if it didn't work out.

20

KAAVI

Two Months before the Wedding

I HAD EXPECTED at least a little pushback from my parents about Spencer's proposal, but I supposed they had been more concerned about my approaching spinsterhood than they let on, because they welcomed him into the family with open arms.

"If he's the reason why you turned down all those other boys, then why didn't you say something?" my mother asked, as she flung her arms around me for the first time in years. Not even a hum about the fact that he's not a Sinhala Buddhist, one of the key, overwhelmingly racist, traits that were stressed during those teatime drop-ins.

It turned out that Spencer knew how to play his cards a little better than I thought. He'd visited Sri Lanka twice before he proposed—to consult on the setup of Pink Sapphires, he had said—and he'd spent a significant portion of that time getting to know my family. I'd barely paid attention as he had conversations with my father about setting up a business, and complimented his way into my mother's good graces. He'd dropped enough hints about being in love with me that my father had started to take pity on him. Even

Tehani liked him enough to help him plan the whole proposal and convince me to invite him up onstage, which was truly a revelation.

The next few days were well and truly a blur. There were announcements to be made, social media to be updated, photographs to be taken (very important, given how Spencer and I didn't even have a single photograph together to begin with), and of course, I had to put in a rush order to have my ring replaced. Apparently, Tehani had a hand in the ring Spence had proposed with, so I guess I could forgive the bland princess-cut solitaire on a white gold band. Thank god Fonseka Jewellers had their own workshop and were able to get an appropriate ring out for me quickly.

And then, of course, my mother dropped a bombshell on me.

She'd checked with her astrologers, as was expected, and all four of them came up with the same BS about the most auspicious day to get married being just three months away. I'd looked at Spencer when my mother made this announcement, expecting some resistance. Bad enough we rushed into this engagement, but to rush into an actual marriage? I had thought we'd have a year, maybe even two, to ease into it. Surprisingly, Spencer was completely game. He put his arm around my mother, gave me a chaste kiss on the cheek, and said he couldn't be happier.

So with everything that was going on, it really was no small wonder that a few things on the business side got neglected.

I arrived at the Pink Sapphires office a little earlier than I normally did. There was a fair bit to catch up on, after all. I'd taken some time off work to deal with the whirlwind that was our engagement, but I had no doubt that Lakshi and Danushka would be able to handle things without an issue.

Which is why I was surprised when I was going through this quarter's financial summary.

My family might've lacked warmth and compassion, but one thing I was taught to do from a young age was to follow the numbers. My father taught me about balance sheets when I was ten years old. I barely needed a calculator to make sure things added up just right. And I know I might sound flippant with my spending, but I'm usually certain of exactly how much is in my bank account. There's a reason why the rich stay rich, you know.

And so I knew the moment I started flipping through the report that something was wrong. I checked the last page and saw the head of finance's stamp and signature. This document had already been checked and approved. That was weird. My dad insisted that all Pink Sapphire's profit and loss accounts (well, there's really no profit—we are a charity after all) be run through his main finance team, and that was headed by Mr. Ananda. I sent him a text right away.

> **Mr. Ananda, good morning. I need to meet you re: last month's p&l. When can I stop by your office?**

MR. ANANDA'S OFFICE was on the same floor as my dad's, at the very top of the building. I'd tried to get the floor for myself—the light up there was truly stunning for shooting content—but my father had flatly refused. I think Tehani might have had something to do with that, which was a bitch move on her part. I have a feeling she's been eyeing that floor for when she finally gets it together and launches that clothing line she won't shut up about, but she'll have to fight me for it, if it ever comes to that.

"Hi, *Thaththa*," I called out, hoping to make it directly to Mr. Ananda's cubicle without any distractions, but my father waved me in.

"Good news, *Duwa*! The Mount Lavinia Hotel said they can block out the whole place for us," he called out, a little louder than I would have liked. My father never did know the meaning of the word "tact." I just gave him a small smile, tucked my chin down, and mumbled loudly that it really wasn't necessary. I couldn't have our staff thinking I was some kind of spoiled brat, could I?

"Have you met Chamara? He's helping us out with the interior for the new outlet."

"How do you do, Chamara?" I said, dutifully, to the young man who turned beet red and didn't meet my eye. I hoped he wasn't giving us some ridiculous quote or something. My father was really going over the top for this new showroom, probably because he wanted to show off to Spencer.

Mr. Ananda had a junior-level cubicle, even though he'd taken the head of finance role since Mr. Sekar, who'd held the position since before I was born, retired. I asked my father once why Mr. Ananda was kept in his tiny cubicle, when Mr. Sekar's corner office with a view that rivaled my dad's was still empty, but he had just gestured dismissively and said Mr. Ananda was not ready. And looking at last month's financials, maybe he was right.

I'd barely spoken to Mr. Ananda in the two months since he had been promoted (and perhaps never before that either), so he looked quite surprised when I rapped on the glass.

"Hi, Mr. Ananda, are you busy?" He hadn't responded to my text this morning, so I thought I'd drop by anyway. He was from my father's generation, the one where mobile phones were an annoying puzzle to solve rather than an aide that made your life easier. I wouldn't be surprised if he hadn't even seen it.

"Well, yes," he said simply, his eyebrows furrowing beneath his bald head. No *Good morning*. No *Nice to see you, boss*.

"I texted you, but you never replied, so I thought I'd drop in." I made sure the smile never left my face and that I kept my voice steady. Who the hell did this guy think he was?

"Yes. I didn't reply because I wasn't sure of my schedule. I have a report due to your father tomorrow. Perhaps we could speak after that? I'll try to slot you in for later in the week."

Was this asshole seriously trying to blow me off?

"No, Mr. Ananda, let's speak now. I need some information cleared up urgently."

"I'm sorry, Kaavindi, it will have to wait."

"Excuse me?" My voice rose just a fraction. Just enough for a few of the staff around his cubicle to take note.

Was he out of his mind? Everyone who worked at the Jewellers called me Miss Fonseka, even Mr. Sekar, who'd seen me in my school uniform when I was a child. Only the girls at Pink Sapphires got to call me Kaavi because of this whole team-building bullshit I was trying out. I knew Mr. Ananda was new, but he's got some balls if he thinks he can treat me like this.

He just stared at me with an exasperated glare, his mustache twitching.

"I don't care if you're busy, Mr. Ananda. When you submit a report to me that's full of mistakes, I expect you to stop what you are doing and pay attention. It's not my fault if you're not able to manage the pressures of this job."

"What are you talking about?" I finally had this imbecile's attention, though I didn't care for his tone. I could tell that most of the staff had stopped what they were doing and were trying to be discreet about listening in on the commotion.

"Last month's P&L, Mr. Ananda. It has your signature right here, see?" I spoke slowly now, patronizing him on purpose. That'll show him to be rude to me in front of my employees. "You've made some significant mistakes in the calculations, which is what I've come here to talk to you about. But since you seem to want to avoid me, I can only assume that you are out of your depth here, and not competent enough to handle our financials the way Mr. Sekar did."

My voice was loud now, making sure everyone surrounding us could hear me. That'll show him to throw his weight around. I was fed up with older men like him not giving me the time of day. Thinking I was some spoiled brat just because I was the boss's daughter. It didn't matter that I was spoiled; what mattered was that he got the numbers wrong, and I spotted it. I might be the boss's daughter, but I was sharper than his pompous ass.

Even his shiny bald head turned pink.

"Give those here." He all but snatched the folder from me and leafed clumsily through the pages.

"I don't know who signed off on this," he said, finally, "but it wasn't me."

I burst out into laughter.

"Typical," I snorted out. "Can't own up to your mistakes and so you're claiming that you had nothing to do with it? Listen, Mr. Ananda, I can put up with your rudeness for the sake of the business, but I won't allow you to muck around with the company accounts. If this is just for my charity I can only imagine what a mess you've made of Fonseka Jewellers."

Taking the financials from him, I turned and made my way directly to my father's office. No one got away with treating Kaavindi Fonseka like that.

21

KAAVI

Two Months before the Wedding

"So, you just, like, had him fired?" Tehani asked, jealousy dripping from her voice.

I exhaled, reaching out from my ridiculously comfortable bed at the Marina Bay Sands in Singapore for the glass of Moët that sat on my bedside. One of the perks of traveling out of Sri Lanka was the unapologetic day drinking.

"Fuck off, there's no need to give me shit about it, okay? The guy was a douche. He had it coming."

"*Thaththa* just agreed to it?"

"Why wouldn't he?" I shrugged. The truth was that my father was a little harder to crack than I'd ever let Tehani know. He insisted that we couldn't just throw out our head of finance, especially now that Mr. Sekar was gone. That it left Fonseka Jewellers far too vulnerable without someone overseeing the accounts closely. I got it, of course, but I couldn't be the laughingstock in my own company. I had insisted, and when that didn't work, I might have fabricated a bit of what happened to make it seem like it wasn't negligence that caused Mr. Ananda to sign off on my report, but dishonesty. And that was one thing my father would not stand for.

"Well, who's going to do our accounts, then?" Tehani nagged. I honestly wished she'd just shut it. The only reason she was even on this trip with me in the first place is because she'd managed to convince my mother that I shouldn't go wedding dress shopping alone. Like I ever needed anyone else's help. Besides, the whole point of the trip wasn't for me to go nuts on the shopping (I mean, it would happen anyway, but it wasn't really my motive) but to get away from the nonstop wedding planning.

"We'll manage. If things get really out of control, *Amma* can always step in, no?" And while I'd detest seeing my mother every day at the office, no one could argue that she was the sharpest out of the lot of us. She'd helped my father with his bookkeeping from the day they got married. It was only then that Fonseka Jewellers really started to grow. Sure, my father's family was well-off before—I doubt my mother would have agreed to marry him otherwise—but it was only after she joined the ranks that they became well and truly rich. My father liked to joke that my mother was his lucky charm. I knew better. With brains like hers, you didn't really need luck. Too bad societal pressures forced her to be a stay-at-home mum and shift her focus to so much mindless gossip. If she'd been in charge, we'd have taken over the whole damn country.

"Are you fucking serious?"

"Why the hell do you care so much? Did you have a crush on him or something?" That should irritate her enough.

"Come on. You know I've never even met the guy. He'd just started, no? *Thaththa's* driver told me."

"Oh god, Tehani, you really need to stop gossiping with the help." What the hell would people think if they saw her hobnobbing with a driver?

"You're starting to sound like *Amma*. And you know Mr. Ananda's wife's sick, right? Cancer, stage four, I heard. He probably needed his job, Kaavi, what with the medical bills and all."

"Well, he should have thought about her before he was such a colossal dick to me." I nonchalantly chugged down my champagne while she rolled her eyes and started to text someone.

The room felt very quiet. I didn't know his wife was sick. If I did, I'd have—well, I guess I wasn't sure. I took out my phone and sent a hasty email to Lakshi, who worked at Pink Sapphires.

Hey, could you remind me to call Mr. Ananda when I get back? I need to check in on some misplaced files with him.

The least I could do is offer him some money to hold him over until he finds another job, which I'm sure wouldn't take very long anyway. According to my father he was well qualified, despite his inability to spot basic mistakes.

"So, your appointment at Trinity Gallery is at three, right? What are your plans after?" Tehani asked.

"I'm meeting some friends from university for dinner and drinks."

"Oh, okay. Then I'll make an appointment at the spa and order room service, if that's okay with you?"

"Why wouldn't it be?"

Thank god she didn't ask to tag along and make me have to come up with another string of lies.

My phone beeped right on cue.

Reservations made for 7 p.m.
Hope you're ready to have your
brains fucked out. xSteve

Let's hope this asshole's moves in bed were better than his supposed dirty talk. After all the chaos since the engagement, I deserved to blow off some steam.

22

KAAVI

Four Days before the Wedding

THE DAYS LEADING up to the wedding were more stressful than I could've imagined. I didn't know how time sped up the way it did. It's not like I was having fun. You'd have thought I would have enjoyed it—the picking and choosing and shopping. I've been the center of attention my whole life, so it's not like I wasn't used to it. I just wish I could shake the sense of dread that had made itself at home in the pit of my stomach.

I finally got a morning that was relatively free, so I spent it filming a whole load of content. My follower count was slowly ticking upward, and I would be stupid to waste this opportunity. I wore the pink silk robe that had just arrived from La Perla; thank god for my forwarding shipping box. It cost me an arm and a leg in customs tax, but there really was nowhere decent to shop in Colombo, and I'd already shot with the clothes I'd bought during my trip to Singapore.

I had my hair twisted up into an artfully messy bun. It only took about a million bobby pins and half a can of hair spray. Of course, I spent an hour making it look like I wasn't wearing makeup. That my glowing skin was just the result of being in love. Of—insert air quotes—pre-wedding bliss.

I climbed back into bed and messed the covers up around me. I held up my iPhone with the ring light attachment and took a selfie.

Finally, some downtime relaxing in bed x Wedding prep is tough work! I posted.

Then I set up my tripod to shoot a video. I spent about twenty minutes talking about my pre-wedding skin prep routine, making sure I mentioned the products I was being paid to endorse but never really used because they made my skin break out. I can't imagine anyone actually believing this bullshit—my skin was the result of weekly facials, a cocktail of imported serums and elixirs, a solid layer of foundation, and a ton of cash to blow. Any moron who thinks there's a miracle product for looking this good has been smoking some shit.

I eyed the arrangement of pink roses that I had delivered last evening. They were missing something. I pulled out a note card and a pen.

I can't wait to marry you. Love, Spencer, I wrote. I stuck it on the arrangement of flowers and filmed a quick Boomerang opening up the card. Perfect.

Was I laying it on a little thick? Sure. But I'm only giving everyone what they wanted. It's like a service, really.

And for what it's worth, I wasn't always like this. Everyone goes on about it, so I guess it must be true—I was a dreadfully boring, shy child. Throughout college all I ever posted were pictures of landscapes and black-and-white photos of mundane things like shadows. Things that I thought made me seem mysterious and arty and cool. It all happened one day by accident. I'd moved to Chicago and was depressed AF (your best friend suddenly cutting you off will do that to you) and had just done my makeup for a night out with my friends from J.P. Morgan. I think it was Red who took the picture and bullied me into posting it on my Instagram.

I guess it was easier to boss me around back in the day, because I did, and then forgot about it until I woke up the next morning. I'd usually gotten ten, maybe fifteen likes on my landscape photos. When I checked my phone, I had seventy-eight, and it went up to ninety-three through the day. Along with comments—which foundation was I using? Were my eyelashes real? Could I post a tutorial? With each *like* a piece of my heart felt glued back together. With each comment a little bit of my emptiness evaporated. I didn't have to be this insipid, sad girl. Not anymore. I could build myself up to exactly who I wanted to be, one post at a time.

I never thought back then that a picture on Instagram would lead to everything I had today. That I would finally build my empire around it.

I know that everyone and their grandmother has an opinion on social media—how it's "fake" or "performative." Well, I'll just ask you one thing: What part of life isn't performative? From the image an intern portrays at work to be taken more seriously, to the beggar on the street who pretends to have varying ailments to extract some change for the day's meal, everyone is playing a part. Props to anyone who's managed to monetize it.

I checked the time. Damn it.

I was going to be late for my sari jacket fitting. I had just selected my outfit when my phone beeped.

We need to talk. Call me.

Fuck this bullshit. Seriously. Like I didn't have enough on my mind.

But still, I was about to dial when I heard my mother's shouts travel up the stairs.

Really, woman? For someone who's always on my case about keeping up appearances, she regularly managed to pull some ridiculous, dramatic bullshit in front of her annoying friends.

I sighed. I'd better go out there and do some damage control.

I guess it wasn't the worst thing. I looked great in this not-trying-at-all, five-hundred-dollar robe, and it'll be nice to have one more chance at showing it off.

I went down the stairs, ready to smooth over whatever it was my mother was on about when I saw Amaya.

I couldn't believe it. This was certainly not good. I guess I could understand my mother's hysterics now, but I didn't have the luxury of reacting. Those aunties were watching us like animals marking their prey. They would love a dramatic scene, wouldn't they? Something they could call their gossiping friends about and have a good old chin-wag, all at the expense of my mother. No way I was giving them that satisfaction.

"I invited her," I said to my mother. Thankfully, that shut her up.

I had to admit, I was curious as to why the hell she'd suddenly rocked up after lord knows how many years. Maybe she thinks I was backstabbing her by marrying her ex, but hey, she screwed me over first. I hope she doesn't decide to tell anyone about how she dated Spence. That'll really mess things up for me.

But there was only so much I could focus on. My phone kept vibrating in the pocket of my robe, and there was a call I really needed to make.

Making my way upstairs again, I'd have thought Amaya would take a hint, but it looked like she followed me as well.

I didn't have time to get wrapped up in her drama now. Amaya had made it very clear over the last few years that she didn't give a fuck about me or our friendship. I had far more important things to worry about.

I went into my bathroom and ran the shower. Hopefully, that'll be loud enough to drown out my conversation.

"What's going on?" I asked as soon as he picked up, making sure I kept my voice low.

"I'm doing great. Lovely to hear from you too."

"Cut the bullshit, Mike."

"Can you meet me today?"

"Today? You've got to be kidding me! I'm drowning in wedding prep."

"Oh, trust me, sweetheart"—I rolled my eyes—"you're gonna love what I have for you."

"Can't you just—?"

"Kaavi?" Amaya called out.

Fuck her. Seriously. If I didn't have Mike to deal with I would have stormed back into my room and told her to get lost.

I yelled out some bullshit excuse, my mind already a million miles away.

"Listen, I don't have time for this," his voice was low too. "Meet me at Cinnamon Grand. Text me when you're on your way." The asshole hung up.

It was all I could do to keep my shit together for the rest of the morning. Amaya tagged along, still oblivious that I didn't really want her there. The fitting with Andre needed to have ended, like, yesterday, but he was taking his sweet time about it and I let him have his way. He was upset enough when he heard I was wearing a Hayley Paige dress for my reception—I actually thought he'd pass out when I told him. I mean, Andre was the best designer in the country, but all that meant in Sri Lanka was that he was a big fish in a pond the size of a puddle. I needed a showstopper dress for my showstopper wedding, no offense to him. But I sucked it up and tried not to look too impatient as he tried to strong-arm me into an elaborately beaded straightjacket.

My phone buzzed again.

Where are you?

It's not like I was on holiday, Mike.

Andre and his assistant left to find a necklace or something, leaving me with Amaya.

It was my first time truly alone with her in years. Since she just up and vanished, leaving me so worried that I'd gone to the police, checked every hospital in Northern California, and couldn't eat or sleep for weeks, only to learn after what felt like a lifetime later that she was living in my own house back home. You tell me that's not the most ridiculously selfish bullshit you've heard.

Anyway, I'm not the whimpering little loser who followed her around all my life, only to be left a pathetic mess when she cut me out. I wanted her to know that. I wanted her to see how I've changed. How confident I am now. How I am everything. How I *have* everything.

"What do you think?" I asked. I knew the answer. It felt delicious to rub it in. I looked amazing. It wasn't just Andre's and his tittering assistant's gasps of delight—I had eyes. I don't know who circulated the memo that it was unbecoming of women to appreciate how they looked. Probably some insecure man. I mean, I worked out every day. I haven't eaten anything deep-fried since last year. I spent an inordinate amount of time and money on my skin, hair, makeup, nails, and outfits. It is only right that I'm allowed to look in the mirror every once in a while and feel fantastic.

"You look amazing." Bitch, I'm a fucking ten. I wanted you to know that. I wasn't the stupid, shy little girl who came running to you all the time. You couldn't hurt me anymore.

I kept my mind solidly on that until I hopped in an Uber and made my way to meet Mike.

23

KAAVI

Four Days before the Wedding

WALKING INTO ANY public establishment in Colombo was a giant pain in the ass. Chances are that you'd bump into someone you knew. Literally every head in the building turned toward you the moment you entered, sizing you up, wondering if you were worth their time to say hi. Not making eye contact was the key. People were only obliged to say hello if you smiled at them first, so I kept my gaze stubbornly on my phone. If I didn't see anyone, I couldn't be accused of ignoring them, right?

The Cinnamon Grand lobby was laughably indiscreet. It's pretty much guaranteed that the who's who of Colombo would be swarming around, but I guess this wasn't Mike's first time.

I found him sitting in a corner tucked just out of sight, a baseball cap angled low on his face. As if that gave him even the smallest shred of anonymity. I would have laughed if I wasn't so irritated. Any disguise he could have come up with was useless. Mike was white. He stuck out like a sore thumb anywhere in Colombo. Luckily, the hotel lobby wasn't too busy today.

"Hi there, sweetheart," he said, as I sat down across from him.

"Seriously, Mike?"

He gave me a cheesy grin and I tried my best not to let my exasperation show. Mike was doing me a favor, I reminded myself. Sure, I was paying him, but there wasn't really anyone else I could ask, and he knew it.

"Seriously." He held out a large folder but pulled back as I reached for it.

"You sure you want to know what's in here, sweets? No going back after this." I glared at him, pissed-off at how childish he was being, until I noticed him looking serious.

Mike was married to Karen Walker, who was the head of a large NGO in Colombo and had pretty deep connections at the American embassy. Karen's job did most of the heavy lifting, and from what I could tell, Mike simply bounced around from five-star hotels to beachside bars. He had some experience in security, or intelligence, or something, because he'd taken a break from doing shots of arrack and chain-smoking to run some checks on an American hedge fund my dad was interested in investing in at the time, and my dad said he did good work.

And so when I wanted a background check run, discreetly, I figured he was the best person to do it.

Don't get me wrong. There were worse things than marrying Spencer. I think back to my classmates—most of them married already, with a child or two to boot. Husbands who have affairs at the office that the wives turn blind eyes to, probably because they were fucking someone else on the side themselves. Colombo society was nothing if not incestuous. Everyone was related to everyone some way or another, which made love triangles even more complicated than they typically would be.

But that's why my deal with Spencer felt comforting in a way. And I certainly wasn't under any delusions. It definitely was a deal.

I'd pushed aside my doubts and embraced it, like brides were supposed to. Colombo society was going to think I was knocked up for sure, but I guess they'd shut up when there was no baby nine months later.

Then I got a call from the lady who managed Pink Sapphire's donations in the US. A check had bounced, she said. It was probably nothing. Just a bookkeeping error. But the check was from Spencer's company.

It was just a tiny, nagging thought that started in my mind. Pretty soon it started to itch, and then it started to fester. I was paying attention to things that I never thought about before—

Who was picking up the bills for everything? Mostly me. It didn't make sense to pay international charges on his credit card, he said, and I agreed. I mean, his money was going to be *our* money soon. I didn't want to be wasteful.

Where was he living? At one of the swankiest apartments in Colombo, owned by my dad, who said that family shouldn't have to pay rent.

Was he paying for the wedding? He claimed he was—at least for the homecoming portion of things, as he should. But as far as I knew, my dad had paid the deposits for everything because Spencer hadn't transferred his money across from the US just yet.

My dad was building us a house.

My dad was giving him the reins on our new showroom.

It seemed like a much too convenient arrangement, if you asked me.

But maybe all of it was just in my head, which is where Mike came along. I'd reached out to him two weeks ago and asked him to run a background check on Spencer. I was sure that everything would be fine. That it was just pre-wedding cold feet kicking in. That this was all some sort of misunderstanding and Mike would clear everything up and I'd go along with my marriage of convenience like I had planned.

But all that changed this morning.

There was no way Mike would be so persistent if all was well.

I yanked the folder out of his hands and opened it up. There were pages and pages of accounting information that would take me at least a few hours to study.

"What's the CliffsNotes version, Mike? What was so urgent that you made me ditch wedding planning and rush over here?"

"Go over the accounts in detail, sweetheart, and you'll see for yourself. But your suspicions were right. Your boyfriend's broke. I hope your dad had you sign a prenup."

Prenups weren't really a thing in Sri Lanka, but that was mostly because we didn't have to split our assets down the middle or anything ridiculous like that if we were getting divorced. Besides, my dad had Colombo's best lawyers on retainer—it wasn't like Spencer could take me to the cleaners on my home turf.

I took a deep breath.

Okay, so he was a gold-digging asshole who was using me for a sweet ride.

Was I surprised? Maybe not.

Could I leverage this to my benefit?

That was the more interesting question.

I thumbed through the documents.

"How bad is it? Low checking account, or seriously in the red?"

The look on Mike's face told me what I needed to know.

Fuck me.

"And his businesses?"

"Kaavi, he'd been bought out a year ago, though I can't seem to find a trace of the money anywhere. His current start-up has been defunct for months. They've even filed for bankruptcy."

Fuck you, Spencer. If this shit ever got out it would ruin me. At least he could have told me so we'd come up with a plan or something.

"I've asked my friend to keep up with the checks. This is just the financial part of it. You know, stuff that's left a paper trail. There's a whole other side we need to check out. In my experience when someone's in it as deep as him, it's only a matter of time before something else starts coming out of the woodwork.

"Oh, and one last thing."

There was more?

"Do you know what his relationship is to someone named Zoe? Zoe Bassett?"

"Zoe?" I repeated. "He's never mentioned the name. Who is she? Like an ex-girlfriend or something?" Spencer and I didn't really talk about our exes. One of the many things we've tiptoed around because, hey, when you've heard your now-fiancé bone your then-best-friend in the next room, you don't ever really want to talk about it.

"No idea. She had a police report filed against him last year, but she's dropped the charges recently."

"What for?"

"No clue. She's got herself a pretty high-end legal team by the look of it. Everything was buried, and we can't seem to track her down either. Look, it could be nothing. Maybe he owed her some cash or something. My guys are on it, of course, but I'd keep my eyes open if I were you."

24

KAAVI

Four Days before the Wedding

MY MOTHER TREATS even the simplest of parties like the queen is coming to tea, so I had no doubt she would go over the top for this "small get-together," as she and my dad called it. When I got back, the house was overrun with service staff and setup crew and extra hired help.

"For god's sake, child, where on earth have you been?" My mother descended on me the moment I stepped inside. "Never mind. Just go and take a look at the table decor. Tell the florist whether you like it. I personally think it should be taller, but he keeps saying that guests get annoyed when they can't see past them when they are sitting down."

I didn't really have time to dwell on this news about Spencer. I had to deal with flowers, and then table setup, and then my mother wanted to talk to me about the layout of the buffet. I wanted to tell her to just get on with it. It was fine. It was all fine.

But it wasn't all fine.

My fiancé was lying to me.

Sure, we didn't have the most rock-solid relationship to start with. But I'd thought we could have been a team. I mean, look at my mum and dad—a strong example of teamwork if I ever saw it. Sure, I'd never seen them so much as hold hands, let alone kiss, but they'd built this fantastic life for me and my sisters. Maybe it wasn't what you saw in the movies, but it was a hell of a lot easier than ugly crying and chugging down bottles of wine when you got your heart broken.

But now this sneaky little shit was hiding things from me. Things like being broke. I mean, I honestly didn't care about the money—my dad had plenty of it for me, for him, and for our entire neighborhood if necessary. It was the lying that truly pissed me off. Well, that, and what the fuck was I supposed to do if it got out?

How the hell was I supposed to deal with this? The wedding festivities had started. It wasn't like I could call all of this off. My mother would kill me. Hell, my family's name would be dragged through the mud—I'd let her kill me.

Spencer and I had been doing a delicate little dance from the moment we got engaged. We made the necessary public appearances, of course, but we also kept a careful distance. In true Sri Lanka style, all this was easier because it was unheard of for him to stay at our house until we were officially married. He visited daily, but it was mostly to have tea or watch cricket with my father. He gave me a chaste kiss on the cheek whenever he saw me, and he was a fucking dream whenever there was an aunty around. We were cautious, as we should have been, given how, oh, you know, we were never really dating to begin with.

I weighed out the pros and cons. Since money wasn't the issue for me (hell, I may be many things, but a gold digger is certainly not one of them), and canceling a wedding that was just a few days away would be a shitstorm of epic proportions, maybe I could use this as leverage. Let Spencer know his bullshit wouldn't fly with me.

I have to admit, after feeling so off-kilter these few months, it felt good to finally have the upper hand again.

Spencer showed up to the party right on cue, dressed immaculately in the shirt and trousers I'd had sent over. It was as if he knew, too, because he was carrying a large bouquet of Stargazer lilies, which he presented to my mother with a flourish, giving her a warm kiss on the cheek.

"Spencer!" Nadia shrieked, running up to him. He produced a single lily from god-knows-where and handed it to her, amidst the *awws* and *oohs* from the few guests who had already started to arrive. She wrapped her arms around his knees while he reached down, tickling her as she squealed.

He smiled at me as I walked down the stairs.

"Darling," he said, kissing me delicately on the cheek.

"Watch the makeup," I whispered back.

"You look breathtaking, as always."

I gave him a little smile, and he offered me his arm. We did a small walk through the garden, greeting the guests that were making their way in. Everyone told us how great we looked together, and how happy we must be, and how we would make the most beautiful babies.

I spotted Amaya, sitting at a table with a group of aunties. I hoped she wasn't running her mouth off about her relationship with Spencer. She said she'd keep quiet, but it's not exactly like I could trust her, right? Fuck, all this business about Spencer being broke has thrown me for a loop.

I finally couldn't take it anymore.

"Let's go out back for a moment," I said, during a brief pause between making small talk with guests.

"Out back? But, darling, your mother would kill us if we didn't greet everyone like we promised her."

His bullshit saint talk didn't fool me. He was avoiding me. Here we were, about to spend the rest of our lives together, and this son of a bitch was actually trying to avoid me?

"I need a break," I said, walking away. I knew he'd follow. He was the devoted husband-to-be. He'd never let his bride go unattended.

The two waiters having a smoke in our back garden scampered off quickly when they realized it was us. Otherwise, it was empty, thank goodness. The last thing I needed was for someone to overhear this.

"What's going on, Kaavi?" I guess the *darlings* were only reserved for when we had an audience.

"When were you going to tell me?" I went for nonchalance, but he could tell there was an edge to my voice.

Spencer dropped my hand and turned to face me.

It glimmered between us—the fragile, intangible puff of smoke that held us together. The facade, the need, the advantages of tying the knot. One wrong breath, and it would shatter.

But I didn't want it shattered tonight. Not right now.

"Spencer, I know about your business in San Francisco. I know you've filed for bankruptcy. I know you're broke. All I want to know is why you didn't tell me."

I kept my tone light. I wanted to hear what he had to say first.

He took a moment to answer.

At least he had the decency to look ashamed.

"How did you find out about that?"

"One of your checks bounced, so I called in to figure out why." It was only half the truth, but that was enough for now. He wasn't the only one who could hold his cards close to his chest.

"Look, I know I should have told you. I've been meaning to. I shouldn't have put it off."

"Is that why you want to marry me, Spencer? Because you're broke?"

"No." His voice was forceful. A touch louder than it should be, and he realized it too. We both looked out at the garden, just to make sure.

"No," he said, again. "Look, I've apologized for this a million times before—the way I asked you to marry me. I mean, I thought it was what you wanted, you know. You were always talking about what a pain it was that your mother was always on your case, and how frustrating Colombo society was, and how a marriage of convenience was all you needed."

I had said those things, I supposed. I just wasn't expecting a fucking proposal out of it.

"And look, I should have told you about my company. I know. I mean, I've hinted at it a few times, you know, trying to work up the nerve to tell you."

He had?

"If you did, Spencer, I must have missed it."

He put his hand under my chin and lifted my face so my eyes met his.

"You don't think I wanted to? Jesus, Kaavi, all this, it only works because we are friends. You know. We were friends first. That's what makes it special."

"Exactly. Which is why I don't understand why you couldn't have told me."

"Because it's all so much, okay? Your family. This life. How do you think it makes me feel, being welcomed into all of this when everyone thinks I'm some super successful millionaire? It's so intimidating, Kaavi. Feeling like I'm not good enough to be here. That I'm not good enough for you. That nothing I ever do will be enough."

I knew what that felt like once. Never feeling like you're good enough. Sure, everyone thinks I have it together, but the truth is that it's fucking hard when every single turn you make is examined and judged and gossiped about.

"So, you sold your shares in your two old companies, and are in the process of shutting down a third. Is that all?"

"Yes, I'm sorry."

"And your personal finances?"

"I have some of what my parents left me, of course. I'm just, well, let's just say I'm not as magazine-cover wealthy as everyone here seems to think."

I sighed.

"Why the hell couldn't you have told me sooner?"

"Why do you think, Kaavi? I was scared you would leave me. That you would hate me. That your family would hate me and I'd lose everyone in an instant."

He tucked a stray piece of hair behind my ear. He looked so earnest. Like a little child who got lost somewhere. It must have been hard growing up without parents. I thought about my huge house, and my mum and dad who always had my best intentions at heart, no matter how misguided they were. I was so very lucky.

"It still doesn't excuse you lying to me, you know."

"I know. I'm so sorry. I know. I promise this is it, okay? You'll never find me lying to you ever again."

And with that, he kissed me.

Not the bullshit, let's have a show for the aunties peck. A full-on kiss. The kind we had when we were smashed out of our minds and the world around us evaporated as we stumbled into a hotel room somewhere. I let myself melt into him.

So he lied. But he also got caught. Now he owed me. And if there was one thing you learned about doing business, it was always better to be a creditor than a debtor.

He leaned me up against the wall, and I felt his hands push into the silky neckline of my dress. I reached up and bit his lip.

"God, you're hot," he murmured, pulling away from my mouth and trailing kisses down my jaw. "We need to get away from the crowd more often."

"You better not fuck up my hair," I whispered. He trailed his hands down my arms and pinned me up against the wall. I fucking hated it when he did that. He always wanted to be in control. And so did I. Maybe that was why we worked in some fucked-up way.

We heard a door slam and pulled away quickly. Just in time, too, because a waiter in uniform walked out with a crate of wine bottles.

"Sorry, madam. Sorry, sir." He practically ran away as soon as he saw us.

"We'd better get out there, huh?"

Spencer smiled back. "Sure. I just can't wait to do more of this, you know."

Of course he fucking couldn't.

I pulled my phone out and flipped the camera onto selfie mode, checking my hair and makeup. Shit. I'd have to fix my lipstick the moment we got back inside.

I had a text from Mike. Just a reply from when I texted him earlier today. But it was enough, somehow, to shake me awake.

"Hey, Spence," I tried, making sure my voice was relaxed.

"Yes, darling?"

"I've been meaning to ask. There's someone that's reached out to our team in San Francisco about making a significant donation. I think the last name was Basket or Bassett or something like that. Is it someone you've managed to rope in?" I smiled widely in false gratitude.

A beat passed. Something shifted in the air.

And then Spencer smiled back.

"Nope. I don't think so. If there's a new donor, it's all down to you and your brilliance."

He offered me his arm and I took it. We made our way back inside, where I excused myself and went upstairs to touch up my makeup.

It felt nice to be alone. To be away from everyone. Even if it was for just a moment.

I smoothed back my hair and gave it a spritz of hair spray.

Then I took out my phone and texted Mike.

I need to know who Zoe Bassett is. Let me know
as soon as you find anything.

It took a liar to know a liar, that was for sure. And it took a liar to know when the other liar's mask was starting to slip.

25

KAAVI

Three Days before the Wedding

I DREAMED THAT I was standing in the grand ballroom of the Mount Lavinia Hotel. The large chandelier sparkled down, bathing me in light as I stood in front of a full-length mirror. I was alone, but I was in my Hayley Paige wedding dress. My hair hung down in loose curls. My makeup was simple, except for a bold red lip—the color of blood.

I was a vision. Completely stunning. It was a pity that I was alone. Someone else ought to see me looking this good, or it'd be such a waste. I turned around, admiring myself, when I noticed a small spot on the hem of my dress. I was bending down to look at it, when I noticed another spot, and another, and another. Little red droplets were starting to splatter on me, as I looked around, trying not to scream in frustration, trying to figure out where they were coming from.

And suddenly, there he was—a body. Dead. Stone-cold. Purple lips and gray skin. Reaching for me. Choking me, while I spluttered blood. I could smell him. Rotten fish and maggots and the rusty metal of blood.

I couldn't breathe. I couldn't see. My dress weighed a million pounds and held me in place—giving him full control. Letting him have his way. Letting him win.

I opened my mouth to scream, but blood leaked out of my throat. It ran down in rivulets, soaking my dress, which only grew heavier. This was the end; I just knew it.

So when I was woken up by screaming, I thought it was my own. I sat up in bed confused. No, the screams were definitely coming from downstairs.

I rolled out of bed and pulled on a robe, rushing to find out what the commotion was.

It was my mother, I realized halfway down the stairs. Oh fuck me. Don't tell me I almost broke my neck getting down here because of one of her little episodes. The hotel probably ran out of caviar or something ridiculous like that.

But still, the house was full of relatives and friends who had flown down for the wedding, and it simply wouldn't do to have her screeching like she'd lost her marbles.

"*Amma*," I hissed, when I reached her. I looked around, expecting to see a trembling maid, or some other messenger she was in the process of shooting, but it was just my dad, sitting on the sofa, looking like he was as sick of her as I was.

This was strange. They never yelled at each other. At least, not out in the open like this. Their fights were usually a combination of silent treatment, simmering glares, and passive-aggressive comments spoken aloud to other people.

"You!" she yelled, when she saw me. "You're the cause of all of this. *Lajja naddha?*" Aren't you ashamed? "This is all your mess."

"What?" I asked. I looked to my dad.

"What's going on? Fiona, are you okay?" It was Aunty Geetha, who had flown in from the Gold Coast in Australia. She'd been staying in one of the guest rooms. Great, just what we needed right now.

"Of course I'm not okay, you know—"

"Fiona." My father stood up, his voice booming over hers. "I think we should go upstairs, hmm? To my office?"

"I can't bel—"

"Now!" And he stood up. "Geetha, please excuse us. It seems we have some family matters to attend to." Aunty Geetha was left with her eyes bulging and mouth open. She'll be on the phone the very second we leave.

The door to Laura's room banged shut as we made our way upstairs, so she probably overheard the whole thing also. What the hell was my mother thinking? We've spent years making sure we kept up appearances, and then she just decides to fly off the handle like this?

"*Thaththa*, what on earth's going on?" I tried to keep my voice level. There's nothing that my father hated more than emotional outbursts, which is probably why he has more regard for his chauffeur than his wife.

"Sit down, both of you."

We did as he asked, my mother quiet now but still looking like she was about to explode.

"I got a call today from your mother's friend, Josephina. You remember her, don't you?" He was speaking directly to me, so I nodded.

"She seemed quite aghast with some information she had received. Information about Spencer."

"Spencer?" My pulse quickened. What the hell could it be? Had news about his company's bankruptcy spread so quickly?

"Yes, about his family."

"His family? *Thaththa*, I've told you, his parents are both dead."

"It doesn't appear that way, *Duwa*."

"What?"

"Josephina had apparently been delivered some information anonymously"—he eyed my mother—"which I don't quite believe, but still, she said she called me directly and had her driver drop these off." He patted to a plain white envelope sitting on his desk. "She said I must have already known about it," he snorted, "but that she was doing the honorable thing by coming to me first."

"The honorable thing." I rolled my eyes. "What does it say, so?"

"Why don't you take a look for yourself?"

I gave him a look, but curiosity got the better of me and I pulled out the contents of the envelope. They were printouts of newspaper pages, mostly, all reporting about a Jeremy Spencer. I looked at the dates.

"His father?" I asked.

"Yes." They were all articles about various arrests, made over many decades, the most recent being five years ago. Spencer's father, it seemed, was very much alive, and still serving out his sentence in prison.

There was a line in one of the articles, which was highlighted—
Jeremy Spencer's wife, Sharon Spencer, who has been missing since her release from California Pacific Rehabilitation Center after being charged with the illegal possession of a controlled substance, was not available for comment.

"And his mother is—?"

My mum squeaked at this. "She's a drug addict, Kaavi! Can you believe this? An addict in the family? *Haiyyo*, I won't know where to hide my head. How could you do this to us?"

But I ignored her.

"How do we know if this is true?"

"So you weren't aware of this?"

"No, of course I wasn't aware."

"*Haiyyo*, this is the problem with marrying a foreigner, I tell you," my mother started up again. "If he was a Sri Lankan, then at least we could have found out about him. Asked around. Checked his background."

"*Amma*, you're the one who insisted that I marry him right away."

"Enough now, both of you." My father beat my mother to her reply. "There's only one thing left to do."

Call the wedding off? Would it be so terrible? We could tell people that my father had a change of heart. It would be the talk of the town, of course it would be, but it would all die down eventually, right?

"And what is that?" my mother huffed.

He looked at me again. "Give Spencer a call. Ask him to come here at once."

26

Three Days before the Wedding

IT TOOK SPENCER about a half hour to get home, during which time I got a few more details of what happened this morning. Turned out that Aunty Josephina, that nosy bitch—I didn't buy her bullshit story about an anonymous delivery at all. She'd probably hired a PI or something—had sent over the package to my father, and then called up my mother directly afterward to "ask what she thought."

Of course, my father, logical as he was, had no intention of telling my mother about any of this until he found out if it was true or not. He was accosted by her when he was trying to have breakfast, which was when I heard the yelling and rushed downstairs.

I tried to count the number of houseguests who would have overheard. So much for keeping this shit under wraps. My mother was usually so smart and calculating, but the way she'd just fly off the handle like this was a major weakness. And not only to her.

"You better keep your mouth shut, you hear me, Fiona?" my father warned, before Spencer entered the office.

"Good morning, *Thaththa*, what's wrong?" Spencer asked.

"Morning, *Putha*. Would you mind sitting down?"

All this bullshit and they were still calling each other dad and son? I gotta hand it to Spencer: he really could be even-keeled during the rockiest of situations.

"I received these documents today. Could you please take a look at them?"

All three of us watched Spencer as he leafed through the contents of the envelope. It felt like he was shuffling them for a million years. My heart was beating so loudly I was sure everyone could hear it. Why the fuck was I so nervous?

After going through everything, Spencer gathered up all the papers, put them back in the envelope, and stood up.

"*Amma, Thaththa*, I want to thank you for all your kindness. You have been nothing but perfect parents to me from the time I proposed to Kaavi. Parents that, as you can see, I was never lucky enough to have. I thought my luck had finally changed, but I see now that that is not to be the case."

"What are you saying?" my father asked, the wrinkle between his eyebrows deepening.

"This is why you asked me to come here, isn't it? To tell me that you are ending our engagement? I must say that I'm not surprised. Ashamed, yes, but not surprised. I also wouldn't want my daughter, if I'm ever so lucky one day, to marry the son of a convict and a drug addict." He looked at my mother, whose face was beet red as she refused to meet his eye.

"Spencer, we didn't ask you here to end anything. We asked you here to find out if this is true, and if it is, why you felt you had to lie to us?"

All this time I held my anger at bay. This fucker promised me, just last night, no more lies. And here he was, caught in another. I mean, he didn't deny it. He was ready to leave. So let's just fucking let him.

"Yes, *Thaththa*, I mean, yes, sir, it's true. I'm sorry I didn't tell you before. It's just that I was so ashamed. When I look at Kaavi, when I look at your beautiful family, all I see is perfection. And I am not my parents. I haven't seen them or wanted anything to do with them since I was sixteen years old. In my mind, they are as good as dead."

My mother winced, and Spencer caught on.

"I'm sorry, I know we aren't supposed to speak of our parents this way. But they have done nothing for me. Every cent I earned was my own. Everywhere I've gotten, I've gotten because I've had to push myself. So, yes, in my mind, I'm on my own. That's how I've always felt. And then I met Kaavi—and all of you, and I thought, well, maybe I didn't have to be on my own anymore? Maybe I could have the only thing I've ever wanted? A family. That's why I never told you, sir—"

"Now, there's no need for all this 'sir' business," my father interrupted him.

"Sorry. I—" Spencer blinked back tears. "That's why I never told you about my parents. Because I was scared that you would never accept me if you knew the truth. That you would judge me by the actions of the people who never even knew me, let alone cared for me. And now I've gone and messed everything up. I'm so sorry. I'll leave the apartment and check into a hotel. I'm happy to pay for any deposits you might have to forego and—"

"Spencer"—my dad rose to his feet also—"enough with this talk. We are not asking you to end this engagement."

He's not?

"We just wanted to get to the bottom of things. If we are going to be family, we aren't to keep secrets from one another, you hear?"

Spencer let a single tear roll down his cheek. What a fucking performance. He'd lied to me about his parents just yesterday.

"Yes, sir, I mean—yes, *Thaththa*."

"I don't tell many people this, but my father"—he gestured behind him at *Seeya's* picture—"was a terrible drinker. Heart of gold, but that was his one weakness. Could never give up the bottle. And when he drank, my god, he turned into something, well, something quite terrible."

What? *Seeya*? I guess Spencer wasn't the only one good at keeping secrets around here.

"We never talk about it, of course. But I vowed, the moment that Kaavi was born, that she was never to feel the way I did. We are not our parents, Spencer, and I respect a man who has made his own way in the world. We would be lucky to have you in our family."

He reached out and gave Spencer a big hug, thumping him on the back the same way my heart was thumping in my chest.

I glanced over at my mother, and she looked absolutely livid. But I knew she'd never go against him. Not about something like this. She glared at Spencer, my dad, and most of all me.

I knew what she was thinking—that I should have known better. My mind went back to everything Spencer told me last night. About his parents dying and leaving him money. About why he couldn't tell me about his bankrupt business. About why he wanted to get married in the first place. About how he would never lie to me.

Fuck, I hate it when this happens, but my mother was right. I should have known better.

---⁕---

27

KAAVI
Three Days before the Wedding

I STOOD THROUGH my dad's bullshit speech, all heart and gusto, put on for the benefit of our nosy houseguests. I held Spencer's hand. I went along with everything. I didn't know what the fuck else to do. Maybe I could talk to my dad later on today. Maybe I could convince him that this whole thing was a con. That Spencer was a con artist. A broke, lying con artist who got caught in his act and still managed to weave his way out of it. I can't believe I fell for his bullshit in the first place.

I thought I was being so smart—finding a way to keep my mother and the rest of Colombo happy while still being able to live my life. And here I was, about to marry a broke liar who's clearly in it for my family's money.

I looked around at the guests, all of them lapping up my father's words. I even spotted Amaya in a corner. Why the hell was she here today? I thought back on her chatting away with the various aunties last night. What if she was the one who fed the information to Aunty

Josephina? But then my gaze fell on Spencer and it didn't seem as important anymore.

"We should go for a walk," I mumbled in his ear the moment my father finished.

"Yes, of course," was all he replied, leading me outside. We sat down on a bench under the large mango tree.

"People inside can see us, you know," I reminded him.

"I'm counting on it," he replied.

He was waiting for me to take the first shot. I could sense it.

Well, no one ever accused me of shying away from a fight.

"You're full of shit and you know it. Just because you've got my father wrapped around your finger, don't think for a second that you've fooled me too."

Spencer looked upset. He rubbed his hair and looked agitated but didn't say anything.

"You were smart—I'll hand it to you. The proposal I couldn't turn down, the cozying up to my parents, but I really hope you don't think, Spencer, that I'm afraid to end everything. Because I could."

"Then why haven't you?" His voice was cold. Deathly cold. I'd never heard it like this before. The look on his face, the uneasy way he was tugging on his hair, it was all a show. His voice was composed. He was in total control.

"Why haven't you?" he asked again.

I was too surprised to answer.

"I know why, Kaavi. It's because you'd do anything, and boy do I mean just about anything, to keep your pristine reputation intact. It makes it so easy to figure you out. You'd rather die than lose face."

I forced a laugh.

"If you think you can coerce me into a goddamned marriage by holding my reputation hostage, Spencer, you are far stupider than I thought. This is Colombo, remember; this is my town. Would it cause a scandal? Sure. But a few months and a few large donations to various charities, and maybe a huge party, is all I need to make everyone forget. No. This bullshit ends now. I want you gone by tomorrow."

I started to get up but Spencer grabbed my hand.

"Sit down, Kaavi. I'm not done."

"Oh, but I am."

"Sit the fuck back down and listen to me or you'll fucking regret it."

Who the hell did he think he was?

But he hadn't loosed his grip on my arm, and I couldn't push him off without causing a scene.

"Now you listen." His voice was evil, but his face was the picture of a pleasant, devoted fiancé. What a fucking sociopath. "You will marry me, like we planned. You will forgive me for hiding a few details of my past. Your father accepted my reasons, and they should be enough for you."

I snorted.

"You have some nerve—"

"If you think I've spent my time in and out of Colombo just helping you out with your charity, well, that's sweet. But I'm no idiot, Kaavi. Do you think your father is the only one who runs background checks?"

I laughed.

"What do you mean? You ran a background check on me? I don't have a fucking thing to hide except that my engagement is a goddamned sham."

"Not on you, Kaavi. I just happened to stumble onto something very interesting about your father."

I was caught off guard for a moment.

"On my dad?"

"Yes. I don't think he ever intended on me seeing it. I'd just dropped by his office quite late and unannounced one day when I caught wind of it at first. And then a little more digging and, well, let's just say that no one likes to be caught with their pants down."

"Oh please, Spencer." I rolled my eyes. "If this is about some woman or the other that he's been with over the years, or, well, even right now, it's really no big deal." And I was right. You didn't get to be where we were without some rumors flying around. I'd heard it all—that Nadia was the love child my father had with a mistress, that my mother had a lover that my father had killed, whatever you could come up with, the gossips had been there before. I steeled myself.

"This is Colombo—nearly every man in my father's position has a mistress. If you've got information about some woman—"

"It's not a woman, Kaavi. It's a man."

I choked.

"You're bullshitting me." There was no fucking way.

"I don't bullshit, Kaavi. You should know that. Not when the stakes are so high." He pulled out his phone, tapped around, and showed me the screen. It was an image of my father with another man who looked familiar. I think I had seen him before, maybe it was at the office? Yes, it struck me. The interior designer. My father had introduced him to me the other day.

But regardless of who the man was, this was a picture my father would never want getting out. One that could destroy him in a place like Colombo. His reputation, my mother's, my sisters', and most of all my own will be dragged through the mud. And this would stick. He'd struggle to live this one down.

"This won't fly, Spencer, you know that, don't you? This is Colombo, not the US. We have connections here. Hell, we're fucking royalty here. You think that you, a nobody who's not even from here, can just waltz in and threaten us? You've got to be fucking kidding me."

He swiped left and kept swiping. The pictures kept getting worse. There was one—it looked, well, if you spun a story just right, it looked quite forceful. Like my dad was hurting him.

"I think this one's the winner, Kaavi." Spencer read my mind. "This young man he's with, I happened to have a chat with him. He's willing to come forward, you know. To tell everyone and anyone that your father forced him into this. That he was exploiting him. He's willing, if he had the right support, to hire a lawyer and press charges. Now, I know you lot have your connections, of course. Could probably bribe a judge or do whatever to get this buried, but not before word really gets around. Think of what this would do to your family."

I stayed quiet. Fuck, did this son of a bitch have me?

"I know you'd never in a million years let that happen. You'd sooner die than let your family's name and business be ruined. Especially if it risks your father going to jail for assault. Especially if it risks you losing all this." He swept his arm around, indicating my house. My home. My family.

"So it's pretty simple, Kaavi. I'm not a total asshole. Our initial agreement still stands. I will be a loving and devoted husband to you, at least in public, just the way you like it. And I get, well, I get the kind of life I could have only ever dreamed about when I was starving, being jostled around foster homes, and working my ass off. There's no way in hell I'm losing all this just because you had a change of heart."

28

KAAVI

Three Days before the Wedding

THERE WAS ONLY one person left to speak to, and she wasn't going to like it one bit.

I'd seen my mother leave the house in a huff, slamming the front door on her way out. When she gets upset, there's only one place where she takes refuge—the spa. I paced around my room like a wild animal until she returned. One of the newer maids must have been in here earlier because a few things weren't where they were supposed to be and my bedspread wasn't smoothed out the way I'd instructed. I straightened it out, restless, and shifted the picture frames back to their usual spots. There was a stray piece of paper on the floor as well—*Kaavi, please call me. We need to talk*, it read. The handwriting looked familiar, but there was no name. That was weird. I checked my messages to see if any of the girls from Chicago had tried to get in touch, but I honestly didn't have the energy to deal with any more drama. I was up to my neck in it as it was.

My mother had just gotten back when I knocked on the door of her bedroom (she calls it her "dressing room," and while it did hold enough clothes to dress a small population of heavyset women who loved all things colorful and sparkly, she wasn't fooling anyone by pretending she still slept in the same room as my father).

She opened the door, all shiny and smelling of sandalwood, and whatever Zen-like feelings she was able to muster appeared to vanish the moment she saw me.

"What?" she barked, though for once she used her brains and kept her voice low.

"Can I come inside?"

I didn't wait for her to answer and pushed my way in.

"What's all this now?" she asked again, crossing her arms in front of her.

"I need your help, *Amma*, okay?"

"Why don't you go and ask your father?" Her voice was full of sarcasm. The only thing my mother did better than throwing parties was hold a grudge.

"Look, I'm sorry, okay? I promise I didn't know."

She didn't say anything.

"I swear! Why the fuck—" She gave me a glare. "Why on earth," I adjusted, "would I agree to marry someone from a background like that? It's clear now that he's using me for my money. For our money. There's no way he could live a life like this in the US."

"Are you sure it's just money he's after?"

"What makes you think that?"

"Because if he joins this family, he gets more than just money. He gets security. He gets support. He gets an entire new life. And normally, people who are in search of a new life do that because they've done some bad in their old one."

Just great.

"So if you feel this way, why did you encourage me to marry him?"

"I didn't—"

"Oh, come on, *Amma*. You welcomed him with open arms. I'd have been married off the same day he proposed if it were up to you. You didn't even care that we weren't dating!"

"You weren't dating? But you spent so much time together. And he told me he had been in love with you since university."

"That's bullshit, *Amma*. Just because we worked together on the charity it doesn't mean we were involved. I mean, come on. I know you grew up in the Dark Ages, but even you can't be that dumb."

She faced me then, anger dancing in her eyes.

"Now here, you listen to me. When you chose your university, did you ask me? When you applied for jobs, did you think to ask, even for a moment, what I thought? You work, you run your charity, you travel around the world, and not once did you ask—*Amma*, what do you think? I'm just here to throw parties, and entertain the wives of the men your father does business with, and clean up everyone's mistakes. To clean up all your mistakes. So, no, Kaavi. I didn't know you weren't in a relationship with him, because it's not like you ever tell me anything anyway. And now you come and ask me for my help? No, you got yourself into this mess, now you get yourself out of it. And don't think, for one second, that I'll let you run out on this wedding and destroy all the years I've spent holding this family's place in this society. You think it's been easy, with the rumors and the whispers and the jealousy? But I've held it together. For the sake of this family. And now it's your turn to do the same."

With that, she stalked into the attached bathroom, banging the door shut after her.

I OFTEN GET asked how I manage everything I do. How I'm a director of a company that turns over millions, while running a successful charity, while managing multiple social media accounts and maintaining a presence as an "influencer," while also working out, eating healthy, and being so fucking perfect it makes you want to scream. And if you come up with some smart-ass comment about how it was easy for me because I have my father's money, I'll slap that smug grin right off your face. Sure, he helped me out at first, but how many parents help out their kids when they have money to spare? And how many of those kids built award-winning, successful charities? So what if I got dealt a good hand? People with so much more, *men* with so much more, have fucked it all up. But not me. I've managed to do it all.

And the reason for that, if you must know, is that I am able, I believe more so than the average person, to compartmentalize. I can remove myself emotionally from most situations while I search for solutions. You might say that makes me cold, but I say it makes me smart. Besides, no one would ever accuse a man of being a cold compartmentalizer. We get fed too much of that genius, billionaire, playboy, philanthropist bullshit. Men are allowed to fuck around, more so when they are rich. No one ever asks a man how he maintains his waistline while running a company. Men marry trophy wives all the fucking time. Why was it so wrong that I tried to seek out a trophy husband?

The only difference was that my golden trophy turned out to be cheap old brass underneath his glossy exterior, and actually had the audacity to blackmail me.

I couldn't do anything that would mess things up for my dad. It would shatter him, and frankly, it would be shit for business. I can't believe I didn't have a clue though. I mean, I knew he and my mother had literally no love life. I just didn't think . . . But, then, what did they know about me? I guess we were all in the same boat.

Maybe it would be better to just marry Spencer? I'm marrying him in Sri Lanka, after all. I could always put safety measures in place. Make sure I'm smart about where I move my money, if that's what he was after. I'd have to keep all this bullshit about his company going belly-up and his disastrous family life under wraps, but knowing everything was out in the open now made it easier to control the narrative. If it came down to it, we could always say that Spencer liquidated his company in San Francisco to work more with the charity. That he was searching for a more meaningful life.

And then, after riding out all the publicity my Insta will get after the wedding, I could keep a low profile for a few months. I won't even have to publicly announce the divorce for a while. This is what high-profile couples in Sri Lanka do all the time—they allow themselves to drift apart. As long as I can keep Spencer from making a stink, I should be okay. Actually, now that he's showed his hand and I know what his real motivations are, all this should be much, much easier. If it's money he wants to walk away, well, I happened to have a fair bit of it, even though it pains me that I'm in this position because of him. But still, I had to keep my emotions aside. Like my mother said, I got myself into this mess, I had to get myself out of it.

I pulled out my phone and sent Spencer a text—

Deal on. You better hold up your end of the bargain.

He might have won this battle, but there was no fucking way I was letting him have access to my kingdom. I will win this war. It just might take a little longer than I thought.

29

KAAVI
Two Days before the Wedding

Now that I'd made up my mind to go through with the wedding, I had another fucking headache to deal with—Mr. Ananda. It turned out that Tehani was right and his wife was really sick. Who would have thought? She was so sick, in fact, that she'd passed away a week after her husband was let go. Talk about a rough patch, huh? I'd checked in with Danushka, who was usually up to date on all office gossip, and it turned out that Mr. Ananda had to transfer his wife from the private hospital she was in to a government one, since their medical insurance got canceled. It wasn't technically my fault. I mean, she still did get medical care, right?

I felt bad, though, and sent him flowers and a note with my sympathies. I'd even stupidly offered to pay an extra month's salary before I'd gotten an angry phone call from him blaming me for everything. The inadequate care she received at the government hospital, he claimed, resulted in his wife's premature death.

I'd laughed then, perhaps insensitively, because grieving aside, that was a ridiculous thing to say. I'd politely told him that my offer

of an extra month's salary still stood, but if he wished to discuss anything further it would have to go through my lawyers. I'd thought
he would have left me alone after that. That he was hysterical because of his loss, but would come to his senses after he calmed down.
I've been waiting for him to calm down for weeks.

First, he had shown up at my house during the cocktail party,
screaming that he wanted to see me. For what? I had no clue. Thank
god the staff had the sense to get rid of him.

And this evening, when I'd hurriedly picked up a call from an unknown number thinking it was something wedding related, it had
turned out to be him. I only managed to duck into the bathroom at the
Mount Lavinia Hotel lobby in the nick of time, and it took me more
than a minute to calm down before I made it out to my bridal shower.
Given everything that was happening, I wasn't really in the mood.

I used to love these events. It definitely gave me a ton of content
for my Instagram, that's for sure. And it was nice to see all the
comments—*Kaavi, you're so beautiful! Kaavi, where did you get your
dress from? Kaavi, tell us about your makeup routine?* Seriously, everyone
thought this shit was real. My makeup routine is three different
types of foundation and fifteen minutes on the Facetune app, bitches.
Calm the fuck down.

But now, well, if I was being honest, it was exhausting. Sure, I
loved being the queen bee, but the amount of work it took to keep
my throne drained me. There were times I caught myself fantasizing
about getting away from everything. Just jumping onto a boat and
sailing off far, far away.

But then I looked around the party—the exquisite food, the sparkly cocktails, the random booths, the fawning young girls all crav-
ing a piece of me. I'd have to die before I gave all this up.

———

FINALLY, SOMEONE ANNOUNCED that it was time we move to the beach. I breathed a sigh of relief. The "after-party" will be a completely different type of exhausting, but at least everyone will be too smashed to remember if I was perfect or not.

I let the crowd move out before I joined them. Pulling out my phone, I dropped Mike a text—

> **Anything new?**

I wasn't expecting a reply, but the phone pinged back right away.

> **When are you signing the marriage certificate?**

What the fuck was wrong with him?

> **The day after tomorrow, Mike. Stop fucking around.**

> **I might have a lead on Zoe Bassett. Will have more information for you tomorrow.**

> **Tomorrow is the religious ceremony. Work faster.**

> **Tomorrow morning is the best I can do. Sorry, darling. Where are you now?**

I've checked into the Mount Lavinia Hotel. Just
call me, okay? Don't just show up here. My
family and relatives are everywhere.

Sure thing, sweetheart.

Mike?

Yes, love?

Do I need to be worried? I typed out, but hesitated. I was sounding
like a whiny, needy bitch. Whoever this Zoe is, I can figure it out.
I've come this far, haven't I?

Just hurry the fuck up. I hit send.

My head was starting to hurt. I felt inexplicably nervous as I
walked down to the party. I wished, well, I haven't actually wished
for this in a while, but I wished I had a friend. Someone I could talk
to. Someone I didn't have to calculate my moves around.

And that's when I crashed into Amaya.

I was surprised that she'd turned up here today, just like I couldn't
understand why the hell she'd decided to invite herself to all the
wedding festivities. Maybe if I didn't have so much going on with
Mr. Ananda and Mike's information, I'd have been more upset about
her. She was the one who disappeared, after all. She was the one who
threw out our friendship like it was some dirty old rag not worth
saving.

But maybe she knew something about Spencer? Maybe she had
information that would help me? Give me something I could use
against him if I needed it.

I thought about what happened between us, all those years ago.

How she was so upset with me. How she stormed out of the house, never to talk to me again, and all because—it happened so long ago that I couldn't fully remember all the details.

All I remember was that she and Spencer had broken up, for perhaps the millionth time since the spring. It was just after our graduation, so Amaya and I had rented out a new apartment. She was supposed to be starting her internship right away, but I was moving to Chicago in two months to work at J.P. Morgan. I remember feeling scared. It was the first time we would be well and truly apart. I was different then. Fearful, timid, afraid of my own shadow.

She'd asked me not to tell Spencer where we'd moved to. I wasn't, under any circumstances, supposed to give him our new address. But he'd shown up when I was returning my cap and gown, and he was just so heartbroken, and they had already ended things and gotten back together so many times that I just caved and gave it to him.

I'd returned home a few hours later to find a livid Amaya storming out of the building. She screamed at me that I'd chosen him over her and left. I didn't understand. I'd just been trying to help her.

I didn't see or hear from her again until she showed up at my house.

Did she have every right to be mad at me? Sure, I guess. I didn't know what went down with Spencer, of course. Had something happened? Something bad? At the time, I never thought it was possible. Spencer was everyone's hero. He was the only guy who hung out with us on girls' nights. He was our designated driver. Our bodyguard when we got too much attention at a club. He'd treated Amaya like a heroine from a romance novel. He was a good guy.

He was a good guy to me, too, until he wasn't.

"Ams? You okay? You're not leaving, are you?"

She nodded.

I should have just said it. That I wanted her to stay. Instead we had some rubbish back-and-forth about my mother bugging her and her insisting that she was tired.

That was until she blurted out that I can't marry Spencer.

But it wasn't what she said. It was the way she said it.

So much entitlement.

For years growing up I was stunted in Amaya's shadow. She always got what she wanted. She was bossy, sure, way before it was politically incorrect to call women bossy. But she used to order me around. Tell me what to do. I spent so much time and energy trying not to upset her. She was fearless back then. She'd taken the fall for me, too, sometimes—when I thought I was in love with a teacher at school and she pretended like she was the one dating him to discourage gossip and I could spend time with him. At the time I thought she was being my friend. Now I knew that she was using my mistakes to control me.

And here she was, telling me what to do again.

"You can't marry him, Kaavi. I was with him for four years, okay? You can't marry him."

Not a request. An order. A stake to her claim.

I guess some things never changed after all.

I gave her a little smile. She wasn't the boss anymore. I was in control.

"I knew that's why you showed up here. You're still in love with him, aren't you?" I didn't care if she was, to be honest. She could have him if it meant both of them were out of my life.

"No, it's not like that. You don't understand."

I don't understand? She broke my heart, worse than any asshole man ever could, and now I'm supposed to be the bad guy?

"I should have known. Really. Look, you'd cut me out of your life, okay? I've tried so many times to reach out to you. I wanted to talk to you about it, of course I did. But come on, Ams, after everything we've been through together you just decided to stop speaking to me. And why? Because I tried to help you all those years ago?"

I hated this. I fucking hated this. I'd made a promise to myself when she left. I'd put up my walls, tall and strong, and no one was getting over them again. And here I was, explaining myself to her again, pleading with her again.

"Help me? You ruined my life!"

Here she was again. Making it all about her.

"What the hell do you even mean?" I hissed. "You're losing your mind, you know that? You've completely lost it. I mean, you just show up here, following me around, completely uninvited—"

"I'm not uninvited."

Was this bitch high?

"What the hell do you mean? How the hell could I have invited you when we haven't even spoken in five fucking years?"

"You invited me, Kaavi. You said you wanted me to come. You even lied to me about your parents wanting me to be here."

Yep. She's lost it. Completely batshit. I just needed to get away from her. I had bigger problems to worry about. I didn't have time for this unhinged bitch from my past. I can't believe I actually thought about opening up to her.

"You've lost your goddamned mind. Everyone said it, I just didn't believe them."

She grabbed my arm, screaming at me to listen to her.

This was the limit.

"Are you threatening me, Amaya? I'll listen to you or what, huh? Or what?"

I'd been threatened way too many times in the last forty-eight hours, and I wasn't taking this shit anymore. She needed to shut up and get out of here.

"Or what, Amaya? You'll kill me like you killed Gayan Peiris? Huh? Is that what you'd do?"

That should do it.

"Yes! I'll fucking kill you before I let you do this. You hear me? I'll fucking kill you."

Damn, and I thought *I'd* taken it too far. Mentioning Gayan was a low blow. We both knew that. It was just a stupid teenage accident. I just wasn't expecting her to react like that.

"Well, there you go."

She tried to explain but I didn't care. I told her to stay the hell away from me and my wedding. I couldn't deal with this anymore.

I stormed off toward the beach, but I didn't make it to the party.

I found a quiet, unlit spot and took my shoes off.

Then I waded into the ocean, until the water was to my waist. It wasn't cold. The Indian Ocean was never cold. My dress billowed out around me. Thank god I'd had the good sense to book out the whole beach so no one was around.

I took a deep breath, the deepest I'd taken in a long, long time. Then I lowered myself into the water, and screamed.

No one could hear me. Just the way I wanted it.

30

KAAVI

Day of the Poruwa Ceremony

THEY SAY A little bit of nerves is normal before you get married. We see it on TV and in movies all the time, right? Though most often it's the groom that fears commitment and runs away, and we've already established that Spencer is going nowhere.

But it wasn't commitment that I feared. No way. I don't think anyone has the discipline to commit to something the way I could. I mean, think about it—I've committed to my entire perfect way of life, haven't I? I've committed to flawless hair and pristine skin and an even squeakier-clean reputation. People look at me and wish they were me. If you think, even for a moment, that doesn't take lifelong commitment, well, why don't you give it a try and see how it works out for you?

And in the grand scheme of things, I don't mind committing to Spencer. He's perfect on paper, blackmailing tendencies aside. We could set off on exactly the kind of marriage I wanted—unencumbered by ridiculous expectations of eternal romance and marital bliss. Please. All you need to do is look into the hollow eyes of new parents or couples that have passed the honeymoon period to know that nothing lasted. What lasts is stability. Comfort. Potential companionship with a person you didn't have to keep comparing to a past version of themselves. You know, when their waistlines were trimmer and they acted like the sun shone out of your behind.

I've never believed in soul mates. I've never needed a man to make me feel complete. I'm plenty perfect on my own. Marriage was just window dressing. A decorative element in a society that places far more value on how things look rather than how they make you feel. No one cares if you're married happily, after all, just that you have a husband.

My nerves weren't a mess because of the commitment. Or my strategically prescribed new life.

My nerves were a mess because my groom was a liar, and someone hated me enough to actually burn my wedding dress. It was probably Amaya, getting back at me for what I said yesterday. Well, fuck her. I don't care what the fuck she pulled. I could deal with her bullshit later.

When my phone rang at 6:30 a.m. the morning of my Poruwa ceremony, I was showered, dressed in my bedazzled robe that read *Bride*, and sipping on my coffee.

"Mike," I said, in way of greeting.

"Kaavi, hi, I hope I'm not waking you up. I wanted to catch you before— Today IS the big day, right?"

"Today is the ceremonial day, yes. And you didn't wake me. What's going on?"

"It's not good, Kaavs."

We weren't close enough for him to call me that, but I let it slide. There were bigger fish to fry.

"Tell me." I steeled myself.

"There's a reason Zoe Bassett was so hard to get ahold of. She's, well, she's gone into hiding."

"What do you mean, hiding?"

"I mean she's afraid for her life. We still haven't been able to talk to her, but my colleague spoke to her best friend. She'd been dating Spencer for about two years. Zoe's very well-off, according to her. Had a nice trust fund set up by her grandparents before they died. A trust fund that Spencer tried to help himself to, apparently."

I was clenching my fist so hard around my phone that it bit into my hand.

"And?"

"She'd been trying to end things for a while, but apparently Spencer had been, well, look, there's no easy way to say this. Spencer had been violent toward her. Put her in the hospital. She'd even filed a charge, but dropped it for some reason. Her friend claims she was blackmailed. Anyway, she managed to get away. She's changed her name now, and is trying to recover."

"When did she leave?"

"Early August, the year before last."

Just before Spencer met me at the reunion. I'd been his meal ticket right from the start. How could I have been so blind?

"Look, Kaavi, from what she said, he's a lot more dangerous than you'd think." Didn't I know?

"Don't worry, Mike. It's not like I can't take care of myself."

"I've heard a lot of people say that, Kaavi. I just hope for your sake that you know what you're doing. Zoe was, well, from what I heard, she had to spend a large chunk of her trust fund on a plastic surgeon. Please be careful."

31

KAAVI

The Night before the Wedding

I DRANK A lot of champagne and thought long and hard about what my options were. The day passed by in a blur. The makeup, everyone fussing over me, the various people who traipsed in and out of my room, telling me over and over again how lovely I looked, what a beautiful bride I was. The exhausting photo shoot that I cut short because I just couldn't put myself through it.

On top of all that, I had to appease a heartbroken Andre, who wasn't buying what happened to "his" dress. He probably thought I'd destroyed it on purpose so I could just wear the Hayley Paige, but honestly, I didn't have enough energy left in me to care.

And then, the Poruwa ceremony itself. I smiled, I did all the rituals, I was perfect. I *am* perfect.

"Glad you decided to keep up your end of the bargain," Spencer whispered in my ear as he wrapped the necklace on me. It felt like a noose. "I was worried you'd have a change of heart and run away in the night."

I smiled sweetly so the crowd wouldn't notice anything amiss. I was just a happy bride, enjoying my big day.

"Kaavi, look, I'm sorry, okay?" He was whispering, also with a smile on his face. "I didn't ever mean to make you feel trapped. I care about you. I want this. Just give me a chance. You'll see what a perfect husband I'll be."

If my bouquet trembled in my hands, no one seemed to notice.

I excused myself from the crowd as soon as I could. It wasn't easy. All the guests had to be greeted, elders had to be worshipped, and even though the main festivities were tomorrow, that didn't stop the Sri Lankan uncles from taking maximum advantage of the open bar and busting out moves on the dance floor.

I was passed around from table to table, making small talk, listening to aunties gush over how I looked in the traditional Kandyan *Osariya*. I hung on to Spencer's arm—my husband. Married in the eyes of tradition though not yet in the eyes of the law. He was disgusting, and I didn't want to be anywhere close to him, much less touch him, but I just needed to get through this evening.

That's what I kept telling myself.

I just needed to get through this evening.

"Kaavindi *Baba*, I'm so happy for you." That was Seetha, grabbing both my hands with a huge smile on her face. "I only hope Amaya *Baba* will be as happy as you are one day."

I had forgotten all about Amaya after Mike's phone call, but who could blame me anyway?

"Thank you, Seetha. I must get going now."

"*Baba*, do you have anyone to help you change? Would you like me to stay back?"

"That's okay, Seetha. I'll manage."

That was sweet, albeit a little strange, but Seetha was always a strange woman. Neither Amaya nor I could ever really figure out what was going on in her head. To be honest, it had always freaked the fuck out of me, especially after Gayan's drunk driving accident. It was cruel of me to accuse Amaya of killing him yesterday. That was just a rumor, of course, and wasn't Colombo ripe with those? We'd just been surprised that Gayan was as drunk as they made him out to be. We'd all been pretty inexperienced drinkers back then, and Gayan, as always, was more interested in trying to get into my pants whenever Amaya was distracted.

The exhaustion from the past few days had settled into my bones. I had just made it past the guests and was almost inside the main hotel, when I saw someone lunge for me out of the corner of my eye.

I gasped, sidestepping, my bouquet dropping to the floor.

"Kaavindi!" Mr. Ananda cried, lunging for me again.

He smelled of arrack and his eyes were bloodshot. Thankfully, one of the drivers had seen the commotion and appeared out of nowhere, pulling him back. There were no other wedding guests around to see this, thank god.

"Why are you here?" I hissed.

"I need to talk to you. To make you pay for what you did." He struggled against the man holding him.

"Anything we discuss will be through lawyers," I said, turning away. I couldn't deal with him right now. Definitely not today.

"You bitch," he spat. "You've had everything in your life handed to you on a silver platter. You just float on with your head in a cloud, with no clue how the rest of us suffer."

"I really am sorry about your wife, Mr. Ananda. I've told you that. But there's nothing that can be done now."

"You just wait. You'll have what's coming to you soon. You'll see." He reached behind him to the small of his back, fumbling to pull out something from his waistband.

"What's going on here?" My mother's voice rose over the commotion, and suddenly two more drivers appeared from god knows where. One of them stepped in front of me, while the other grabbed Mr. Ananda's arms and twisted them behind his back.

"*Podi* madam-*wa athulata geniyanna.*" Get small-madam inside, my mother said, and I was swiftly escorted back to my room.

It was when I was locking the door that I realized how much my hands were trembling. Two threats in less than twenty-four hours, a sociopath husband, and a burned wedding dress. Everything was starting to snowball. I can't have that. I need to be in control.

I tried taking a deep breath, but that was near impossible in Andre's skintight sari jacket. And I had gone and rejected everyone's help in getting changed because I just wanted to be alone.

I pulled off the sari fall—the fabric that draped over my shoulder—got rid of the frill around my waist, and finally managed to wriggle out of the skirt. Then I stood in my underskirt and contorted myself into the strangest positions to reach the buttons on the back of my blouse, but with no luck.

So when someone finally knocked on the door, I threw it open gratefully. Perhaps it was someone from my family checking in on me? I'd even bully a room service boy to help me out if it came down to it.

But it wasn't any of them.

"What are you doing here?" I asked Amaya, who looked like she was about to faint.

"I need to talk to you, Kaavi."

"Well, I have nothing to say to you. And I asked you to stay the fuck away from me."

"It isn't that. Listen. It's important—"

"Look, I honestly don't care, okay? I have bigger issues to deal with right now." I tried to shut the door in her face, but she stuck her arm out and pushed her way inside.

"Hey! What the—"

But my words died in my mouth as I saw the knife in her hand.

"We really need to talk, Kaavi."

I gulped.

This bitch was crazier than I could have imagined.

AMAYA

Interview Transcript: Amaya Bloom (abbrev. AB)

Date: January 25, 2020

Location: The Mount Lavinia Hotel

AB: My name is Amaya Bloom. I live in Los Angeles, though I'm currently staying at my family home at 75 Gregory's Road, Colombo 07.

EP: Miss Bloom could you please explain to me what you were doing at the Mount Lavinia Hotel on the night of the twenty-fourth? It is our understanding that you were disinvited from the wedding.

AB: Yes, I was disinvited. But Kaavi is my oldest friend. I hoped she wasn't serious when she asked me not to come. Besides, I had already booked and paid for my room many weeks ago and didn't want it to go to waste.

EP: But you did not attend the Poruwa?

AB: No. I requested a room with a seaside view and watched from my balcony instead. It felt wrong not to respect her wishes on her big day.

EP: But you did visit her room later on that day?

AB: Yes. I did. I wanted to apologize.

EP: To apologize for what?

AB: For—well, it's a long story. All of it. But mainly I wanted to apologize for everything that happened at the bridal shower, and to tell her the truth about what happened. Why I stopped talking to her so long ago.

EP: Did Miss Fonseka appear normal to you, during this visit?

AB: To be honest, no.

EP: Would you please elaborate?

AB: She appeared distraught and upset. Mainly with her fiancé, Matthew Spencer. She spoke to me about leaving him. She said she had an air-ticket booked to Singapore, and intended on flying out early this morning.

EP: You are certain of this.

AB: Yes. That is what she told me. She said she would contact her parents when things settled down.

EP: If this is the case, Miss Bloom, may I ask why you delayed informing her parents or the authorities of such vital information?

AB: Because she asked me to. She didn't want it getting out until she was gone. She was afraid.

EP: Miss Bloom, I'm sure you are aware that there were signs of an attack in Miss Fonseka's room. During our investigation, we were able to take an inventory of Miss Fonseka's belongings. Among them was her passport.

AB: Her passport was in her room?

EP: Yes. And the night guard on duty claims that she never left from the main entrance, which she would have to do if she were to leave anytime before 6:00 a.m., as all other entrances would be locked.

AB: [Silence]

EP: Miss Bloom, would you mind telling us about your relationship with Miss Fonseka?

AB: I can't believe this.

EP: What can't you believe, Miss Bloom?

AB: That this is happening. Kaavi and I have been friends since we were children. We grew up together. We went to the same school here in Colombo. She even decided to apply to universities in the US with me instead of going to the UK like her parents would have preferred. We were like sisters. We remained close through university, which is where I met Spencer.

EP: Yes, Mr. Spencer. You were romantically involved with him, am I correct?

AB: Yes.

EP: You must have been jealous, then? That your friend was marrying your boyfriend?

AB: I was not jealous. I was scared.

EP: Scared of what? Of losing your boyfriend? Is that what motivated you to hurt Miss Fonseka?

AB: No. I— Listen.

[Pause]

[Takes deep breath]

Let me start from the beginning. When I first met Spencer I had just turned nineteen and had never really been in a serious relationship before. He, well, he took care of me. I wasn't ever taken care of much growing up. My mother died when I was young, as you must have heard by now, and my father never really wanted anything to do with me. Spencer was this handsome, dashing man who paid attention to me and, well, I suppose you can imagine the rest. On the surface, we looked like your run-of-the-mill couple. We were in love. We were happy. He was friends with my best friend.

EP: Could you please get to the point, Miss Bloom?

AB: Y-yes. That's what I'm trying to do here.

[Pause]

He was, well, I guess you could call it controlling. It was nothing significant, at first anyway. He had a preference for how I

dressed. He hated it when I wore high heels, or makeup, for instance. At first, he would say that it was because I didn't need it
to look beautiful, but then he used to get, well, almost irritable
if I ever even wore lipstick. And then one day I came home to
find that he had thrown away every bit of makeup I owned.

It escalated from what I wore, to who I spoke to, where I went. It's
all a bit cliché now, of course. I didn't see it at first. It was almost like, well, like those rocks that get shaped by a river.
How could something as soft, something as beautiful as a
river have the ability to change the complete structure of
something as hard as a rock? Because I was as hard as a rock.
I'd lost my mother. I'd survived. I was indestructible.

It was only when I saw a photo someone had taken of me on my first
day of college that I realized how much I had changed. If you
spoke to anyone from my childhood they will tell you how out-
going, how "bossy," how full of life I was. And then I was afraid
to leave the house without him. To make any decisions at all. It
was even more terrible because I was paying for everything. For
his share of the rent, starting capital for his various businesses,
for his—um—I guess you could call it a cocaine habit. He—he'd
struggled—with his addiction, though he'd never call it that, of
course—over the years. He said he only used it as a coping mech-
anism. And he'd get upset if I ever spoke back to him. Said I was
going on a power trip because I felt I owned him. It couldn't be
further from the truth of course. But his ego was fragile, and I
didn't want to hurt him. He was all I had.

And what started as requests, and gentle berating, and subtly putting me down, then grew to much, much worse. I—well, I
don't think I need to spell it out. I tried to end things with him
many times. I fought back, you know. But it was—well, you

never think it could be you, you know? You hear stories about women in abusive relationships all the time. You always wonder why they never left. You never think it could be you. I never thought it would be me either. Even when I was in the thick of it. I didn't—and I can't even believe this when I think about it now—but I didn't even realize that things were so bad for me. He never hit me, you see. Not outright. There was grabbing, I think he might have choked me once, but I justified it to myself. He was just trying to calm me down because I wouldn't stop crying. He was trying to stop me from walking away. He was forcing me to stay, to talk about our fight. That was healthy, right?

EP: And was Miss Fonseka aware of your turbulent relationship?

AB: No. Not at all. I went to great lengths to hide it. So did Spencer, I guess. She knew we argued, of course, but Spencer never spoke to me the way he did when we were alone around her. Around anyone else really. To Kaavi, I must have just looked like an overly emotional girlfriend. Crying all the time. Breaking up with him one day and taking him back the next.

I—well, Spencer didn't have it easy, either, you know. His family was never there for him too. It was one of the things we bonded over. I wanted to be a safe space for him. Like he was for me.

I must have done an excellent job covering it all up, though, because when it came down to it, she took his word against mine.

EP: Please explain further.

AB: It was the end of my senior year, the day after graduation, and I wanted to end things with Spencer for good. We were moving to a new apartment, so it felt like the right time to make a clean break. I ended things and asked Kaavi not to tell him our new address. She did.

When Spencer showed up at the new place with flowers, he assumed, just like Kaavi assumed, I suppose, that I hadn't really meant it. That this was just the threat of a breakup and not a real one. He played me this song on his phone, and chased me around the living room as I tried to back away from him. He was—it was not like the other times. He'd been angry before, sure, but this time I thought he'd kill me.

[Pause]

I'd never been that scared. After a few hours, after I pretended like things were okay, I managed to convince him that I needed something from the store, and the moment he left I just took my passport and my purse and ran. Kaavi was just getting home as I left the apartment, and I—well, I was very, very angry with her for giving Spencer our address. I should have told Kaavi then. I mean, I knew. Of all people I had known what Spencer was like. How charming he was. How he could have coaxed information out of her as easily as taking candy from a baby. But I was so hurt. So angry. I blamed everyone. I blamed Kaavi for giving me up. My parents for abandoning me. I blamed myself for letting things get this far. I told her that I hated her and never to speak to me again.

I waited at the airport for fifteen hours until I could get a flight to Sri Lanka. I was terrified he'd find me while I waited. I hid in the bathroom for almost the entire time.

And then I got home, but I was afraid that he'd follow me all the way here, to Colombo. So afraid that I couldn't bear to live alone in my house. I told everyone that there had been a break-in at my home, and turned to the only family I ever had, even though Kaavi and I weren't speaking to each other. I moved in with them—it was just for a while, at first. They didn't know what had happened. Just that I was going through a bad breakup and needed to recover. Mrs. Fonseka was the first person to realize I was pregnant. They were less than thrilled, as you can imagine.

EP: And was Matthew Spencer ever made aware of this?

AB: No. I never wanted him to know.

EP: Before he attacked you, you said you wanted to leave Mr. Spencer for good. Was there anything else, apart from the abuse, of course, that helped you make this decision?

[Pause]

Miss Bloom?

AB: Remember I told you how he hated me wearing makeup? How he liked to control what I wore? I didn't really connect the dots until later. He didn't want me wearing makeup because he hated me looking grown-up. The same with high heels. And the clothes he wanted me to wear were always, well, they were girly. And young looking. I—I didn't think much of it, at the time anyway. Who cares if your boyfriend insisted you always wore white cotton panties when you finally felt like you were important to someone? Like you finally had a place in this world?

It happened right after I graduated—I used his laptop while he was in the shower and an email popped up with a link that routed through a bunch of sites. And I knew I shouldn't snoop but something felt off and just—well—and I found—well, I still don't know exactly what it was I'd found. The extent to which it went. Just that it contained children. That it was very, very wrong.

That was when I knew that I absolutely had to leave. He didn't know what I had found. When he got out of the shower I just

told him that I never wanted to speak to him again and then I
left. But he found me, as you know.

[Pause]

This is why—well, this is the main reason why I flew back here.
To stop the wedding. Not just because I didn't want Kaavi to
marry him, but most importantly, because I needed to keep
him away from Nadia. I know I agreed to stay away from her.
To not interfere in her life—with all their lives. And I don't
have this pining to be a mother or to step in and take her away,
which is probably what Mrs. Fonseka thinks. I can see she's
happy there. I just want her to be safe. I needed to keep her
away from him. I've seen the photos of Spencer with the Pink
Sapphire girls too. He shouldn't be around children.

EP: But why not come clean? Why not simply tell everyone what
you knew?

AB: [Pause] What proof did I have? Spencer is, well, he's this perfect man. Everyone loves him. I could see it from half a world
away. If I showed up here, screaming that he was some sort of
pedophile, I'd have just been the crazy ex-girlfriend who
wanted to ruin this perfect wedding. Don't tell me you didn't
think that to begin with. Don't tell me that you didn't think I
was here because I was still in love with him, or because I was
obsessed with her.

EP: Is this knife yours, Miss Bloom?

AB: Y-yes. I gave it to Kaavi. Last night. For her to defend herself.
She was trying to leave him.

EP: We have a video that Miss Fonseka recorded on her phone.
Would you like to see it?

AB: She—she left a video?

[Kaavindi Fonseka's voice fills the room]

If someone is watching this, then chances are that I'm already dead.

I don't even know why I'm recording a video. Call it a force of habit. Maybe later on I'll see it and it'll be hilarious. But tonight, well, [nervous laughter] this isn't the kind of nerves I was expecting the night before my big day.

I'm having my dream wedding. I'm tying the knot at this beautiful hotel where my parents got married. Where I spent so much of my childhood playing down by the beach. I should be out of my mind with joy.

And maybe I'm wrong. Maybe I'm just being paranoid. But I've had this feeling for a while now, that things aren't right.

Maybe it's just—

Hang on.

[Whispering] I hear footsteps.

I think someone's outside my door.

[Knocking]

Oh god.

[Louder] Who, um, who is it?

[Whispering to the camera] They aren't saying who it is.

[Knocking again]

Oh god, here goes.

AB: [Pause] Her face. She's only showing the right side of her face.

EP: Is that what stands out to you, Miss Bloom? Because I would have thought—

[Interruption]

Security officer: Miss Padmaraj, please come with us at once. There's been a situation in room 311.

EP: [Standing] Room 311? Isn't that . . . ?

Security officer: Yes, madam. That's the groom's, Mr. Spencer's, room.

32

AMAYA

The Day of the Wedding

ALL THE DEEP breaths and counting to five and checking for numbers didn't reassure me. Things had gone wrong. Things had gone very, very wrong.

I'd known it this morning, and I knew for sure when I saw the video. If we were still sticking to the plan, then why on earth didn't Kaavi just name Spencer in the footage? Why did she just keep it vague? Was she trying to screw me? I thought back to how angry she'd been with me up until then. She was definitely trying to screw me.

I was certain Miss Padmaraj was going to have me arrested.

I was so sure of it that I'd already started grasping for straws, spilling out my heart, trying to figure out how I could get out of this.

But then a security guard barged in during the middle of my interview and I was forgotten, for the time being at least. I didn't even have to look at the numbers to know that luck was on my side.

Miss Padmaraj stood up and rushed out of the room.

"*Mey* miss-*va mehe thiyaganna* please," she barked to one of the younger-looking security guards on her way out. Keep this lady here please. He looked scared out of his mind at being acknowledged directly by her, but nodded, his eyes wide.

The rest of the guards followed Miss Padmaraj, and I was suddenly alone, my mind reeling. A situation in Spencer's room. What was it? Had he finally come clean? Had he hurt himself? Had he tried to escape?

Escape.

It was like a light bulb went off in my head.

I wasn't under arrest. Not yet, anyway. I could leave if I really wanted to. The young guard was just outside the door to this conference room, which was left open in the rush. Not high-security by any sense of the word. Good.

I checked my watch. I had been left here for about five minutes.

The deep breaths I took calmed me down.

I hated having to do this, but there was definitely no other choice.

Holding my head high and my shoulders back, I stepped out of the room.

"Miss Padmaraj called me," I said in my most American, non–Sri Lankan accent. "She wants me to come down and join her."

The panic on the security guard's face made me feel like a real villain. I knew what I was doing. *He* knew what I was doing. I was playing my Colombo 07 Privilege Card. The card I hated everyone else in this town for playing. Where I would use my perfect westernized English and the wealth I had the luck of being born into to make someone else feel so small, so insignificant, so afraid of their status in life that they felt that they had no choice but to let me do what I wanted. Rich kids, the children of the politically connected, did it every day. Standing in lines, stopping for traffic cops, following procedure in public administration buildings wasn't for them. For us.

We'd breeze by in life, while security guards like the one who was stuck with me today feared for their jobs. Because a complaint against him to a higher-up that I would no doubt have connections to would take away his livelihood in one swoop.

But now wasn't the time to let my conscience get the better of me.

He hadn't replied. He was probably trying to figure out what he should do.

"Do you want me to call her?" I asked, pulling out my phone. "What was your name again?"

"Miss, *mata kiwwa ne yanna epa kiyala*." Miss, she told me not to let you go.

"I'm sorry?" I raised my eyebrows at him, even though I knew very well what he was saying. Another trick of the rich and ridiculous. Because not understanding your mother tongue was somehow an increase in social status. I suppose we can thank colonialism for that.

"Miss—*ah*—" His face was red and I felt guiltier than when I burned Kaavi's dress.

"Okay, look, if you want to try and stop me, then go ahead, but I'm leaving."

And with that, I turned and rushed down the stairs.

Thank goodness this wasn't the US. Even most branches of the police didn't carry guns, let alone security guards. And this one wouldn't dare lay his hands on me.

But I could unpack my class privilege later—when I wasn't about to be arrested for murder.

He might have been following me, but I didn't look back. I ran out of the old wing, into the courtyard entrance of the hotel property. From here, it would be easy enough for me to slip out from somewhere. I'd probably be able to jump in a *tuk* once I got onto the main road. I didn't have any money on me, but Seetha would probably be able to sort me out once I got home. It'll be fine.

Except the entrance was swarming with hotel security.

"*Koheyda mey yanneh?*" Where are you going? A security officer who looked far more serious and far more confident than the one upstairs called out to me.

Luckily, the very guard I had slipped away from moments earlier showed up next to me.

"Padmaraj Miss *kiwwa ekkan enna kiyala*." Miss Padmaraj asked me to bring her.

"Hmm," the older guard said, walking away.

I had no choice but to be marched toward the new wing. The bravado I had thrown in the face of the poor officer was evaporating along with the ocean breeze. I had no idea what to do now.

We walked through the lobby and into the elevator wordlessly, until we got off on the third floor. Eshanya Padmaraj was there with a gaggle of more security, while one of the hotel guards sat on the floor with his back propped against the wall.

"*Mama dakke nah*, miss. *Kawuda pitipassen avilla mata gahuwa. Tika-kata kalin thamay sihiya aavey.*" I didn't see anything, miss. Someone snuck up from behind me and attacked. I only gained consciousness a little while ago. He looked like he was on the verge of tears.

"What happened?" a voice boomed down the corridor.

Mr. Fonseka barged down, his face red and dripping with perspiration.

"Nihal, you're not supposed to be here," Eshanya Padmaraj responded, trying her best to sound calm but clearly frazzled by his appearance. She hadn't seen me yet, thank goodness. Perhaps I could slip away in this commotion.

"What do you mean I'm not supposed to be here, Eshanya? I

asked you to come to get to the bottom of this. To figure out what happened to my Kaavi. And now I'm told that my son-in-law is missing too? What's the meaning of this?"

I had been backing away—hoping to make it to the stairwell next to the elevator we had used, but I stopped in my tracks.

So Spencer was missing also? Had he managed to attack the guard and slip out? Or had someone else attacked him?

"What on earth is going on?"

It was Mrs. Fonseka this time.

"Fiona, where the hell have you been? I've been looking all over for you. I was just about to come in search of you when . . ."

"What has happened to Spencer?" Mrs. Fonseka wasn't about to be distracted.

"Nihal, Fiona, listen, we are trying to put things together, but you aren't making it any easier by being here. And it appears that the guests are not safe in their rooms either."

"So you think Spencer was attacked?"

"That certainly is a possibility, but we have no way of making sure with the guests all spread out like this."

She turned away and punched something into her phone.

"Hello, Mr. Ferdinand." I recognized the name of the manager who searched my room this morning. "We need to move all the guests over to the main ballroom now. Please inform your security. Yes. This needs to happen right away." She paused for a moment.

"I don't care if the ballroom hasn't been arranged, Mr. Ferdinand. They need to be moved now."

When I grow up, that's exactly the kind of woman I want to be. One who knew what she wanted and wasn't afraid to get it. I just wished we were both on the same side.

"*Ahuna, nedha? Okkoma* guest-*la tika vahaama* ballroom *ekata geni-yanna. Kaale nasthi karanna epa, ahuna neh?*" Did you hear me? Escort all the guests to the ballroom immediately. Don't waste any time, understand?

And then her eyes fell on me.

"What are you doing here?"

"I—" I tried. But she had bigger things to deal with right then. Like a missing groom to match her missing bride.

"Just get her to the ballroom with everyone else." She waved me away. "You also, Nihal. I'm sorry, but it's for your own good. There might be someone dangerous on the loose in the hotel, and I need to make sure you're safe."

Mr. and Mrs. Fonseka both nodded and allowed themselves to be led, along with me, back downstairs and to the main ballroom.

There were already a few guests making their way there. All of them whispering, suspicious.

"What's going on?" they whispered.

"I heard she's dead."

"I thought she'd killed herself."

"I knew it: she has run away."

And still, in the middle of all that—

"I love your shoes, *aney.*"

"Haven't seen you in so long. My, you've lost weight."

"Do you think they'll at least have the lobster station open for dinner? The room service food was horrendous."

This was all just entertainment to them.

I felt like screaming. I needed a moment, just a small moment, to be alone. To think things through. To figure out a plan.

I hung back on the staircase and stubbed my foot against the edge. I was hoping the cut I made on my toe this morning would sting, but the sneakers I had on padded my wound too well. I bit the inside of my cheek instead. It hurt, just not nearly enough.

This is not what Kaavi and I discussed last night. This is not how things were supposed to turn out at all.

I took a moment and ducked into a quiet corridor. The hotel security were too busy with the crowds, so it was easy enough for now.

Trying to take a deep, centering breath, I thought back to yesterday.

"I KNOW. I know you don't want me here," I had said, my voice coming out all high-pitched and breathless. "But please, you have to listen to me."

"For fuck's sake, Amaya, I don't have time for your bullshit right now." It had caught me by surprise again. The way she sounded. Not like she spoke on her Instagram Lives, or in front of a crowd of people. She had sounded rougher, somehow. Mean.

"No, listen, please. I know you think I'm some sort of nutjob who flew over here to ruin your big day—"

"Like you didn't try?"

I felt my face redden. She was right. I burned her dress. I was here to stop the wedding. But not because of what she thought. I wasn't here because I was in love with Spencer. I was here because I loved her. And Nadia. And yes, even the rest of her family. I was here because I couldn't bear the thought of a monster living with them, making himself at home, being close to my child.

I had to make her listen to me, at least one more time.

And if she didn't—well, I knew Spencer's room number. I had the knife. I'd probably be caught. I'd probably end up as one of those slimy, disgusting headlines. *Jealous Ex-girlfriend Stabs Groom to Death the Night before His Wedding.* But I didn't care. Let everyone blame me. I didn't give a hoot. At least my family would be safe.

"Please, just give me five minutes. Okay? Five minutes and then if you tell me to I'll be out of your life for good. You'll never see me again, okay? I promise."

Kaavi suddenly looked tired.

"I never wanted to not see you, you know? You're the one who just disappeared."

"I know. But please listen?"

She went over to the minibar and pulled out two miniature bottles of whiskey and tossed one to me.

Relief flooded through me.

I twisted off the top and downed the entire thing in one shot. Well, I tried to, at least. The whiskey burned when it hit the back of my throat and I spluttered, managing to spill a fair bit of it onto my white T-shirt.

Kaavi raised an eyebrow at me, the way she did if I did something stupid when we were kids, and had tossed her head back and downed it in one go. Always more graceful, always more elegant. Then she threw a fresh T-shirt at me.

"Put this on. There's no way I can concentrate with that giant stain on your boob."

I did what she asked. I've always done what she asked.

She sat on a chair and crossed her arms.

"Go on, then?"

I didn't sit. I paced around her room as I told her. I told her what things were like with Spencer. About how he treated me through college. About how I loved him in the way you do when you don't know any better—so deeply that you lose your sense of direction. That it was nearly impossible for me to find my way back. That I knew I had to, after what I found out about him. The thing to finally break the spell. Or the curse.

I told her about the abuse, my eyes trained on the floor, my voice rational and robotic. Those things happened to a different girl. I wasn't her. Not anymore.

I told her how her parents took me in when I showed up at their doorstep, a broken shell of who I used to be, and begged that they didn't tell her I was there, just in case she was still loyal to him. Just in case she told him where I was and he found me again.

I didn't tell her about the baby, but we weren't best friends all our lives for nothing.

"Nadia?" she asked, and all I could do was nod. Something flashed through her eyes—was it understanding, or hurt, or rage, or recognition? I don't think I'll ever truly know.

"And that's why," I finished, feeling heady, probably from the nerves but also from finally being able to talk about it after so long, "that's why I came. Because I couldn't have him hurt you—hurt all of you, but especially Nadia—the way he hurt me."

Kaavi was quiet. It was disconcerting.

But still, I gave her a moment. This was big news; I knew that. I basically told her that the man she was about to marry was the thing nightmares were made of. She probably had a million questions for me, even if she believed me.

She did believe me though. I knew it the second I finally looked her in the face.

And she didn't have a million questions. Just one.

"Why didn't you tell me?"

"I tried, so many times. But you were so angry with me for disappearing, and your mother was so upset about—"

"Not now. Why didn't you tell me then?"

"I think maybe"—I faced her full-on, my eyes searching out hers, years of things unsaid—"I was afraid of appearing weak. Of not being in control."

She blinked. And then she shook her head.

"Well, I've really gone and gotten myself fucked, haven't I?" She rubbed her eyes.

"I'm sorry. Maybe you think you love him, but I promise you, you deserve better."

Kaavi sighed.

"You don't know the half of it."

"Then tell me, Kaavs. Let me help you. You know I will. You know you can trust me."

"Okay, look, I have an idea. I—well, let's just say that I've had my own suspicions about Spencer. I've been thinking of a way out of this for a while."

I could have fainted with relief. Of course Kaavi was smarter than I had given her credit for. Of course she'd caught on to the fact that Spencer was a scumbag.

"But why can't you just leave him? Call the whole thing off. Your parents would understand."

"My parents? No way. They are part of the reason . . ." she let her voice trail off. "My parents won't be of help, Ams. I'm on my own. And anyway, I can't let Spencer get away with all this. He needs to pay for all his bullshit."

This did not feel right. Didn't she know that she couldn't get the better of him? She might be smart, but he was dangerous.

"What do you mean?"

"Listen, I'm just going to, well, I'm going to disappear for a while, okay? Tonight. And I'll need you to cover for me. Please don't say no."

"Of course I'll cover for you, Kaavs, but where are you going?"

"I'm going to fly out to Singapore. I'm getting my flight arranged now as we speak. Now listen carefully—everyone's going to lose their shit when they realize I've gone. You'll probably be questioned. I don't want you to lie. I want you to tell them—anyone who asks—what you've told me about Spencer, okay? About him being such a class A dick."

I found myself nodding. She was leaving. Thank god she was leaving.

"Let me come with you." The words slipped out before I even thought about them.

She smiled at me but didn't say anything. For a second there, I saw her. My best friend. The girl who listened to my dreams, who was my only family.

"I just—it's been so long. I don't—" I felt my voice wobble and paused to get it back under control. "I don't want to lose you again."

"You'll never lose me, Ams. You never did, okay? What, you think that just because we don't speak to each other for a while that we're not friends?"

"Five years is more than a while."

"Hey, I'll be fine, okay? I need you to stay here and handle things for me. People need to know who Spencer is. Just give me some time to get on a plane and get out of here."

After everything I had done, I could give her that.

"I'll be fine, okay? Now here's the plan. I'm going to call Spencer in here."

"What? No!"

"No, calm down, listen. He has to be seen coming in here. Where's your room, again?"

"Upstairs, around the corner."

"Perfect. I want you to go now, and call room service. Have them deliver something to your room. Tea, or something that won't take long. The waiter will have to pass by my room to get to the stairs. Hopefully we can time this right and the waiter will see Spencer."

I didn't like it one bit.

"And then when he leaves, I need you to come back. To help me get everything together. Think you could do that?"

I could do that, sure, but I felt like I was about to throw up.

"What if Spencer—what if he puts two and two together, Kaavs? What if he figures it out?"

"He won't. Don't worry."

"You don't know him like I do, Kaavi. He can be dangerous." An idea suddenly popped into my head. I pulled out the knife I had put away in my bag. It looked juvenile and ridiculous in this five-star hotel room, but it would serve its purpose, if needed.

"Keep this."

Her eyes went from the knife to my face a few times. I could almost see her try to work it out—why I would have a knife from home with me today.

But if she thought it was strange, or downright psychotic, she didn't say anything. She just took the knife from me and set it in her desk drawer. Perhaps she just wanted the blade away from me as soon as possible.

But then I saw her eyes glint.

And I knew I wasn't going to like whatever she was about to say next.

"Ams, I need one more favor from you, okay? Not now. After Spencer leaves. I need you to do something so that everyone believes, without a doubt, that Spencer was a terrible, abusive asshole. So that everyone knows that I had no choice but to get away."

I instinctively looked at the time. 11:11 p.m.

"Of course. Anything." And I meant it.

There wasn't a hint of humor on her face when she asked. She was hard, cold, and unbreakable—just like the engagement ring that sparkled on her finger.

"After Spencer leaves, we're going to have to wreck this room so it looks like I've been attacked. And I'll need you to punch me in the face."

I TOOK ANOTHER deep breath, willing myself into the present.

The crowd had died down around me. They were all probably at the ballroom now. I leaned against the wall.

Think, Amaya. Think.

There has to be a way out of this.

But my mind kept finding its way back to her. To the way she looked in that video.

What was she getting at? Why didn't she just name Spencer if she was trying to shift the focus onto him? Why didn't she show her face with the bruise I'd left on her cheekbone? Did she even intend for someone to watch the video, or had she left her phone behind by accident? Was she unable to take her phone with her because she was attacked, or hurt for real?

I tried to remember everything she said, and a part of it flashed back into my mind.

I'm having my dream wedding. I'm tying the knot at this beautiful hotel where my parents got married. Where I spent so much of my childhood playing down by the beach.

An idea flashed in my mind. It was barely an idea actually, more of an inkling. The guard had said she'd never left the hotel. Dead or alive, she's got to still be here.

33

AMAYA

The Day of the Wedding

GETTING DOWN TO the beach wasn't so difficult now that most of the security had moved over to guard the entrance of the ballroom. I had to be careful, of course, and I did duck behind a large pillar once, but on the whole, I managed to get to the shore without too much incident.

I pulled out my phone, but the battery had died. I had no way of checking the time. I kept my eyes half-closed anyway. I didn't want to see any unlucky signs.

I crept down the path that led past the beach huts where the bachelorette party had taken place. Then farther down, beyond the kitchens. There was no one around. Ghosts like me were free to roam around this abandoned beach unhindered.

I could see it, farther down. The small line of changing rooms that no one used anymore after the new ones were built during hotel renovations. They were mostly defunct, and I had no idea why they weren't torn down. I didn't know if Kaavi was in there or not. But if she hadn't left the premises and every inch of the main building had been checked, this was probably the only option left.

And I was right. There were two trails of footsteps imprinted onto the sand. Someone had come down here not too long ago.

I would have liked to have some cover. To have something that hid me from where I needed to get to. But there was just me and the open stretch of beach. I paused and took a deep breath. I had only counted to three when I heard a shout.

There was little choice left. I put my head down and ran over, my heels kicking the sand out behind me while the wind and the waves graciously muffled any sound I was making.

Slowing down as I reached the line of changing rooms, I surveyed my options. All the cubicle doors were closed. I reached out and tried the handle of the one closest to me. It was locked, and the knob was slimy—some sort of moss having grown on it during years of neglect. But I could hear voices now. Crying, maybe, or some sort of a whimper.

Making sure I was quiet, I slunk down past the doors. There was still moss on each of the handles, except for when I got to the very last one. The voices were louder now. Someone was inside.

I didn't have a weapon with me. I would have done just about anything to still have my knife, but there was no choice now. I had to see what was going on.

I twisted the knob and the door swung open.

"Well, it's about fucking time." Kaavi's voice was like a slap across my face.

"Kaavi! You're all right? You haven't been hurt? Everyone's been so worried—"

"Amaya, what the fuck are you doing here?"

My eyes finally adjusted to the darkness of the small room in front of me. It took me a moment to notice the man slumped over in the corner.

"Spencer?" I called out.

"Amaya!" Kaavi said in return.

"Did he do this to you? Did he hurt you?"

"Amaya, god, you've got to help me. She's crazy." Spencer's voice was a rasp.

"What's going on?" I turned to face Kaavi. She looked livid.

"What's going on is that you need to get out of here right now. Just go outside and hide or something."

"No way. I'm not leaving you."

"Amaya, seriously."

"Leave while you can," Spencer mumbled. "She'll kill you too."

"Don't be ridiculous, Spencer. Kaavi's not going to hurt me. Or you. Are you, Kaavs?" But she didn't meet my eye.

"Tell me," she addressed Spencer now, "tell me why I shouldn't just kill you. After everything you've done?"

"I haven't done anything, Kaavs. All I wanted to do was give you the life you wanted. That's all. I'm sorry if, oh god, I'm sorry I did some fucked-up shit to get here. Look, we'll call the whole thing off, okay? I'll delete the pictures. We'll just put it all behind us. You have to understand that I never meant to hurt you."

"And what about Zoe Bassett, Spencer? Did you never mean to hurt her too?"

Even in the dimly lit room, I could see Spencer pale.

"Zoe? She's just an ex-girlfriend. I don't know what crazy shit she's told you, but I've never done anything to her."

"Like you never did anything to hurt me?" The question was out of my mouth before I even thought about it.

It was the voice he'd just used—placating, gentle, seeking out forgiveness. I'd heard that voice before. I'd fallen for that voice before.

Seeing him here, on the floor, helpless—it brought out a wave of something in me. I'd blown Spencer up as a monster in my head. A powerful, cruel monster who was always able to hurt me. Just the memory of him had been enough to knock the wind out of me. To make it hard to breathe. To make me tremble. And here he was, more than five years later, just a man. Just a man who was trying to hurt again.

"Why don't you tell Amaya the truth, huh, Spence?" Kaavi spat. "Tell her how you went to our college reunion after Zoe dumped your ass and moved away, because your funds had run out. You needed a quick buck, didn't you? And you figured the best way to do it was to try and worm your way back into Amaya's life again. I'm right, aren't I?"

Spencer didn't say anything, and my body went cold. Would I never be safe from him?

"But Amaya didn't come to the reunion, of course. I was there instead. Open and ready to be your next victim." She snorted. "The thing you should have learned along the way, Spence, is that I'll never be a victim. And definitely not a victim to a two-faced, abusive pedophile asshole like you."

"Kaavi, please, you have to—oh my god!"

It was only when I heard the panic in his voice that I saw it, glinting in Kaavi's hand. A gun.

Where the hell did she get that from? Mahesh said it was near impossible to get one in Sri Lanka.

"Look, I need you to just shut the fuck up and—"

Kaavi was interrupted as the door burst open once again.

It was the bald man I'd seen outside her house on the day of the cocktail party.

"What the hell is going on here? You asked me to meet you and I—"

"Mr. Ananda. Fucking finally."

Bang!

The shot was so loud my hands reached out on their own to shield my ears. But I couldn't close my eyes.

Mr. Ananda's face was frozen as he collapsed, first onto his knees, and then backward onto the ground.

Kaavi stood over him, her eyes wide, breathing hard. She was shaking like a leaf.

She turned over to look at me, panic starting to etch itself onto her face, when suddenly she was falling also. Using what just happened with Mr. Ananda as a diversion, Spencer had managed to get onto his knees and tackled her to the ground.

"You stupid bitch." His voice was devoid of all the softness and weeping from earlier. "You think you can just get away with this bullshit?" He was wrestling with her now, trying to reach for her gun.

"Amaya!" Kaavi called out, desperate.

She didn't need to tell me twice. I launched myself onto both of them and strained to get a grasp on the gun myself. Everything became a blur. I was only vaguely aware of a shoulder against my neck. A knee in my back. An elbow to my face. And then finally, my fingers brushed against something cold. I reached for it with everything I had. It was almost out of my grasp, but then it was between my fingers.

And I felt Spencer on top of me, like he had been so many times before. He was trying to pin me down, his face contorted in the same way that still gave me nightmares.

"You're pathetic," he heaved.

I closed my eyes. My fingers pulled the trigger.

Bang!

I don't know if his eyes actually went wide with the realization that I killed him, but that's my last memory of Spencer.

"I'm. Not. Pathetic." I gasped, heaving him off me. "I am strong. I am brave. And I'm fed up with your bullshit."

Kaavi was pulling me to my feet but I barely noticed. I aimed a kick at Spencer's body. It hardly did a thing, but it finally felt like a release. The monster was dead. The monster was dead because I killed it.

I felt a tear slide down my cheek as Kaavi took the gun from my hands and wrapped her arms around my shoulders, holding me close, so close that I could hear her heart pounding.

"You're okay," she kept saying, over and over. "You're okay."

She moved the dead man she called Mr. Ananda and then she adjusted Spencer's body as well. I was dizzy. Reeling. About to pass out.

"You're okay," she said again, and she held my hand as we made our way down the beach.

The sun was starting to set. I could see people, in the distance, making their way over to us. They'd probably heard the gunshot and figured out where it came from. Mr. Fonseka led the pack of them, followed by Tehani, and the wedding guests and hotel security. They were coming. Everyone was coming. I was about to be caught and put in prison and I didn't even care. My monster was finally dead. Nothing else mattered.

But Kaavi kept dragging me forward, and just before the crowd got close she leaned over and whispered in my ear.

"Just let me handle this, okay? Everything will be all right."

As soon as everyone caught up to us she collapsed on her knees.

"I'm fine," she called out, tears gushing down her face. "I'm fine. I'm okay. I was attacked, but Amaya saved me. Amaya saved me."

34

AMAYA

The Day of the Wedding

KAAVI SAT, WRAPPED in a blanket on her parents' bed at their suite in the new wing of the hotel. I was on a chair, to her right. Eshanya Padmaraj sat in front of both of us, though she looked uncomfortable as the rest of Kaavi's family hovered around her, protective and upset.

"Please tell us everything from the start, Kaavi."

"Okay, yes." She was speaking in her Instagram voice again. Modulated, low, and alluring. Inviting everyone into her. Pulling us in.

"So, last night was a little, um, shall we say emotional, for me. I was just getting ready to marry Spencer, and while I do love him, it had just struck me that I was about to marry a man that I hardly knew anything about." Her eyes sought out mine. I knew what she wanted. I stayed quiet.

"I called Amaya. I asked her to come to my room. Just to talk, you know."

"I thought you and Miss Bloom were no longer friends?"

Miss Padmaraj's interruption brought sighs of annoyance from the rest of the room, but Kaavi gave her a small, tired smile.

"We've been friends since we were children, Aunty Eshanya. Yes, we did have a small falling-out, but we spoke about it and have since made up."

"I see." Something about Miss Padmaraj's tone was off, but that didn't stop Kaavi from going on.

"So, Amaya and I spoke—we had a lot of catching up to do—and then she left. I was feeling much better, of course, but I did still have a tingle of nerves. I thought it would be nice to go for a walk."

She held up her hands as she heard her mother's gasp. Her daughter going for a walk alone after sunset was every mother's worst nightmare.

"I know, *Amma*. I know. I'm sorry. Oh gosh, you can't believe how sorry I am. I just thought, you know, this is a five-star hotel, with so much security. And we'd booked out the entire place, right? So I didn't think it was such a big deal."

"You went for a walk, and then?" Miss Padmaraj asked, trying to bring the conversation back on track.

"That's when, I guess that's when Mr. Ananda grabbed me. He clamped something down on my mouth and put something, it was a hood or a pillowcase maybe, over my head so I couldn't see. But I knew I hadn't been dragged out too far. I knew I was still on the beach.

"He locked me up in this dirty little shack—I think it might have been one of the old bathrooms or changing rooms or something that the hotel doesn't use anymore. And then he left me there. I—I don't know why. I thought maybe he was speaking to one of you—" She looked over at her father, who shook his head. "I don't know. He'd been after me for money, you see. I think he'd become quite unhinged after his wife's death. Blamed it on me for some reason. He showed up at the Poruwa also, you know, but security had escorted him out. And once before as well, at the cocktail party we threw at our house. So he definitely had a lot of issues."

"And what happened next?"

"Well, I was there for lord knows how long, until Mr. Ananda showed up again. He looked even more deranged than before. He said—" Kaavi's voice broke a little. "He said he was going to make me realize what it was like to lose someone I loved. Just like I'd done to him. He made me call Spencer and tell him where to come. He wanted me to tell him that he would kill me if Spencer alerted anyone. I didn't want to, you know—I wanted to keep Spencer safe, but—"

Miss Padmaraj nodded.

"That was probably why he overpowered the guards and left his room."

"When Spencer got there, Mr. Ananda, he—" Kaavi burst into sobs then, her whole body heaving.

"I would have been next, I'm sure of it," she gasped, reaching out for my hand. "But then Amaya showed up. She managed to tackle him, somehow, and all three of us were struggling to get ahold of the gun when it went off. It was an accident, wasn't it, Amaya?"

"We were only trying to get the gun away from him," I replied in a voice that wasn't my own.

Kaavi continued to sob, her face in her hands.

"The gun was loud. I was so scared."

Her parents rushed to her side, her mother pulling her close and her father letting his own tears fall as he rubbed her shoulder.

I looked over at Miss Padmaraj.

"Maybe we should give them some space?"

35

AMAYA
One Week Later

SHE WAS PLAYING outside in the garden. Her nanny was sitting next to her while she poured imaginary tea into the delicate real china tea set that lay on a low picnic table. Both of them were wearing fairy wings. Her smile was so bright that I could barely look at her.

Nadia—the real reason I came back here. I couldn't have Spencer around her. I did everything I could back then to keep her safe. I wasn't about to stop now.

A part of me longed to go up to her. To say hello. To say goodbye.

But she was happy and peaceful and had no idea what the real world was like. I let her be that way. It was a choice I made five years ago, and despite what Mrs. Fonseka seems to think, it's not one I regret. I am many things—I am stronger than I give myself credit for, I am fiercely protective of the people I love, but I also need to heal. And healing is a solitary journey. Not one worth disrupting a childhood for.

I checked the time. 11:11 a.m.

I whispered a goodbye that no one would hear. My biggest gift to Nadia was the life I had always wanted for myself.

Turning around, I saw Tehani a few feet away from me. She'd been watching me, judging from her expression.

"Don't worry, I'm not going to kidnap her or something, if that's what you're concerned about. I just wanted to get one last look at her before I left."

"I—I wanted to speak to you really quickly, if that's okay?"

"I think you've said enough, to be honest."

I had heard, because every bit of the investigation had been dragged open by gossips and well-wishers and aunties and uncles, about what Tehani had done. How she had invited me to the wedding. How she had pretended to be Beth. It's a good thing that everyone was so focused on Mr. Ananda's attack because Tehani would surely have been made out to be a straight-up sociopath otherwise.

It felt like my heart was ripped out all over again, when I heard about Beth. To think I had spent so long speaking to someone, opening up to them, telling them my innermost thoughts, all to find out later that it was a lie. It hurt to even think about it. It was excruciating to have to speak to Tehani now.

"Okay, look, I just wanted to apologize, okay?" Her tone was defensive, so I started to leave.

"The truth was that I wanted what you and Kaavi had, okay? I wanted a friend too."

Something about the way she said it made me pause, though I still didn't turn back to face her.

"All those things I said, not all of them were lies, you know. I know I gave you a different name. And different circumstances, of course. But look, all the real shit I said, you know, the stuff about how I felt so comfortable opening up to you and all that, that wasn't a lie. Okay?"

I still didn't say anything. I couldn't if I wanted to.

"Please believe me. You—you were my friend."

I turned around slowly. I don't know what she was expecting. A hug? A tearful confession that it's okay, that I forgave her for tricking me when I trusted her with things I never thought I'd tell anyone? That it's all right that she thought I was a murderer? It was all I could do not to imagine myself breaking off her long fake nails and sticking them straight into her eyeballs.

I tried to do what I did best. I took a deep breath. I counted to five. But that was the old me.

"Fuck off, Tehani."

I walked to the car without looking back at her. Then I pulled out my phone and sent a text.

> **Alexander, hi. I'll be back in the US soon. Shall we meet on Friday? I was thinking we could do drinks at the hotel bar first, if that was all right with you?**

He could whip me for my insolence if he wanted to, but I suddenly felt brazen. It was time for me to move forward one way or the other. It was time for me to start taking back control over my life.

> **I would love nothing more, Clara. I'll send a car for you at the usual time.**

Good things were definitely coming my way.

36

KAAVI

"You didn't need to come drop me, you know," Amaya said, giving me a small smile. We were both sitting in the back of the car while my mother, who was having trouble letting me out of her sight, sat up front with the driver.

"It's fine, I told you. It's the least I could do, after everything you've done for me."

The truth was, I would breathe a little easier once she was safely on her flight back to LA. All loose ends tied up. Any chance of what she knew coming back to bite me in the ass subdued, at least for now.

"I have something for you," Amaya said, pulling out a box.

"What's this?"

"Open it so."

It was a box of photographs of us from when we were younger. I hadn't seen most of them in years.

"Thanks, Ams, these are great."

"Thank Seetha. She's the one that hoards everything like her life depends on it."

I laughed.

"I'm going to post a throwback album of these on Insta. You mind?"

She looked at her watch again and shrugged. "Sure, why not."

In a way, it was kind of nice having her back in my life. My mother, however, disagreed vehemently, even when Amaya and I explained the truth about what Spencer did to her. I think she still thinks that Amaya will swoop in and insist on taking Nadia away someday. Amaya has assured me that she wants nothing of the sort. She never wanted children, she said. She wanted Nadia to be safe, of course, and she knew the best place for her was with my family.

Still, I could hear my mother audibly release the breath she was holding as Amaya hugged me, gave her an air-kiss, and wheeled her suitcase away.

"You think you could hold in the celebrations until her plane takes off, at least?" I asked, rolling my eyes. A porter was watching me, though, so I gave her a big smile to tone it down.

"Don't you think you should be nicer to me, after everything that happened?" she countered.

I sighed.

It was only a matter of time before she rubbed this whole thing in my face. I knew it.

"Keep your voice down," I said, making sure I was still smiling. "Let's go to the Airport Garden Hotel and have a drink." She was smart enough to agree. There was no telling who would overhear us if we spoke at home.

The hotel was about ten minutes away, and it took about another ten minutes for our drinks to show up. My mother was quiet the whole time. Quiet and smug. Waiting for the right moment to strike.

"Well?" I asked.

"Well what?"

"You have something to say, no, so say it."

"I think you're the one with things to say, Kaavindi. Like how about *thank you, Amma.*"

"Oh please." I rolled my eyes. "You were saving your own ass as much as mine."

"Language, Kaavindi. And I did save your *ass*, by the way. Your plan was abysmal. You should be keeping flowers at my feet and worshipping me for what I managed to do."

"So you managed to get me a gun, *Amma.*" I snuck a quick peek around, but no one was within earshot. "Thank you. There, are you happy now?"

"I had hoped for a little more gratitude than that."

I suppose she was right. I mean, she got me into this mess, but she sure as hell got me out of it. Call it mother's intuition, but she guessed I would try to run the night before the wedding. Or maybe she planned on getting rid of Spencer ever since she heard he was broke and his dad was in jail—who knows? I had just made it out of my room when I found her, waiting for me, hands on her hips and absolutely livid.

"You're right. I'm sorry. Thank you."

"I couldn't believe how stupid you were, getting Amaya tangled up in all of this."

"Yeah, I didn't realize how volatile she was. It was a long shot, anyway, but I figured she could be a backup plan. In case Mr. Ananda didn't show for some reason. She was the only one who figured things out and showed up at the beach, after all."

She sighed.

"Still, it was stupid to involve someone else."

The truth was that if I was good at compartmentalizing, I was excellent at planning. I've said a thousand times before, I always, *always* had options. And once again, luck came knocking on my door. Amaya helped me "hatch a plan" and was fully ready to go along with it. And it wasn't the worst plan either. I would say Spencer was abusive and leave.

The hardest part of that whole thing was getting him to come down to my room. To act as if everything was okay. To kiss him. To feel his disgusting hands on me. I thought he got suspicious a few times, especially when I "accidentally" scratched his face while he was feeling me up. But men think with their dicks, so he wasn't distracted for too long.

But after Amaya helped me destroy my room, gave me a massive shiner, and left, I changed my mind. This wouldn't work. It made me out to be a victim—a weak damsel in distress. Not a great narrative at all. And besides, Spencer was oily enough that he'd probably find a way to slither out of any accusations. And what if he leaked the images of my dad out of spite?

Could you imagine what that would do to my reputation?

No, I needed a better plan. One where I came out on top, like I always did. And that's when my mother showed up. She all but laughed at my ideas and gave me a better one. Then she convinced my father not to call the police right away, telling him that it would ruin our family name, and had him use a third-rate security company instead. Thank god, because there was no way this whole charade would have ever held up under a serious investigation. She also pretended she had no idea who Mr. Ananda was during her interview, so that he wouldn't get called in for questioning instead of showing up at the beach. She even managed to get me a gun, though it was touch and go for a while there.

Amaya was my backup in case Mr. Ananda didn't work out. In

case he didn't respond to my message and meet me at the shack on the beach. That's why my recording was so ambiguous. I hadn't quite decided who the true villain was yet. No way could it have been Spencer. At least, not to the real world. I could picture the headlines now—*Groom Attacks Bride the Night before the Wedding.* I'd have been a fucking laughingstock. Everyone always blamed the woman for letting it get that far. Why wasn't she a better judge of character? Why couldn't she just leave? If only things were ever that easy.

Of course Tehani had to almost ruin everything by drunkenly staggering to my room while I was in there with Spencer, but fortunately Amaya knocked her out. That whole debacle got swept away, thank god, along with all accusations against Amaya. She did come out the hero in this. She should thank me, really.

"Well, everything's done now. Things can go back to normal, hopefully. I'll just use all this press to get another endorsement or something. Things always work out for the best."

"No need to get cocky, Kaavindi. Be prudent. You'll probably need to be in the months to come."

"What do you mean?"

"I can't believe you haven't noticed. I thought we'd taught you better than that, but then, you have been distracted, I suppose. Fonseka Jewellers has not been doing well, Kaavindi. So much so that I've had to dip into your charity fund from time to time."

I raised an eyebrow at her.

"You're the one who messed with my accounts?"

"And I was surprised it took you that long to realize. You're slipping, Kaavindi."

"I had someone fired because of it."

"And look how useful all that turned out to be."

I took a sip of my drink.

"You really are a piece of work, you know that, *Amma*?"

She sighed. "When will you grow up and stop getting yourself into trouble, Kaavindi?"

Enough with the fucking dramatics already.

"What do you mean, *Amma*? Look, I'm grateful for your help, I really am. But I've taken care of myself all this time, I'm not about to stop now."

It was her turn to roll her eyes.

"Are you really that idiotic, child? Do you think you just magically maintain your flawless reputation when you are flying around the world sleeping with god knows who? Do you think that your little problems from your teenage years miraculously went away?"

I swallowed.

"What do you mean?"

"Oh, don't tell me you never figured it out?"

But I had no clue what she was talking about. I raised an eyebrow at her.

She shook her head.

"And here I was, thinking you were the smart one. Tell me, Kaavindi, what do *you* think happened to Gayan Peiris?"

Gayan? The boy who died in a drunk driving accident?

"I have no idea what you are talking about. We were at Amaya's, and he'd had too much vodka. Amaya and I barely drank back then; we were mostly pretending."

"And did you give a second thought to that bottle of vodka you just *happened* to stumble on that night you were sleeping over at Amaya's? I know you were just trying to impress her and that horrible boy, but I always wondered why all the sleeping pills I had dissolved into the alcohol never knocked you out."

I frowned.

"I knew that useless bastard would drive back home. All those stupid boys did. Just like I knew that the two of you were getting together behind Amaya's back."

There was no way she could have known that. We had been so careful.

And did that mean—?

"You drugged him?"

"I did what I had to do. Imagine what it would have done to you if it got out that you were sleeping with your best friend's boyfriend? And at that age? Kaavindi, you would have been ruined."

My palms felt damp and I rubbed them against my trousers.

"I took care of that physics teacher you were misbehaving with, too, by the way, if you'd like to thank me for that as well. You know, the only thing I'm grateful for is that you were quiet and well-mannered enough that you didn't call attention to yourself like Amaya did. With behavior like that, it was easy for everyone to suspect her. At least I've taught you to be discreet."

I rarely felt lost for words, but I honestly had no idea what I was supposed to say.

"Are you really all that surprised, Kaavindi?"

I suppose she *had* managed to get a gun, help me kill my fiancé, and pin the blame on someone else. Maybe I had to give her a little bit of credit.

"So why do you hate Amaya, then?"

"Come on, Kaavindi. I didn't hate Amaya. It was actually quite useful having her around when you were younger. She always took all the attention away from you in the best possible way. But when she showed up pregnant, well, your father took pity on her, and my astrologer always did say that it would be lucky for me to have three children, so it all worked out. I just wanted her out of our lives. She'd served her purpose."

I wanted to be angry. I wanted to be outraged.

But how different was I from her, actually?

They say we all eventually turn into our mothers. I was well on my way there.

We heard drums beating in the distance, and someone blowing a conch shell horn.

"Oh look," she said, standing up. "Seems like there's a wedding happening. Let's go take a peek at the bride. At least some daughters know how to make their mothers happy."

Acknowledgments

To my friend and agent, Melissa Danaczko, whose support and advice has always been invaluable. Thank you for all your encouragement and for always believing in me and, most importantly, in my thinking couch!

To my amazing editor, Jen Monroe, whom I can always count on for the best ideas! Thank you for being so wonderful to work with, and for not being (too) disturbed by all my strange suggestions.

To my brilliant marketing team, Jessica Mangicaro and Elisha Katz—and to my rock star publicity team, Loren Jaggers and Stephanie Felty. I was so thrilled when I found out that we would be working together again that I did a (terribly uncoordinated) happy dance. Thank you for working so hard to get this story out into the world.

To Candice Coote for all your help in bringing everything together!

To Emily Osborne for, once again, creating such a beautiful cover that I can't stop staring at.

To my production editor, Jennifer Myers, and copyeditor, Marianne Aguiar: I know it couldn't have been easy navigating around all the Sri Lankan–isms in this book. Thank you for your sensitivity in making my character voices as authentic as possible.

And to everyone at Berkley and Penguin Random House who helped bring *You're Invited* into the hands of readers. I'm so grateful for you!

To the wonderful team at Hodder & Stoughton, especially Bethany Wickington. Thank you so much for all your support and hard work across the pond!

To the lovely team at Stuart Krichevsky Literary Agency for being such a pleasure to work with.

To Crystal Patriarche and the team at BookSparks for all their help in getting the word out about this book!

To my ever-supportive Berkletes, who have cheered me on every step of the way.

To my amazing friends and family, who love me even when I'm an antisocial hermit that never keeps in touch with anyone when I'm writing.

And as always, to CJ: I know this book throws shade at weddings, but there has never been a moment in the last twelve years when I haven't been thankful that I married my best friend.